America Attacks

A "Nelson's Men" Series
The Korean War

Book III

By Dennis Kennelly

America Attacks
Copyright © 2020 Dennis Kennelly
ISBN: 978-1-970153-27-9
Library of Congress Control Number: 2020925758

La Maison Publishing, Inc.
Vero Beach, Florida
The Hibiscus City
www.lamaisonpublishing@gmail.com

Patriotism is supporting your country all the time, and your government when it deserves it.

Mark Twain

Introduction

As a backdrop, the United States state of Florida is about 40% *larger* in landmass then **South Korea** and share a similar characteristic of being a peninsula surrounded by deep ocean waters. From there on, they are as different as the Sun and the Moon.

Korea had been a Japanese province since the early 1900s. As part of the Japanese surrender in 1945, it was divided in half to appease the Russian leader, Stalin, who entered the war against Japan three weeks before its capitulation.

This political decision was made by ill-informed people who had little knowledge of the region, with a slight understanding of communism, and for the most part, had an isolationist view of the world.

Only the military had any strategic foresight. But new President Truman was learning on the job and his advisers knew what the American citizens wanted --- their men home, peace, and no new taxes. They focused on reducing debt and cutting defense spending to do it. They wanted America to return to traditional values.

The military lost its voice and suffered dearly over the last five years as each of the Service Branches budgets was cut to the bone.

Although South Korea came under General Douglas MacArthur's overall command, his focus was Japan, where he was considered an unofficial Viceroy. One could see how a backwater like Korea could go unattended.

`

On June 27th, two days after the invasion by Communist North Korea, on June 25th, 1950, America's President ordered the United States military to attack the North Korean invaders *that had crossed the border and were actually in South Korea*.

It was excellent political news. Mostly to send a message to Russia's leader, Stalin, that we would fight against his Communist expansion.

Stalin ignored it, as he and the North Koreans knew we had nothing to fight back with, and they were right.

Their strategy was simple. Confuse and lie to the world, proclaiming this was a civil war where South Korea had been the aggressor. What they planned was to overrun the South in a few weeks and pronounce that a country unlawfully divided, had successfully been unified.

It soon became apparent to America's military and political leaders that the under-armed Republic of Korea (ROK) Army was no match to repel the invasion and was rapidly crumbling from superior firepower. The fate of the young nation was at risk.

The rapid enemy advance dominated thoughts of South Korea's ability to survive. Advised of the threat to Japan and the whole of the South Asia region should South Korea be overrun, President Truman acted. Three days later, on June 30th, the President ordered *total* US involvement, unrestricted bombing above the 38th parallel of North Korean military targets, and the sending of U.S. ground forces to Korea.

United Nations involvement swiftly followed with General Douglas MacArthur named commander of all U.N. forces in Korea.

It was almost too late.

At the start of the invasion, America had about six hundred soldiers in all of South Korea.

Except for the forty or so Army veterans stationed at Colonel Nelson's clandestine listening posts, the remaining forces were mostly administrators and trainers. The survivors of the invasion at Colonel Nelson's four listening Posts and his inspired team back at Eighth Army headquarters helped delay the avalanche of a determined enemy.

Kick the hornets' nest at your peril.

As depleted and short of most everything, the American military machine started to get its system into gear. Enough veterans remained in all services to deal with impossible odds and labor through bad times. Much American blood would flow before America would be ready to attack, but attack America would.

This book is the beginning of that story, but also a continuation of the heroics of Colonel Nelson's men, led by First Sergeant Rusty Fabino.

From the Author

Although a work of fiction, this story reflects the time and attitudes of world events. Actual time frames and depictions of noted military and political leaders are facts. My story and its characters are a product of my imagination.

The story of Korea goes much deeper than just the first fight against an expansionist Communist regime. It reflects on how America viewed it's standing in the world at the end of WW2 and how that morphed into its present-day Super Power role. Korea set the stage for America to fill a void that no other country could and had a cascading effect on American foreign policy to the present day.

Long forgotten, the men who fought here wondered why they did.

They were warriors, but few recognized what they had accomplished and endured.

America didn't win.

Our soldiers battled to a tie, a truce. It wasn't even considered a **War**: *It was considered a police action*!

Some police action! Tell that to the families of the dead and wounded. They were just young men ordered to fight, thrown into the harsh reality and brutality of front line combat.

U. S. Deaths: Total In-Theatre - 36,574
U. S. Wounded in Action - 103,284
There were No parades.

Sixty-Seven years later, there is no Peace Treaty.

In 2020, the United States maintains a military presence of over 23,000 men/women in Korea

Somehow I hope to bring some recognition of the valiant efforts these men made in a long-ago fight for our country, in a faraway land for a noble purpose.

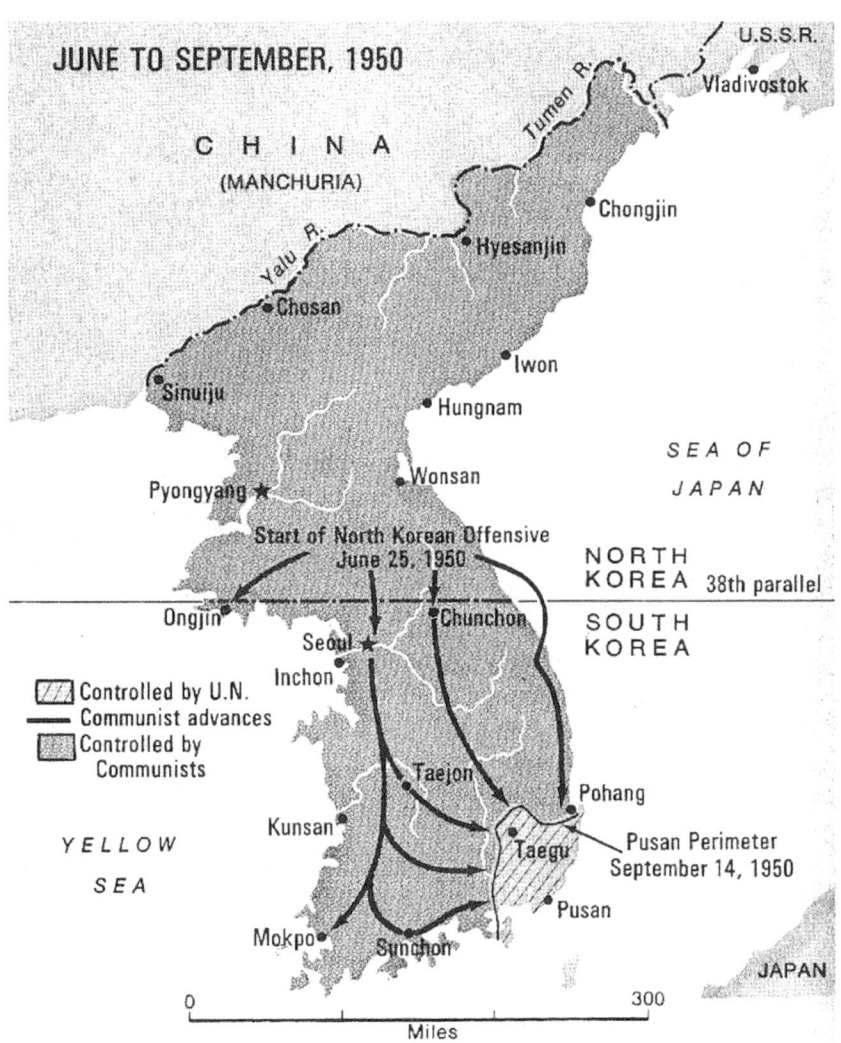

Prologue

It's been eight days since the communist North invaded South Korea. Their superior weapons and excellent training quickly overwhelmed a brave but under armed South Korean resistance.

Their forces have now captured the capital, Seoul.

Caught up in this drama since the beginning is a small secret America A-Team.

American Colonel Nelson, head of G-2 (Intelligence) operations for Eighth Army in Japan, is the commander of this secret group because of his role in establishing four hidden listening posts with Top Secret CIA equipment along the 38th parallel.

Rusty, leader of the most extensive Post, survived the invasion with most of his reinforced unit along with the secret CIA equipment. They've been fighting as a guerrilla force ever since and have been successful in inflicting significant damage to the enemy in many battles, and slowing their advance.

Rusty's team had just returned from a difficult mission to a mountain cave ten miles east of Seoul. The elaborate mission plan, designed by a Master Sergeant Nick Beloit, back at Colonel Nelson's headquarters in Japan, resulted in the demolition of the last two remaining bridges over the Han River, just south of Seoul. This action should delay the enemy's further advance south by days, if not a week or more.

They needed to move.

x

Chapter One

Rusty leaned against the cave wall and thought of this most recent spectacular success. Knocking down those bridges. Damn! That was special! How much providence was involved in making that happen?

It certainly couldn't have happened without these South Korean guys assigned here in this cave to spy on Seoul. No way, he thought.

Meeting C J and his four-man signal unit. Lucky for us C J speaks fluent English. Surprised, he's only a sergeant, being as smart as he is, and is also the nephew of the head of South Korea's Military Intelligence, their Army's G-2. His uncle, Colonel Oh, also happened to know Colonel Nelson, my boss, G-2 of America's Eighth Army. What were the chances of all that coming together?

Rusty thought this was something as he nodded off.

Above the loud noise of the downpour, Red called across the short distance in the cave, "C J! Will this weather hold us up from leaving later or slowing our schedule?"

"This rain will not slow our journey. We're good to go!"

Red nodded, closed his eyes, tried to sleep, but became introspective.

He wondered why he was still alive. Grateful, but speculated that this might be his last mission. From his landing in Normandy with Rusty to crazy special ops with then Major Nelson, he had fought through the worst that the Nazi's had to offer and only picked up a scar on my jaw. I'm a lucky bastard!

But now, he was worried. Over the last eight days, he was surprised to experience that the worst had gotten worse, and maybe there was a more profound evil for him yet to face.

Exhausted, he finally shut out those terrible thoughts and fell asleep.

At 1400 – (2:00 PM), C J led the men out of the cave.

"Just another summer day!" Said a sarcastic Joe as he stepped out of the cover of their mountain hideout into a rainstorm. Last, in the column, he followed Arron, who turned at the comment, "At least it ain't mortar rounds!"

The column of twenty men set off down the backside of a mountain, just east of the capital city, on a three-hour journey to their escape boat and raft. Loaded with weapons and as much ammunition as they could carry, the going was slow.

Colonel Nelson's headquarters ordered Rusty's team to the city of Osan, a difficult fifty or so miles away. Their secret CIA communications equipment has played a vital role in the teams' continued survival as well as impacting the critical need of delaying the enemy advance.

They had to go to one-quarter rations, as their food supply was insufficient for the expected two-day trip. At least they were rested. After almost forty-eight hours of continuous fighting and moving through demanding terrain, they had gotten a solid six hours of sleep this morning.

Leading the column, C J, the Korean sergeant who headed up the ROK signal unit at the mountain, thought of these strange new American soldiers he'd fought with these last few days. His mind wandered further back to his past.

Although raised in a displaced Korean family in Australia and educated in excellent English schools, he'd met few Americans. When he and his uncle returned to Korea after the Japanese surrendered, he enlisted in the new South Korean Army. It was then that he started meeting Americans, as they were his military trainers. But for the most part, at that time, these Americans just wanted to go home.

His military uncle had shaped his thoughts and pushed him to excel. A student of history, his uncle, believed early on in his youth that one day Korea would be a free country if men worked hard at making it happen. He instilled this same desire and motivation in C J.

Unbeknownst to the American occupying forces, a small core of Korean military veterans formed. A small number had fought against the Japanese as resistance fighters, but most fought *with them* to survive, but all hated them. C J's uncle had connections and relatives in both camps, and he rose quickly to the head of the table in this new group. They became political and allied themselves with the favored American choice that sponsored Syngman Rhee, in the country's first *"FREE"* election.

Then the killing started. C J reeled at the memory. Young and ignorant, he was ordered to kill the enemies of the state, and kill he did. The Americans just stood aside, not knowing what to do. No guts, these guys, he thought. After a while, he figured out what was going on and didn't like it.

Confused, he sought answers, so he went to his uncle, who was now a star in the new Korean Military General Staff. Major Oh then, now Colonel Oh, G-2, head of South Korean Army Intelligence, he listened to C J's questions and his concerns.

C J remembered his words said to him that now seemed so long ago.

"C J! Korea has been sheltered by oppression for many hundreds of years. This country has only known hatred and abuse. The gods have let loose that pent-up anger, and it now needs a harsh hand to bring back civil order. It will be a painful process. Mistakes will be made, and wrongs will occur, but it must happen. Try to understand it! Most of all, keep the goal of a free and independent Korea utmost in your mind!"

Those words said by his uncle had sustained him through the worst. He saw something emerging that raised his belief in his new country.

He came back to the present and thought about this oddball American group.

Rusty, this American Army guy, never met a leader like him. Almost like me, so he's a first sergeant, yet he commands like a general. Well, no, that's not right. He leads! How? Damn, if I know! Never seen a leader seek advice like that. Asking his team for help? Americans!

Then there are the other leaders. I don't know how that works, but it does somehow.

I like Red, another first sergeant, a cautious fellow, think he's Rusty's XO. I'd want him by my side.

Then Tully. The Ranger. How'd he get here? Another first sergeant! He's crazy! Smart. An unusual leader. He somehow fits in.

I can't figure out how the rest of the men seem to all have input. Maybe I'll find out if I live through what's coming.

Behind C J in the column, was Rusty, Red, and Tully. They'd been quiet for the first hour because of the torrential rains. The downpour now tapered off enough to hear without shouting.

"What the hell does Colonel Nelson think we're gonna do in Osan?" Said a skeptical Red. "And how many US troops are going to be there?"

"Just hope there's a battalion or two of Rangers!" Quipped Tully.

"An armored division would be better!" Said Red.

Rusty was annoyed because he too had significant misgivings about their objective and was in the dark about what was coming but didn't show it. He said, "We follow orders! Nelson hasn't steered us wrong yet! Stop talking like a bunch of privates!"

Quiet for a moment at Rusty's rebuke, Red called back. "Guess you figured out that we're joining the front line. No more sneaking around in the bushes and getting them from the rear. Our turn on the wall. We'll now be facing them full on."

Rusty stopped, turned, and in a calm voice, said, "We've been on the wall, damn it! We will stay on the wall until Colonel Nelson says otherwise. Let's stop talking about unknowns and get the hell out of here!"

Two hours later, they reached the bend in the Han River behind the mountain, found the boat and nearby raft. The ancient craft held fourteen of them plus equipment, was shaped like a canoe, pointed at both ends but longer and wider than a typical American model. The raft, made of big logs, made it stable, was able to hold the rest of the men and equipment, albeit somewhat underwater.

With ten paddles, the boat and trailing raft made slow but steady progress across the Han and down into the southern tributary, as they followed close to the eastern shore staying in the wash, out of the primary current going north.

"Based on what Muzich said, I think we got maybe close to three hours to the PBY." Said C J. "It'll be dark, so we'll need to get the flashlights on about then."

"How long after that for us?" Asked Rusty.

"Depends." Said C J. "On the current. It should be weaker farther down. Then, of course, we must avoid obstacles, like trees or sandbars. It's probably a thirty-mile run. I think we're making a mile, maybe a mile in a half an hour against this current. We'll pick it up when we drop the men off at the plane and ditch the raft. So, if all goes well, around 0900 (9:00 AM) tomorrow."

"Then how long is the march to Osan?" Rusty pursued.

C J never encountered a man or men like these. They want to know everything, and they want to know it NOW.

"Rusty! We have a lot of time to think about timing. Let's get to A, then to B, and then wonder about how and when we get to C."

Rusty laughed. "I am a pain in the ass sometimes!"

C J jerked back. "No, you're not! A good leader keeps searching for options! I wish we had more like you!"

Rusty felt his sincerity. "Listen, C J! Your country has YOU! And your uncle! And plenty more great men! Don't go off like that. I'm nothing in this great drama unfolding. You're the future! Learn! Now lead us to the Promised Land!"

Chapter Two

Sunday, July 2, 1950 - Day Eight of the Invasion
Japan - Eighth Army Headquarters – G-2 Operations
Section – Conference Room – 1630 – (4:30 pm)

After the A-Team had been dismissed by Colonel Nelson a half hour ago for a well-earned night's rest, Master Sergeant "Nick" Beloit lingered at the conference table. Having just completed a successful operation, he couldn't relax. He started going through new low priority cables from General Church's command in Korea. He came across orders given to General Dean's 24th Infantry Division, whose Colonel Smith's battalion was assembling to head to Osan. Then he found more cables.

Nick's mind swirled with confusing options, like a chessboard with too many Bishops, but not enough Pawns!

He sat back and thought about what was unfolding. He jolted up and went to the projector, searched through the 8" x 10" transparencies till he found the one of Osan taken from five thousand feet on a clear day; it showed all.

Nick sat and studied it. After ten minutes, he said out loud, "Idiots! What the fuck were you thinking?" He shook his head in disbelief.

He picked up the phone to Colonel Nelson.

"Nelson!" Said the weary Colonel, about ready to fall into his cot.

"Sorry, Colonel! Nick here. Sir! Osan is going to be a slaughter!"

"What? I'll be right there! Call back the rest of the team!"

Nelson didn't hesitate. If Nick sounded the alarm, it was severe.

He was back at their conference room in ten minutes, where his XO, Major Hank Jarvis, was sitting down. Lieutenant Larry Cole and Captain Sam Haran immediately followed him in.

Not one for quipping, Captain Haran, known as the *Professor*, said, "I for one, thoroughly enjoyed that rest! What's up?"

Colonel Nelson leaned into the table with a distressed look. "Go, Nick! What's wrong?"

"Decided to go through current cables we overlooked earlier while everyone was getting their beauty rest." He smirked. "I'm jealous. All right! I couldn't leave."

"Noble!" Said LT Cole, not smiling.

Nick turned to Cole. "This is your baby, buddy! Your plan! And it's been mucked up!"

Larry Cole froze in disbelief. "What are you saying?"

"Your plan, on staging a rolling defense down the main highway, starting at Osan, has been transformed into a fixed defense at all cost!"

"Holy shit!" Said everyone in the room.

Stunned silence prevailed as the group collected their thoughts.

Nick broke it.

"An hour ago, General MacArthur relieved General Church's Advanced Korean Command and appointed General

Dean, commander of the 24th Infantry Division, as head of all forces in Korea."

Nelson leaned back in his seat, not entirely digesting this new information. "General Dean just got there! What! A few hours ago?"

Then Major Jarvis stood up. "He's a damned division commander!" His face turned to beat red as he said it.

"Sit down, Hank," Nelson said calmly.

"We're all tense! But we will conduct ourselves as leaders. It should've been Eighth Army! Our General Walker put in command, but it wasn't. I'm the only one here that knows General Dean, and I'll attest to his leadership abilities and combat experience."

Pausing, Colonel Nelson continued.

"Without disparaging General Church, who is a good leader but without any combat experience. General MacArthur's choice was a sound one. Dean's division is on the ground or will be fully in a few days. And he's there as of today. Furthermore, you must know that this is only temporary. We will join this fight in short order. Now let's get on with helping General Dean!"

"Nick! You started this discussion! Finish it!"

"Sir! Don't shoot the messenger!" He said in his deadpan style that brought smiles to the table, breaking the tense mood. He then rose and went to the projector, slipped in the film, and pointed to the wall where Osan's topography was precise from five thousand feet.

With a five minute detail of how he thought Colonel Smith's battalion would establish their defensive positions, he further detailed how the enemy would proceed to envelop them and destroy Smith's force. Nick ended with the assessment that this would take a day, two at the most.

"Nick, you continue to amaze me. You are the best tactical analyst I've ever met." Pausing, Nelson thought about these new orders for General Dean.

"General MacArthur has finally realized the seriousness of North Korea's advance and is willing to sacrifice significant American casualties to slow it down. We can't counter that order, but we can offer some advice. Now that we know we're staying at Osan longer than our plans originally intended, we need another plan. Let' get to it!"

Chapter Three

Sunday, July 2, 1950 - Day Eight of the Invasion
Korea - Taejon Airfield – One Hundred Miles SE of the Han
River – 1630 – (4:30 pm)

Captain Stands stood and watched the military machine in action from the edge of his hanger door. Cloudy, no rain, but hot as hell. The fickle weather had changed. From monsoon rains and reasonable temperatures to hot, humid, and just overcast.

Known as Wild Bill, Captain Stands was a three-time Ace flying P-51's in Europe. Refusing promotion and rejecting absorption from the Army Air Corp into the new Air Force, he stayed with his friend, Colonel Nelson, in the Eighth Army, as a Special Operations person. Nobody knew what that meant but Nelson. It kept Wild Bill out of a system that not only did he not belong in, but one in which he wouldn't function properly. He called Nelson his "favorite" Colonel. Nelson knew what he'd done for him in the War and since. Captain Stands would do anything for the Colonel and knew the feeling was reciprocal.

The C-47 transport planes kept landing, thirty soldiers per with lots of boxes of ammo. He'd seen this before, in France. Desperation! Teenagers were piling out of the planes, newly enlisted, peacetime occupation troops from Japan, with not a clue of what they faced. He wanted to scream.

Turning back to the hanger, he called out, "Come here!"

Billy, the sergeant mechanic, jumped, Arnie, his assistant, came off of the crate where he was sitting, and George, the Post # 1 survivor, stopped sharpening his special knife. All gathered around Wild Bill standing near *Just Due*, his rebuilt P-51. This crew had brought this abandoned plane back to be a fighting demon.

"We're getting some company tomorrow with any luck. George, a few of your friends from Post # 4 are coming in. They blew up the Han River Railroad Bridge yesterday. Hell of a job, I understand. You'll be joining them. For what? I don't know. But I'm expecting orders as well. We'll have to wait, like the little clogs we are in the big machine gearing up for the big push." He said sarcastically.

Uncharacteristically melancholy, Captain Stands continued. "I'm honored to be with you and watch what you've done to bring this magnificent warbird back to fight again. I know he will honor you. I thank you!"

He then walked off toward a corner by the entrance as the men were left to wonder at his words.

Wild Bill knew what was coming, and it much distressed him. When the big war machine started up, the small things, individual people, and units that could have prevented the death machine from starting all fell to the side. He knew it was going to be all-consuming. Tears filled his eyes. It was out of his control.

Stands heard a commotion just outside the hanger. Men were shouting, then what sounded like punches connecting to bone brought him running outside and then to the side of the building where he saw a man sitting on top of a guy lying on the ground, hitting him repeatedly in the face.

"Stop!" Wild Bill yelled, then pulled out his .45 pistol and chambered a round. The distinctive sound of the 1911 automatic sliding click made as a shell was chambered brought the fight to an end.

"Get off him! Don't mess with me because I'll shoot you. Slowly now, move."

The soldier rose, "He's a goddamned coward! A stupid asshole officer! Got my friends killed, and I want to kill him!"

"Back off and shut up!" Wild Bill went to the guy on the ground. He wasn't moving but was breathing. He'd been in enough fights to know his nose was broken and maybe his jaw, but he wasn't in critical danger. Lieutenant's bars shined like a lighthouse on the unconscious officer's shoulders. Captain Stands shook his head and said to the standing soldier, whom he then realized was a non-com. "You're screwed!"

The Captain, still holding his forty-five, walked over to the soldier, who stood defiantly with hands still clenched and stared at the sergeant and thought that this poor bastard got a straight ticket to hell.

Billy came rushing up just then. "What's going on? You okay, Captain?"

"Yeah, Billy. Find a medical team and bring them here fast! This officer's seriously hurt."

Looking at the sergeant, Stands said, "You make a stupid move, and I will shoot you! Understand?"

"Yes, sir. Got no beef with you, sir. My name is Engle, Dan." The adrenaline rush was fading; he noticeably relaxed.

"Before shit rains down on you, Sergeant, you better tell me what's going on! I hope you pray to God that he doesn't die because then, it's out of my hands. I heard what you said about this officer. So tell me how he killed your friends!"

Curious men gathered around them, wondering what happened, everybody was nervous.

Engle went to his knees and let out a huge breath; the final release of his anger complete. Hurt and loss were the only things left. Captain Stands knew this feeling well, holstered his pistol, and kneeled next to the sergeant. Somehow he knew the officer deserved everything he got.

"I got coffee inside the hanger. Let's go in and talk."

An hour later.
Japan - Eighth Army Headquarters – G-2 Operations Section – Conference Room – 1630 – (5:30 pm)

Major Jarvis hung up the phone. "Colonel, you're requested to meet with General Walker in his office, immediately."

As he proceeded to the meeting, Nelson wondered why it was urgent. Was it General Dean taking over command of Korea? Things were happening so fast; he didn't have a clue. Roll with the waves, he thought.

"Thanks, Jim, for coming so fast. Got a scotch neat here. Sit and relax. I'm going to tell you a story, but first, we need to have our drink."

They toasted.

"I've only met General MacArthur a few times; both were cordial. I never spoke with him on the phone; it was always through his staff. Until today."

General Walker poured another round.

"I've been mulling over our discussion since his call to me this morning." He lifted his glass and took a big swig.

"MacArthur got details of how you planned and executed those successful missions against the hard targets. Like the Kaesong Railroad Bridge near your Post that a North Korean Company had seized before the invasion and your men recaptured. The one that everybody thought was a South Korean uprising. Then the Cheorwon Bridges you destroyed, and the North Korean General's HQ compound you demolished. And of course, your most famous accomplishment, the destruction of the Han River Bridges. Finally, to top off these incredible achievements, you organized the destruction of an east coast railroad tunnel twenty miles above the 38th parallel in North Korea. MacArthur mentioned that most officers would take a career of accomplishing any one of these challenging assignments, but you did them all in just a few days."

Nelson said nothing.

"He even recognized your foresight in setting up those secret Border Posts. Although he alluded to insubordination but said he admired your spunk. In other words, it's okay if things turn out fine. Lots of high praise from God."

"I'm flattered." Said Nelson.

"Jim, he was honoring you. He's recommended you for the Silver Star."

Nelson sat still, stunned. Then responded, "My team did these things; they deserve the medals!"

"You're right! And some will get them. But not now. That's not how it works. The fact is, you lead men, you hired them;

handpicked each one. You approved the plans and the operations and finally got these plans approved through our maze of inter-service obstructions. God bless you! That alone gets you a medal. You deserve this, Jim."

The General poured another round.

Nelson felt there was something else.

"MacArthur wants more. And his suggestion, well, that's not right. His order has confounded me for most of the day. Jim, he wants you to set up a Special Operations Command within your G-2 Operation organization within Eighth Army."

"What does that mean?"

"He has recognized your ability, Jim. You know how to pick leaders, thinkers, and doers, and your long career attests to that record."

General Walker took a sip from his drink and continued.

"We have nothing in our command structure to do this. Nothing in MacArthur's, heck, we've got nothing in the whole Army that can do what you've done. We had pockets in the War, OSS, Rangers, Raiders, but they were all fragmented. Not one of them was ever brought into the big picture. Maybe because the big picture was so big, or maybe there was resentment by the commanding generals, who knows. But this war is different. That's what we talked about."

Nelson sat back, digesting what his friend and mentor had just said.

"Jim, you'll have free rein to plan your missions! He's authorized you to have direct command of whatever force you'd need, handpicked of your choosing, and recruited from any Command or Service. You wouldn't have to jump through hoops to get things done. It'll be your show!"

"What did he say to you about your role, General?"

"We spoke about it, Jim. You report to me. The rest is between him and me."

"If I understand this correctly, this would be a sub-section under your command. So, if I screw up, both of us go down?"

"Would you think our Emperor would possibly diminish his aura by being directly linked to a failure?"

Nelson nodded.

"Sir, does it need to be an officer to command this Special Operations Unit?"

"You're something, Colonel! As far as General MacArthur or I give a good hoot about who's in command? Don't care if he's a janitor! If you pick him, it's good! You're responsible!"

"Sir, as you well know, I already have an unofficial Special Operations Unit, and I have a close relationship with our CIA partners. Does MacArthur know about this?"

"He doesn't care about who or what you have or what and whom you deal with, just what you can continue to contribute."

"So General, he doesn't know about the CIA?"

"No, Jim, that's a secret we need to keep to ourselves."

"When does this new order take effect?"

"Orders are being issued as we speak. You got this new command. The name is NSOPU, and it's TOP SECRET. Only a very select few will know any details about it."

General Walker paused, thinking about his final words.

"Colonel, you've got something that few men have ever even dreamed about; use it wisely, as I know you will. Any Command that receives a directive from NSOPU is to comply as if General MacArthur himself ordered it; that instruction has already been issued."

Lifting his glass in a toast, a somber General Walker said, "Jim, you deserve the medal, and I trust you. Now do what you have to do! Your orders are to slow these guys down, whatever it takes!"

His A-Team was at the conference table when he returned. Nelson looked somber when he sat down.

"Anything?" He asked.

"Yes, sir." Said Major Hank Jarvis. "Captain Stands called from Taejon airfield with a situation. I thought it might help us. Involves a KMAG (Korean Military Advisory Group) sergeant beating up his KMAG lieutenant for abandoning his position and subsequent slaughter of his South Korean unit they were training. Wild Bill thinks highly of this sergeant, thinks this Lt should be brought up on desertion charges or just shot. He wants this sergeant; believes he knows this area better than anyone. Thinks he can make a difference!"

"Go on!"

"He's been training ROK troops south of Seoul for three years and knows the landscape. He's half Hawaiian and Korean; speaks Korean fluently. Lastly, he has a Bronze Star and two Purple Hearts from his Pacific Island adventures. And oh, he thinks KMAG MP's are coming to arrest him. He asked for advice?"

Colonel Nelson had not yet resolved his feelings from his meeting with General Walker.

"Get back to the Captain. Wild Bill is an extraordinary judge of character. Let's go with it. Tell him that this sergeant is now part of Special Operations Command, G-2 Eighth Army, and he's untouchable. Verification only with me."

Nick didn't miss much. "Is this a new command structure, sir? I thought it was only a ruse for a while?"

Nelson leaned back in his chair and realized he had to come clean with his team, but not now. He needed some time to digest what just happened.

"We'll talk more about this later. Until then, it's still a ruse, Nick."

Chapter Four

Sunday, July 2, 1950 - Day Eight of the Invasion
Korea – On the Han River Southern Tributary, Somewhere
South of Seoul - 2230 – (10:30 pm)

They'd cast off five hours ago. Prevailing winds had shifted early on, now bringing hot, humid weather from the southwest, out of the South Pacific. Temperatures had risen into the high eighty's by late afternoon. The night had brought a deep blackness thick with humidity; it hadn't rained in a while. It was sticky hot and slow going but uneventful.

When they left, there was nothing but high grass on either bank. If you looked up, you saw high mountains near to the east and farther, lower ones to the west. Circling birds in the west were often seen, far off in the distance. Other then than that, they saw no living thing. It sent a strange and ominous feeling through the men.

The boat paddlers were not used to this hard, constant motion, using their arms and the strain to their backs this way. Red soon realized what this extra exertion was having on the men and so established a half-hour shift where four men would slip into the refreshing water and trade places with the guys on the raft.

Sometime after dark, Arron and Larry, and two others had just gotten into the raft. They felt refreshed by the brief dip and were relieved to stretch out flat on the raft. The air was still with not a whisper of a breeze. The only sound around them was from the dip of the paddles and push of the water from them, and the drag of the raft through the river.

Arron whispered over to Larry, "Ever been scared of quiet like this?"

Larry didn't answer. Yeah, he thought. A long time ago. The basement flashed through his brain. He tried to block it out as he had all his life. I'M NOT GOING THERE!

"I get the willies, Arron." Pausing to change the subject. "Wanted to ask you about the fish you caught for us at the Post. Man, you made delicious stuff! How'd you know what was good?"

Arron sensed he hit a nerve. Funny, he thought. Been with Larry about a year at the Post and don't know anything about him. Considering this thought further, maybe the jokes on me; nobody knows anything about me either.

"Larry, remember that time, think it was three or four weeks into setting up the Post when we all came down with the craps. Well, I never said anything, but earlier that day, my grenade fishing expedition landed this huge weird looking fish. It must've been fifteen pounds. So I made a stew from it. Larry! I tell you, I crapped my brains out like everyone else. Trial and error was my secret. So far, nobody's died from my cooking."

"You mean you don't know anything about these fish or animals you've been feeding us?"

"Didn't say that! Ain't no biologist. Just know how to survive! Trial and error. Good so far, right?"

Larry laid back on the raft. Thought of how he just put his past darkness out of his mind. Wondered about Arron. Right next to him. A guy he never thought much of anything about, and here he was, intruding on his deep hidden feelings. What did he experience? Does he have nightmares? How did he survive his parents? The war?

"I'm a tech engineer, Arron. Don't know shit about survival. Just know how to blow things up."

"Damn! You sure are good at that explosive stuff. I don't even know where you're from Larry, but I can tell you're on my side. We're fighting Northern crazies, and that's all that matters!"

"Yeah, Arron, I'm on your side. I never figured out much about life, but I hate stupid. These guys from the North are idiots thinking they can take on America. Hey, what about you, what's your story?

"Not much to tell. I grew up poor on a farm just north of Miami. That's where I learned to survive off the land, fish, hunt, and cook. Joined the Army in 1940 when I turned 16, lied, of course, but I had to get out of my area because of an unfortunate incident with a Northern Yankee salesman. I did really well, and by 1943, I was dropped into the German-occupied Balkans with two other guys to train and fight with the local resistance. That was some lousy shit, but I survived. My two team guys didn't."

"I would've never guessed you've been through so much, Arron. You're always joking around. Guess you never know about someone."

"Hey, Leyden, I never asked you how you got involved in this mess. You just flew in with Muzich and those guys with all those explosives to blow the bridges." Asked Tully.

"Just lucky, I guess." He laughed. "Seriously, this mission was put together on the fly by Master Sergeant Nick Beloit, who needed someone he could trust. I was his combat partner when Nick got his foot blown off by a Japanese land mine in the big war. He called, and I came running - end of story.

"What about you, Tully. How the hell did you get your Ranger ass get involved here?"

"It's kind of a long story, but I'll try to make it short. My squad was all vets of the war from various units and had been together for the last three years in Japan. Our Ranger Battalion was attached to an Army Division. Both commands had terrible leadership and rated at the bottom of every exercise. It was apparent our squad wasn't going to see any action for a while, but if we did, we felt we wouldn't last long because of these ill-trained officers."

With a laugh, Tully recounted meeting Red in Japan at a Weapons Review Analysis, where they became friends and learning of his deployment to Korea and involvement with Colonel Nelson.

"So, after talking to my men about what was going on and what could happen in Korea, my squad decided, as a unit, to follow my leadership and see if we could go to Korea."

"So that's when I volunteered my squad to Colonel Nelson."

Not a sound of war as they slowly passed south. Crickets and the gurgling river passing over an intermittent obstruction were the only sounds they heard.

Rusty leaned into Muzich. "You sure you can get your plane off the sandbar?"

Still hurting from the wound he received piloting his PBY with reinforcements and explosives to blow up the Han River bridges, he was irritable. The stitches in his arm hurt, but he had refused further pain medications from Marty, the unit's combat medic. He knew he had to fly, he said, "I know my shit, Sergeant!"

"Thank you, Navy Commander John Muzich, for putting me in my place! And that's first sergeant! But I don't give a good crap if you're an admiral! I only care if you can get my men out of here! Can you?"

Muzich flinched at the criticism, and let out a breath, "Feel like shit, Rusty! Sorry. Didn't mean to come at you like that. Don't like being questioned. I do that enough to myself. But yeah! That bird is like a bulldozer! She'll power off of any stinking sandbar!"

"Don't want to leave you stranded is all. We can't wait until daylight to make sure you get off."

"I know. Got a fallback plan if stuff happens. We kept an emergency six-man inflatable in the rear of the plane. I need to check it, but I think it's undamaged. We could follow you down the river if you leave the boat exposed on the river bank where you exit."

"Muzich! You're a determined Commander. If you say your bird will fly, well, I'm a believer."

During the journey, Rusty ordered that the men leaving on the PBY would take only minimal supplies. They would only take their 45 caliber shoulder pistols. The rest of their weapons and ammo were to be left in the boat for them to take.

Working the tiller in the rear of the boat, C J checked his watch. "We're nearing where the plane should be."

Rusty called out, "Tracker! Lights on!"

Tracker had been leaning over the front of the boat for the last hour, trying to hear the water passing against the plane. A Chippewa Indian from Minnesota, he had unique skills and great senses.

He started searching the darkness with his flashlight. A half-hour later, he spotted it in the middle of the river.

"There!" He yelled, pointing his light on the plane.

They hit the sandbar a few minutes later. The men were happy to exit, stretch, and relax a minute. But only for a minute.

"Move fast; this is not a picnic area!" Said Red.

Leyden became the onsite director of the plane. "Gregg! Go left with the flashlight along the side. Check for holes, obstructions. Phil! You got right! Muzich! Check inside!"

J P came up to him. "What about me?"

"Go up top and check for nests in the engines or anywhere else."

"What kind of nests?"

Leyden was thoughtful, thinking he was still in the jungle. "Just be careful. Snakes! Big vipers! Rodents! Could be anything!"

J P felt he was jesting. "Long as this baby doesn't rock!" He laughed and climbed. J P had a dreadful fear of motion on any body of water, even a stream.

Muzich came out a few minutes later and met Rusty by the front hatch. "Inflatable looks undamaged. Everything looks ready to go."

"Hope to see you soon! Good luck, Commander Muzich." Rusty shook his hand and left.

Marty came over to Muzich, who was leaning against the hatch. "Get that arm looked at first thing! Good luck, sir!"

"It's been an honor to have served with you, Marty." They shook.

Red found Leyden, shook his hand, and said, "see ya," then ordered his men back into the canoe boat. The parting was subdued among the men. They didn't think they'd meet again.

As the canoe pulled away, Leyden, about ready to board the plane, yelled into the dark. "Tully! Kickass!" He heard a grunt.

Leyden stood there for a moment and realized his new responsibility. Being with Jack, leader of Post # 4, when he died on the Han River Bridge, added to this unwanted burden. Now he was responsible for the remainder of Jack's surviving command, Gregg, Phil, and J P, to try and keep alive. A chill went up his spine when he realized that he wasn't sure that he could. He also wondered whether he'd make it.

Chapter Five

Except for a short dinner break, they labored through the evening. They signed off on the CIA secrecy documents, organized the pickup of the CIA secret equipment, and arranged their transport to Captain Stands at Taejon Airfield.

Master Sergeant Nick Beloit insisted this one secret mission plane also carry as many 30 and 50 caliber machine guns, 60 mm mortars, and ammunition that it could bring. He ordered out men and trucks with MP escorts to warehouses to deliver them for the scheduled morning flight. It took Nick the better part of four hours to get this all arranged. He was exhausted and frustrated but said nothing.

His efforts did not go unnoticed by the rest of the team sitting around the table. Although all were working on something, nobody was working as intensely as Nick.

"Maybe we should take a break!" Said Colonel Nelson, as he got up and stretched his legs, the group followed, a few formed a simple line to the coffee maker. Nick went to the back wall map depicting an aerial photo of Osan, Korea, from five thousand feet.

Nelson grabbed two cups of coffee and walked over to Nick. "Here. Tell me what you see."

They both took sips of the steaming black coffee. Nick nodded.

"Sir! Ever since I heard our forces were to take a stand and fight here, I've been sick and said so. Been racking my brain trying to figure out how we could do that ever since? I can't!"

"Then stop trying!"

"Sir!"

Nelson felt he needed to address the entire team, so he turned and spoke.

"Listen up, everybody!"

"This Team developed a rolling defense plan for our forces to intercept the enemy at Osan and show them that America has arrived. Slow them down on that main highway by harassment and interdiction. The plan wasn't designed to stop the advance, just slow it down. But the military leadership outside of our command structure ignored this plan."

He paused to weigh his thoughts.

"We need to think past this battle developing — six hundred men at Osan against an Army. You've done your best here. I don't believe that we can do a damn thing in the next few days to change what's going to happen. We can help, and we will, but the outcome is all but certain."

Nelson became calm and walked to the back of the room.

"I'm changing up the A-Team structure as of now!"

The semi-groggy members around the room snapped awake.

"General McArthur and our General Walker have authorized a new unit within my command section. It's Top

Secret, and you now are so advised. You have all signed CIA documents. They are far-reaching, and yet they go beyond the CIA, as they encompass ANY TOP SECRET document or disclosure."

Composing himself, Nelson paced.

"You are not to discuss with anybody outside of this room anything said from here on, period. I had to say it. I know you wouldn't, but pillow talk, etc. We all know the ease of slipping by accident. Okay, that crap had to be said."

"So now, I present my dilemma to my trusted Team. We must split the group. The picture is getting too big. Eighth Army is about to get fully engaged in this war, and it needs a dedicated G-2 staff to support it, that's us. But another task has been given to me, us really, that transcends this responsibility. MacArthur called it a fancy codename, I call it an Emergency Response Effort. Because without it, MacArthur, our General Walker, and I think our Eighth Army G-2 efforts will be in vain."

The Team was transfixed.

Nelson then detailed the pending orders and his discussion with General Walker.

A long-dead silence ensued. Finally, Major Jarvis stirred in his chair.

"Sir. A suggestion. I've been working directly with all Eighth Army Division G-2 unit leaders for the last many days and would like to expand that staff. I could take that leadership responsibility. Free you up to do this other thing."

"I hoped you'd come forward, Hank. I didn't want to order you."

That got a smile from the Team.

Nelson stayed stoic, then asked, "Who do you want from this team?"

Major Jarvis was taken by surprise by the question and got flustered. "Colonel, do you know what you're asking me?"

Nelson, not showing anything, said, "Major. Hank, you're one of the smartest judges of men I've ever met. So, yes, I want your assessment and your choice or choices."

"Damn it, Colonel!" The Major had never been put on the spot like this. He was feeling uncomfortable. Facing this handpicked team of the best men he had ever assembled and now having to pick among them was an impossible task. Which ones would best contribute their incredible talents to what we need now?

Jarvis regained his composure, thought about that long ago Genie, who granted one wish. Might as well seize on that, he thought.

Major Jarvis sat up straight. "Sir. Respectfully, I would request the entire A-Team, but I know that would do a disservice to you. So, my wish is to take Lieutenant Larry Cole and Captain Sam Haran."

Nelson smiled. "It was a trick question, Hank. Sorry, but I wanted to confirm your thinking. As much as I hate to part with Lt Cole, I believe he'll best help you and Eighth Army in the mission you initially hired him to accomplish. But I need Sam."

The room again became silent.

"So, to be clear, this secret unit will be named '**NSOPU**' and will be separate from G-2, but we will work together. I'm Commander of both, as Head of Intelligence. Hank, you will build your staff as you see fit, you are now Deputy G-2 of

Eighth Army operations, and we will meet daily. All ongoing G-2 field operations are your responsibility, as my deputy. This other new role I have taken on is under this unit's umbrella, but with a separate leader, me, at the moment, so you're all involved in one way or another, and I will need your support. Do I have it?"

Lt Cole was the first to respond with a "Holy Shit! Are you kidding?" Then he realized the room was quiet and slunk back in his chair.

Then the group started clapping their approval.

Hammering next to them interrupted the celebration.

"Thanks for your support. General Walker wastes no time," alluding to the noise; "he's building a separate section next to ours for this new secret Command."

Chapter Six

Sunday, July 3, 1950 - Day Nine of the Invasion
Two Hundred Miles off the East Coast of Korea
Aboard Aircraft Carrier USS Valley Forge (CV-45) – 0600 –
(6:00 am)

After the briefing, Commander of Flight Operations, Art Dixon, stood facing his pilots. The wall chart at his back depicted the North Korean target area, some four hundred miles away. It was in great detail.

"I'll admit to you that I've never ordered a flight into combat, but I'm good at my job. Most of you have never been in combat, but you, too, are trained well and know what to do. We have a good plan. You've studied it. Any questions?"

Squadron commander of the A -1 Skyraiders, Lieutenant Commander Charles Blackford, "Blackie," raised his hand. "Sir, I know you said the weather over our primary target should be a lot better than here, but what if it's not, and the secondary objective is closed in as well, what do we do?"

"Sorry if I wasn't clear, but you are then authorized to seek targets of opportunity on your return. Not breaking formation but only seeking breaks in the weather for your group to interdict enemy activity."

"Thank you, sir."

"Anyone else?" No response.

"Trust your instincts! Good luck!"

Blackie walked out with his wingman, Archie. They'd been together since '44, flying Corsairs off of the deck of the USS Hornet (CV – 12). They'd both loved that plane, but after the war, they signed up for test pilot duty, mostly to stay in the service. Blackie's wife had sent him his divorce papers in '45, before the end of the war. Archie had no family, so he said, and had no interest in returning to civilian life.

Among many planes, they tested the A – 1 Skyraider. They loved it. Thought it was the best, far superior to any for close-in tactical ground support. They were convinced, and so was the Navy.

A – 1 Sky raider

The Jet age had arrived during this same time, putting the final nail in the WW 2 Corsairs future. Blackie and Archie wanted no part of this new jet age. They liked the beauty of an excellent propeller plane and loved the in-your-face exhilaration of ground support operations.

The Skyraider kept them out of the jets, and because of their experience, they became trainers. They were the best Skyraider trainers. When the first squadron was formed and became active, Blackie became commander, and where Blackie went, Archie followed.

Blackie's squadron of these new A-1 attack aircraft landed on Valley Forge in the summer of '48. A jet fighter squadron of Grumman F9F Panthers arrived soon after that. The Corsairs had not been replaced yet and were still aboard.

Valley Forge was one of the last of the Essex Class of Fleet Carriers, started in late '44, she was commissioned in '46 and fully outfitted in early '47, she was new but old. Not designed for the modern jet aircraft or the new capacity required of more advanced maintenance requirements and aircraft ordinance, but she still was a beautiful machine and performed like the Queen she was. Per her Captain.

Blackie waited for the "Man your Planes" order and wondered about this mission. High top escort by jets? Damn! My old Corsairs following in as fighter-bombers. Me flying a new combat mission after five years! In a brand new plane! Old and new. How can I feel old at 28? But I do. Next to him was his best friend. "Archie, do you feel old?"

"You got the jitters. It's been a while, but you always got them before a mission. Yeah, I feel old. What's the average age of our squadron, maybe 22? Remember when we were them?"

"Pilots! Man Your Planes."

After taking off in light rain, they got up to cruising altitude above dense clouds for most of the hour and a half run. The group held integrity and saw occasional big breaks in the weather. Blackie was encouraged.

The city of Pyongyang, on the West Coast in North Korea, was their target. Only fifty miles north of the enemy's main line of attack, it was a central marshaling infrastructure of rail, storage, and a large airfield.

Approaching at 20,000 feet, the break in the clouds brought a big smile to Blackie.

"Leader to Squadron! We'll follow our plan. **A** Flight follows me to target airfield! **B** Flight to the railyards! **C** Flight to storage buildings! Tally Ho!"

Blackie dove, Archie followed his leader. Blackie's four 20 mm autocannons were devastating as he strafed the sitting unprotected enemy planes. Pulling up, performing a tight turn, he focused on a string of hangers near the end of the runway. Leveling off at 600 feet, he started dropping his five 500 pound bombs among them.

While making a full turn, he headed toward the refueling tanks on the far side of the field, he glanced to his side and admired the fine work his flight had accomplished so far. Smoke and flames engulfed a large segment of the area.

At three hundred feet, the fuel depot came up fast. Firing ten rockets in quick two-second intervals, Blackie then climbed quickly. The fireball created was a sight.

As Blackie's squadron reformed heading home, every flight leader checked in with no losses. One received minor damage by ground fire. He felt relieved and exhilarated.

This new Skyraider he'd tested and recommended performed even better than he thought. What a weapon, carrying an 8000 pound payload, like a bomber, yet it performed like a fighter. Damn! I like this plane.

Switching his radio channel to his Top Cover group of Panther jets, he was surprised to hear a lot of chatter about their victory above them. He figured out they shot down two Russian-built Yak-9 fighters trying to come down on us.

He knew of this Yak plane, the most significant Russian fighter plane in WW2. Comparable to our P-51 Mustang, but faster. They would have made mincemeat of us! I'm starting to acquire a real fondness for our Jets, he pondered this life-saving engagement.

"Thank you, Panther's," he whispered.

Without much fanfare or, in fact, even an acknowledgment, Valley Forge launched the first Carrier attack of the Korean War on North Korea. At the same time, its Panther Jets scored the first air victory of an American Jet in this new era.

Chapter Seven

Sunday, July 3, 1950 - Day Nine of the Invasion
Korea – On the Han River Southern Tributary, Somewhere
South of Seoul – 0845 – (8:45 am)

It was a hot, humid, bright morning, about forty miles further south from the plane drop-off when C J found the place he sought, a narrow clearing on the western shore. They pulled up and thankfully stretched out for a while, finally unloaded everything onto the river bank.

Organizing the bundles, ammunition belts, and sacks, then securing them together to carry on their backs took some time. They were human donkeys, as most infantry were, when their trek to Osan began, under a brutal sun with C J's *Three* at the lead. Both C J and *Three* knew Osan very well, but *Three* grew up there.

Three got his nickname like the other two men in C J's unit, *One* and *Two.* It was because they didn't speak or understand English, which made communications with the newly arrived American's impossible. But they were very bright, show them something once, and they knew how to do it, plus they were brave, as the last mission at the Han Bridges just proved. *Two* didn't make it back.

As they moved off the flat river terrain and progressed into the higher grass, they could sense the gradual rise and see remote groups of hills. The pathway soon turned to rock and mud; they forded a few minor streams. A distant mountain and rolling outcroppings were all they could see. The hot sun turned to cloud cover, providing some relief to the high temperatures, but the humidity was oppressive. Thankfully, there was no rain.

The idle chatter amongst the men had ended long ago and settled into a sullied silence of occasional grunts and curses when someone tripped or fell or whose foot got stuck in a mud hole. They continued going higher into the foothills, experiencing greater height after every undulation. They saw nothing for three hours until they approached the first summit.

Halting the column, C J saw signs of humanity. Friend or foe? He waved back to the men to bring up support. Rusty and Foxy were five men back and came forward.

"Someone is around here, not sure who. We need to scout."

Rusty nodded to C J. "Foxy, get Frenchy, Snake, and Tracker."

Moments later, they rushed up and knelt. "We may have company? Split up. Foxy, you and Tracker angle south, Frenchy, take Snake to go northwest. We're moving ahead slowly. Go!"

The landscape was barren rock and brush, with gullies and crevices. Once off their sort of path, it was rough going for the scouts. They had been chosen well for this mission. Both Foxy and Frenchy spoke Korean, and Tracker and Snake were extraordinary recon experts.

Off the crest of the summit, down a few hundred yards in a gully, Tracker dropped silently and pointed further down into a ravine, it led to a large cave. Men and women were milling about in a large group. Weapons were visible. The uniforms of some of the men looked like ROK uniforms, other men had all types of garb, from pheasant to banker suits. Some of the women had babies and young children.

"Must be a hundred people!" Tracker whispered, bewildered at the sight from their perch.

"Get C J and Rusty." Ordered Foxy.

Ten minutes passed before Rusty and C J arrived along with Frenchy and Snake, who had spotted nothing on their mission. The rest of the team was coming up behind them, taking up positions.

"Not enemy." Said C J to Rusty. "But running and scared. We need to be careful."

C J had told Rusty and the men about South Korean's President's obsession with Communists and his broad interpretation of what that meant; how he dealt with them before and after the free election. Anyone who opposed him was labeled a Commie, and, after the election, C J and other Special Forces disposed of the leaders of these Commies in the short but bloody civil war.

This attitude continued as the South Korean Army retreated. Syngman Ree, South Korean's President, took the low road, had little character, and was often characterized as a thug as heinous as Chicago's uber-thug, Al Capone.

C J recounted the last order he had received from his command before he lost communications. His President ordered retreating ROK units to round up and kill suspected Communist sympathizers so they couldn't help the advancing enemy.

The team had seen horrible things from both sides, knew fearful people on the run didn't much care what side you were on, you could be a threat, like any cornered animal, they'd fight.

The men watching talked about how to approach this group without causing alarms of possible retribution as Army deserters or collaborators as communists?

Frenchy realized the dilemma and had a solution. He crept up next to Rusty and C J, looking down on this group.

"Rusty, I'm the only real American that speaks Korean. We have no identifying anything about who we are, but I'm totally white, not half and half like Foxy, speak English and Korean, and I think I can march down there without causing an *OK Corral* fiasco."

Rusty and C J looked at each other. Neither had a better idea.

Rusty nodded, "A damn Ranger! Frenchy! You guys are crazy, but damn it if you don't have brains too. I'm becoming quite fond of you. Okay, go for it."

Frenchy moved off, made his way down toward the cave. Unspotted, very near the mass, he rose, his Tommy gun raised high above his head. In Korean, he spoke, "American! No harm to you! I come to help!"

He started walking into their lair.

The reaction was swift. Soldiers grabbed rifles or pulled side arms and formed a line around him.

"Anyone speak English?"

An officer stepped from behind the line, his pistol still holstered. "Who are you?" Spoken in proper English.

"American Army Ranger, sir." He saluted, the officer returned it.

"Frenchy is my name. I and a small secret American unit have been fighting from the border since the invasion. My unit is on the bluff with all arms trained on this camp should you do me harm. As I said, we wish only safe passage, whether you come with us or stay here. We're just passing through and want no trouble. That's your choice."

"Where are you going? Why would we follow you?" The ROK officer, now recognized as a captain, then turned and shouted to his men. "Lower your weapons. He's a friend."

Thinking fast, Frenchy remembered the ruse Foxy played on the ROK regimental colonel when they first met, to gain respect.

"Thank you, Captain. My colonel will answer your questions. May I bring him down here to discuss your concerns and our mission?"

"How many men do you have?

"Sorry, Captain. My colonel's name is Rusty. He's disguised as a low rank as fitting our secret mission. I'll bring him down with a few of his key men, and he can answer all your questions. All I can tell you is that America is here and we are part of them! We aim to fight for your country."

"Go, bring them in." The captain said with the first hopeful thought he'd had in a while.

Chapter Eight

Sunday, July 3, 1950 - Day Nine of the Invasion
At the Same time - Korea – Taejon Airfield – One Hundred
Miles SE of the Han River
0845 – (8:45 am)

When it pulled up, Arnie jumped out of the truck he was working on at the front of the hanger, ran to the rear of the arriving vehicle, lowered the hatch and exclaimed, "You've arrived at a sacred place! Rejoice!"

Inside the truck, the men had just landed in a shot-up PBY on a lake a few miles away. They'd been ordered back from their impossible mission from Rusty's team after being instrumental in blowing up the Han River Bridges.

Commander John Muzich, the Navy pilot, was first to jump down with a wince. His arm still hurt like hell from the wound he suffered after his plane was damaged by AA fire when he flew this very team into a blind river landing near the mountain hideout they just vacated.

Tech Sergeant Tom Leyden, leader of the assault team on the bridge and now the new leader of the Post # 4 team, jumped next and said to Arnie. "Only fucking rejoicing I'm doing is if there's a bunch of big steaks on the fire!"

Survivors of Post # 4 followed, Phil, Greg and J P were happy to get off the truck. Their leader from Post # 4, Jack, was killed on the bridge next to Tom Leyden. He was on their mind when they landed. Talking amongst themselves about how Jack's end impacted each of them, they surprised themselves by their consensus. Of course, they missed him, but knowing him, they reflected that he went out the way he would've wanted, in a battle, for a worthy cause. They came to peace with that thought.

"Listen up!"

After his yell. Captain Stands saluted them, didn't wait for a return. "Heroes are welcome to my humble surroundings, come in, relax. I'll see if I can make you comfortable. Sorry, but steaks are not on the menu this morning. Maybe tonight? But we have coffee, real eggs, and bread, go in and eat."

He walked up to Commander Muzich, a fellow pilot. "I heard you did some extraordinary work up there. Get some food, and then I'm taking you to the hospital to get a real specialist to have a look at that arm."

"Thanks."

Later, after he returned from the hospital, Captain Stands surveyed his new arrivals and walked over to the steak guy, intuitively knowing he was their leader.

"My friends call me Wild Bill, what's yours?"

He stared at him. "Tom, or Big Tom, Leyden, from Queens, NY."

"I can tell you're an old hand at this war shit, Big Tom. You got something coming up, due in here in a bit. Don't have a clue what it is, but for a heads up, it's on a special plane due in this AM for MY EYES Only, concerning you, Leyden."

"Thanks for the grub, Captain. Can we sit, may I see a map of where in the hell I'm at?"

Pausing, Leyden asked, "You have an Eighth Army Air Force patch on your flying jacket, I thought that was absorbed into the new Air Force command?"

"I have maps. Let's sit over there."

They settled on boxes at the corner of the hanger. Nearby, Leyden noticed the P-51.

"That's as beautiful a fighter as I've ever seen. Yours?"

"He's *Just Due,* resurrected recently from the graveyard by my great crew, and now he's my warbird. I fought with this plane just recently, but I have a long love affair with the P-51, a magnificent fighting machine."

Tom felt as comfortable with this officer as he has ever felt with any new soldier in arms he has met. Wild Bill felt the same about Big Tom. Both knew they'd been through it and didn't have that ego crap that usually went along with it, rank or no rank, they figured they were equals, professionals.

The Captain spread out his area map on the crate box.

Chapter Nine

**Sunday, July 3, 1950 - Day Nine of the Invasion
Korea – At the Cave, Rusty's Team Meeting with ROK
Soldiers and Civilians - 1300 – (1:00 pm)**

Frenchy led the group down; his hands held his Tommy gun high above his head. Rusty, Foxy, and C J followed with weapons slung from their shoulders.

As he got close, Rusty recognized the bars on the ROK captain and stopped, saluted. The captain returned it then said, "I understand you are a secret unit and show no rank. Are you a Colonel?"

"Captain! I'm an American Colonel that has fought a secret war against the North Koreans since the invasion. Now I don't know why you're here, and I don't give a good crap. Whether you're running from the fight or reorganizing, that's your affair." Rusty paused to look around and continued.

"I want to pass by without trouble from you. We're heading to Osan to join up with American Army regulars to try to slow the North Korean advance."

"I would do you no harm, Colonel. My concern is about my own country's rabid anti-communist troops, and special enforcers of perceived deserters."

"We are neither."

"How many men do you have, Colonel?"

"Not enough."

C J saw the captain's unit arm patch and spoke up. "The Capital Division saw a good deal of action right down into the streets of Seoul, were you there?"

"The sixty-three men here are all that's left of my two hundred and fifty man company when I brought them across the Han River. They fought bravely. I don't intend to sacrifice them for a lost cause." Looking over at C J, "Sergeant, why are you with these Americans?"

"Captain, first, I love my country and don't think the war is lost. Second, my uncle is G -2 of the South Korean Army, and he ordered me to join them."

"You're a fool, Sergeant, to believe an old man, and that anyone cares for us. America will not waste any of its men when defeat stinks the battlefield."

C J bowed his head. "I'm ashamed of you, Captain. You're educated and appear to be a warrior, but you are afraid. You have no faith, and without faith, you are of no use to your Country or your men, so go and tend to the fields, save your men, escape facing the harsh fact of maybe dying. Accept living like slaves under communist rule, just as we did with the Japs. Is that your wish?"

The captain stood, stunned by this sergeant's words.

High on the bluff, Tully watched the actions through his binoculars with Red by his side, lying prone behind his 30 caliber machine gun.

"What's going on?" Red was anxious.

"Still talking, everybody looks calm. Wait! The leader is speaking to his group. They're stirring, gathering gear and weapons. The civilians are packing. Frenchy is coming back up here. C J and Rusty are talking with the ROK leader. It looks positive, Red."

Frenchy soon got to the bluff and reported to Red and Tully about the colonel ruse employed and that this group would join them on their trek to Osan. Told them that they were starving and that the ROK soldiers had seen much battle and death and were demoralized. He wasn't sure if they'd fight or run. He had no thoughts about the civilians nor how they were going to survive.

Chapter Ten

Sunday, July 3, 1950 - Day Nine of the Invasion
Korea – City of Pusan at the Tip of Korea – Earlier that Day

The city of Pusan was in chaos. Even though military order had been imposed a few days ago, no overall progress had been made to break up the log jam for the US Military as enormous quantities of supplies and soldiers poured in. It was catch as catch can, and not many were catching anything.

The harbor was vast, but dockage was limited, and facilities were antiquated. The port swelled with ships with no place to unload. Ships unloading had difficulty getting transport of the material out of the area. Troops disembarking had limited places to assemble, nowhere to feed them, and few means of available transportation to take them to the front.

The airport was the same. Once a small International airfield by any standard, in a few short days, it became one of the busiest airports in the world. And a significant bottleneck; same story as the harbor. Adding insult to all the chaos, the first arriving American officers and engineers mistreated the local Korean labor leaders, much like their Japanese oppressors did just a few short years ago. Operations at the docks and particularly the railroads, slowed considerably.

Army Logistics Headquarters in Pusan

The phone rang.

"This is General Walker. I want to speak to Major Jorgen, Head of Logistics!"

"After a few seconds, he was connected. "Major Jorgen, sir. How can I help you?"

"Is Captain Zelts on your staff?"

"Yes, sir, and he is troubling. Very unorthodox, I'm glad you read my recommendations about him."

"Is he there in your building? If so, please bring him into this call."

"Yes, he's here. Just rebuked him on a fantasy he had. I'll get him, sir."

A few minutes later.

"General, I have you on speakerphone, with me is Captain Zelts, as you requested."

"Good!" A pause.

"Mister Zelts, you've only been a captain only a few days, what have you learned?"

Taken aback by the question, but pissed off at his asshole boss for ignoring his proposals, he said, "Sir, Captain's bars aren't enough."

A pause on the speakerphone. "I thought so too. Major Jorgen! You've established a new record for an officer in my command receiving the most complaints in the fewest possible days. I don't suppose you had any in-theater experience during the war?"

"No, sir, stationed at the Pentagon during the War, been out here about a year."

"Thought so. Pack your things, Major. You're fired!"

"What! I'm following orders and procedures; you can't do this!"

"I'm sure you're good at staff logistics, Major, but not in the field. I'll put you in for full retirement. Now please leave immediately."

He got up and left, the door slammed.

"Captain Zelts, I've got to start landing my Army in Pusan. Right now it's so mucked up I fear sending any more of anything. Tell me, if I made you in charge of the entire Pusan logistics situation, what are the first three things you'd do today?"

"Wow, General." Said the young ex-Lieutenant, now Captain of only a few days. "Besides begging for additional men and material," and without pausing, "I'd do the following:

1) I'd take the only three large empty barges we have in the harbor, fill them with sand and gravel and build a new pier. We have some bridging equipment and a large amount of *Marston Mat* steel planking material we use to construct temporary airfield runways. That'll give us two more ships we can dock. It'll take two days."

2) "I only have ten bulldozers. All but two are working on building outer defenses. I'll stop that and bring the remaining eight back to pave additional runways and exit roads at the airport. I can get them started late today."

3) "We pissed off a good deal of local Korean labor leaders when we came, mainly the railroad guys. We have suffered because of that. We need to get the rail system working. I will personally go and apologize to them and hopefully give them monetary

compensation, that is, if I can get approval from somebody outside of my command structure."

"That's what I like about you, Zelts. You got the answers to serious questions, anticipate, and are not afraid to break the rules. Although, your note to me about this situation could be construed to be insubordinate. But I didn't take it that way, mainly because you suggested a more seasoned logistics leader."

"General, I didn't mean to get the Major fired. It's just that things are so bad over here, and I know lives are at stake."

"Enough! You're what's needed there NOW! I've issued orders, should be there already."

"I promoted you to Major. You're in Command of all logistics surrounding Pusan."

"When we hang up, I want you to detail the top three things you need to be sent to you, ASAP, include money for the locals. Send this list to this unit, NSOPU, write it down. Now, this unit is TOP SECRET, and I mean it! I'll call them to give them a heads up and stress the urgency of your needs. Otherwise, anything and I mean anything that gets in your way, you are to call my XO, Colonel Harris directly."

"Good luck, Major Zelts. Don't disappoint me!"

Major Zelts sat back, humbled, and scared. Never before had he ever felt the weight of real responsibility. He then sprang forward, determined, grabbed a pencil, and started writing the immediate needs of his new command.

Chapter Eleven

Sunday, July 3, 1950 - Day Nine of the Invasion
Korea – Task Force Smith entering Taejon – 1600 – (4:00 pm)

Colonel Smith's partial force set out early from Pusan. The train that was to take them wasn't ready, with no known time when it would be, so they scrambled to find anything with wheels. The convoy was a makeshift of vehicles of what could be bought or stolen. Some military vehicles, others impounded civilian trucks and trailers. Anything that could run was added to the caravan to transport them north. The almost 200 mile trip to Taejon took over eight hours.

More units were following after they disembarked and would have the same transport problems. Colonel Smith was also to meet additional forces flown into Taejon. It was a nightmare of planning.

The advanced unit rolled into Taejon in drizzling rain. Colonel Smith reported to General Church, who, although he was just replaced as Commander of all forces in Korea by General Dean, Colonel Smith's Division commander, was here on the ground. General Church was the guy in charge right now and gave Smith his marching orders.

Colonel Smith was disgusted with these orders but had no way of contacting his boss, General Dean, to try to change them.

`

His jeep driver and longtime friend, First Sergeant "Whitey," Dillon, drove Smith to the airport to meet the just arriving troops.

He found only a company of riflemen and became somewhat depressed that no heavy weapons were with them. The rain became more substantial, so he walked over to a nearby hanger for cover. Behind him, he heard. "You lucky bastards! You get to fight in all kinds of weather that the gods determine."

"What?"

"Just saying how envious I am of the Army's ability to fight in any weather and kill the heathen."

It was then that Wild Bill saw his Colonel's Eagles. "Sir! You must be Colonel Smith; I didn't know. I have a surprise for you inside."

Laid out on the interior side of the hangar floor was copious amounts of heavy weapons and munitions.

"What's this? Who in hell are you, Captain?"

"These are yours, compliments of a Master Sergeant, Nick Beloit, at Eighth Army G- 2 headquarters. I never met him, but I sure do like his style. As to the rest, well, I'm just doing my thing."

"Got a message here for you as well." He went to a table and lifted an envelope, then yelled, "Leyden! Need you!"

"Top Secret, Colonel Smith, for your eyes only." The captain said as he handed over the envelope. "Got a bigger one, and this was enclosed. Mine was interesting reading."

Tech Sergeant Leyden came up to Wild Bill. "Is this about our new orders?"

"Think so. Got to wait till the Colonel here reads his message."

Finished reading, Colonel Smith yelled to his sergeant, "Whitey! Come here!" Then he joined up with Wild Bill and Leyden. "You Leyden?"

Leyden and his new arrivals had had time to get something to eat, get a hot shower, and don new utilities, including boots, also sent by Master Sergeant Beloit.

Colonel Smith had no idea who Leyden was or where he'd been, but he looked like he just stepped off of a plane, all nice and clean, and he was a Tech Sergeant.

Ever one for pissing off an officer whenever the chance presented. "You can call me Tom, sir."

Wild Bill smirked at the remark, admired Leyden's balls. He was just like him.

"Can that bullshit, Sergeant! You've got some TOP SECRET crap with you, and I'm to escort you to some damn hill on my way to a fucking suicide mission, so if you show disrespect again, I'll have Whitey here but a bullet in your ass, understand?"

Leyden relaxed. "Apologize, Colonel. Rare to meet an officer that knows the score."

Whitey changed the scene by focusing on the weapons displayed. "Sir, these are a great addition to our strength. I'll get them parsed out."

Wild Bill interjected, "Colonel, I need to speak with you for a minute, privately."

They moved to a corner. "Colonel, I don't know what was in your orders, but my orders are to make sure that you understand how important your TOP SECRET escort duties are for these guys. They're special, been doing dirty work for many days, killing those commie bastards. That equipment they carry can't be captured, no matter how many men it costs."

"Thanks, Captain. Didn't know what they've done. Knew about the last part."

"Don't know if your orders say that you're taking on a new assistant communications sergeant, but you are, his name is Sergeant Dan Engle, he's an expert in the terrain where you're going, and he's part of this new Secret Communications thing. I wish I knew more."

"Thanks, Captain."

"My friends call me Wild Bill."

Later in the afternoon

As they assembled for the trip north, Captain Melvin, Commander of Company B, 1st Battalion, detached from the 25th Regiment, 25th Division, came to his 1st Platoon's First Sergeant, "Whitey" Dillon.

"Whitey!" He said in his Texas drawl, "Glad the colonel didn't steal you away from me. He recognizes that anybody can drive a jeep, but few can lead men like you."

"Thanks, Cap."

"You know we got buffalo piss served on shit! Your platoon is the lead scout unit and me at command; we pull out in ten minutes. We are to babysit this other group to a certain hill and make sure they get there safely. We also have a Sergeant Engle; he trained ROK units up this way for a few years, so he'll be our guide and ride with me upfront."

The little convoy assembled in light rain. Whitey grabbed Leyden and directed him and his men to a truck, where they manhandled several crates onboard and then climbed in. He was charged with their safekeeping by his captain.

Leyden's men were all freshly outfitted, clean, fed, rested, and scared shitless. They were unusually silent as the convoy pulled out.

A grateful Sergeant Dan Engle sat in the back of the first jeep, thinking about how lucky he was to have a second chance!

Sergeant George Lopez, the survivor from Post # 1 and the three survivors from Post # 4, had all worked with the Top Secret equipment they carried. They had discussed their new deployment and how best to get this new technology to work for the troops in the field. The orders and instructions were inadequate. But they knew about a few essentials. Phil was an avid techie and had overseen the entire technical operation at Post #4. He had questions.

"So, Sergeant Whitey, my name is Phil, and I have a question. Do you have a command communications vehicle?"

He looked at him with a blank stare. "I don't know."

"It's important. Our ability to help you depends on it, can you find out?"

"So, you guys are on a special mission?" Asked Whitey.

Leyden sat back, felt pressed. "You have no fucking idea of where we've been or what we've done, Sergeant. All you need to know is that we've probably seen more death in the last couple of days then you've seen in your lifetime."

"Sorry if I came off wrong. I've seen my share of horror. I want to see how I can help. I'll find out about that communications vehicle."

Leyden nodded. "Thanks. We'll try to help you, but it will take a little time to set up. I fear for you on this first encounter. I think you're going to get your ass handed to you."

"Yeah, that's what I think, my boss agrees. Been there before, though. Appreciate the additional weapons you brought in."

An hour later, the convoy halted for a piss break.

Whitey climbed back in after the others. "Hey, you with the communication question!"

"Names, Phil! What'd you find out?"

"We got a command Jeep with long-range capabilities. They say twenty miles with a clear line of sight."

"If it works, we're in business. I'll give you our frequency before we leave."

"We can use all the help we can get, thanks."

Chapter Twelve

A captain popped into the room, "Sorry, got an urgent TOP SECRET to NSOPU, you share this space now, so I hope it's okay?"

"I'll take it," said Captain Haram.

"That's our first for this new unit, Sam. Read it."

"From a Major Zelts, Commander of Logistics in Pusan, Korea. On the behest of General Walker, he asked that I request you to employ your extraordinary abilities to break this terrible bottleneck we experience at the only junction in bringing in Eighth Army troops and supplies into Korea. He said to list my needs, although many, my most urgent are as follows:

1) Barges – the bigger, the better, filled with bulldozers and cranes.

2) Seabee's – A division would be best, but I'll take a platoon.

3) Cash - $50,000 in $20 bills to pay off railroad personnel, more if I can get it.

All is very urgent."

Nick was thoughtful for a second, then said, "Hey! Is this that same guy that General Walker promoted at our first big meeting? Man, I thought that was something. But he was jumped to a captain, right?"

"It's the same guy, Nick." Said Colonel Nelson. "Now he's been promoted to major. Zelts must get things done. And then he follows with our first NSOPU challenge."

Nelson paused to collect his thoughts, and finally confronted his doubts about the leadership of this split operation. Having chosen one leader for the G-2 Operation but not the other left him in a difficult situation that was now quite clear. He needed to be commander of all two without the details of running both.

The full A-Team watched and waited as their leader went through his progressions; they knew something was afoot; it didn't take long.

Nelson finally looked around the table.

"Nick, I want you to head up this Secret Group."

The response was spontaneous with clapping and "yahoo's."

"I'm honored, sir, but I'm not an officer. How can I do this?"

"Because I say you can. You're head of this Secret Unit. Any trouble, you come to me, then General Walker. Worse comes to worst, you go to the Emperor himself with no staff in between."

Pausing a moment, "Nick, take this by the balls! I already talked to Captain Haram about this, he's ecstatic that you're the leader, recommended you, in fact. Tactical and strategic, you two are a great team."

"Thank you, boss. I'll do my best!"

"First order of business is solving Major Zelts's problem."

Nick nodded, "Got it, boss!"

"Maybe we need an assistant, secretary type?" Suggested Captain Sam Haram.

"Might have someone in mind." Said Nelson.

As the meeting broke up, Nick and Sam stayed, got up, and grabbed another coffee from the fresh pot, then sat down to plan.

"I'll get the money, Nick. I think you're good for most of the rest. Maybe I can help to get the equipment, buying it from Japanese sources?"

"Get lots of money, Sam. We don't have a lot of Army construction stuff in Japan. We don't have much of anything here. Don't know what a barge costs or a crane, but I do know this is not a competitive bidding situation, not when we want it tomorrow."

"Sam, I want you to call the major manufacturers of bulldozers and cranes in Japan tonight and make deals to buy their inventory, all of it! Wake the CEO's if need be. No haggling, but be firm. Otherwise, we'll take possession as a war necessity, and they can sue the US of A."

"Didn't know you were a lawyer, Nick?"

"I'm just a bastard in the trench kind of guy!"

"Yeah. That's what I like about you!" They both laughed.

Nick's first call woke Commander Wyle at his home.

A groggy Wyle answered the phone.

"Sorry to disturb you, sir, but the fate of a nation awaits your response."

"Is this Nick?"

"Glad you recognize my voice. I need your help again."

Commander Wyle is commandant of US Naval Base Sasebo, Japan, and had just been recommended for the Navy Cross for his action in organizing a secret attack by a UDT unit sent off from a submarine from his base. They destroyed a North Korean train tunnel 20 miles north of the 38th parallel on the east coast. Nick had ordered that operation only days ago.

"Commander, I need Seebee's, and I need tugboats and barges. And construction equipment. And I need it tomorrow."

Fully awake. Wyle knew the reach of this Master Sergeant, Nick Beloit.

"What are you asking?"

"Shit's flying, Commander. You're a hero today; don't let it go. I'm with a new secret unit authorized by General Mac himself. Think you may have received notice about it, NSOPU from Eighth Army is its name."

"Can't recall it."

"I've great respect for you, Commander, that's why I'm asking, but I'm not really asking."

"Hold on, Nick, let me grab a pencil."

A few minutes later, Commander Wyle woke his entire Naval Base by immediately issuing an emergency Air Attack alert and then assigned men to gather what resources they had to fill his list for Nick.

Two hours later, he called Nick back.

"Master Sergeant, my logistics captain asked some questions and made a few suggestions you ought to hear."

"Commander, please call me Nick and start anywhere you'd like."

"Okay, Nick. We have but two Navy tugboats that we can't spare, but we lease much more on-demand from local sources, same with barges. We only lease these; we have none ourselves. Heavy construction equipment is all contracted for on a project basis, but we have some of these manufacturing plants all around our city, usually with dock loading capabilities. I'm faxing you a list of these resources and home telephone numbers of their CEO's as we speak."

"That's great work, Commander; it's much appreciated."

"There's more. We have three fleet destroyers about ready to set out. If you can persuade Seventh Fleet Command to let you borrow them for a day or two, they are much better than tugboats."

"Damn! Now that's a great idea."

"Thought you'd agree, so I put the destroyers on high alert, emergency sailing possibly at dawn, pending further orders."

"Got more. A company of Seebee's arrived three days ago to build out our facilities. They have just settled in and haven't started anything. They're on alert, have light equipment only, so if we could collect the barges and such here, we could get them going in short order."

"Commander, I'm not sure how this stuff works, but I'll put my submission in for you to get a raise!"

"Thanks, Nick, never worked for an Army Master Sergeant before, but this sure has been an honor."

Sam and Nick worked through the night, pissing off Japanese CEOs and military rank in both Japanese and American services.

Commander Wyle and his command did the same. The only two C- 47 planes on his base were alerted to fly at a moment's notice. He ordered the recently successful UDT-Three unit, the one that blew up the tunnel, to pack and load their equipment on one of the C – 47's. These men were exceptional, and Seabee trained, he felt they could help.

Chapter Thirteen

**Monday, July 4, 1950 - Day Ten of the Invasion
Japan - Eighth Army Headquarters – Colonel Nelson's
Quarters – 0430 – (4:30 am)**

"Colonel! Sorry to wake you. Got General Walker on your line one."

"General!" Nelson, not fully awake, "What's wrong?"

"Two minutes ago, I was awakened and informed that MP's were at the Bank of Japan with its President in tow with orders from NSOPU to dispense $500,000 in cash to this unit. Did you order this?"

Now aware and awake, "This order came from my command under an NSOPU operation, then yes, sir, I'm responsible. Let me remind you, General, that I'm trying to save Eighth Army's ass, and you and General MacArthur ordered this on me. These orders are to be obeyed."

"That's all I wanted to know, Colonel. Sorry to wake you."

Nelson got up and took a quick shower, knew the pieces on the chessboard were moving. He wanted to be a player.

Walking in at 0530, Nelson saw Nick and Sam on the phones. Knew they'd been at it all night. They looked like shit. He grabbed a coffee from a fresh pot and sat.

As dawn broke over Naval Base Sasebo in Japan, the combined efforts of Nick, Sam, and Commander Wyle's teams showed as the harbor looked like Times Square on New Year's Eve. Barges were being pushed into peers to be loaded. Singular barges were being towed out fully loaded with heavy construction equipment. It was a beautiful sight that nobody saw.

The first Naval construction convoy for Pusan was almost assembled. At the base airport, a truck pulled up to the C-47 already boarded by UDT Team Three. Chief Petty Officer Drew O'Malley, "Chief," its leader, had received last-minute orders to wait for a particular truck from Tokyo.

When it arrived, four MPs and an Army Captain approached the plane and greeted Chief at the ramp.

"You must be special. Drove all fucking night to deliver a box filled with money for you. Got another huge box in the truck for your base commander. I want to get in on this action, what's going on?"

Chief took this implication to a higher plane; he didn't know anything about any money but knew his superiors.

Chief quickly drew his .45 and put it right in the Captain's face. "Don't know what you're talking about, Captain, but you need to follow orders. Give me what you've been ordered to deliver, and if you fuck with Commander Wyle's box, I'll come back and kill you. Got it!"

Back at the table, Nick looked at Sam, ignoring Colonel Nelson, "How'd you'd do?"

"Got lots of notes, bought a bunch of bulldozers, but damn, I don't know? I'm bout ready to pass out."

Nick finally addressed Nelson. "Boss, we spent a shit load of money tonight and put many balls in motion on this grand billiard table. I hope it will be enough."

"Thank you both, I know you gave it your all."

Chapter Fourteen

Monday, July 4, 1950 - Day Ten of the Invasion
Korea – US Army Logistics Headquarters in Pusan Harbor –
0630 – (6:30 am)

Major Zelts new responsibility pressed hard on him. He prayed that General Walker was right about this new secret unit, so he acted as if it would. He reorganized priorities of his resources, as he told General Walker he would, and so ordered them. Then he spent the rest of yesterday and far into the night visiting with the local Korean labor leaders at their offices or their homes.

Surprised by the warm welcome and change in attitude on news of his boss's removal, he made substantial progress. The promise of immediate cash incentives helped greatly.

Zelts told them of his need to load an artillery company of 105 mm guns and other assorted weapons on a train to Taejon so that American soldiers can try to stop the Communist invaders.

All promised that they would start action that very night.

The flight from Naval Base Sasebo was brief. The C- 47 covered the 100-mile distance in less than an hour. The Pusan airfield was close to the harbor and UDT Three's final destination. The trouble they had on arrival was trying to secure their equipment and then getting transport.

"Fuck all," said a frustrated Chief after ten minutes. "Handy! Get armed and steal a truck. We'll take our stuff with us."

The airbase was in chaos. Handy was back in ten minutes with an Army duce and a half.

Later, after finally finding their way, they pulled up to a dilapidated building with a small sign, **US Logistics.** A place more fitting of an ill-repaired American middle-class home in the burbs.

"Bobby! You and Ray grab that box of money. Handy, you and Matt mind the truck."

Chief pushed through the door, Bobby and Ray in tow. "Who's Major Zelts?"

A sergeant at the desk, stood up, "What's this? Who the hell are you?"

"Fuck off, Sergeant! Just get me Major Zelts."

The building was so small that you could hear anything spoken above conversation level, and this was certainly that.

A bleary-eyed Zelts came out of his office. "I'm Major Zelts."

Chief looked at this skinny young officer and thought of a few derogatory adjectives he could say. Still, instead, he saluted, "Sir, I have a vital box for you and have been asked by the highest authority, for my team, to assist you in any manner of your choosing."

A stunned major returned the salute. "You're Navy divers. Why were you sent to me, and what's in the box?"

"Yes, sir, UDT Three at your service. Our five men are also Seabees. This large box contains cash, US dollars in small denominations."

A big smile broke out on Major Zelts face. He then grabbed Chief's hand and shook it. "Thank you! Thank you! Please come into my office, and oh, isn't this one hell of a 4th of July!"

Chapter Fifteen

Monday, July 4, 1950 - Day Ten of the Invasion
Korea – Task Force Smith in Taejon – 0900 – (9:00 am)

The morning was miserable, with intermittent heavy rain. Colonel Smith was in a quandary; he'd heard nothing yet from his advance unit sent to Osan, a mere 50 miles away. Worse yet, he had no idea where his Artillery Company and other heavy weapons units were. He felt naked, started to despair. Then straightened up, thought of this special operations unit that was just attached, and figured they must have encountered a delay at their drop off point.

Colonel Smith found his second in command and asked if he'd received any word from Captain Melvin.

"No, sir. Not sure their command radio Jeep has the range to reach us from Osan."

"I was hoping they would call in before they got that far. Shit!"

The train whistle ended any further conversation.

Colonel Smith gathered a few members of his command and hustled over to the nearby train station and saw flatbeds loaded with 105 mm artillery guns and jeeps with mounted recoilless rifles. Soldiers were piling out of boxcars and gathering equipment. The Colonel wanted to kiss somebody.

If he only knew that it was the lowly Lieutenant Zelts, who but ten days ago, was promoted to Captain and then just yesterday promoted to Major, in a logistics command that made this train possible.

Smith's Task Force moved out two hours later.

Earlier that morning.

Captain Melvin's small convoy of two jeeps and four trucks made slow but steady progress up the crowded road filled with refugees headed south. As they got closer to Osan, Sergeant Engle and Whitey moved to the first jeep to signal when they had reached their secret units mountain drop-off point.

Staff Sergeant Leyden pointed out the location from a topical map supplied by Colonel Nelson's command. It was about ten miles south of Osan and had a clear line of sight to that area; Sergeant Engle knew it well. Smaller hills permeated the valley highway, but this hill dominated the terrain for many miles to the north.

"Stop here! That's the hill we want."

Staff Sergeant Tom Leyden was in a foul mood as he jumped out of the truck into a rainstorm. He looked up at this mountain; it was steep and muddy. Realizing that they would need to make multiple trips to get all the equipment and packs up to their new home, he cursed. "No fucking way!"

The men started to unload the truck as Leyden went up to the second jeep and, standing in the rain, yelled through the vinyl flaps.

"Captain! I need ten of your men to help me carry this secret equipment up this goddamned hill."

First Sergeant Whitey Dillon and Sergeant Engle were also standing in the rain next to Leyden. Whitey spoke first.

"Sir, this is a special unit; the sooner they can get set up, the better for us. We can leave a truck, the men can catch up to us."

"Jesus, Whitey! We don't know what we'll find? That's a big piece of our unit."

"Captain, if we find bad shit up there, ten men ain't gonna make a difference."

Shaking his head, the captain knowingly smiled. "How come you're not an officer, Whitey?"

"Didn't marry right, sir."

Chapter Sixteen

Monday, July 4, 1950 - Day Ten of the Invasion
Korea – Rusty's Group Entering Osan – 0700 – (7:00 am)

Rusty's small command had swelled considerably with the addition of the South Korean soldiers from the cave and pickups along the way; now almost two hundred troops plus another two hundred or so civilians of all ages.

On a hill, a mile just outside of Osan, Rusty and C J huddled. Having surveyed the town and surroundings, they concluded the enemy hadn't arrived yet.

"I know of some secret warehouses." Said C J.

"I hope that means food and weapons?"

"Yes!"

"Does *Three* know where they are?"

"No."

"OK, we'll hold here. You take Frenchy and Joe to the weapons warehouse. Tell your *One* where the food storage place is and have Foxy and Marty join him. Take portable radios, call in your findings. Keep both a secret until we know what we got."

He also ordered Tracker to do a deep recon to the right and Snake to pass through the town and circle the west side. He gave Snake a radio and told Larry to monitor the three in the field and to stick close to him in case something came up. Rusty then gave orders to the group to stay on the bluff until the scouts reported back.

C J's team scurried through the northern backstreets of the mostly deserted town. Osan was large by Korean standards, housing a population of over 20,000 people, was located behind a small mountain, just off the main highway that ran from the Capital to the southern coasts.

C J recognized an overgrown dilapidated metal wire gate entrance off an obscure alley. "This is it!"

Skeptical, Joe said, "You sure? It looks like it leads nowhere."

"Exactly! My uncle brought me to this place when we received independence. He thought civil war might break out. Told me this was a secret stash that his group of Korean officers had hidden from you Americans and your sloppy bookkeeping. They didn't know what side America would take. It was an insurance policy."

Breaking through the gate, they had to make their way in a dense five-foot tall brush that led into a large compound of three buildings. They broke the chain on the first and entered the cobwebbed warehouse to see stacked boxes of all sizes from end to end.

"Sacre bleu!" Shouted Frenchy. He loved showing off his Canadian French whenever possible.

"Holy shit!" Said a delighted Joe. "Are the other two buildings the same?"

"I hope so! Never been in any of these before." Said a smiling C J.

Frenchy didn't wait to see the other two buildings and called in, "Larry! Tell Rusty we might be able to arm a regiment. Only opened one of three buildings, but we got stuff, haven't seen any heavy weapons yet, but I'm hopeful. The town looks deserted; I'll call you when we're finished."

Foxy called in a few minutes later with positive news about their discovery. C J's *One* led them to a large hidden building filled with C, K, and D combat rations plus other canned foods and grains. Again, no hostiles.

Rusty didn't know how close the enemy was and was troubled by his lack of orders. His new command had taken on something he'd never envisioned. Most of his group were starving and the majority of the ROK soldiers had no weapons.

"Red! What do you think?"

"You don't need my advice. You get us into that town and feed these people and arm the soldiers. Stop asking me stupid questions!"

"I rely on you, Red. Now you make sure we're covered with a tripwire guard out there with our guys, so we don't get bushwhacked."

"I'll wait until Tracker and Snake check back and then figure out our situation. I've never let you down before Rusty! Won't now!"

Rusty led the ragtag group into Osan, found *One,* who then directed them to the food building.

The radio crackled, "Snake!" Said Larry as he passed it to Rusty.

"What! Great! Bring'em in, we're in the town."

Two jeeps and three trucks pulled into the center of the city. Snake led a group up to the vehicles as troops piled out.

Rusty stepped forward, saluted. "Captain, First Sergeant Rusty Fabiano welcomes you to Osan."

Getting past the scruffiness and obvious hardships this group showed, he saluted back. "Who the hell are you guys?"

"It's a long story, but the short version is that we've been fighting these bastards since the invasion, and we're here to help you if we can."

"By any coincidence, do you know a Tech Sergeant named Leyden?"

"Oh, man! How do you know him? We blew up a bridge together a few days ago, not far from here."

"Damn!" He updated Rusty on Leyden's team and approximate position.

The group moved into a covered deserted open-air shop of some sort and found a table so they could view their map on. C J's *Three* and new arrival Sergeant Engle knew the area well, so they started their defense planning.

Time was pressing. Earlier, the captain sent a jeep messenger to let his colonel know it was safe to bring up the main body.

While they were planning, Red sent out lookouts, one in particular, to the mount above the town that commanded an eight-mile approach from the main highway. He also established a reinforced roadblock at a small pass just north of the city, manned by Foxy, Dean, Joe, and Arron, who was assigned the bazooka.

"Red! Are you serious?" Said a really annoyed Arron. "We've been lugging this weapon around since we left the Post, ten days ago, and I've been doing most of the lugging."

"I was wondering who was going to start the bellyaching. What do they always say in a murder mystery? The butler did it! Well, in this case, the cook did it."

"Damn you, Red! I'm just letting off steam, been too quiet, and I'm nervous about what's coming."

"I know. We're been here before. It always sucks before it starts."

Not long after, the haggard Korean unit, now fed and newly armed with American M-1's and Thompson submachine guns from the liberated warehouse, came marching down the main street, to the main highway, it's captain at its lead.

They met Rusty and Red at the intersection. As they approached, Rusty saw a swagger. Damn! He thought, maybe they'll fight.

The captain halted his unit, approached Rusty, and saluted.

"You Americans are hard to figure out. But I like your spirit, don't know yet if you'll hang in there, but I've changed my mind about defending my country. It took a sergeant from my homeland to wake me. Thank you for bringing him to me. Where do you want my men positioned?"

"I'm honored to fight with you, Captain. This battle is only a battle, and I'm pretty sure we'll lose this one. But delaying them is our main goal plus being able to stay alive to fight again. I've set up a roadblock just north of the town; you could help there."

"A realist! Odd to find one among Americans. I hope your government doesn't disappoint you."

As his column approached the roadblock position, Foxy called out halt, as he did not recognize the ROK captain. And then he did.

"Come! Sorry! Captain, I didn't recognize you."

"We're all jumpy. Foxy, is your name, right? We're here to help you protect this highway."

"Yes, sir. Good memory."

The captain ordered his men to disperse in defensive positions and then stayed at the roadblock with Foxy.

The flow of refugees was a daunting task at the roadblock. Thousands of ordinary people were fleeing their hamlets and farms. They were scared. Word spread quickly of the cruelty of these communist invaders and their numerous atrocities on their march south.

Set up as a tripwire for the advancing North Korean Army, the roadblock also served as a routine check to ensure no weapons were smuggled in behind their lines by infiltrators.

A commotion stirred in the congested refugee group in front of the roadblock. A mounted South Korean officer, his horse obviously under stress, ran through the crowd and pulled up at the barricade.

He spoke Korean, "Let me through! I'm an officer!"

"Let me handle this," said the ROK captain to Foxy, as he grabbed the reins, he asked, "Where're your men, lieutenant!"

The rider's eyes shown the light of someone who'd seen a ghost. "Behind me!" He said, "But we must go fast!"

He pulled the reins out of the captain's hands and leaped forward to escape.

The captain yelled for him to stop, but he didn't, so he then pulled his .45 from his holster and shot the horse out from under the lieutenant. The distraught officer went flying into the mud.

South Korean soldiers came running from the rear, up to the roadblock and started yelling, they were angry, believed this captain had shot their lieutenant.

When they saw the lieutenant rise from the mud, they calmed down.

The captain and two of his men helped the mud soaked officer walk back to the group of gathered soldiers. He was dazed but not crazed as before, wondered what had happened. The officer's men surrounded them and told the captain how brave the lieutenant had been; that he saved most of their platoon under heavy artillery fire, but suffered a near miss that knocked him unconscious as they withdrew. They put him on this horse, and he'd just awoke as they approached the roadblock and broke free from his guide.

"Where were you?" Asked the captain.

"The industrial district of Suwon, sir. About ten miles north." A sergeant called out. "They're not far behind us. They've got tanks!"

The captain directed his two men to take the lieutenant and his men to get food and then to rearm. He told them to find the American combat medic he'd met, to attend to this officer and for them to stay close to this hero.

As they left, Foxy came up to him. "That was something, Captain. You're a natural leader. Thought for sure you were going to shoot the deserter."

With a slant of his head, the captain bowed. "Thank the gods I missed! Another lesson I just learned about assuming."

Foxy called in his report to Rusty.

Later

Tracker returned from his extended, broad scout mission of the Northeastern (right) side of Osan and found Rusty and the newly arrived advanced American recon unit leaders in a house looking at maps.

Tracker entered the room, had a presence that was hard to describe. It wasn't physical because he was slight of build. Maybe it was his jet black hair with eyes to match or his dark complexion. But it was something in his persona that projected a unique quality that everybody felt. They took notice.

"Got a bad feeling, boss!" He announced without waiting for an introduction.

"Go on, Tracker, what is it?" Said Rusty.

"Got far up the road to a logical block point we could establish. But there's a pass about a mile on the flank that the enemy could use; they could envelop our defensive position. No defense is possible to that pass. Can't see how we can hold this enemy with limited forces."

"Show me." Asked Captain Melvin.

Tracker pointed at the map, showed the flaws and possible flanking maneuver that would entrap the entire defense.

Sergeant Engle spoke. "He's right, I trained in this area, and he pinpointed the best defensive positions but also pointed out the weakness. That pass he's talking about leads up a narrow valley between a dense forest. With enough troops, heavy weapons, and artillery support, it could be defended, but we have none of those. My training maneuvers assumed we'd have a full division to defend this strategic position. A 600 man Brigade just ain't gonna cut it."

Chapter Seventeen

**Monday, July 4, 1950 - Day Ten of the Invasion
Korea – The City of Osan - Colonel Smith's Task Force
Arrives – 1130 – (11:30 am)**

In a drizzle, Colonel Smith met his recon units' commander, Captain Melvin, near the center of Osan.

Having already briefed the colonel via radio about what the captain found and that he had two local experts of the area working on a defensive scheme made the greeting brief.

Colonel Smith ignored the captain's request for him to meet with the soldiers planning the defense.

"I have maps, Captain, and we have a plan. No need for second guessing. We're running out of time."

First Sergeant Whitey Dillon had accompanied his captain out to greet the colonel and became upset at his dismissal of the captain's efforts. He couldn't let this go.

"Colonel, sir. May I speak?"

"Jesus, Whitey. What?"

"Sir, you'll have all the time in the world when you're dead. But I don't think your men think like that right now. So, I suggest you take a few minutes to listen to what experts of this area have to say. And, oh, sir, there's an American special operation unit that's been fighting these guys since the start, they might have some insight about this enemy."

`

Task Force Smith's main force was slowly pulling into the city. It would be a while before they needed additional orders from what they had. Colonel Smith realized he'd be stupid to ignore his most trusted and experienced non-com.

"Damn it, Whitey, let's get out of this rain."

Whitey turned to Captain Melvin, "Sir, let's take the colonel to Rusty."

Captain Melvin entered the room and announced Colonel Smith.

The ragtag group stood to attention and saluted.

"Please relax." Said Colonel Smith, after returning their salute.

"I haven't seen a more battle weary bunch of soldiers since December '44, when my Tank Company broke through the siege of Bastogne. My first sergeant tells me you've been fighting since the beginning. I hope you've been giving better than you look."

The men laughed. Rusty spoke first, "Sir, we sure as hell would like to think we've done pretty well."

"Are you the officer?"

"I'm First Sergeant Rusty Fabiano, sir. The rest of these men are my equals, all first sergeants. We've never had an officer in our command in Korea, but we follow orders from our boss in Japan, at Eighth Army, Colonel Nelson."

Stunned, the colonel found a seat. "I know Colonel Jim Nelson. A damned good man and a fine judge of character. He's number one under General Walker. I'm now impressed."

Captain Melvin spoke up. "Sir, these men know that secret team we dropped off. They say that they, with them, blew up a bridge south of Seoul a few days ago."

"Is this true?" Asked an unbelievable Smith.

"Your friend, Jim Nelson, planned it all, sir." Said Rusty.

"Damn good work! I hope we can score a victory here as well."

"We had some serious help, but sure as shit, we kicked some ass there."

Colonel Smith nodded and, from his satchel, pulled out his plan for his defense of Osan and put it on the table.

"This is what intelligence gave us, and then we formulated a plan."

"Captain Melvin filled us in on your orders and command strength." Said Rusty, "We were hoping you were leading an Armored Regiment, Colonel; I guess you were too."

"I'm lucky to be leading these mixed units that were ready to go on such short notice. Only six hundred or so, but I'm hoping we can put up a good fight. Tell me what you think of our plan?"

"Before I do this, Colonel." Said Rusty. "I want to make one thing clear. We're here because my boss, Colonel Nelson, ordered my team here to assist you, and I will do that. But that's all I'll do. Because sir, you are going to get crushed here, and I'll not be part of it."

Dismayed by his circumstances, Colonel Smith responded, "I'm fully aware of my role here, Rusty. And like you, I don't want to sacrifice my men to stupidity to make a purely political statement. But sometimes, it has to be done. Besides, I have my orders, but if you can help me in any manner, I'm all ears."

After reviewing the plan, and taking a short break, they conferenced around the map.

"Colonel, Red is my number one and has proven his ability in tactical planning, both offensively and defensively, so I asked him to do this review. Red!"

"Sir, I'll start by saying that we have experts with us that know this area and have been here most of their lives. So the good news first.

"With your force level and meager local terrain intelligence, your plan is well thought out."

"Your plan is absolutely correct in identifying the critical bottleneck here."

Pointing to a location three miles north of the town on the main highway, where, after it winds through foothills, the highway rounds a bend through a constricted pass, and finally emerges where the road becomes open.

"It is at this bend that the enemy is most vulnerable and a great place to stage a determined defense. So, the placement of your artillery company just south of the city is excellent. It's six miles away from this funnel, almost max range for your cannons."

Red continued. "A large field on the westside is the first view the enemy has from this pass; this is important for your anti-tank units to be well hidden in this field."

Tully interrupted, "What type of bazooka's do you have?"

First Sergeant Dillon spoke immediately. "Same crap we had in the last war, the 2.5mm rocket weapon."

"Okay!" Said an angry Red, looking at Tully. "We'll hold off any comments until this review is over."

"Let's get back to this highway bend. I'm calling it a pass, and your plan got it right as a choke point. When the enemy makes the complete turn from the bend, they have the open field on the westside and now a sloped ridgeline on its eastside. I like how you positioned a good deal of your infantry and heavy weapons on the ridge, particularly the mortar platoon."

Red stopped.

"Now for the bad news."

Colonel Smith, sitting on a crate, looked at Captain Melvin and Whitey when it dawned on him that the two men he was looking at and the man he was listening to were his age or older and probably witnessed more war, blood, and stupidity that he could ever imagine. But I'm in charge.

"Please hurry, Red. We're about to be attacked."

"They'll be time enough for dying, Colonel. It now just depends on how many. I hope we can figure that out here, sir."

"You're facing experienced, battle-tested troops that outnumber you by a wide margin. They have superior firepower in tanks and artillery. I'd advise you to prepare for a quick withdrawal so that you can fight again."

"Those are not my orders. I know this is not an ideal plan, but I've got to do the best I can. My command represents America's resolve to fight! Not skirmish!"

Colonel Smith abruptly stood.

"Thank you for your input." And he left with his captain and Whitey.

"What happened?"

"Don't know, Red. I'm as confused as you." Said Rusty.

"God almighty!"

Tully, off to the side, said, "He didn't want to hear any more bad news. Red, as my daddy once said, "If you don't ask, you can't help stupid. That colonel never asked us one question about our experience fighting this enemy. Not sure he's worth our effort."

Rusty was also disturbed by Smith's reaction. "You've got a damned good point, Tully. But Colonel Smith is facing his command's death, if not his own. He deserves our respect. We bring the only possibility of avoiding his Brigade's complete slaughter."

"I'm going to talk to First Sergeant Whitey." Said Red.

Rusty didn't hesitate. "Tully and I are going with you."

Later

The weather maintained its dreary surprise of a downpour to drizzle throughout the morning and now into the afternoon as the full Brigade arrived, took their positions, and started digging in.

Colonel Smith's headquarters established a prominent presence on the back of the ridge overlooking the entire expected battlefield.

That's where Rusty's team finally found Whitey, "How did you know how to find me here?"

Red laughed. "I figured out where Smith's headquarters would be. Since your colonel thinks your shit doesn't stink, he'd want you close! And damn if that's exactly how I feel!"

They both laughed.

After a brief about what they hadn't told the colonel about, they convinced him to set up a short second meeting with the colonel.

It began awkwardly. "Glad you're here." Said Smith.

"Since you have a decent force with you, I want to use you as my fire brigade as a reserve unit just south of town, in case they breakthrough."

Rusty said nothing.

Settling down, Smith asked about positioning his anti-tank units.

Tully, feeling off at that last suggestion, asked, "You got HT (Heat, as in anti-tank) for your recoilless rifle jeeps?"

"Don't know! I have no experience with this new weapon. We unloaded them so fast I didn't check their ammo. I'm lucky I got anything."

Tully frowned. "Colonel, if you ain't got Heat, those guns are then infantry support and should be in the rear as artillery. What about the bazookas? Whitey said you didn't get the new 3.5 inch models?"

"What new models? I've only got the standard 2.5-inch ones we used in the war."

Red spoke. "Colonel, we fought these Russian T-34 tanks. Without HT, the jeep recoilless rifles are useless against them. The old 2.5 inch bazookas can only be effective if you take out the tracks, but they'll not destroy them."

Colonel Smith looked at Whitey, "Get this information to Major Lavelle, (Smith's second in command) First Sergeant."

"Wait! Before you leave, Whitey. I must tell your colonel about the enemy's long-range artillery." Said Rusty. "When the invasion started, we defended a fortified Post miles behind the 38th parallel and were subjected to fierce shelling from heavy caliber long-range cannons. These big babies fired earth shattering explosives from some 18 miles away. If their advanced troops run into any resistance in Osan, they'll set up these cannons and destroy every living thing in their path, and then just walk in."

"Thank you for your help, Rusty, but I have my orders."

Rusty stood. "Sir, I think you are either very brave or foolish to ignore what is obvious. As to the use of my forces, I'm not under your orders. My goal will be to prevent you from being outflanked, and then withdraw."

Rusty, without saluting, turned, and left the bunker. Red and Tully, in an awkward moment, saluted and followed.

A Little Later
Red and Rusty were sitting at a table discussing how they should deploy their men when the South Korean captain came in. "Rusty, may I speak with you?"

"I'll check on that item." Said Red, as he left the room.

"Of course, Captain, please sit. What's on your mind?"

"You're not a secret colonel, are you?"

"No, Captain, I'm just a First Sergeant, sorry for the ruse."

"You damn well should be a Colonel! You're a great leader. I'm proud to follow your command, First Sergeant. I want orders from you for my troops. With all the pickups on the way and the men that volunteered from the roadblock, I now have over three hundred South Korean soldiers. All are fed and re-armed. I think they'll fight."

"Thank you. I don't even know your name?"

"Captain Kim Dae-Jung, Commander of A Company, 2nd Battalion, 8th Infantry Regiment, Capital Guards Command. That's my title, but that's not all I am."

Rusty thought of the upcoming fight and thought of this man. He'd fought this enemy, as he.

Captain Kim continued, "No sir, a man is not judged by his title or his status, only by his actions. I'm but an ordinary man that has seen much. But when men in battle stand and praise their leader, well, that's something to be recognized! Your guys did that, and that lieutenant from the roadblock, his men did that. I hope he recovers."

Rusty nodded, "Captain Kim, I'm honored that you joined us and privileged to fight by your side. Let's see how best to get the men positioned."

They then moved to a building that had a ground floor office of some sort. It looked like it had been a lawyer's office as it had a conference area in the back and multiple office spaces without doors. It was severely damaged, apparently trashed by an angry mob. There was a second floor. Off in a corner room, Tully, C J, Tracker, and Red sat on the floor and ate C- rations.

Rusty heard the chatter and stood in the doorway with Captain Kim.

"We have plenty, Rusty. Get some while you can." Said Red.

"Good idea!" He and Kim grabbed a box and sat, opened the food, and started eating.

All were quiet.

"So, Red, what do you think of our Colonel Smith?" Asked Rusty, concerned by the long silence.

"First off, he's not **OUR** Colonel. He's a veteran officer who only experienced victory with superior forces and lots of support. Granted, he's smart, but he has no idea of what's coming at him. Plus, he's one of those guys that take orders, literally, you know, like that *hold at all costs* shit! He'll get his whole command killed here! For what, to slow these Commies down! For a few hours! I call that nuts."

"Tully! How about you?" Rusty asked, showing no emotion from Red's response.

"He didn't ask one question about our engagements with the North Koreans. Not about their tanks; or their tactics. Nothing! If Red didn't tell him about the bazooka's, he wouldn't even know how to defeat these tanks! Jesus! Rusty! You never, ever heard me tell you, nor have I ever told my men to run from a fight in my Ranger life. But I say let's get the hell out of here!" He paused a second. "Although, I do want to fight next to that First Sergeant Whitey; I think he's a born again Ranger."

Captain Kim had never experienced anything like this. "Is this how American soldiers view their officers and obey orders?"

Interesting question, thought Rusty, as the group awaited his response.

"Yes and no, Captain. We are a complicated society. Yes, we discuss our leadership openly because our lives depend on them and their decisions. And No, when ordered, we follow them; well mostly, unless they are deemed grossly wrong."

That brought a chuckle to the Americans.

Rusty didn't smile and looked at both Red and Tully.

"You both have made your points, and I agree. But Osan is just the opening battle in a delaying action. Colonel Smith knows the scoop; you're not giving him proper credit. He knows he's going to get badly mangled. He'll probably become a scapegoat, but he's going to follow his orders to delay this enemy. So stop with the shit about him."

"Now, about us." Rusty continued. "We're not under Colonel Smith's command, and we are out of contact with our colonel. Our compelling orders from day one has been to slow the North Korean advance. So here we are, on the front lines, where Red said we'd be just a few days ago."

Red looked at his long-time best friend with wonder. The confidence he radiated, at particular moments like this, when he spoke to the core of the issue, he couldn't believe Rusty was just like him, an Army First Sergeant.

"We will plan, as we have always planned, our battle operation. But not as trench diehards. We aim to follow our orders. Delay! But survive to delay again and again. We'll try to help Colonel Smith's command, but our objective is to fight and withdraw with minimum casualties."

Red brightened, "Let's look at the map again!" He hoped he might find something to help this pending disaster from happening.

Commotion at the front entrance announced the arrival of Tracker and Sergeant Dan Engle.

"About time, you showed up, Tracker. Figured you got lost." Said Red.

"Good thing I like you. Making fun of *real Americans* can be dangerous."

"Found a serious problem!" Said Engle to the group.

Rusty, now fully alert.

"What!"

"I trained my South Korean units in this area for months about two years ago." Said Sergeant Engle. "To the east of Osan about two miles, foothills rise into the eastern side of the mountain north of the town into a wide elevated wedge. It opens into an open valley that then contracts at the base. It's maybe a mile long. They call it the Eastern Valley."

"Back then, it was only accessed from the south. But we found that the locals cleared trees, built an entry point from the highway, and cleared a rough path into the valley. It's not on any maps, but the enemy will find it."

"Good job, Engle! Tracker, keep a close watch on our new friend." Red said as he rubbed his hair.

"If it's okay with you, we'd like to scout the eastern bluffs and go deeper north." Said Tracker to Red.

"Okay, but Engle … don't let him take any scalps." Red was serious.

Chapter Eighteen

Digesting this new intelligence, Red studied the layout for a good hour, talked to Rusty, and Tully about some ideas then came to a consensus on a course of action.

Rusty decided that with this new information and plan, it was worth another effort with Colonel Smith.

The revelation of the Eastern Valley opening and its potential to outflank Smith's entire position stunned the colonel and left him speechless, trying to digest the ramifications.

Watching, Rusty never felt more helpless.

"Colonel, you have been put in a position where you will forever be vilified for whatever you do. Fight to the end and slaughter your men or fight and quickly withdraw so that you can fight again. You'll then be accused of running."

"Running! America hasn't fought a war like that since George Washington. The Army teaches that the 'Alamo' was one of our most significant victories. How sad that glory is valued more than lives."

"You're an extraordinary man, Rusty. I wish there were more of you. I appreciate your concern for me, but really for my men. I have great respect for your efforts to save as many of them as you can."

Pausing, then looking Rusty in the eyes, he said.

"But here's the rub. The moment we dug into the forward positions and established that three-mile point north of Osan as the line of our defense, we fucked ourselves out of any possible organized retreat if things go sideways."

"Of course, it's the only place we have a chance of holding them, but this East Valley Intel, well, if they get behind me, I'm screwed."

"Colonel, this enemy is fierce. They will come at you, nonstop. They aren't afraid of dying. I hope you can hold your highway position."

"Colonel Nelson ordered me to assist you, sir, and so I will. I'm taking my men and the South Korean troops I have to guard your flank in the Eastern Valley."

"That would be greatly appreciated. I'll have Whitey set up communication with you."

"Good. But I'll warn you, sir. We'll not stand and fight, we'll only try to slow'em down, then we're out of here. I suggest you do the same."

Rusty wished he could contact Colonel Nelson and tell him how bad this battle looked. But he had no idea where the closest relay tower was to use his secret communication equipment. The Korean cable relay station in the city was demolished by retreating South Korean forces and Colonel Smith's command communication jeep was nonfunctioning for unknown reasons, so he couldn't contact Leyden.

He'd had no time, nor did he know where Leyden was, even if he was only ten or so miles away. The effort would probably be in vain anyway, the enemy was at the door and was about to break it down.

(*The Japanese constructed the Korean Cable before they invaded China in the 1930s. The communication cable was built deep underground along the main western highway from the tip of the Korean border with Manchuria to various relay stations down the entire Korean peninsula to the city of Pusan where it went into the water and came out at Japanese Headquarters in Japan. This cable was vital for fast communications, as Japan continued their aggressive war in China.*

In 1945, the Korean Cable was cut off at the 38th parallel, but remained operational from that point south, connected to America's Eighth Army headquarters in Japan.

When the CIA invented the VLF secret communication and spying equipment in 1950 that Rusty and Leyden were carrying around, the CIA intuited that Korea was to be the next hot spot, as in bullets and bombs. Not many felt the same way except Colonel Nelson.

The equipment was so exceptional it broke accepted academic norms by many levels. Nobody had explored the Very Low Frequency universe in depth before. The CIA did, and the results surprised even the jaded.

In effect, they discovered that VLF (Very Low Frequency) signals, generated by a small amount of energy, could travel almost forever in a modestly expanding straight line. It was like an old Morse code signal machine.

That was one discovery, but the next one and its machine changed everything.

*This device could pick up multiple radio frequencies within ten miles or more **and could** relay each frequency in real-time to a line* *of a sight receiver using this VLF technology. So in effect, if you know your enemy's code, you could listen in in real time.*

Based on that, the CIA, knowing that Colonel Nelson was committed to erecting four secret listening Posts below the 38th parallel, decided it first needed to receive these signals in Japan. It decided towers were the easiest and cheapest way, so they constructed a string of towers on top of Koreas' Central Mountain range. Each tower had large conical receptors/transceivers placed in multiple locations around the tower. They then devoted all its energy on trying to figure out how to utilize this new science effectively back at CIA headquarters in Japan.

The day before the invasion, the CIA broke the North Korean military code. It was now possible to listen in on direct orders to field units.

From the very beginning, VLF communications existed with Colonel Nelson's G-2 section at Eighth Army headquarters and the CIA.)

With full trust in Red's input and his instincts, Rusty authorized him to plan the defense of the Eastern Valley defense. He also liked Tully's uncommon idea about establishing a quick escape, using stolen vehicles.

Thinking about it, Rusty figured they'd need ample supplies to help them survive when they escaped with a long journey to safety.

Rusty radioed Captain Kim to execute that discussed plan. A small team came to steal trucks from Smith's various units at the rear of Osan and then take them to the food and munition warehouses. They were then loaded and moved just to the east of the town, where Rusty had established their main escape trucks.

The men moved out to the east side of the city and headed north up the rising hill. Arron, ever the civil war make-believe historian, said, "kind of reminds me of my great uncle telling me about his journey up the Shenandoah Valley when he attacked the Yankees."

"I don't think that went well for your uncle, Arron." Said Ranger Dean, the sniper, right beside him. "If you must speak, I want to hear about your next stew. I can still taste your last one. But please, no details."

Joe and Marty walked together. "I told you. Your fears are just what we go through. Here we are again, Marty, and it'll be okay. Or it won't! It's out of our hands. You okay with that?"

"Yeah, Joe, I've come to terms with that, thanks."

Before the last few battles, Marty, the combat medic, had increasingly become fatalistic. Joe, the ever calm Flatbush Brooklynite, encouraged him to face reality with acceptance.

Mario and Snake had paired together as they followed the line. "The two of us, buddy, we're gonna do some shit tonight!"

"We got no orders! What the hell are you talking about?"

"Just got a feeling. You'll see!"

With the sky jumping around from partly cloudy with some light to dark clouds and heavy rain, there currently was a light rain falling as they ascended the rear of the Eastern Valley. Once on top of the hill, the small valley came into full view.

It was a horrible defensive position with little cover. But it had a steep slope and held the high ground.

"Shit!" Was Red's first reaction after taking in the full scene, then stopped and took a hard, long look at the area. He saw how the lower pass opened like a funnel into this narrow valley. Damn! His mind went ping-pong. We should go close to the funnel at the choke point, but we'll be exposed when we'd have to withdraw. That unit would be wiped out. If we let them advance too far up the valley, they'll flank us; same result. Fuck all! His mind screamed.

Rusty watched Red go through his mind progressions and saw him become transfixed. Rusty called out to his team leaders

Around Rusty and Red, in the open field, in the light rain, the key men gathered. Tully, Foxy, Tracker, C J, and the new arrival, Captain Kim.

"Never saw you like this before, Red. Explain!" Asked Rusty.

"Just focusing is all!" Red deadpanned. "Glad you're all around because I'm not entirely sure how this will play out."

He reviewed his thoughts, his plan, and his doubts.

"Tanks can access this passage at the bottom but won't be able to come into the valley because of the mud. They'll get stuck at the funnel, I think." Said C J, who had scouted the valley to the main road. Captain Kim added, "We brought up a lot of weapons and munitions from those other two warehouses C J found. All Japanese. Smoke grenades, regular ones too, of course. A number of their T- 99 light machine guns with their heavy ammunition. And, thanks to C J, we got some of their *Knee Mortars*, type 89, the best damn close in weapon ever invented."

"What!" Said Red, "Holy Shit! Don't fuck with me now! You're serious, right?"

Tully had no idea what was going on, hadn't heard anything about Japanese weapons, but he was encouraged.

"You didn't know? Yes! We have these weapons, Red." Said Captain Kim, feeling stupid, thinking how many times ASSUME has killed.

Kim thought that C J told Red what was in the other two warehouses, and C J had assumed Kim did the same.

Tully and Red, although they fought in Europe, knew about these weapons from the seminar they attended in Japan, about the best weapons of the war. It was where they'd first met.

The Knee Mortar was a simple weapon, fired by one man; it was devastating. A barrel length of only 10 inches with a total length of just two feet, the Type 89 mortar weighed 10 lbs. It fired a one and three-quarter pound 50mm high-explosive shell. Other shells available were smoke, incendiary, and flare projectiles. Its range could be adjusted by holding it at different angles. It was effective from 390 to 2,130 feet. It had to be braced by a hard object when fired, like a tree root or rock; if it was a leg or thigh, the recoil would break it. After the war, studies revealed the effectiveness of this deadly weapon and concluded that 40% of all infantry combat causalities in the Pacific Theater were caused by its use.

"This changes EVERYTHING!" Red yelled. Excited, he grabbed Captain Kim. "Do your men know how to operate these weapons?"

"Some do, many fought with the Chinese, as I, against the Japs and used their weapons against them. They're simple; I'll get my troops to instruct the ones who don't know."

Red knelt on the Valley ground, with his knife, he cut into the grass and mud to create positions. "Captain Kim! Here's how I want you to place your men. Please order these dispositions in detail to your unit leaders."

As Kim was about to leave, Red grabbed his sleeve. "Captain! This defensive position is going to fall on you. Many of us are going to die here, Americans and South Koreans, but you're going to bear the brunt. Are you prepared?"

For the second time, Captain Kim faced another first sergeant.

"You don't know what I've suffered, and I have no idea what you've endured. Let's say it's even. We've been through hell, the both of us. And still, here we are. Will we both go into the fire? I'll fight till we can't fight anymore. Does that satisfy you, First Sergeant?"

"You better! My family here in this field depends on you."

As he walked away to order his men to follow Red's orders, Kim wondered who the American leader is? He thought Rusty was, yet, this Red, commanded this upcoming battlefield like a general. The dispositions are masterful. But I wish we had more men! As good as the plan is, we will not stop them. I think I'll probably die here. Then he raised his head and looked into the darkening sky and thought, better than dying in a cave or on the run in a ditch.

Invigorated, Captain Kim went about ordering his men to dig deep foxholes and get bushes for cover. He found experienced men to train the novices on the Japanese weapons. Encouraging them that this was not their last stand, that they would fall back in order. They had a plan, trust me, he said.

He prayed that the plan would work.

Chapter Nineteen

Monday, July 4, 1950 - Day Ten of the Invasion
Korea – Colonel Smith's position, Three Miles North of the City of Osan – 1800 – (6:00 pm)

Persuaded this was an ideal ambush point, Colonel Smith deployed some of his meager forces on the high ridges above this pass.

When he found out his six recoilless rifle jeeps had but three rounds of HT (Heat - anti-tank) per jeep, he ordered their company commander to take good aim at the tanks and then get the hell out of there.

His artillery company was also short of munitions and had nothing but HE (high explosive) rounds. The 105 mm guns were good but required a direct hit to knock out a tank.

Smith didn't have an adequate communication signals group. He had no extra signal units to his command beyond his basic battalion structure, yet, he was given an artillery unit that was not connected to an infantry battalion system. Then there was the mortar platoon, another attached unit with no sync; he had no way to communicate with these units. Smith was angry.

The old WW2 radio equipment they did have, worked about as well as they did five years ago, which was spotty at best.

`

And old hand at FUBAR, the Colonel ordered the use of the ancient war communications system, human runners. But it was difficult for the runners because of the unfamiliar rough territory and the distances.

From his Command Post, he was two miles behind his first line of defense and two miles away from his artillery battery.

As the sky grew darker and the rain gained intensity, Colonel Smith became morose and started thinking about past defeats. Lt Colonel Bill Travis at the Alamo, heroic, but defeated and killed. General Custer, ignorant and impulsive, got his whole command wiped out. Will I go down in history as a fool or a hero?

"Sir!" Said First Sergeant "Whitey" Dillon. A squad from his platoon, was now assigned to CP security and communications, "Updating communications and dispositions, Colonel. We got hardwire and portable radio to all platoons at the pass, radio only to the Recoilless Rifle Company, but we're experiencing problems with them and runners only to the mortar platoon.

"We have no communications established yet with the Artillery Battery. We're working on a jeep system to get there; runners aren't gonna work, it's too far."

"Thanks, Whitey. What about Rusty's group?"

"Sir, they're on their own in the Eastern Valley. It's too far to communicate with them by any means."

"Jesus! What if they get overrun? How will we know?"

"You're kidding, right, Colonel?" Whitey got a sick feeling in his stomach.

Chapter Twenty

Monday, July 4, 1950 - Day Ten of the Invasion
Korea – Rusty's Command in the East Valley North of the
City of Osan – 2100 – (9:00 pm)

They had furiously dug foxholes for many hours all along the valley, in carefully planned areas and sequenced to perform according to Red's plan. Cut down bushes from the nearby hills camouflaged positions.

The men were exhausted but in good spirits and settled in their foxholes.

About a quarter-mile up from the main highway, a dirt entrance path entered the pass and gently rolled around into a funnel that slowly opened entry up into the valley.

Just beyond this entrance, off in the northeastern corner, in a deep foxhole dug into a line of bushes, next to a steep rise, Red, Rusty, Foxy, and *One* stood in the rain.

"I don't like you being here, Red. You sure you got to do this?" Asked Rusty.

"No! But I got the only bazooka that can knock out a tank, and I know how to shoot it. Plus, I planned this whole goddamned defense, and I think we can get the hell out of here when we must!"

"Jesus, Mary, and Joseph!" Quipped Foxy, "I'm counting on you!"

"You sure *One* knows how to load this bazooka?"

"Yes, damn it! I'll show you."

Red raised the weapon.

Red called *One's* name and said, "Fire."

One drew a rocket out of his back carrying sack, armed it, and shoved it into the tube, wrapped the ignition wire around the firing pin, and tapped Red on his head, textbook; about ten seconds.

"Damn!" Said Rusty.

Red turned to *One* and bowed in recognition of excellence. *One* smiled, bent back.

Rusty said, "Glad that's settled. Hey, where's Tracker? And how long has Tully's Team been out and where are they?" He was losing track of time.

"I sent Tracker to scout into the hills east of us and make sure no surprises await our withdrawal."

"Tully's group left about an hour ago. They're near the main road, at the entrance to the valley. Can't imagine these bastards wouldn't send out scouts ahead of their main force. Don't want them coming up here, finding our little surprise."

"Not questioning you, Red. Now listen to me! You are not to die here! This battle is a bullshit exercise in trying to delay; you and I know this. We talked about this; we will fight, but we will pull back. Don't get that Irish temper going. You've done a fantastic job in planning here, but it's not Red's last stand, and it's not ours!"

"Shut up, Rusty! I know."

Rusty didn't shut up, "This fight is lost before it begins. You and I got a lot more fights ahead of us, and I need you!"

Red slumped back in the foxhole. "Yeah! I hope so. Been an honor serving with you in case things go, you know."

ROK Captain Kim jumped into their foxhole. "Red, I've inspected all your locations of my troops, and they are as you directed."

Rusty laughed. "Trying to take my command, hey, Red!" Then he turned face to face with Captain Kim.

"Captain. I need to remind you that we Americans and your South Koreans will get our asses kicked here, despite the brilliance of my second in command and our American forces on the main highway. They will bear the brunt of this attack and will suffer the most. But our intentions are not to sacrifice our troops, but to make a good accounting of ourselves and live to do it again. Is that clear!"

Captain Kim saw the anguish on Rusty, wondered again about these Americans. Thought about who the better general was and who Rusty was really talking to, and who was leading the Americans on the main highway?

Kim acknowledged Rusty with a grunt then left, knowing what he and his men had to do.

"Time for you to get the hell out here, boss." Said Red, to Rusty.

As Rusty was climbing out of the foxhole, he turned, "Foxy! You're in charge of this crazy Irish bastard!"

Foxy was quick, "I'm from Chicago, and that's an impossible order!" They hauntingly laughed.

Foxy, Red, and *One* settled into the trench. Their position had the best direct shot at anything coming up through the small pass. Red had set up staggered lines of foxholes across this valley, starting at his position. He called it the Zulu defense. Nobody knew what the hell he was talking about until he described it in detail.

Red was a student of tactical warfare, although only a non-com, he was recognized as one of the best, certainly by Rusty and recent experiences confirmed that to the rest of the team.

Foxy had been quiet much longer than his usual self and asked Red, "I'm now speaking for my Confederate friend, Arron, who's not here, but he, nor I, have ever heard of any Zulu defense in the Yankee War, or any war for that matter. Would it have helped Arron's South?"

After a year of this, Red got annoyed. "Foxy! Arron has been a pain in my ass about this Confederate shit! Are you taking up his cause? Cut it out. You, nor he, no more care about that war, then I care about what happened yesterday."

"Don't mess with my distractions! It keeps me sane."

Red reconsidered, "Sorry, Arron sometimes pisses me off. Don't you start?"

"But I got you thinking about something other than what's about to happen, didn't I?"

Red stayed quiet for a time. "You just stay focused and don't worry about what's on my mind, okay?"

"Just making conversation to pass the time, Red. Just tell me when to run."

Leaning back against the foxhole wall, Red thought about nights like this. His fight in the **Battle of the Bulge** in the big war, being overwhelmed, struggling against incredible forces, retreating, trying to save his men, and yet fight. He fortified himself; maybe my time has now come. I've cheated death for damned sure, so, if anyone's listening up there, I'm still not ready!

As the night wore on, constant rain changed to intermittent clouds with dappled light from a three-quarter moon that allowed for decent visibility.

Joe had quietly slipped off to find a worthy spot on the eastern valley ridge, about ten feet off the valley floor behind a downed tree.

Sniper Dean decided to find his piece of real estate. He climbed the east ridge, 50 yards behind Joe's site, and 30 feet higher, found a well-sighted location behind a rock formation, then built his tent shelter for his sniper rifle in case it decided to rain again and settled in. He thought about what would come around that Valley funnel first. It didn't matter to him. Mechanized, infantry! The fucking Pope! He'd kill what he could, and then he was going to get the hell out of this trap.

Then he worried about mortars and artillery.

Tully's Team down at the Main Highway path entrance leading into the Valley – Same Time

Mario and Snake teamed up and went north up the highway about a quarter-mile past the pathway entrance and got behind a big boulder just off the road.

"I told you." Quipped Mario, as they settled in. An ideal spot, they could see anything approaching from either direction.

Snake wasn't impressed. "So, if you can see the future, what happens next?"

Mario was in a somber mood, as this strange night, rain then moonlight, then clouds, made him even more uneasy.

"You and I, buddy, we're a killing machine! We'll do this night, right!"

Tully and Frenchy were 100 hundred feet directly across from Joe on the other side of the pathway, both 300 feet up from the road entrance.

Frenchy was a Ranger and had served with Tully from the beginning of the invasion of Europe. They'd experienced crap weather, rain, snow, freezing, and sweltering hot, but tonight he felt different. Maybe it was this strange country that he'd been in all of 10 or 11 days, he couldn't remember exactly. Perhaps it was the almost non-stop fighting. He felt weird.

"Tell me, Tully, and don't give me your usual bullshit! Are we gonna make it out of here?"

"Jesus, fucking Christ, Frenchy! After what we've been through, we should've been dead a long time ago. So consider this good behavior, and we're on borrowed time. Now, as to this shit-hole situation we're in, I want to remind you that we Rangers have occasionally broken off attacks at the front and then attacked to the rear. You and I experienced that at Bastogne, remember?"

"You saved us there, and no, I'll never forget that. But I'm asking about *now*."

"I think our plan is good. Think Ranger, Frenchy, and we're the best!"

Across from Tully and Frenchy at the Valley Entrance

Joe sat in his hidden spot, soaked from the earlier rain but comfortable in his position. He reflected on the last many days with wonder. Except for the Frankenstein like scar on his forehead, that was it. Damn, he thought, I got into a war I didn't even know was about to happen. Shit happens, he thought.

He liked being alone here, it was good cover without worrying about a foxhole buddy or his squad, but he was anxious anyway. He'd grown attached to his new family, a strange mixture of Army and Ranger comrades. Yeah, he thought, my family. What was going to happen to them, or me, this night? Or tomorrow. Damn! We've been through shit and escaped death more than any group, or any man has a right to expect. Are we that good? Or just damned lucky? Maybe we're both? I sure as shit know I was both to survive Flatbush Avenue and then Okinawa. So maybe it continues? He settled back, tried to quiet his mind, and listen for danger.

The rain started again and made the only sound.

Rusty got back to his CP up the valley. The trench was in the center near the top, shaped in a U. It commanded a complete view of the valley. He got in the ditch with Larry, who operated the radio, with C J next to him. Beside him were the four men he'd ordered back.

Ranger Moose carried the only automatic rifle, the BAR. Surprisingly, he'd never said a word to Rusty or, for that matter, hadn't talked much to anybody, surprisingly said, "No disrespect, Rusty, but I belong at the spear! Not at the ass!"

Rusty laughed. "Moose! That's why you're back here, so we don't get their spear in our ass. Now you, Arron, and *Three* go back and guard our escape route."

Marty was relieved he was staying in the CP. His combat medic skills would surely be needed soon. He was tired of being so overprotected by his comrades. Grabbing his gear and rifle, he prepared his mind. Waiting, it might be hours he thought, then fury, fear, and death will come! Jesus! I think I'm going crazy!

"Larry, who do we have contact with?" Asked Rusty.

"Down the valley, we have Red and Captain Kim. Heading into town, we've got our escape team, Arron, Moose, and *Three*. I can't get Colonel Smith's CP or anyone else."

"Have you tried contacting Leyden?"

"No. We didn't set up our equipment. Didn't think we had enough time or if it would have made a difference."

"Right. Who did you put in charge of that secret stuff?"

"Arron."

"Jesus!"

Chapter Twenty One

Monday, July 5, 1950 - Day Eleven of the Invasion Korea – Tully's Advance Team just north of the Valley Entrance – 0300 – (3:00 am)

Just off the highway, behind the boulder, Snake's eyes flew open. Not asleep, he was in semi-conscious mode, as most experienced combat vets learned to sleep for long periods.

Mario heard it too and only moved slightly.

"Our guests have arrived." Whispered Snake. "You take the north."

Mario moved to the north edge of the boulder. He couldn't see in the pitch darkness and the rain, but he had excellent hearing.

Snake did the same on the south side of the big rock and had the same problem. But he also heard an engine. Only one he thought, small, maybe a scout car? He was closer to the highway than Mario and started to catch Koreans talking as they passed. They spoke softly, but they had to elevate their voices to communicate above the noise of the rain. He had no idea how many soldiers were on this road. He guessed from a low of 10 to a high of 30, maybe a squad to a platoon.

He smiled. No Tanks! Not the main attack! Just scouts!

`

The end of the column stopped in front of Snake. Mario slid next to Snake and whispered, "They passed me, no one behind them."

Snake whispered back, "This is the tail of the column. I think they found the Valley path. Trying to figure out what to do."

Mario said, "Guarantee, they're gonna split. They'll send a small unit up that path, but the main unit is going down that road, they're not our concern."

Snake knew his orders and said, "Okay, let's follow them and take out anybody going up the valley path. Then we'll come back and think about these other assholes."

"I like how you think." Mario said, always in the mood to do some dirty work.

They waited until they heard the column move, then slithered down to the road, moved to the path entrance to the valley, and crept up, trying to find the scouts going up.

Snake counted his steps from the entrance path, then grabbed Mario, and pulled him close. "They got a good head start; they must've cut guys from upfront to go up this path."

"Shit!" Said Mario, "Now we got to find'em and not get killed by our own guys."

Snake tugged Mario's arm, "We can do it! Let's go fast."

They figured the enemy would spread out in a V formation, so they each took an edge with a plan to roll them up. They got very close before they heard the rain hitting the North Korean's rubberized slickers. Lucky dogs! Thought Mario, they got rain gear. Reconsidering, he knew these guys were not going to be so fortunate after all.

Mario was the first to run into the first soldier, knocking him down from the rear. Both surprised, Mario had the jump and the knife. It ended quickly and silently. He then moved off at an angle to the next.

The second and third guy went down easy, but, as he reached for the fourth soldier, he stepped into a deep hole and started to go sideways. With presence of mind, he grabbed something as he fell. A strap, maybe, he didn't know, but it was enough to take the man down with him, actually, on him.

The enemy's rifle came down on his helmet with a bang, and he let out a yell as Mario stuck his combat knife in his chest.

Boom! A muffled shot. Mario lay still not knowing who fired.

He heard Snake's distinctive whistle; he whistled back in his code.

They crawled out and met, fearful their men would get trigger happy after the sound of the shot.

"Had to shoot that guy after you started dancing with your killing partner! That's all of 'em, let's get out of here."

Retreating to the valley path entrance, they talked about what to do next. Sitting in the rain, in the dark, they discussed killing the rest of this enemy scout team, which they figured numbered at least 20 or more and having some vehicle.

"They're not going to be happy when their guys don't show up." Said Snake. "They may go up this path to look for them?"

"They'll stop here sure enough. But we got shit! We can't take on these guys head-on. Can't even see where good cover is!"

"We got grenades! And surprise! What happened to you up there? This is not like you, Mario, snap out of this!" Snake slapped him across the back of his head. "You and me, buddy! The best killing machine, ever!"

"Hey, assholes!" Came a familiar voice out of the dark.

Tully and Frenchy joined them, "Heard the shot and you guys whistling. How many?"

Mario answered, "We got ten up the valley. Think maybe twenty or more reconning down the road towards Colonel Smith's positions. We're thinking of fucking them up when they return."

Tully smiled in the dark. "Rangers! If only we had enough! But four is better than two, and I like the idea."

"I feel stupid talking to a shadow, so I gotta ask, you bring anything special with you?" Asked Mario.

"Besides Frenchy! Yeah, we both have an extra pouch of Japanese grenades, and each of us has their Type 99 light machine gun, thanks to C J."

Neither Snake nor Mario knew anything about these Japanese weapons.

"Are they good." Asked Snake.

"Very!" Said Tully. "Let's get a plan together. And we need to take a prisoner or two."

They waited, each man had moved into planned positions. The rain stopped and the clouds lightened with the moon filtering through here and there, improving visibility significantly.

Tully was the only man who had fired the Japanese light machine gun. A simple weapon, much like our BAR (Browning Automatic Rifle), but it had a higher rate of fire and held a top-loaded 30 round box of ammo, not the 20 round clip that the BAR had. The best feature about it, though, and the one that would pay off big tonight, Tully thought, was that it had a muzzle flash suppressor. It was a feature that was unique to this Japanese infantry weapon in the big War. It didn't reveal the firing position of the shooter's flash like all guns usually exhibit when fired. A feature that killed so many Americans.

He and Frenchy had lots of extra ammo boxes and grenades.

The highway road at the Valley entrance was somewhat narrow on the valley path side. There was an off-road ditch on the near side for drainage, with a bank that rose sharply into dense underbrush and trees. Tully and Mario took up positions behind some rock formations on this high side, about a hundred feet *south* of the valley path entrance.

A small meadow opened on the other side of the highway, the west side, and ended at a group of low hills, some 300 yards away. The field appeared benign, with overgrown green grass and knee-high weeds, but the recent incessant rains had turned it into a dangerous swamp. A man would quickly sink up to his waist and get stuck. Of course, this was not visible at this point.

Mario and Snake found their spot just north of the valley path. Mario, with his Tommy gun, set up off on the west side and Snake, with a bag of Japanese grenades and his Tommy, sat behind a dead tree stump 50 feet away on the entrance side, up a small incline.

Time moved slowly for the waiting men. Now it was nearing 0500 – (5:00 am). No gunfire. Everybody wondered if this was the pre-advance attack? Would the enemy suddenly appear at their rear? Did Colonel Smith's troops take this recon team out? Where the hell are these guys?

Low gear engine noise got Tully's attention. They were coming back. He didn't have to move a twitch; he was ready.

As anticipated, the column stopped at the valley path entrance. Five soldiers fanned out at the path and knelt, rifles up.

Only shadows were visible, and Snake still could not make out what the vehicle was, but he didn't care now as he pulled the pins on three grenades and tossed them in rapid succession at this mysterious beast. He then grabbed his Tommy and opened up on the knelling troops.

Tully opened fire immediately. Mario was hurling grenades as fast as he could pull the pins. Soldiers usually do what is human nature; run the other way from danger. That's when Frenchy raked the entire west side of the column. He couldn't see them but knew they were there and kept reloading his box ammo.

The grenade flashes illuminated some of the road areas and highlighted exposed soldiers. It wasn't much of a firefight. The little resistance was quickly suppressed.

It became still, except for whimpering and anguish calls amongst the wounded.

"Let's go," said Tully to Mario. "We need to find a live one."

Frenchy moved toward the burning overturned vehicle that was casting enough light to see a decent perimeter around it. Three bodies lay to the side, two had deep wounds, but the third had but a head gash, and he was an officer.

Deciding to check him out, he was breathing. He faked being a fellow communist and spoke Korean to him. Not responding, he slapped him awake. He tried it again, told him they had to get out of here. Groggy, the officer replied, told him to get the American captives because they were vital to their mission.

He wanted to cut his throat but knew he was an intelligence asset, a big one and didn't want to carry him, so played along for as long as he could.

Off to the side, he told Snake what he learned, who found Tully, who discovered the two dead Americans among the bodies.

The Rangers left no enemy suffering.

Chapter Twenty Two

Monday, July 5, 1950 - Day Eleven of the Invasion Korea – Rusty's CP at the Head of the Valley – 0600 – (6:00 am)

Another cloudy, dreary morning greeted the soaked and weary soldiers of the Eastern Valley of Osan, as they called themselves. Foxholes filled with mud and water, they had to sleep leaning against the mud walls. Their cover was cut tree and brush and did not shelter them from the rain. The dirt front from their foxholes was washed away by the rain as no sandbags were available. Not much of anything was available but raw grit, supplied only by them.

"Rusty! Got Red!" Said Larry as he handed the portable to him.

"Go!"

Red relayed what happened at the valley entrance earlier. He and Foxy were still interrogating the North Korean officer but figured they got it all and told him that he sent a runner with the two dead GI's dog tags.

Red ended the call with, "Jesus, Rusty! You're right. They're coming hell-bent on rolling over all of us! I get it! Good luck!"

Rusty grabbed Larry, "As soon as Red's runner gets here, we're going to Colonel Smith's CP. We got a jeep?"

"It's a mite distant, but yeah, unless they stole it back."

Colonel Smith's CP was typical of regular Army, behind the front, with a tent and cots for sleeping above the mud.

Rusty entered the colonel's tent, saw him sipping hot coffee with his major, and introduced him as Major Mark Lavelle, looking at a map.

Rusty had a scowl on his face, raised his hand to show dog tags in his palm, and then threw them at the colonel, "Here are the dog tags of two of your men. Captured, sleeping at their posts, then killed. My men eliminated an enemy recon platoon that captured your guys. We interrogated one of them, an officer."

Smith looked at the disheveled, soaked, and angry first sergeant in disbelief.

"What do you mean? Was that your firefight in front of our positions an hour ago?"

"Who else? We're guarding the northeast valley so you don't get outflanked. That was my best four-man recon team that took out that platoon. Good thing, too, since they mapped out all of your positions."

"Christ!" The Colonel was stunned. "They had us? You did it with four men?"

"Right! As I told you before, you don't know shit about my men or me, nor do you have any idea of what we got now or where we are. Frankly, Colonel, I feel sorry for you. You got handed a shit stick, and all I'm ordered to do is help you as best I can. But! And I mean but! My orders are to survive and keep fighting."

"Sergeant, I don't take lectures from sergeants."

"Sir, in a few hours, 20,000 North Korean soldiers will be coming around that highway bend with tanks. Are you fucking serious? I give you five, maybe six hours before your entire command is wiped out. Call your boss, big Mac, ask for a few divisions!"

"And sir, it's First Sergeant."

Despondent, Colonel Smith knew the score, didn't like to be reminded of it by this non-com. He sat back in his makeshift seat.

"I'm sorry, First Sergeant."

"That was one great job you did out there, thank you, Rusty! I somehow think I underestimated your tactical command skills and experience in theater. Can you defend the East Valley?"

"No offense, sir, but it doesn't matter now. I have a token force, as you, maybe 300 hundred or so with no heavy weapons, guarding your right flank northeast of you in the valley. I think we can hold for a few hours until they concentrate their mortars and artillery. Then we're out of here. That's fair warning, Colonel. You must move out as well, or else you'll be enveloped and killed."

"I'm in command of this battle, First Sergeant! I'll tell you when to withdraw."

"Colonel, we have no communications, no hard line communication stuff with us at all. I've told you what I'm doing! I now notify you, sir, that your right flank in the eastern valley, that which you didn't authorize me to defend, that I will withdraw all my forces after any heavy attack, and I advise you to do the same."

"I'll remember your name, First Sergeant Rusty Fabino. Do you have any other suggestions?"

"Yes, sir." Pointing to a map on the colonel's desk. He pinpointed to the location of the valley path entrance on the highway. "That should be your first artillery target. The meadow on the right is quicksand; nothing gets through there."

Colonel Smith stood. "Never met a non-com like you, Rusty! You should be an officer, but I haven't decided what rank you should be. Good Luck!"

They saluted.

Chapter Twenty Three

Monday, July 5, 1950 - Day Eleven of the Invasion
Korea – The Battle of Osan Begins – 1100 – (11:00 am)

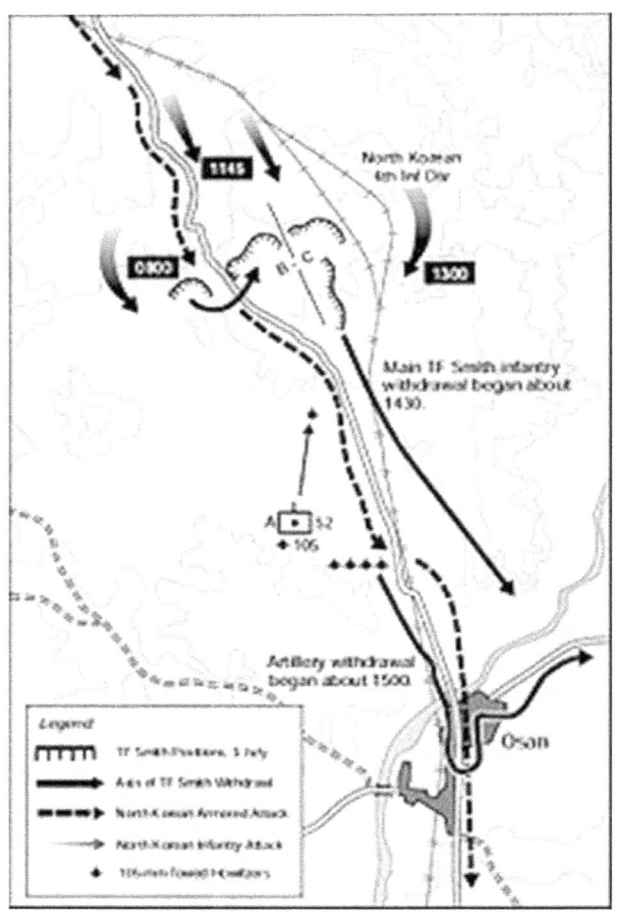

Rain poured. Thick clouds darkened the day as if it was near dusk, not sunrise. Since the short but intense firefight a few hours ago and then the discovery that two of their own were dragged off and killed ran through the ranks. Anticipation of impending doom raced through the green American soldiers dug in at the thin line of resistance, just off the highway, on a ridge north of the city of Osan.

Experienced non-coms roamed the positions trying to steady the men. Officers were mostly new and unseen.

Colonel Smith worried about his lack of communications with his artillery company and the rest of his command in general. Runners were too slow but were all he had.

The disappearance of First Sergeant "Whitey" Carlton disturbed him. He ordered him to command a squad of his 1st Platoon to be security for his CP. The real leader of the team, a competent sounding veteran sergeant, told him that Whitey just went off to inspect the rest of his platoon at the front line.

Whitey found his platoon on the second defensive line, nearer the highway. They had decent protection he thought, with adequate separation. The platoon lieutenant huddled in a foxhole with his radioman and two soldiers; Whitey jumped in.

"You good, sir?" Whitey asked the newly minted West Point LT.

"Good to see you, First Sergeant. Yeah! I think we're gonna give'em hell!"

Whitey grabbed the LT and pushed him against the foxhole wall.

"Sir, my platoon's survival depends on you! You get them the hell out of here before you get overrun, because you will be, if you delay. Hell is coming down on us, sir! You best have no fucking illusions!"

He saw fright in his LT's eyes and decided to disregard his orders to return to the CP. His men were more important.

Over on the west side of the highway, directly across from Whitey's platoon and about a hundred yards from the bend in the road, was the recoilless rifle jeep platoon positioned parallel to the highway, in a mostly open field. Unlike the meadow north of them, this area was rock, with small contours, ravines, and some large outcroppings that afforded some concealment.

They'd spent the last many hours hiding their jeeps with brush and any camouflage they could find. The crews gave up their rain gear early on to protect the slim rocket ammunition they had from getting wet and potentially compromising the rocket's contact points.

In a rush to get these six mounted weapons to Korea, there was no room on the C – 47 transport planes for their loaded ammo trailers. The four-man crews had to unbox the ammo crates from ammo trailers at the airport and place the loose rockets on the floor in the jeeps. They only had room for eight rockets, so their LT told them to load 4 HT (anti-tank) and 4 HE (high explosive) rounds. They had to make do.

The crews were well trained on the weapon, but none had seen combat.

Their LT was farther back in a seventh jeep with the platoon radio that didn't work.

The sounds of clanking tank treads carried far in the calm, rainy morning. It was like a lightning strike on the pitchers diamond in the World Series.

Everything stopped for the American troops.

At the first sounds, Snake and Mario ran from their exposed positions on the highway and headed up the valley pathway, signaling to Tully and Frenchy to move back as they passed their location. They didn't move.

The eerie and frightening sounds of the tanks approaching made a few of Colonel Smith's soldiers run. Sergeants grabbed some and tried to bolster the rest, but fear was pervasive.

With a clear view from his CP, Smith watched the enemy column round the mountain road, coming directly down the highway, exposing themselves to his positions. The first vehicle was an old German WW2 half-track, followed by three Russian made T-34 tanks. All flanked by tight infantry lines.

It was at this point that his orders had been to open fire, but nothing happened. Another tank started to come round the bend. Colonel Smith started screaming. "Fire! Somebody fire, goddamn it!"

As if someone heard him, mortars started thumping. The explosions signaled to the artillery battery to commence firing. Their last orders given were to shoot farther to the rear of this column, into the junction of the valley path road, then walk it back. They only had HE (high explosive) shells but nothing to kill a tank unless they got a direct hit. They opened fire.

The men in the recoilless jeeps were stunned by the progression of armor moving across their front. They saw at least a hundred soldiers walking next to the vehicles on their side of this column.

It quickly dawned on them that the jeeps had no infantry support upfront or anywhere around them, and the enemy was a hundred yards away! They froze.

The mortar explosions broke their momentary lapse. They fired! All six jeeps, almost in synch, at point-blank range! They couldn't miss and didn't. The half-track just blew apart. The second vehicle, a tank, must have been hit in its ammo storage locker, as its blasted turret blew ten feet in the air. The second and third tanks burst into flames. A fourth tank had just rounded the bend but was not fully exposed and only received a glancing blow off its side.

As impressive a weapon as the recoilless rifle was, its flaw lay in its name. The very system that allowed the gun to be mounted on a jeep and not recoil made it a very vulnerable and a dangerous weapon to its crew.

Corporal "Howie" Akard, in charge of jeep # 2, was closest to the highway and had just fired the shot that missed killing tank # 4. He knew that firing the rifle would release an enormous cloud of gases that allowed the energy to be released in the air and not in the recoil of the gun. But it was like setting off a flare in the night for all to see.

"Go, go!" Howie yelled, "Move, or we die!"

The four men jumped into the jeep, and it took off.

Tank # 4, now more than halfway round the bend, by chance, had its main gun aligned directly on jeep # 2 and fired. The jeep disappeared in a cloud of smoke and dirt.

The few surviving North Korean flanking infantry around the tank column rose and charged the remaining jeep positions as they started retreating.

The jeep platoon LT watched the horror unfold. jeep # 3 didn't make 30 yards before it succumbed to concentrated gunfire and rolled to a standstill. Jeep # 4, against orders, stopped after driving about 50 yards and decided to fire another shot, this time it was HE against the advancing soldiers. It was effective and killed many, but fruitless. The crew died in a withering hail of bullets.

The young lieutenant wanted to puke.

The remaining three jeeps retreating were making good progress but then stopped because a large number of soldiers were running towards them. The LT's jeep, at the lead, panicked, "Are we flanked!" He called out! To no one.

The guys in the jeeps knew they were dead when they saw the soldiers coming and froze. But then, these attackers weren't firing at them. Then they saw some American helmets and South Korean uniforms and M-1 rifles.

Sergeant Bob Dare, on jeep # 5, jumped out and signaled to the other Jeeps to stand and fight as this unknown force of troops came up to them and started firing at the charging enemy.

It was a small, but a capable, motivated force that stopped the North Korean soldiers dead in their tracks.

A somewhat crazed South Korean lieutenant, whose horse was shot out from under him yesterday, and who was hospitalized, had fully recovered and escaped his confinement to organize his troops and a local resistance band of misfits that turned the tide at that moment.

Chapter Twenty Four

Monday, July 5, 1950 - Day Eleven of the Invasion
Korea – The Battle of Osan Continues on the East Side of
the Highway - 1115 – (11:15 am)

Sergeant Whitey heard the thumps and saw the mortar detonations. The enemy vehicles started to explode. Smoke from across the highway told him that the jeeps were engaged.

Without orders, the men on the ridges and foxholes opened fire on the enemy troops. Unlike the soldiers on the other side of the column who received no small arms fire, the massive volume coming down on the east side from the Americans caused panic among the North Koreans astride the tanks. Tanks burning behind them, mortar rounds detonating among them, and overwhelming firepower coming from above, they started to run.

At 200 yards or less, they became easy targets for Colonel Smith's men. Fewer than half made it back to cover behind the bend in the highway. Artillery detonations to their rear column caused more fear.

Tank # 4 had now fully pulled out from the bend and entered the field on the west side of the road to support the now halted infantry attack on the jeeps. It kept firing at the line of resistance but wasn't doing much damage. Jeep # 6 kept shooting at it and finally destroyed it on the third shot. But that was their last anti-tank rocket.

Mortars on Whitey's side of the highway shifted aim and started impacting enemy troops threatening the remaining jeeps. Realizing they were exposed and with no tank support, the North Koreans made a hasty retreat to the road ditch and then back to the road bend.

Colonel Smith had watched the battle and saw his error. His left flank was severely exposed. He called Major Lavelle, who commanded his small reserve force of a reinforced platoon, some 50 men.

"Mark, get your reserve over to the field on the west side of the highway, 200 hundred yards or so back from the bend. Bring those jeep guns in behind you. Bring that bazooka squad with you. Nothing gets past you, or they'll flank us! Got it?"

"Colonel? When do we pull out? We just killed four tanks! I think they got a lot more coming and they haven't fired an artillery round yet. Sir! How long do we have to stay?"

"Goddamn it, Major! You just follow my orders!"

Chapter Twenty Five

**Monday, July 5, 1950 - Day Eleven of the Invasion
Korea – The Battle of Osan Continues on the Eastern Valley
Pathway –Rusty's Position - 1200 – (Noon)**

Earlier explosions farther down the road meant the start of the battle to all in the valley.

The constant clanking sounds of tanks passing nearby left Tully and Frenchy cold on this hot and rainy day.

Friendly artillery explosions that impacted the area earlier scared the bee-Jesus out of them, as the rounds came close. They did some damage to the enemy as they heard secondary explosions from the road. It then became quiet as Smith's artillery started walking its way back to the bend in the highway.

"I think we should move now?" Said Frenchy.

"For once, I think you got it right! Go!"

They ran up the left side of the valley and stumbled into a crowded trench.

"Glad you finally took my advice!" Said Mario with a grin.

Snake smiled at Mario's side, but the other South Korean soldiers in the trench weren't smiling. They just showed fear and resolution.

Tully went over to one South Korean guy holding a Japanese light machine gun. He showed him his much smaller

Thomson sub-machine gun and patted him on his helmet. They looked at each other, and both smiled.

Another ROK soldier at the end of the trench was resetting his 'knee mortar', as the rain had weakened its initial position. His friends decided their life depended on finding something to secure the recoil of his weapon and so went out to scout around and eventually found a large rock that they dragged back and secured against their foxhole back wall so that he could brace his weapon against it, allowing him to fire it accurately.

These South Korean soldiers were exhausted and frightened. America's presence bolstered their spirits, but they saw little deterrence to the tidal wave flowing over their country, yet, somehow, they knew this was different. They were not going back to that same Japanese like rule. They've tasted some freedom and liked it.

The enemy unit entered the bottom of the valley funnel in an orderly manner and hadn't spotted the camouflaged foxholes or trenches, but then something spooked them. A bugle blew, and all at once, a full company of 200 North Korean soldiers came running up the narrow path, turned and started to spread out into the valley.

Sniper Dean fired first, killing the lead officer.

Red's first line of his Zulu defense cast off their bush cover, was entirely comprised of South Korean soldiers, and immediately raked the charging enemy with a fierce volley from their Japanese light machine guns.

Twenty-five men firing almost point-blank, each with a 30 round box of ammo firing at 800 rounds per minute, can kill a lot of men in a few seconds. Snaping out the second box, ready to insert the third box of ammo, the corporal in command of this first trench yelled to ceasefire. He didn't see anything moving, and nobody was firing back.

Red watched this opening with pride and some surprise. He wondered why the enemy charged like that, but more importantly, what were they going to do next.

"Red! Got Rusty for you." Said Foxy, as he handed over the portable.

"What!"

"Lots of noise down there, glad you're alive, what's up?"

"Just getting started. They're gonna get real pissed soon. Prepare to run. Don't call me again!"

A much more organized force slowly made their way through the path, made the turn, spread out, and proceeded in proper jump and cover in squad formations. The funnel was getting crowded.

Red figured they now focused a least a battalion on this valley, and so far, they committed two, maybe three companies.

He needed to modify his plan to meet the changing tactical situation, so he huddled with Foxy and **One** to relay his instructions. They immediately took off, **One** to the second defense line where the men mostly had Knee Mortars, and Foxy to the first defense line.

Both shortly returned to Reds trench with the OK sign.

Within a few minutes, the second line opened fire with their 'knee mortars' on the spread out, but not dug in, enemy infantry, and kept shooting.

The panic and havoc on the North Korean troops was immediate. Unlike typical mortars that have a high shell trajectory and thus make a screeching warning sound before impact, the Knee Mortar was a low trajectory silent killer; it just exploded without warning.

At the start of the detonations, and as the enemy tried to retreat, defense line one came back into action. If you stood to run from the mortars, you were cut to pieces by the machine guns. Stay, and you died in a mist of smoke.

The engagement lasted but a few minutes, and then the valley grew quiet as a few remaining survivors slithered back.

As Red estimated, a second enemy company was eliminated. Don't you be patting yourself on the back asshole, his mind said. Keep focused, damn it. Lot's more to go. Get to it!

Besides the screaming of the enemy wounded, the battlefield was quiet. Distant rumblings told of the battle unfolding on Colonel Smiths' front.

Silence was a timed event in Red's tactical mind. It made him nervous that it was just too long since they wiped out that last attack. So he decided to act and shot off a flare, signaling Phase Two.

Line Three commenced firing smoke shells from their 'Knee Mortars' to hide Red's first two defensive line withdrawals. His foxhole stayed.

Joe figured he could do some damage if he remained and ignored the signal. He'd not engaged the enemy at the outset, although they were near, he thought waiting might achieve better results. He always believed he could do more; it drove him.

Joe heard Sniper Dean's opening shot, realized he wasn't too far behind and above him. It was comforting.

Like Joe, Dean preferred fighting alone and relished his unique sharpshooter abilities. But this continuum of killing was starting to create a small crack in his wall. Sitting there, thinking about how many men he's killed, he then switched his mind over to how many friends he watched die.

No, that's not right, he thought. I didn't make friends. That wasn't right, either. Shit! Stop thinking, he screamed into his mind, and then it popped out, totally at of the blue, still screaming, *Protect your family!*

"Damn!" Dean sat stunned for a moment at the revelation of his thoughts. Now determined, he got back to business.

From a distance, the screaming sounds were but a moment of warning and then impact, two seconds, maybe. The explosions were mortars that walked up the Valley for a few minutes and stopped. It didn't do much but make more foxholes and made the recently vacated ones bigger.

All got quiet in the Valley as dull explosions shifted over to Colonel Smith's area.

A tank rumbled up into view. Red thought about what C J said about this not being a tank friendly valley, well, he was wrong. "*One*! Fire!" Red positioned the bazooka as *One* loaded it and tapped his head.

Enemy infantry started to spread out around the tank. Red fired at 100 yards. It took three seconds, and the tank stopped with a muffled explosion. Then the turret hatch blew off in a fiery flume.

Joe let the tank pass and got behind the second group coming up the Valley. When he heard the tank get killed, Joe started tossing the Japanese hand grenades. Found it ironic and amusing that he was using the same weapons that killed so many of his fellow-men on Okinawa.

Joe's mind just went somewhere else as he continued to move on the North Korean troops. Now running and shooting his Thompson, then diving to the mud to reload. Tossed two more grenades and passed through the enemy column, and jumped into a large bush at the corner of the Valley edge.

Sniper Dean moved his sniper rifle around the enemy positions and spotted movement at the edge.

"Joe! You fucking idiot!" He whispered, "Always thought we were very much alike!"

Dean followed Joe's crazy moves and killed a few trying to get a bead on him. He was dumbfounded at what Joe just did.

Red saw the tail end of Joe's run and confirmed what he had all along suspected; that Joe was possessed. Foxy almost fired on him, thinking he was a crazed North Korean. He was half right.

Red fired another flare, signaling the 'knee mortars' to fire high explosives into the enemy positions.

"Time to go, Foxy!"

"I've seen enough! Thought you maybe wanted to stay and see a little more fireworks? Glad you don't!"

As the detonations got underway, Foxy and *One* followed Red out and ran up the Valley to the next defensive line.

Joe thought it was time to vacate his little drama party excursion. Wondered why he did that stupid run up the column. He planned to toss a few grenades than move off, right! Where did that crazy shit come from? It just happened. Why did I do that? Do I have a death wish? Joe's mind calmed as he thought about his actions while crawling up the valley to friendly lines.

Chapter Twenty Six

**Monday, July 5, 1950 - Day Eleven of the Invasion
Korea – The Battle of Osan Continues on Colonel
Smith's Highway Position - 1300 – (1:00 pm)**

The initial bloody nose at the road bend caused a momentary pause in the advance down the highway until a very pissed off enemy colonel radioed his artillery battalion that was positioned four miles in his rear, to open fire.

The North Korean artillery barrage on Smith's first defense ridgelines was not intense but sure was effective. It caused few casualties but created panic among the many green troops. The shelling didn't last long, maybe ten minutes, but long enough, as anyone would attest to a concentrated bombardment.

Private Roy Klein huddled deep in his shared foxhole with his buddies, Harry and Wayne, when the bombardment ended. They were all shaking, scared as never before, but they felt lucky. Screams and calls for medic resonated through the momentary silence.

Only six months out of basic training and after only one month in the 24th Division, Roy and his friends were 19 years old and didn't know shit from Shinola. Each from different parts of the country, they had joined the Army for varied but compelling reasons, never thinking they'd soon be fighting in some obscure war. Only friends for the last month, they became close as they discovered they were all misfits in one form or another. Roy had knocked up a 17 year old girl, and the judge gave him three options, marry her, jail, or the Army. The other two also had less than patriotic motives to sign up. No money or legal issues.

And here they were.

The silence was suddenly broken by heavy machine gun fire that roused them out of their semi stupor. Tank sounds coming out of the road bend got them motivated to look out of their foxhole.

The sight was chilling.

Enemy infantry were pouring out of the highway bend, coming up the slope, attacking their lines.

Tanks were moving into the fields on the right. A lone tank made a turn towards them and fired.

Explosions from mortars impacted all around them.

The attacking infantry was spreading out, gaining ground, not stopping, and shooting at a high rate of fire.

The three men, shaking, fired their M-1 rifles at the attacking troops. Fellow soldiers were abandoning their positions in panic, running past, or getting cut down in front of them. Roy's M-1 clanged empty and he dove down to reload when a hail of bullets raked the top of his foxhole. It sprayed muck and grime on him and his face.

"Jesus! What the" he could hardly see but saw his friend slide down the side of the foxhole. If he didn't know that his friend was beside him, he would never have guessed who he was. He had no face, not much of anything to his head. Realizing the stuff on his face was his friend's fluids, Roy vomited. Reeling from this and wiping away the blood and gore from his face, he saw that his other friend's body was lying on the other side of the foxhole.

He realized that if he hadn't ducked to reload, he'd be dead as well. Shaking, Roy got out of the foxhole and ran.

Tanks bursting out from the highway bend were the last straw for many, as they started to abandon their positions. Dense concentrations of attacking enemy troops climbing the ridge broke the American lines into a full-fledged flight to the rear.

Colonel Smith lost control of his forces. He ordered a general retreat to anybody who he had communications with, which were few.

A long line of tanks flowed through the field, killing his remaining jeep platoon. Enemy infantry at their side attacked in force.

The bazooka platoon aligned behind the jeeps were at near point-blank range to the tanks. As warned, the old 2.5-inch bazooka could not penetrate the heavy armor, and Colonel Smith saw his men, try and try as bravely as they could to disable the tanks, were overwhelmed by the enemy without doing any damage to the tanks.

Captain Melvin's reserve force of 50 men, sent to help the bazookA-Teams, realized it would be suicide and withdrew. Melvin led his men south to retreat towards the artillery company.

Enemy tanks regained the highway passed their initial burning armor, and entered the city limits of Osan, behind Colonel Smith's forward positions.

Smith's artillery company, positioned just west and south of Osan, panicked when they saw the tanks coming down the road, about three miles in front of them. Their major was a veteran and rallied his gunners.

"We will fire on these bastards!" He directed his six 105 mm cannons to fire their remaining ammunition on the tanks, knocking one out. Then the tanks fired back. Their assault troops started spreading out, forming an attack formation.

The artillery gunners kept firing until their major figured the enemy troops were getting too close, so he ordered their guns to be spiked, then grabbed what they could and ran to the vehicles sheltered south of town.

At the ridgeline, Whitey watched the enemy stream out of the highway bend, spreading out onto the slope, like aunts. His platoon would be overrun unless they moved quickly. Whitey took charge when his LT froze. So he ordered his men back some, they were holding, but things had broken down fast after the artillery and mortar barrage.

As the fight raged, the enemy penetrated the first line of trenches. Whitey realized this fight was over. Whitey screamed to his men, "If you want to die, you will just run! To live, you will fall back in order and fight!"

"We go! Now!"

Whitey led his platoon. Run and stop, fire! He trained his squad leaders well to do this. Other noncoms tried to control their men to stem the panic, but amidst the charging enemy and mortar explosions, it was difficult. Men carried wounded on their back; others grabbed their arms and dragged them. Some were left.

They were retreating toward Colonel Smith's CP.

Chapter Twenty Seven

**Monday, July 5, 1950 - Day Eleven of the Invasion
Korea – The Battle of Osan Continues in Rusty's Position in
the Valley - 1300 – (1:30 pm)**

Red couldn't believe what he was watching as the enemy emerged out of the 'Knee Mortar' barrage. The early estimate he made of a battalion fighting here was wrong. It's a goddamned regiment! At least 2,000 men, not 600.

"Shit!" He said out loud. The enemy was taking heavy casualties, but they were persistent, smart, and there were a whole lot more of them then he had.

He radioed Rusty, told him he thought it was the end.

"You got this battle, Red! Glad you see it that way. Now get out! I'll get our rear in motion."

Red than radioed Captain Kim. "Captain! I'm ordering smoke and mortar now so you can get your men out. We'll follow our retreat plans. Good luck!"

Red fired his last flare.

That was it for the valley defense. Now it was about not being overrun. But it all depended on the discipline of the men.

Just as the valley force initiated its smoke and 'knee mortar' withdrawal plan, the enemy charged. Enemy mortar explosions started hitting the valley lines in the rear. Bugles blew from different formations throughout the valley.

Watching from his CP, Rusty was horrified as the situation clarified. It appeared that the enemy had a new reinforced unit that looked like a regiment, all charging through the smoke. His stomach convulsed, thinking about his men. Two thousand men! Oh, shit. We're dead.

Then something extraordinary happened.

On a high eastern hill at their rear, overlooking this valley, came a high volume of incredible ordinance, decimating the advancing line of troops. Bodies kept exploding apart, falling in a sweeping arch threw their lines. It was like a scythe from the sky just swinging, back and forth, blowing apart anything it hit. It stopped the enemy advance cold and killed most of the first 500 or so.

Red jumped out of his foxhole, ordering all to follow. Captain Kim didn't question providence and did the same. The entire # 3 line ran like hell to their escape route.

Rusty had no idea what had just happened but thanked whatever God had intervened. He led his CP command out to help the wounded to the waiting trucks. Marty, the combat medic, was fully engaged with trying to patch those severely wounded. It was a heartbreaking job.

They didn't have much time, and they didn't have enough trucks.

"Rusty!" Said Captain Kim abruptly, as he stood next to the loading convoy of trucks. "It's been an honor fighting with you. I'll take my men through the rice paddies and head south. I hope we meet again. Good luck, Colonel!"

Rusty smiled at the compliment as the Captain walked away and then yelled after him, "Kim, you're a good leader. Survive! Your country needs you." He waved goodbye.

As trucks started pulling out, Tracker jumped on the driver side of the third truck driven by Ranger Moose.

"Jesus! Tracker! You scared the shit out of me! Where the fuck you've been?"

"Been saving all palefaces asses. Where's Rusty?"

"Back at the loading point."

"See you later." Tracker hopped off and walked back to the last trucks getting loaded.

"Hey, chief!" Tracker yelled as he saw Rusty get into the cab of the last truck.

"Get in. Damn good to see you!" The truck moved off. "That was you, wasn't it?"

He smiled. "Got lucky scouting around in the hills. It was really Sergeant Engles' idea to look over there. He kinda remembered a training exercise done around here a few years back."

"Is he on another truck?"

"We got ambushed after we made all that noise, just leaving. Two scouts. Got the sergeant with a head shot. I scalped both."

"We found an abandoned Quad M45 all covered up on this hill overlooking our valley. Like someone prepositioned it for an enemy attack like we had. Must have sat there a few years. The trailer tires rotted out, and the battery was dead. But it was fully loaded. Figured it might fire if we could get a battery."

"Ah! So that's why one of our trucks was dead."

"I hope you appreciate the heavy haul of that stinking battery back up that hill. I just got to admire some things you white people make. That fucker started right up and didn't jam. Think it did some good?"

"Jesus Christ, Tracker, you saved our asses!"

"Thank Sergeant Engle. Knew his shit. I liked him."

*The **M45 Quadmount** (nicknamed the "meat chopper" for its high rate of fire) was a weapon mounting four of the "HB", or "heavy barrel" .50 caliber M2 Browning machine guns mounted in pairs on each side of an open, electrically powered turret. Each gun had a 200 round magazine attached in a drum. All four guns could be fired at once or the upper and lower two fired separately.*

On Colonel Smith's side, it was pure panic. First Sergeant 'Whitey' Dillon led the remnants of his platoon to the CP. The entire withdrawal from the ridge defensive positions was a combination of keep running and, or, a more disciplined run, drop and shoot that was directed by experienced NCO's, like 'Whitey.' But they didn't have enough of those NCO's.

Whitey stopped his men just outside the CP to get his colonel and jumped in. It was empty.

"Damn it." Quickly exiting, he yelled, "to the trucks!"

They ran.

But getting to the trucks proved to be impossible for Whitey's platoon as the enemy sealed their route when tanks entered the outskirts of the town and closed the highway.

Fortunately, the tanks had little infantry support, so they halted, thinking this might be a rouse to lure them into a trap.

The delay was just long enough to allow most of the survivors of Colonel Smith's command to filter out of Osan.

America's first land engagement with this new enemy was a disaster.

Chapter Twenty Eight

**Monday, July 5, 1950 - Day Eleven of the Invasion
Japan – Eighth Army Headquarters - Colonel Nelson's G-2
Conference Room – 1800 – (6:00 pm)**

"Any word from Leyden's team?" Asked Nelson.

Major Hank Jarvis, now Deputy G-2, nodded. "Yeah! I finally got word a few minutes ago that a convoy of Smith's escaping artillery battery was stopped at the base of Leyden's mountain by a lookout. It's as we expected, Colonel, it was bad. This unit was overrun but was able to spike their cannons and escape as tanks passed them and entered Osan. They know nothing of Colonel Smith's force or much of anything."

"So we know nothing about Rusty's team or of Colonel Smith's, except that enemy tanks are in their rear and captured Osan. Fuck all to hell!"

The Major got up and went to the projector, turned it on to the film on the glass. The blowup on the back wall was an ariel photo of this area from 5,000 feet, on a bright day.

"Colonel, as you can see, there are many escape routes out of Osan, east, south, and west." He pointed out the ways. "Rusty's team has C J, a local, who knows these roads. Colonel Smith, well, I don't know, maybe Rusty advised him?" Pausing.

"We do have positive news out of this shit, sir!" He said as if delivering news to the grieving relative that the recent death of the beloved left a partial inheritance.

Nelson didn't say a word, just gazed, hoping for something.

"Sir! Leyden's team and equipment are now in sync with CIA Japan and working through the last issues, but mostly resolved. They're picking up messages from enemy division headquarters down to battalion level. Osan taught the CIA a lesson. They discovered that when multi divisions share the same area, as in Osan, the number of radio frequencies that need personal monitoring double or triple. CIA got caught short on that, realized they were understaffed, but they're beefing up quickly."

"Anything useful, Hank?" Asked an unsmiling Nelson.

"We've identified the two attacking divisions. Two of their best, sir. Our old foes that overran *The Post*; the NK 105Th Armored Division and two regiments of their 4th Infantry Division. These are experienced soldiers transferred back from China and were highly trained by the Russians."

"Their intercepts relayed a sharp but brief encounter with our forces. They thought American forces would put up a better fight. They are encouraged. CIA concluded that the enemy forces were consolidating at Osan for the next push south, tomorrow."

Nelson stood up. Thinking of his friend, Colonel Smith. "Shit!" He moved away from the table and thought of Rusty and his team and the grand drama unfolding.

"Hank, bring in the rest of our team." Ordered Nelson.

From the next connected cubicle, the Secret Ops unit of NSOPU, Master Sergeant Nick Beloit, leader of this command, entered first, followed by Captain Sam Haran, fondly known as the Professor.

It was funny that they all took their old seats around the big conference table. But it was only a day since they split.

Nelson's G-2 team, now headed by Major Hank Jarvis, sat next to his key planner, Lieutenant Larry Cole.

Nelson stood up and walked to the rear of the room, where a large wall map of South Korea hung. "Let me begin by saying that I know everyone here has given his 110% effort. Otherwise, you wouldn't be here, so this isn't a pep talk. What I want is for you all to come together and *pull something out of your collective asses* .... Kind of discussion... of what the hell we do next!"

Nobody laughed.

"You've all been briefed on the latest. Thanks to Nick's efforts, the Pusan bottleneck is clearing up and has allowed the rest of General Dean's 24th Division to land. Elements of his 34th Infantry Regiment has started to move into blocking positions south of Osan. His 21st Infantry Regiment is getting ready to move up as well."

Pausing, Nelson ran his hand through his head and then focused on his men.

"General Dean's 24th Division is going to be chewed up and spit out, one regiment at a time. We know this." He turned to the wall map and pointed out the blocking points ordered by General Dean, all good, but inadequately defended.

"Today, recognizing the tenuous situation we face, General MacArthur ordered the 25th Division to embark for

Korea. The division will probably take a week before they are engaged."

"Our strategic analysis, the ones you have continually all prepared, and that we have continued to send up the chain of command is starting to be read by someone. God bless whomever!"

"Also, General MacArthur has come to realize that what we have is not enough, thanks, I think to our efforts. So he has released deployment of the 1st Cavalry Division to General Walker, who, within a few days, will assume command of all Eighth Army forces in Korea, and that's secret!"

The men at the table clapped. "Finally, some good news!" Said Nick.

Nelson put his hand up to stop the happy.

"It's not enough!" Yelled Nelson. Calming his demeanor, he spoke, "At the rate of the enemy's advance, we will run out of time. Pusan harbor, despite our efforts, cannot handle landing another division. But we must! It's coming down to Pusan. I think we can't stop them until then. General Walker had it right way back, when he said, 'Pusan is our Alamo,' but he wanted a different ending! So" pausing to collect his thoughts, "let's talk."

The one-footed Master Sergeant, Nick, didn't disappoint. "Sir! I've been talking to MacArthur's staff about an alternative to landing the 1st Cavalry in Pusan. I told them it would be a disaster. Sent them plans that Sam and I developed for an amphibious landing up the east coast, just north of Pusan. The landing may be opposed, but then, if the enemy is there, it will be the opening battle to save our foothold in Korea."

Colonel Nelson smiled. "What was their response?"

"As the appointed leader of NSOPU, General MacArthur's baby and one he authorized, well, my recommendation was well received."

"Bravo!" Exclaimed Major Jarvis.

"I second that, Nick." Said Nelson. "Good work! But will it come in time? And will it be enough?"

Nick looked despondent at the question and answered.

"It depends on so many things, sir, so I can't give you a definitive answer. Can we assemble the necessary LST's and other assault ships in time? Can the South Korean division's remnants on the East Coast Highway delay the steady enemy advance south long enough so it won't interfere with our landing? Will the 24th Divisions delaying tactics be enough to allow the 25th Division to deploy?"

Sam, the Professor, interjected. "Nick isn't clairvoyant! Nor is anyone here, so Colonel, stop asking stupid questions."

That brought a turd into the room. After a pause, Sam continued.

"I mean no disrespect, sir, it's only frustration, that I'm sure mirrors your own. But when tasked to do the impossible, with unlimited power but with no resources, well, if one were religious, one would start praying. But religious or not, we have not given up. Nick & I have scoured the universe of our contacts and beyond, trying to do something to halt this enemy advance. We have promising ideas and will continue to explore all possibilities. That's what you directed us to do, sir. I hope we will not fail you."

The room remained quiet for a brief time. A telling moment for all and it hit Colonel Nelson hard as he realized that no matter how brilliant or courageous his team was, they were fighting against the clock and US resources. The lack of both was a monumental mountain to climb.

"Thank you, Sam." Colonel Nelson said steadily. "I don't like being defeated in battle and losing men as I did today. Colonel Smith is my friend and a part of Eighth Army. My Post team is missing in action. But the bigger picture prevails and overwhelms me sometimes, as I see a potential massacre of our forces in Pusan if we can't hold this enemy."

Emotion caused Nelson to pause. "I'll say no more."

Chapter Twenty Nine

**Monday, July 5, 1950 - Day Eleven of the Invasion
Korea – Hilltop of CIA Intercept Leyden's Team, South of
Osan – 2100 – (9:00 pm)**

Having just been relieved by Phil, he walked through the drizzle of rain into the mountain top camp that had the only shelter.

"Good work down there getting that info from those guys, Sergeant Lopez. We got all vital Intel right off to Colonel Nelson." Said Staff Sergeant Leyden.

"Fucking tanks! And no HT! What the hell, those poor bastards had no chance! "

"Am I going to be assigned to your weird command indefinitely? I thought I was going to fight!"

"Buck up Lopez. I know you've been itching for a fight. You'll get your chance. But nobody said it was going to be a fair fight."

Leyden laughed. "You don't know shit about us and what we're doing, but I'll tell you that we'll hit our little shit-storm soon enough, so be patient my little hellion, you'll have your fight."

"Tom!" Greg called, "Got a message that Dean's 34th Infantry Regiment is moving into positions around a town called Chonan, not far from here. CIA wants us to stay for a while and then move south a few miles so we can monitor further enemy movements.

Staff Sergeant Leyden wasn't a strategic guy. He'd experienced war on the front lines with his best friend, and the best infantryman he'd ever met, Sergeant Nick Beloit. Nick showed him how to anticipate, sense trouble, and maybe, by osmosis, he also became savvy, just like Nick.

And so it dawned on Leyden.

"Jesus Christ! We're only a few miles south of this town, and that's only a few miles south of Osan, that's just been captured."

"And they want us to move *just* a few more miles away? Fuck them!"

Leyden possessed the most advanced technology in the world at intercepting radio transmissions, then transmitting those a thousand miles away, then finally getting feedback.

Leyden had never feared anything before, but this realization of his responsibility to guard this Top Secret equipment hit him hard. He now knew it's potential.

In the dark and continued drizzle, under the shelter, the team met.

The original survivors of Post # 4, from day one of the invasion, Greg, Phil, and JP sat in the mud across from Leyden. They all were on the same mission of blowing the bridge over the Han River, where Jack, their commander at Post #4, was killed. Replacing Jack proved difficult for Leyden, but the difficult days that transpired gained him respect and trust among the men for Leyden's judgment. It was now official, Leyden was their team leader.

Sergeant Lopez was the odd man out in this team. Thrust into this mix at the last hour. The lone survivor from Post # 1, escaping through enemy lines, rescued by Wild Bill and then brought into this mission because of his desire to avenge his comrade's slaughter. He was determined, resourceful, and an experienced fighter.

Many situations ran through Leyden's mind, as he sat with his men. He became confused. The rain added to his anxiety about being responsible for losing this Top Secret equipment to the enemy; his mind started to swirl. Then he lost it. Leyden yelled at the top of his lungs into the rain. "You Mother Fuckers! I've met you before! You subterranean creatures from hell! I will kill you!"

Greg, sitting next to him, grabbed him. "Sergeant! Tom! Snap out of this!"

Pushing Greg off, Leyden regained his senses and shook his head. "Shit!" He sat there, shaking his head and got quiet.

"Not used to having the world on my shoulders. Now I got you guys too! We're going to get the hell out of here!" Catching his breath, "Phil! Contact Nelson, tell him we must evacuate. I can't have our secret equipment captured. Ask him where we should go next. After that, we break camp and head down the mountain."

J P, always the yin in the yang, asked, "We got a lot of shit to carry, Sergeant! Are we getting a ride?"

Tom finally laughed, breaking his intense focus. Knowing J P's affliction for anything water-bound, responded, "You will not enter a boat, J P, I assure you. But we may have to fight our way onto a truck."

That left J P and the rest of the team wondering.

Phil got on the secret Morse code VLF sending equipment, and with Greg on the portable electric crank, sent the message.

"Lopez!" Leyden called over to him. "You and J P break down our camp and get down the mountain. Get us a truck. We'll be along in a bit."

Chapter Thirty

Monday, July 6, 1950
Day Twelve of the Invasion Korea
Rusty's troop Southeast of Osan – 0500 – (5:00 am)

The ten trucks they stole drove all night, albeit very slowly, guided by C J and his *Three*, through the back roads into the central mountain passes. The circular dirt roads left all comprehension of distance traveled to the imagination. East then south, then north, then east and then south again, with numerous obstacle stoppages. It was hellishly nerve-racking.

Then they came to a small river and halted.

Rusty ordered a break and chow. The men piled out of the trucks and assembled in small groups around guys who knew how to cook lousy rations into something eatable. Their last meal was 24 hours ago, so they feasted.

Red and C J roamed through the groups, did a rough count of the men and weapons in the dim dawn light. Besides their original 20, they brought another 100 or so South Korean soldiers from various units that fought in the Eastern Valley. They had an additional 15 wounded that their combat medic, Marty, was attending too.

"None of Captain Kim's troops are here." Said C J.

"I know." Said Red. "Rusty told me he led his men south into the rice paddies. He knew we didn't have enough transport to get them all out."

"I hope we meet up with him again. I think he's a great leader."

"C J! Listen to me." Red grabbed his arm. "You are the leader of your country's troops here. Take charge of them! You're ready to command! Their lives depend on you!"

A deadly silence lasted but a few seconds.

Red continued, "C J, you may not be fully aware of how many lives you have influenced over the last few days. From waiting for Rusty and our team on your mountain top hideout, to helping us destroy the Han River Bridge and then leading us to escape up the valley. Finally getting us back and then bringing us fifty miles south to help defend Osan. Then guiding us the hell out of there."

"C J! Maybe you'll never get the Medal of Honor, but in my eyes, you deserve it."

A proud young man, C J was awestruck by Red's words. He felt he was failing as a soldier because of the helplessness he felt as he watched his country losing its freedom. But Red's encouragement got him to act, as he then got up and mingled with his countrymen to inspire and promise them that America's support would prevail.

Ranger Tully was not as inspired as he overhead Red. Alone now, "You're a piece of work, you know!"

Red nodded, "That's what people say."

"You're right about C J. A good guy. I like him. The rest of the shit about America's support, well, I'm just not convinced. Why are we even here? This country is crap, and I don't get it!"

"You're a fucking Ranger, Tully. You're not paid to think. Army guys, like me, are expected to fight **and think.** So shut your hole and behave like a Ranger. Leave the thinking to a more advanced species."

Red laughed at himself. Tully mulled it for a second then joined him as he quipped, "Nothing better than being in a shithole than being in a shithole with another crazy!"

Tracker scouted the river bank for a mile east and west, but found no passable alternative. A once dried bed leading off the near mountains was now running fast and wide, twenty feet wide by his reckoning, and no idea of how deep it was, but his experience told him this was not quickly passable.

Although the dawn promised a reprieve from the constant rain, the higher clouds kept rolling in.

Rusty didn't take Tracker's report well. Without another route out of this middle mountain valley country road, his convoy was stuck. Neither C J nor his *Three* knew much if anything about this area.

Tully was mad after having just been reminded of his Ranger status. He wondered why they hadn't started to move yet, so he came up from the rear of the column and stood before the sitting group next to Rusty, C J, and Tracker.

"If there were Ranger's wounded in our trucks, I'd start shooting somebody. But goddamn it! We need to try to save these brave men! What the fuck is the problem!"

Exhausted, Rusty deferred to Tacker and C J, who described the river obstacle.

"Jesus Christ!" Said Tully, "A fucking stream is in our way! No problem!"

Tully abruptly left to find Mario, who wasn't far away, peering over the raging stream, with Moose and Snake.

Tully lashed out at the guys. "Mario! What the fuck are you doing sightseeing? We need to move! Get your sorry ass in gear and get us across this stream!"

Mario moved into Tully's face. "First Sergeant! I've been with you since Normandy! You ever speak to me that way again, I'll hurt you."

Tully pushed him back hard. "You West Coast mountain climbing pansies all go soft at the wrong time! You, of all people, Mario! You're not allowed to lose it when your team needs you! Get moving!"

Mario, deflated at the criticism, wondered what happened and why Tully reacted so…weird.

Moving away, Tully realized how tense everybody was, including himself, after having been run out of Osan, fleeing for their lives. And they all were still distraught; he turned back to Mario.

"We're all on edge, Mario! But I hold you to a higher standard. You're a fucking Ranger!" Tully turned and left.

Chapter Thirty One

**Monday, July 6, 1950 - Day Twelve of the Invasion
Korea – Same Time - Leyden's Team Heading South –
0500 – (5:00 am)**

It took hours for Colonel Nelson's group to get back to them as to where they should position next. Their hill had become untenable, too close to the action, and they had no support. All agreed that the prospect of them doing anything positive was remote, and the risk of losing the Top Secret equipment was too significant.

Staff Sergeant Leyden took the lead on this when he communicated to Nelson that they were abandoning the hill and asked where to go next. He didn't ask permission.

When the answer finally came, everything but the equipment was down the mountain by the highway. Before leaving, Leyden checked his map to see where Nelson's team was sending them. Dismayed, he said, "Fuck you!"

A duce and a half awaited on the empty highway, facing south when Leyden and the secret equipment carried by Phil and Greg arrived.

Sergeant Lopez waived out the window. "Is everything's loaded!" J P came around to help with the equipment, and then they all piled in. Leyden went up front in the cab to join George Lopez behind the wheel.

`

"Good job, George! Any trouble?"

"None. Unless something comes up at my Court Martial."

"As long as you didn't kill one of our own….well, even then, I might be able to come up with something. Let's go!"

"No, no! Nothing like that; just too many trucks for too few men."

"How long is our ride?"

"A while. Why don't you catch a few z's while you can, Staff Sergeant?"

He grunted.

"You watched the 34th Regiment pass you going north through the night. How many tanks did they have?"

"Tanks? No tanks. I saw a single battery of 105's, not much else."

"Just as I thought, they'll get fucked! Goddamned idiots! Shit!" Leyden sat back, angry and discouraged, thinking of his orders and whether he will obey them.

He wanted so much to talk to Nick, his battlefield friend, about his dilemma. Should he obey his orders, which he thought stupid or go with his instinct. Then he remembered Nick's uncanny ability to figure out a battlefield situation and go with his gut and how that saved many lives. Am I as good as Nick? Can I make the right decision?

After driving a good while in silence, they entered a decent size town, just awakening to a dark and cloudy dawn.

"Sergeant! Wake up! Got a town." Lopez pulled to the side of the road.

Activity was everywhere. South Korean troops, US combat soldiers gathering in clumps. Chaotic.

A groggy Leyden awoke just as an Army lieutenant jumped on the side doorstep and shoved his .45 caliber pistol into Tom's face.

"You fucking cowards! You're going the wrong way! I want you out of this cab, or I'll shoot you!"

Looking straight at him, Leyden said, "Easy now, sir. You got this wrong, but we'll get it straight."

The LT eased off and moved to open the cab door, that's when he felt a knife at his throat, "You make a play, and you're dead. Understand?"

The gun dropped.

"Thanks, J P." Leyden got out of the truck and got into the LT's face. "What the fuck do you think you're doing, sticking a .45 in my face? Are you stupid?" He pushed him back.

"You're lucky to be alive, asshole!"

Just then, a major came over with a few men. "Stand down, sergeant! Arrest him!" He yelled to his men.

That's as far as it got, as Greg and Phil came around at the back of the major and his small group with guns drawn. "Lower your weapons," Greg called out low and threatening.

"This has gotten way out of hand, major!" Said Leyden, "Let's not get all stupid here. If we were deserters, you all would be dead. We're not deserters, as this lieutenant stupidly assumed."

"If anything, this lieutenant should be locked up for being stupid."

"I'll have you shot, sergeant! I saw you shove an officer, and now your men have drawn weapons on me. How dare you speak to me like this?"

"Take their weapons," Leyden commanded, "I hope you have a communications hut somewhere, major. Lead us to it, and please, stop being such an asshole."

Chapter Thirty Two

Monday, July 6, 1950 - Day Twelve of the Invasion
Japan – Eighth Army Headquarters - Colonel Nelson's G-2
Conference Room – 1800 – (6:00 pm)

The aftermath of Colonel Smith's debacle at Osan continued throughout the day, compounded by a continuum of setbacks and bad news. Worse was the lack of communications about the survivors and, in particular, no reports from Rusty's men.

Colonel Nelson sat with his two teams around the table and discussed events.

Nelson's deputy in charge of his G-2 operation, Major Jarvis, wound up his assessment of the day's events with the recounting of the FUBAR with Sergeant Leyden's Special Intelligence unit in a small village south of Osan with a small American element of the 34th Infantry Regiment.

"Thank God they figured out they had a clear shot to a mountain tower. They got their secret VLF communication equipment operational and gave us an update. It was like a Mexican standoff. This major wanted to shoot our guys for desertion while Leyden had guns on him, and his guys had guns on our guys. It took me a while to convince this major that they were okay, and it was all a big misunderstanding."

"So, where are they?" Asked Nelson.

"Not where we sent them. Leyden didn't like that location one bit. He said about it, and I quote, 'Are you fucking nuts'!, he went on to tell us where he's going, thinks it's better located with many positives, and where he and the secret stuff won't be captured."

Nick laughed. The one-foot master sergeant, now in charge of Nelson's secret operational unit, was an old friend of Leyden, fought with him, and was with him when he lost his foot in the big War.

"I think something of me may have rubbed off on Leyden; I trust his instincts."

"And I trust yours, Nick." Said Nelson. "You got anything?"

"I had Captain Stands, *Wild Bill,* fly a recon sortie over the Osan area this afternoon. It was mostly cloudy with some rain, but being who he is, he managed to shoot up some enemy vehicles and observe something we haven't anticipated, North Korean troops moving down the Central Valley, east of Osan. Wild Bill thought he saw South Korean soldiers farther south, forming a blocking position. Bad weather then closed in. It's a significant find, sir."

"Damn straight it is. If the North Koreans can get around our blocking efforts on the West Coast Highway, they'll out flak us. Christ! That's good work, Nick!" Pausing, "Now what the hell do we do about it?"

"Call your friend, South Korean Colonel Oh, see what he knows about any of his units fighting there." Said, Major Jarvis. "I also think Rusty's team probably is headed that way; they may be in for a fight."

"Jesus! Nick, you got anything we could throw into this fight?" Asked a frustrated Nelson.

"Maybe, sir!"

"What!"

"Sir, the first of our new plane arrivals are disembarking as we speak. The aircraft carrier Boxer landed yesterday with a 115 P-51's, fully equipped for their fighter-bomber ground support role; they have some trained pilots. I'm trying to contact their Wing Commander. No luck so far, being stonewalled, I think."

"When can they fly?" Asked a subdued Nelson.

"Working on that. There's transport to the airbase, then cleaning off the sea spray, engine checks, and finally loading ordinance. Best guess is some in a day or two, all in a week."

"Keep working on that, Nick."

Nick was more than working on that, but he knew that any success meant having a knowledgeable and capable leader in place, one that wanted the job. He was pretty sure who he wanted but wasn't sure if his man would take the responsibility, so Nick decided to wait for him to ask for it, for as long as he could.

Chapter Thirty Three

Tuesday, July 7, 1950 - Day Thirteen of the Invasion Korea – Rusty's Team somewhere South of Osan in the Central Valley 0200 – (2:00 am)

It took most of yesterday and supreme effort, but the Rangers used the truck winches and local trees to figure out how to get all the trucks across the raging stream. Driving as long as they dared in the dark, with only low lights on, they eventually came upon a small deserted village.

They were surprised when they saw a group of ragtag South Korean soldiers milling about at the far edge, and then discovered a real ROK Army surgeon, a major, with a full medical unit all set up, working on the wounded. There must have been more than 50 men lying about under makeshift shelters away from the central medical tent.

C J quickly established a connection with the major and offloaded their own wounded into his main tent. Marty, Rusty's combat medic, helped the men into the tent. Even though he didn't speak Korean, he bowed to the surgeon and pointed to the man needing the most urgent attention. The major nodded in acknowledgment, saw his medical kit and hand signaled for Marty to stay and help him. Marty smiled and gave him a thumbs up.

`

The journey of the long day brought on frustration and much discussion about what they should do next. With no clear line of sight to a mountain tower for their secret VLF equipment, they were out of communication. Their one operational handheld radio was only good for a few miles at best, and it was losing its battery charge.

They had no maps of this area. The rough description given by the major indicated that they were in the Central Valley, maybe 15 miles west of Osan and 10 miles south. But he wasn't sure. Neither C J nor his *Three* had ever been in this area; they were of no help.

As the morning progressed, a steady stream of disheveled South Korean soldiers entered the village. Most carried a buddy at his side, and some had a man on his back and a few dragged makeshift stretchers.

Around mid-morning, Rusty called his team together and told them that they were going to stay.

It was one of the few times in Rusty's command that he didn't discuss his decision with his inner circle. He didn't want a discussion.

There was silence after his announcement when Joe spoke up. "Are we going to fight? If so, I'm with you!"

Rusty chuckled. Nobody else moved. "I'm not sure everybody shares your Flatbush feelings, Joe, but that's what we're going to do. C J has talked to some of the South Korean survivors trickling in this morning. Their recounting of the fights they experienced is disturbing because their battles are near. These men come from organized South Korean units fighting just north of here. We need to help them."

Red asked the next question. "Do we know how many? I mean, how many good guys versus how many bad guys?"

"It's a given that the enemy outnumbers the South. But the terrain does not support tanks or any armored vehicle and lends itself to great defensive positions. These South Korean soldiers are mostly all from the same division, fighting as units in well-organized defensive lines. They described fierce fighting, often, in hand to hand combat."

Tully called out. "Why here? We know nothing about this area?"

Pausing, knowing Tully was really asking why he should risk putting his men and himself on the line again, in this no-name place, in this shit hole country, that's cost so many of his friend's lives.

Stepping up to his face, Rusty said.

"You of all people, Mr. Ranger. The simple answer is because the enemy is here." Pausing, "The more complicated answer is why we're here in the first place."

"Not sure anybody at Eighth Army even knows what's going on in the Central Valley. Even if they did know the full extent of the enemy's advance here, I don't know what, if anything, they could do about it."

Continuing, Rusty, exhausted, slowly peered around at his men and, in a somber voice, said, "So, as I've said before, this is serious shit right here. If the South caves in, it opens a flanking maneuver on our boys on the Coast Highway and presents a second pincer attack directly south. Now I'm not a genius about the big picture, but that would be a strategic nightmare for our troops."

Tully slowly rose. "We all signed up for this mission, wherever it may take us. I, for one, will follow Rusty. No exceptions! I expect the same from all of you. So, since I raised the main objection about our staying here because we don't know the area, then by God, we should learn everything about it, and that starts right now."

Each man was reaching inside himself to steal away the fear each felt about going back into the line again, thinking about the last time and wondering how they survived. But they'd experienced many battles against incredible odds during the previous 13 days, and they were still here. Much of their success and survival, they realized, was because of Rusty. But a few of their friends weren't so lucky.

After a few minutes of quiet, Red stood up. Known as the Rock, a leader of reason among his men, he addressed the group in his usual deadpan style. "Tell us what to do, Rusty, we're 100% with you."

"I want C J to organize volunteers among the able-bodied South Koreans to lead a few of our men to the front lines so they can recon that area. Plus, we got two truckloads of food and Japanese weapons and ammo that I'm sure those guys could use."

C J jumped up. "Most of these men want to go back and fight! They came back here to try and save their friends. They need a leader to organize them. I volunteer!"

Foxy, the original Post Army guy, and Frenchy, a new Ranger addition to the Post, were Korean speaking, both stood up.

"Some have called me flamboyant," said Frenchy waving his arm. "I am thus." He said with a smile. "But I'm good at what I do. Proud to do what I can. So I will go into the wilderness, as my forefathers have, and will carve out a wedge."

It broke the gloom, the men laughed.

Still laughing, Foxy said, "That's a tough act to follow, but being half Korean, I also volunteer. I think that's why we came here."

Rusty stood stone-faced as the men settled down.

"Don't know when my command became a democratic institution. I'm probably the guilty one, as I respect all input in major decisions. But let me be clear. I am this unit's commander. First among equals. I respect that men volunteer for missions but," he paused, "you're all professionals, and I'll treat you as such. I expect you to do the same with each other."

The men looked around at each other and wondered what the hell Rusty meant.

Red ignored Rusty and ordered C J, Foxy, and Frenchy to roam among the ROK soldiers to round up volunteers and to meet back within the hour.

Red then ordered Tracker and Joe to reconnoiter southeast to find a clear line of sight area to a mountain communication tower so they could use their secret VLF equipment to talk to Colonel Nelson's command.

With a brief training period, the South Koreans quickly became proficient on the Japanese machine guns and 'Knee Mortars.' Two hours later, C J and the South Korean volunteers gathered with about 50 men, loaded to the hilt with supplies, weapons, and ammunition. Frenchy stood near, as did C J's *One* and his *Three.*

Rusty addressed the men before him, while Foxy translated. "You've got great leaders here. Follow them and listen. This is not the last battle. We Americans are here side by side with you, and we will continue to fight. Good luck!"

C J talked to the ROK soldiers as they left. The soldiers started to whisper amongst themselves as they advanced to the lines.

As the column left camp, Mario, Snake, and sniper Dean, fully loaded with supplies, followed up the men walking out, they passed by Rusty.

Snake, being an original Rusty Post recruit, spoke as he walked past him, "Can't leave our guys unprotected. We're not volunteering, Rusty. We've been ordered out by our conscious."

Rusty just nodded. There was nothing he could do but admire his men.

The rest of the day and night passed with much activity as Red organized a defensive line around natural approaches to the village and farther north near the overflowing stream that they had difficulty crossing. Tully helped unload the remaining Japanese weapons and ammunition. He organized their placement to maximize their effectiveness.

"What do you think, Red?" Asked an exhausted but somewhat anxious Tully.

"I'm beginning to see a whole new side of you crazy Rangers!" Red said with a big smile. "You even know a thing or two about setting a decent defense. Nice work!"

It was 2 AM when Red jumped awake to the rumble of artillery explosions. How far away? That was his first thought? Three, maybe five miles? Hard to gauge in these hills with no wind.

"Any of our guys come back?" Asked Rusty, as he came up to Red.

Red was fully alert. "I've been watching and waiting. Nobody came in. This crap is close, Rusty. We need to speed up our timetable and get all these wounded out of here. I mean the whole medical unit."

"Give me a guess Red, how many South Korean soldiers could or would stay here and fight?"

"Most of the non-disabled men went off with C J yesterday. We got maybe 15 men; the rest are mostly wounded or screwed up. They'll help in the evacuation, but no, they can't fight, and I think those 15 will need to escort the wounded should they run into obstacles on that dirt path they call a road."

"OK. Get with Marty and communicate with the major about evacuating now. Use sign language or whatever, but get it started. Those explosions should be convincing enough."

"Man coming in!" Yelled Arron. Rusty ran to the spot. It was Tracker.

"I hate this country!" Said Tracker, anxiously, as he met Rusty.

"Where's Joe?"

"He's good. He's back watching the site we found. We ran into enemy scouts on the way there, twice. I wish we had Foxy along to speak with these bastards; we might have found out something from them. Two, three-man teams, well equipped and with Russian shortwave radios."

"How far is it to this site?"

"It's a fucked-up route, Rusty. Don't know the mileage, but it's about two, maybe three hours from here."

"Get something to eat, then get ready to lead us out."

"Chief! Better if we wait for first light. It'll be much quicker going, and I could use a few hours' sleep."

Rusty relented, as he also wasn't fully decided on his plan as yet.

He found Tully nearby sitting around a kettle of coffee hanging over a fire.

"You don't seem to be too upset about the fireworks, Tully?"

"Grab a hot coffee, Rusty. Probably be the last we'll see for a while. That shit is not happening to us this morning. Maybe later today, or most definitely by tomorrow."

"How can you be so sure?"

"C J and our guys haven't come back yet. My Rangers and your men are not stupid, so I know they're doing their thing. When they show up, we'll know about how long we'll have. They'll give us plenty of time to prepare."

"Jesus, Tully! You have a lot of faith."

"Yes, I know my guys."

Chapter Thirty Four

Tuesday, July 7, 1950   Day Thirteen of the Invasion
Korea – Rusty's Team somewhere South of Osan in the
Central Valley - 0600 – (6:00 am)

The rolling thunder of artillery explosions throughout the early morning spurred on the medical unit's evacuation efforts. By dawn, all the wounded and medical staff were loaded on trucks and headed south on the primitive dirt road that nobody knew where it led, only that it was away from the distant artillery shelling and the threat of being overrun and captured.

Rusty, still undecided on what to do next, sought out Red and Tully for guidance.

"Good job getting the medical unit out, Red. Now I need you and Tully's advice."

He went on. "Tracker and Joe found a location to set up our VLF equipment with a line of sight to a tower so we can connect with Colonel Nelson. Its three hours away. They encountered NK scouts, twice. So I'm worried about just sending out our communication team without a heavy escort. But that would deplete our efforts here if we were to stay. I need your input."

"We ain't going anywhere until our guys come back," said an adamant Red.

Tully followed up with, "As I said to you earlier, we got some time. But to your question about splitting our forces and risking this secret stuff to do what? Tell Nelson he and we have a problem? No! Rusty, I changed my thoughts about this. I think we stay and fight as we have over these many days to delay these bastards."

Just then, noise at the perimeter interrupted the meeting.

It was C J, a wounded soldier on his back, leading some soldiers back. Each abled man in line also carried a wounded soldier.

Marty, the combat medic, was the first to run to them.

Rusty watched his men come in. It was a small column, a few South Korean soldiers, wounded themselves yet still carrying more severely injured. His gut turned as the line ended and realized two of his men were missing.

Tully immediately knew who they were and, for a moment, almost lost it. Both were close friends for many years. But then he saw the anguish on Rusty and went up next to him.

Tully hid his feelings behind his typical bravado.

"They're my men, Rusty, and they're Rangers. Frenchy and Dean are resourceful. It's not their time. They'll be back."

"Don't be an ass, Tully. I don't need reassurance! We either lost them or we didn't. I'm sick about the fact that maybe we did, but I need to know what to do next! Go talk to the men and give me your best advice."

Rusty ordered the remaining two trucks to evacuate the newly wounded. Marty did his best to patch up the not so severely injured and try to save as many of the others as he could with what he had for their escape south.

The debriefing of C J and the men revealed a determined South Korean resistance against a formidable enemy. The ROK troops were brave and had smart and committed leadership, but they were outgunned and indeed outnumbered. Besides all that, they were starving and running out of ammunition. But they were still fighting.

After the debriefing, the men got a hot meal and a few minutes to relax and talk.

C J sat with Rusty, Red, and Tully discussing what to do next.

"I told the South Korean regimental commander about this fallback position." C J said. "Told him it would make an excellent defensive stand. He knows his lines can't hold for too much longer, and he must do something. But what, he's not sure."

"How far are their lines?" Red asked.

"The fighting is maybe 4 miles away, but there's no real lines, just small hills, and valleys, harsh terrain; it's a great defensive battlefield. That's the only reason they've been able to hold the enemy off. But the Commies have superior numbers and are using outflanking tactics that eventually will overcome the terrain difficulties."

Rusty looked around at his men, "Been thinking that maybe it might be more important to get Colonel Nelson involved then us helping the ROK directly now. So I made a decision, we'll all go to the site that Tracker found, update Nelson, and then go from there. We'll leave in an hour."

"Rusty?" C J asked. "We still have more food, Japanese weapons, and ammunition. I want to bring as much of this back to the front as possible. Eight South Korean men just came in, with only minor wounds that will help."

"You're a brave man C J. Okay, but bring back Frenchy and Dean."

Three hours away, Joe had spent the night half-asleep, hidden in a cluster of bushes just off a clearing. The earlier encounters that afternoon with two separate groups of enemy scouts kept him from any deep sleep.

He thought about their trek here, how Tracker had stopped dead on this trail and sank into a kneeling position in front of him. He'd heard nothing but followed Tracker's lead. A minute passed. Then swishing sounds as if low brush were being disturbed. Three enemy soldiers entered their trail 20 feet to their front. Fortunately, they didn't look back down the path, too bad for them. He later thanked Tracker for his sixth sense.

An hour later, it was his turn. Occasional glimmers of far-off mountains kept them on this trail. The trail meandered around, dipping and turning, never giving them that clear view they sought, so they just kept going. After climbing down a ravine, they came upon a stream. Joe got that weird feeling he got when something terrible was near and went rigid. Tracker was behind Joe and froze. Joe signaled to go low. They crept forward to see another three-man enemy scout party resting further up the stream. It was quick.

Alone, waiting for Tracker to return, Joe wondered how many more of these scout bastards were nearby. The faint sounds of thunder echoed through the night; he doubted that these were storms because it wasn't raining, so he assumed it was artillery.

Chapter Thirty Five

Tuesday, July 7, 1950 - Day Thirteen of the Invasion
Korea – Taejon Airfield –Maybe thirty miles from the front
– 0900 – (9:00 am)

Captain Stands, an experienced WW2 fighter group commander and a triple Ace, known to all as 'Wild Bill,' was utterly frustrated by the weather. Worse still was the lack of intelligence for target planning.

The facts that he received were more than disturbing. Inexperienced pilots with lousy preparation combined with faulty intelligence planning wasted the pitifully few air resources America possessed. It seemed that the Air Force continually bombed and strafed more of our own American and South Korean units then they did the enemy.

Wild Bill knew how quickly a pilot could get confused, especially when no ground to air communications were available. He'd been there. But still, he thought, they have eyes! If you got low enough, you could make out the differences. They were just too green and too scared to do that.

Over the last few days, he'd flown many missions on his own, alone, against orders and nobody but his ground crew knew, since he had the only fighter on the base. His efforts, though, were frustrating, mostly because of the weather. Clear targets were hard to spot. The North was very good at hiding, perfecting the art of camouflage to a high level. But it didn't take too much skill to hide under dense, low rain clouds.

Depressed, listening to the rain, he sat staring at his P-51 warbird, 'JUST DUE.' A beautiful machine as was ever created, he thought.

"You feeling down again, Captain?" Asked Arnie, the artist/mechanic who painted the symbol of death, the Death Robbed Man with Sycle on his plane's nose. He and his sergeant, ace mechanic, Billy, had restored the mothballed P-51 from the base south of Seoul, to its current fighting shape.

"God works his plan in strange ways and in his own time. I've tried to influence that timeline and been mostly unsuccessful. So I wait for him to see the light."

Arnie didn't understand, so he thought that a good response might be, "Like the Brass always knows best?"

Wild Bill shot up straight. "Arnie! You're brilliant!" The Captain ran off to the phone.

Arnie was left bewildered.

The Korean Cable relay station connection was in Taejon, where the Cable then continued to two more relay stations and finally ended in Japan, in both Eighth Army headquarters and the CIA campus.

Wild Bill, being the somewhat unorthodox officer that he was, had recently finagled a direct connection from the Korean Cable relay station to his airbase. That's where he went to it now, establishing a link within a few minutes to Colonel Nelsons G-2 command.

"No! I want to speak with Nick Beloit. It's a Korean combat mission call, and it's urgent. Just tell him it's Wild Bill."

After a few minutes, he finally got through.

"Holy smokes! I'm speaking to the man himself! What's up, Wild Bill?" Asked the Master Sergeant.

"Nothing's up! There's **NO** fucking air cover that's doing any good. I need your help to change that!"

"Captain, I know you'd been flying against orders, but shit is happening everywhere, so talk fast."

"Give me a squadron of those P-51's from that newly arrived aircraft carrier, the Boxer. Have those planes fully armed for air to ground combat! Then I need you to arrange ammunition and fuel resupply. And oh, a ground spotter that can communicate with the fucking pilots would be most welcome."

"And I wish I had a damn Marine Division! But great minds think alike!" Said Nick.

"I heard you're working on that! But my request is a whole lot easier. I can do a lot with those planes, damn it! We're in a tight spot. And right now our boys could use some good air support, and, damn it all if I'm not a goddamned expert at that! You got some serious pull behind you, Nick. You get things done! And if my favorite Colonel trusts you, and I know that you know that he trusts me. Well then, it's all settled, just a simple mathematical equation wrapped in divine worthiness."

"Jesus!" Said a befuddled Nick.

"People call me that sometimes, but no, I'm just an instrument."

Hesitating briefly, Nick said, "OK, I'm game. Taejon is now close to the front, and we're shifting air resupply farther south. We think the town is next on the enemy's list and shouldn't last more than a week or so. But that's a lifetime. So, what's the airfield's status?"

"It's beautiful! The radar tower is something to behold. The cafeteria and welcome center are first class!"

"Don't be an asshole, Nick. The transports have left, we got a shit field, but it's operational and has room for a P-51 squadron and support. I wouldn't ask this of you if I couldn't deliver. America's desperate goddamn it! I know it, and so do you. I think I can do some good."

"I'm sure you can, Captain. I'll get back to you." Nick smiled to himself. All along, he had hoped Wild Bill would come forward to plan and lead.

Still wanting a final gut check that Wild Bill could plan and lead a squadron operation if he could get it rolling, Nick decided to talk to Colonel Nelson, who knew Wild Bill from D-Day.

It was a short conversation.

Nick then got on the phone and used his new NSOPU command authority. Nobody but General MacArthur himself could countermand his orders. It shook things up at Air Force Command in Japan. They'd get back to him, they said. Nick followed up his verbal commands in written form, almost immediately.

Nick anticipated a delay and got his expanded team working on the logistics of the support required for an extended active air-to-ground combat mission for a squadron of P-51's operating from the remote airfield at Taejon.

Within the hour, he got what he needed from his team. Having still not received any confirmation of his original orders, he issued new orders, detailing his needs and schedule and demanding an immediate response, or he would, as quoted in his communication, go higher. His message was blunt.

"I'm informed that General MacArthur doesn't much like you Air Force folks, thinks you don't like to take chances. I'll reserve my opinion. But if you ignore my orders, I guarantee that I will come up every chain of your command and screw every one of you out of any promotion, and if I can, I'll kick you out of the service! No pension! No nothing!"

It read on.

"This is war! It's not us against us, but if you make it so, goddamn it, I'll crucify you! Let me remind you! It's about saving American soldiers!"

"Are you sure you want to send this, Nick?" Asked Sam, his deputy.

Master Sergeant Nick Beloit had long ago forsworn any military decorum after he lost his foot in WW2. He'd seen the ignorance of his superiors first hand. Plus, he had a knack for understanding battlefield situations, and he was supported as a hero, as he was, by some big brass.

"Sam, if I'm going to get fired or court marshaled, it might just as well be now, send it because this crap is only going to get worse."

The resistance was fierce, and orders delayed until verified by MacArthur's staff, even though their Air Force command, like all others under MacArthur's Army, had been issued the same orders, "Obey any order issued by NSOPU, as if it came from me."

Nick was a unique person, a rather simple man with no ego. His motivating force revolved around his intense sense of patriotism and desire to save as many of his fellow combat soldiers as he could. These traits prevailed in all of his dealings. He took no shit from anyone who got in his way of saving his country and his men, and took this war very personally.

"Confirmation of your orders just came in, Nick!" Said a smiling Captain Sam Haran, Nick's deputy at NSOPU.

"Four hours! I guess I owe you a buck. Thought it would be five or more; glad I lost this bet. Get hold of Captain Stands and tell him his bullshit paid off, and now he's got to deliver!"

Wild Bill was so excited, he danced around his war machine, 'Just Due.' Singing incoherent words and just being happy at the news that he was, again, relevant, and that he might make a difference. Billy and Arnie watched their boss from a corner, astonished, as they've always been of him, but with a reverence that was hard to describe. Wild Bill's exuberance lasted about three minutes.

Now dead silent after his rejoicing. He stood still for a minute or so, as if in a trance, then he called out, "Billy!"

"Right here, Captain!" He and Arnie ran to him. "You alright?"

"Alright!? What the hell! God has just bestowed a sacred mission to us, here in this wilderness, to do some good. You and Arnie are going to join me on a great new crusade. Fellow warriors, my warbird's brothers, a whole squadron, will join us here. I want you to do your best in welcoming them into this great fight. Now, let's kneel and give silent thanks, with a special mention to a guy named Nick."

Chapter Thirty Six

Tuesday, July 7, 1950   Day Thirteen of the Invasion
Korea – Leyden's Team on a Hill Ten Miles North of
Taejon – 1100 – (11:00 am)

Staff Sergeant Leyden and his team spent the better part of yesterday dealing with assault and desertion charges until he was able to communicate with Colonel Nelson's G-2 operations command directly.

The exchange between Colonel Nelson and the major in charge of this unit was heated, but ended well for Leyden's men. Succumbing to a higher authority, the major agreed to provide a squad of his command as support and a protective element to Leyden's men, with full provisions, indefinitely.

A new location, marked on a map as Hill 102 was to be Leyden's new strategic hill location, ten miles north of the city of Taejon. With an elevation of 1300 feet, it had a clear view up a valley for 10 miles and a partial view up the Main West Coast Highway for three miles, where it met a ridge.

The hill was somewhat steep and a bitch to climb. Leyden and all his team were thankful for their escort, as they made hauling up all their equipment easy and did it all in one trip.

"Are we hooked up?" Yelled Leyden to Phil.

"Go take a shit somewhere!"

Guess not, said Leyden to himself.

Leyden had made sure that his protective squad was disbursed around the perimeter of the hilltop, well away from the Top Secret equipment they deployed. They were not going to find out anything about what they were doing.

Greg was on the portable electric foot generator as lights started flashing from the two main units, the receiver/interceptor of enemy communication signals and the VLF (Very Low Frequency) sender/receiver communicator. The portable generator also charged the built-in batteries in both units so they could operate for two hours without the need for the generator.

J P, off to the side, had been gripping since they started their climb to the top and continued throughout the camp set up. They only had one tent! Why where they here, and on and on.

"Say another word, J P, and I'm going to close your mouth hard!" Said Staff Sergeant Leyden. "Nod your head if you understand. Otherwise, you won't be able to eat for a while."

J P never had any conception of boundaries unless it threatened him. He feared Leyden, knew he would follow through on his threat, so he nodded.

Everybody was on edge as they tried to settle into their new surroundings. The fighting up north was close. They could hear the distant rumble of explosions.

"Tom!" Yelled Phil, "We're got a connection!"

Tom came running. "About fucking time!" Then smiled, "Good job, Phil!" and then patted him on his back. Leyden realized it was the first time any of his new men had called him by his first name, and wondered if that was good or bad.

He looked over at Greg, peddling away on the portable generator, and good-naturedly said, "Keep that up, and you may earn yourself a medal."

"Stick it, Staff Sergeant! Nobody here's going to get a medal. We'll be lucky if they find our body parts."

Leyden was taken aback by that remark because he has come to understand that Greg is the glue and most balanced of the Post # 4 survivors. He wondered, however, about the accuracy of that remark.

"Phil! Establish contact with Nelson and tell them we're set up on Hill 102 as ordered, and commencing enemy intercepts for CIA analysis."

About an hour later, Leyden got up to check the perimeter and see how the escort guys were doing. He couldn't find them. They just took off.

"Nice! Real fucking nice!" Leyden said to no one. He was pissed! Five men alone on a hilltop, he thought; I sure hope some friends come soon.

Chapter Thirty Seven

**Tuesday, July 7, 1950 - Day Thirteen of the Invasion
Korea – Taejon Airfield –Approximately Thirty Miles from
the Front – Late Afternoon**

The first C-47 landed around 4:30 under cloudy skies. It held the advanced team of the 7th Fighter Squadron of the 49th Fighter Wing based in Japan, including its commander, Colonel Malcolm Fredrick.

Deplaning and surveying the field, the Colonel's pent-up anger grew. He'd not seen an airstrip like this since his last combat mission flying out of a semi-mud area on Okinawa, where, just 15 minutes after take-off, he was shot down by enemy ground fire. A broken leg from this crash kept him from further action through the end of the war.

Met by a sergeant, Billy, he was taken to a hanger to meet Captain Stands.

As they met, Captain Stands waited for the Colonel to salute first and announce himself, knowing the Colonel was of superior rank, but he, Captain Stands, was in command. They stared at each other.

"Glad you're a suborn son-of-a-bitch like me, Colonel. Welcome to a great crusade! Most friends and enemies alike call me Wild Bill." He saluted him.

The Colonel was momentarily surprised and disarmed. He returned the salute. "My friends call me Stormy."

"Got a bottle of Johnny Walker Black inside; been saving it for a long time. Let's go talk, Stormy."

They were the same age, both old before their time, battled-tested, warriors, and survivors, yet very different.

"Got your orders, Stormy?" Asked the Captain, with a blank face, as they sat on crates at a makeshift table in the hanger in front of Wild Bill's 'Just Due.' The Captain reached down and pulled out a bottle and two tin cups from under his crate and poured a three-finger slog in each. The silence was deafening as he pushed one to the Colonel.

"Let's toast, Stormy, to survival!"

They both clicked cups and took a full swig.

"Thanks!" Said Stormy. "My favorite drink. As to your question. Well, I think what you're asking is how I feel about **THE** orders? I sense you're a very unusual man, and so I hope you'll allow me a frank assessment of the same orders." He paused for another gulp of Black Label. The Captain did the same.

"You got serious pull that I don't understand, and you're a Captain. And you're a fucking *Army* Captain to boot! I now report to you, an Air Force Colonel to an Army Captain. And you are now in charge of **MY** squadron! How the fuck do you think I feel?"

"Glad we got that settled," said Wild Bill, "Just happy you didn't pull your 45 and did serious harm. Let's have another drink!"

The Colonel was disarmed and started to laugh. "Yes, and maybe a few more."

Over the next few hours, many C-47's arrived with the remaining support crews and maintenance men for the squadron that was due to fly in tomorrow. A few ammunition-laden planes were the last to come in before dark. Fuel trucks driven up from Pusan started coming in at dusk.

During the process of finishing off the bottle of Johnny Black, they talked about the very different types of enemy planes they fought against and their tactics. Wild Bill against the Germans and Stormy fighting the Japs. It was gradual, but as they kept talking, the Captain and the Colonel started to bond.

"But why are you still in the Army?" Stormy asked, still troubled by this.

"There's a long history here that you know nothing about, and it relates to your very first observation that I have serious pull, as you put it." Now somewhat drunk, Wild Bill felt he could confide in Stormy.

"During the War, I did some crazy, off the radar shit for my current boss, Colonel Nelson, now G-2 of Eighth Army. We became friends. He knew I wouldn't fit in with this new Air Force command structure and so he kept me within a classified Intelligence section of his unit. I didn't want a promotion; probably wouldn't have gotten one anyway being things the way they were after the War. Achieving a three-time Ace status also gave me a lot of leeway. But I earned my name; I'm a lone wolf now."

Pausing to drain the last drop in his cup, he finished.

"And that's why you're here, Stormy!"

"Damn, you're a very different man than I thought you'd be. I'm happily surprised. I followed you to the very end. But I lost you on that lone wolf remark?"

"Stormy, the last thing I ever wanted to do was lead a squadron into combat, let alone one I don't even know. No! My hope and my prayers were for God to deliver a leader that would lead his men into a fight that he and I designed."

Pausing now, Captain Stands looked into Stormy's eyes.

"And I believe He has done just that!"

Chapter Thirty Eight

Tuesday, July 7, 1950 - Day Thirteen of the Invasion Korea – Rusty's Team at the New Site Located by Tracker and Joe – Dusk –2020 - (8:20 pm)

They left midmorning and had not encountered any enemy scouts along the way to the site. None the less, the going was slow. The burden they bore was immense as they carried as much ammunition and supplies as they could plus their secret equipment. After they arrived and settled in, Tracker and Joe went back along the path to make sure they weren't followed and found nothing.

Red established a perimeter. Before long, Larry worked his magic and established contact with a visual tower. Moose pumped the petals on the portable generator until lights lit up on the VLF (Very Low Frequency) equipment, indicating they had positive contact with a tower and could send or receive.

"We got it!" Larry yelled.

"Go, Larry!" Rusty encouraged. "We've been out of touch for a long time. Establish contact."

It didn't take long. Rusty, Red, Foxy, and Tully sat next to Larry as he sent the Morse code message initializing access to Colonel Nelson's HQ.

Received and authenticated, Larry proceeded on with his keystrokes.

`

"Location Central Valley, exact unknown. Estimate fifteen miles east of Osan, ten or so south. Enemy fighting down this valley in strength. ROK resistance is fierce, but being overwhelmed. We're five or so miles from the front. Need help!"

Standby! Was the response. They waited and waited, but after two hours, Rusty and his team gave up. Every two hours, someone took turns on the portable to charge the batteries so that they could hear the incoming signal.

Frenchy and Dean had stayed behind, fighting with the South Korean unit when they got separated from C J and their men as the battle had become intense. These ROK guys impressed them, and they quickly bonded. So they stayed through the night.

Frenchy immediately became attached to a South Korean sergeant after he and Dean jumped into his trench during an artillery barrage. Frenchy talked to his new friend through the night, then slept a little. They held a small ridgeline for many hours until they suddenly started to get outflanked. Retreating quickly to another position, the sergeant, running just behind Frenchy, was shot in the head, knocking him into Frenchy and leaving most of his brains splattered on Frenchy's back.

Running behind them, Dean saw both men go down and thought the worst. Dropping to the ground next to the sergeant's body, he knew he was dead, then crawled forward a few feet to Frenchy. Seeing the dead sergeant's head almost gone and all the blood on Frenchy's back had freaked Dean out, as he kneeled next to him and touched him when Frenchy moved and said, "Am I hit?"

Dean checked his back, "Don't see anything but blood. But don't think it's yours. We need to move! Are you hurting anywhere?"

"Won't know till I move. Help me up. Where's my friend?"

"He's on your back."

Segments of the loose line started their retreat. The pullback became frantic, mortar shells exploding among the broad collapsing front and amid the men. The next line of defense was well constructed but spread out as was the last; unfortunately, it too had many open, vulnerable areas to exploit.

That was the point, but they waited just a bit too long to leave and became victims of their cleaver defense scheme.

Dean was cursing as he ran just to the right and behind Frenchy. He liked that sergeant, figured it was a sniper that got him. They made it into a new position about fifty yards away and jumped into the first foxhole they saw. Men were doing the same all around them.

Dean immediately set up and started scanning with his sniper rifle scope to his front, trying to find the sniper that killed this sergeant. He started thinking that maybe his mind wasn't right anymore. He found targets and killed them, but he knew they weren't the sniper.

"Dean!" Frenchy called over. "We're not the French Foreign Legion! They would die in a foreign land because of some honor bullshit code. Despite my affiliation, I say it's time we get the hell out of here!"

Dean stopped shooting. Quiet for a moment amidst the incredible noise. He started laughing, Frenchy just had a way about him.

They slipped off the field into the underbrush, made their way behind the battle to get to the pathway, and headed back to the small village.

At the same time, C J had just delivered the extra supplies to the ROK commander and was leaving, disappointed that the commander had no idea of the whereabouts of the two missing Americans. But before leaving, C J was reassured by the leader that he would soon fall back to their reinforced village position further south.

Not long after, with C J in the lead, his small band of men made their way south along the path, when Frenchy and Dean stepped out from the foliage in front of C J with big smiles on their faces.

C J almost fainted, said something in Korean, then "Holy shit!" Then ran and grabbed their arms. "Thought you were both dead!"

Frenchy lost his smile, and although moved by C J's reaction, his words reminded him of just how close he came. He grabbed C J's arm, "Damn it if you weren't almost right! We got real close out there, C J, fighting for *your* country."

C J thought it was a compliment, and still in awe at finding them. Then he repeated to them Rusty's concern about bringing them out and his promise that he would. He told them how much that meant to him that their American leader cared so much for his men.

Chapter Thirty Nine

**Wednesday, July 8, 1950 - Day Fourteen of the Invasion
Japan – Eighth Army Headquarters - Colonel Nelson's G-2
Conference Room – 0300 – (3:00 am)**

Nelson called in Nick's team to join the full G-2 group. Digesting the latest dire news, they sat around the big table.

"As you know," Major Hank Jarvis started, "Leyden's team intercepted a distant enemy communication between division commanders, one in the Central Valley and the other chasing the 34th Regiment. It confirmed Rusty's most recent messages about the Central Valley threat. The South Korean defensive lines are about ready to collapse; they are overmatched. The good news, for us, is that the North Korean units are reporting terrific resistance and heavy casualties."

"Brave bastards! Worthy of help!" Said Colonel Nelson.

Lieutenant Larry Cole followed with his information. "Reports are that the 34th Regiment is fighting a rolling retreat along the Main West Coast Highway and has found a good defensive position north of a ridge that's three miles north of Hill 102 and they're digging in. The next regiment up, the 21st, is moving toward Hill 102 on the Coast Highway with an ETA of sometime late today, maybe twelve hours or so from now. They have some artillery but no armor."

Captain Sam Haram, (the Professor), Master Sergeant Nick Beloit's second in command at NSOPU, rose.

"As we all have advised General Walker and anybody else who cares to listen; short of dropping a few A-Bombs, there's no fucking way of stopping these major pincer movements. They are starting to push our few forces back into an Alamo situation at Pusan."

Pausing a moment, "With great sadness, I have made decisions in the Big War that, in the short run, caused terrible losses to our men. Not a company of 200 or a battalion of 600. No! I'm talking about a division of 10,000 men, maybe two divisions, or more! But on a strategic level, it saved hundreds of thousands of lives and brought the war to a speedier end."

Colonel Nelson thought of Captain Haram's contribution as one of the principal planners of the Pacific Island hopping campaign against the Japanese in the War. A brute force horrific effort that did eventually end the War.

Looking around the table, he drove his point home, "Those men on the line are doing the only thing we have at the moment, sacrifice and delay. Our focus here must be on the Alamo, Pusan! We can't waste our resources on trying to save these men; we must focus on building a final defense."

Colonel Nelson abruptly stood. "Sam! You, without doubt, possess a great strategic mind. That's why you're here."

"And you're right, but I think your tone is off. What I mean by that is that you're right, in that we obsess about our field situation. But we should, because that's our job as the Intel unit for the Eighth Army. Some of which is on the ground and dying!"

Taking a breath, "But let me remind everybody that the real Alamo, fought so many years ago, was about delaying the Mexican Army to allow General Sam Huston time to gather his Army to defeat and ultimately win the war against the invading enemy. So we're fighting little Alamo's! Buying time, so General Walker and the entire Eighth Army can be brought to bear. Let's not lose that focus."

Nick rose. "We're not lost that dual effort, sir. I think what Sam meant was that we need more emphasis on the final defense of Pusan. His and my efforts have entirely gone into supporting the field operations and trying to bring resources into the trenches to help our insignificant resources to delay the enemy's advance. It's been frustrating! I think he wants to know that our efforts and those dying in the field are not in vain."

It was Major Jarvis who interrupted Nick, who sat when Jarvis started to speak.

"It's obvious that we're all feeling the frustration of events. As second in command of G-2, I'll tell you that nobody feels that more than our boss and nobody works harder to help our Army, so accept reality and deal with it!"

He was angry.

"It's going to get worse! A lot worse! Think! You are the best of the best. Keep doing what you do but get rest when you can, if you can't think right, you're ineffective."

Colonel Nelson calmly asked, "Anything else?"

"Got something going with Wild Bill, maybe later today." Said Nick with a sly smile.

Nelson just smiled and said, "Good luck!"

Chapter Forty

Wednesday, July 8, 1950 –
Day Fourteen of the Invasion
Korea – Rusty's Team at the New Location – 0400 – (4:00 am)

Larry woke Rusty from a light sleep. "Sorry! But we got a message and need to act on it, now!"

Instantly awake, "What is it?"

"It's from a Nick, at NSOPU, under Colonel Nelson's unit. Wants to know if we, or the ROK, have smoke markers at the line of attack in the Central Valley. He's planning a major low flying air-ground attack later today."

"C J! Red! Dam it! Wake everybody!" Rusty yelled. That did it.

C J and the rest of the brain trust came running and huddled around Rusty and Larry. After relaying the message from this Nick, there was silence.

"We left a good deal of supplies back at the medical camp, but I don't know if we have any more Jap smoke grenades." Said C J.

"Did you leave the bandages?" Asked Red.

A lightbulb went off in everybody's head. There were mounds of blood-soaked white sheets among the medical debris left at the camp.

"Hasn't the rain made the rags soaked?" Asked Tully.

Marty, the combat medic, replied. "No. A large number of surgical rags were sealed in body bags because we feared disease."

"Jesus!" Said Red and Tully at the same time.

Rusty did some quick calculations of time. "Larry! Get back to this Nick. Tell him we're got no smoke but will stage a blood rag pole line at the ROK front, with our blood on these sheets. Maybe we can make them smoke but probably not. We'll have a smoke fire BEHIND our lines to identify the general area. Tell him they'll have to get close-in to see the poles. Everything north of them is the enemy. Tell him to start the attack at 1100 – (11:00 am)."

"Red! We leave a basic defense here. Breakdown the equipment and hide it. We'll move out in 20 minutes." Rusty was high with energy.

Arron was within earshot of the last order. "Shit! No coffee today!" He felt terrible for the men.

Red ordered Larry and Marty, to stay and guard their camp. Marty griped again about being left out of the action as the three men sat together. Red told him to shut up and reminded him of his importance as the team's combat medic, should any of them get wounded. Then he gave him his 30 caliber machine gun.

"Only got maybe two boxes of ammo, but it's better than that Jap shit. But that Jap shit you got ain't half bad. You're in a combat zone, and the equipment you guard is vital. It cannot be compromised; you understand that right, Marty!"

Red shifted his gaze to Larry. "That goes for you as well! You guard this stuff with your life! Understand!"

A somber nod by all three signaled Red's departure. But as he was leaving, he turned.

"Larry! I expect you to establish a defensive perimeter here, and, I repeat, guard it with your life."

Red turned and left.

Fourteen men headed out, trying to put a thumb in a crumbling dike, but they were excited.

C J didn't know what a focused low air-ground attack meant against **troops**, but he was going to have a ringside seat at what America's air power could do when coordinated, as it was at the destruction of the Han River **Bridges** not too long ago.

Few had ever seen anything like what a formation of skilled pilots could do with the right bomb load and an excellent plan.

They reached the medical camp area without any enemy contact at around 0700 – (7:00 am); it was full light by then. When Rusty entered the camp and saw Frenchy and Dean, the relief on Rusty's face was noticeable. He ran up and slapped them on the shoulders, cursing them to never go off on their own again, but telling them how grateful he was that they survived. The rest of the men followed the welcome. But they didn't have much time, so they went to work.

The search yielded only a few body bags filled with semi-dry blood-soaked rags but no smoke grenades. What they did find was lots of crates of Japanese ammunition and weapons, left for the South Koreans who hadn't retreated to the position as yet.

Red ordered C J, *One*, *Three*, Arron, and Snake to take apart some of the ammunition shells and dump the gunpowder into a dry bucket he found. They needed to make something big, not a fire but something more like a smoldering smoke generating power plant. With all the rain, nothing natural around them was dry. They didn't want an explosion, just a smoke fire. Red was beside himself.

Tracker came to Red. "You paleface people make me ashamed I'm with you. And I like you, but you are so stupid in simple ways. How do you think us Indians survived through the bitter winters through rain and snow through the ages? I will teach you how to make smoke and fire from wet."

"Don't give me that smart ass Indian shit, Tracker. We don't have time. How!"

Realizing what he just said, he laughed.

Tracker smiled, "I'll make the smoke fire. Oh, the gunpowder idea is good, greatly redeemed yourself."

Under Tracker's directions, the rest of the team went out and chopped down ten foot or higher saplings and trimmed them into poles.

After cutting the poles, they were separated into two groups, one placed next to a large pile of loose blood rags, which was then sprinkled with gunpowder and wrapped at the top of the poles by Rusty's men who immediately took them away. All were heavily laden, mostly with the old Japanese weapons and ammunition, but a few carried food.

Tracker directed the remainder of the assembly of the bare poles. Before leaving, he grabbed Arron and Snake. "I need you two to help me make smoke." He handed over a small bucket. "Arron, keep this bucket of gun powder dry. Stay close to me."

A few minutes later, as they left the village, Arron spoke low to Snake, "Never imagined an *Injin* would trust me."

Looking back at Arron, Snake, who was of Mexican descent, said in a whisper. "Funny!" He said with a smile. "Never thought I'd befriend a southern racist."

An eerie calm hung over the Valley because of the thick fog that settled in all around. It felt unnatural. C J met up with a ROK rearguard unit around 9:30 am.

With about 20 yards of visibility, C J and Rusty were brought to the South Korean commander's bunker while the rest of Rusty's team stayed behind.

Surprised by the American's presence, the commander proceeded to tell C J, who translated for Rusty, that he didn't think a fall back to the village position would work. Very jumpy, he explained that he expected a major attack this morning and thought his men would be slaughtered making a move. He was not making sense, appeared to have battle fatigue, and looked like he might have lost perspective.

His number two, a major, came forward and spoke with C J after the commander went to a back section of the bunker. Acknowledging that his commander was sleep-deprived and somewhat "not with it," he listened to a brief update. The major then understood something big was going to happen, so he brought up the map of their current positions.

As he opened the map, he spoke to C J, who translated.

"We have continually fallen back since the invasion, from just south of the border. Delaying and fighting. Our unit has fought intensely, and our commander has now decided, I think, that this ground is a strategic area. He's hoping for a miracle."

Rusty thought he saw a spark in the major's eyes despite the overall sallowness of being totally fatigued as he went to the map.

"We have five key positions that form a wide U in this valley." Said the major to C J and Rusty.

C J then got up and explained the air attack plan in detail.

The eyes of the major glistened, "*Hope!* You brought me a gift. If only for a minute! I'm grateful to you, Sergeant, and your American friends."

"Let's not get too far ahead of ourselves, Major. We have lots to do." Said C J.

Conferring with Rusty, C J related suggestions to the major.

The major called his runners, waiting outside his trench. He instructed them to guide these Americans to his five main forward positions.

The men gathered after returning from assessing the key positions, and then Foxy took the lead in assigning the pole teams.

The major went to the back section and woke his commander, who had fallen into a deep sleep. "Sir, we will engage the enemy shortly with the help of a powerful American Air Force attack."

As the American teams carried the poles into the five critical South Korean positions, word spread of the air assault against their enemy. It was a much-needed jolt of hope among troops long without it.

Not far behind the center of the line, Tracker organized the building of the smoke fire. Arron and Snake gathered brush and leaves. Tracker built a teepee-like structure from the tree limbs they'd cut. He was hoping to discover a few dead ROK soldiers nearby to cut away any dry clothing they might still possess; to his joy and sorrow, he found many.

Tracker, now stoic, said to Arron and Snake. "Will you two go over there, to the dead men and remove their shirts; I need about 20 to wrap the teepee. Wet or dry, nothing fancy, cut away what doesn't come off easily."

Laying out the medical rags they brought, he laced in gunpowder from the bucket, folded the fabric, and went to the next one, and kept adding more. He made many until the supply got low. But he saved enough for the last part.

Then he built the smoke fire pit within the teepee, layer upon layer, wet leaves, and sticks, then adding the rags with the gunpowder, with lots of space between layers for air and heat to mingle.

Finally, he wrapped the outer teepee with the cut cloth from the uniforms, leaving a large chimney opening on top and a bottom air opening that circled the teepee.

Before he finished, he hunched back and sat in a trance. Building this had brought back memories he hadn't thought of for so many years; starving on the reservation and trying to stay warm. Death was everywhere. Hope?

"Tracker!" Yelled Snake. "You okay?"

Arron, right behind Snake, was less concerned, thought of something else. "So your Indian bullshit about making a smoke fire out of wet crap is going to get us all killed?"

Tracker came out of his thoughts and looked at Arron. "We may die today, my southern friend, but it will not be because of a lack of a beautiful Indian smoke fire."

As he walked away and neared a dead ROK soldier, Arron wondered why he made that outburst on Tracker, whom he considered a friend. Deep down Arron knew. He was afraid.

The early morning fog was still thick. It wasn't raining, but it was hot and humid, with only a slight breeze. Rusty wondered if the fog would lift in time. What was the weather at the airbase? Could the planes even find them?

Early intercepts by Leyden's team confirmed a planned massive push by the North on the ROK lines by late morning. These had not been transmitted to Rusty's men in time before they broke camp.

But this information was transmitted to Wild Bill and his new squadron of P -51's.

After the final preparations, Rusty ordered his men to regroup into assault teams among the South Korean centerline troops. It was Rusty's American Fire Brigade.

Tracker started to make his smoke fire.

It was 1030- (10:30 am).

Chapter Forty One

**Wednesday, July 8, 1950 - Day Fourteen of the Invasion
Korea – Taejon Airfield – Twenty miles from the front –
1000 – (10:00 am)**

Wild Bill and Stormy stood looking out at the fog. "My men
are locked and loaded, but I don't think we can fly in this
weather, Captain."

"You keep calling me Captain, well, goddamn it, I'm going
to start calling you Colonel."

"Sorry! Old habits. This fog is thick, and we're heading
into a valley operation with mountains all around. It could be
a suicide run!"

Wild Bill, with a hard face, turned on him. "Stormy! We're
going to launch in 30 minutes, and I don't give a shit if it's into
the teeth of a fucking tornado."

He started to walk away but turned to Stormy abruptly.
"Our God did not bring your squadron to me to sit on our
asses. We go this morning to fulfill His preordained mission
and smite our enemy. Have faith!"

Stormy was left staring at him.

Wild Bill returned to the hanger and called Nick at
NSOPU's HQ in Japan, hoping for a weather update from his
earlier call.

"The fog you're experiencing is a local thing, Captain. High clouds prevail over much of Central Korea, but ships off the East Coast report no sign of rain, but winds have picked up, blowing your way, east to west, 15 to 20 mph. That should clear your fog conditions shortly."

"Love the report, Nick!"

"Give the shitheads what they deserve! Good Luck!"

"Billy!" Yelled Wild Bill, "Bring Arnie!"

"Boss, we got everything set," Said Billy, Arnie by his side. "**Just Due** is on the flight line, you'll be first off, and he's loaded for bear."

"I know. Both of you have done enormous good work, and I wanted to say thanks. Let's say a silent prayer together that we continue to have success together." The Captain bowed his head. Billy and Arnie did a quick look at each other and then followed their Captain in silent prayer.

They spent the night before studying maps of the Valley, the pilots going over every detail of the attack plan that Wild Bill and Stormy had devised.

Over coffee that morning, Stormy updated his men on the new information they received just hours ago. He detailed the new requirements for locating the general ROK position by pinpointing a smoke signal just behind the South Korean lines and then by further identifying key ROK positions with poles draped with rags placed in front of them.

"We've got to get really low to see these poles!" One pilot called out.

Wild Bill sat, and in his head, he counted one but didn't get any further before Stormy answered.

"And that's our fucking job! Not only is this a critical mission, but it's also about saving American lives on the ground here in this battle! If one of you bomb or strafe our forces in this attack, I'll come down on you so hard you'll never fly again. You get low and kill this enemy. Got it!"

His squadron responded in unison. "Yes, sir!"

Wild Bill was pleased with the response, figured Stormy had earned his nickname coming up through the ranks. For a Colonel, besides his favorite, he started to really like Stormy.

The fog was still thick. The end of the runway was shrouded.

Coming out of the hanger, Wild Bill had a smile and met Stormy in front of his assembled squadron.

"As words that were once spoken to me in England, on my first mission to escort a flight of British Lancaster Bombers to Cherbourg, France. *'Hope you make it mate.'* I say this to you because we all think about this. Well, I'm still here! And so will you be after this mission."

Pausing, "Besides, I've got an inside track that tells me that not only will the fog lift, but we're going to catch these bastards with their pants down. Meet you above the fog!"

The pilots climbed into their ready planes.

The squadron assembled around **Just Due** at 3,000 feet, well above the fog and just below the clouds.

It was 1045 – (10:45 am).

Chapter Forty Two

Wednesday, July 8, 1950 - Day Fourteen of the Invasion Korea – Rusty's Team on the ROK Lines in the Central Valley – 1045 – (10:45 am)

"It's just smoldering, Tracker, it's not making a lot of smoke, nothing!" Said an anxious Snake.

"I've been guided by Spirit, Snake. Never failed me before, stay calm." Despite these words, Tracker was furiously praying to Spirit in his head and soul.

Rusty, Red, and Tully were anything but calm. Foxy was talking to a very anxious ROK sergeant, trying to calm him down.

Earlier, they had surveyed the five key ROK positions and realized what a thin line it was, with the most vulnerable being the center. Hence, the consensus of forming a concentrated Fire Brigade of their men just behind this line. They created three teams as emergency help if needed; they had a plan.

As the hour approached, they realized that unless the fog lifted, this whole operation would turn to shit, and they'd be overrun and probably killed.

As instructed, South Korean soldiers from the five key positions ran out and planted their 10-foot blood rag wrapped poles.

Rusty noticed that he could now see smoke rising from Tracker's signal fire, where just a few minutes ago, he couldn't see the area at all. A light breeze touched his face.

"Holy shit!" Yelled Arron, as a breeze hit the teepee, and a small fire started at its base. Then another, stronger breeze struck, and then the flames below burst, sending a massive plume of smoke up the 10-foot high teepee stack.

Snake made the sign of the cross. Tracker mumbled something.

The breeze freshened and quickly blew the fog away.

It was 1100 – (11:00 am).

Artillery shells began to impact the South Korean lines. The North Korean's commenced their big push to clear the Central Valley.

Everyone on the line waited to hear the American planes. They only heard enemy shells exploding among them. They hunkered deeper in their trenches, most started praying.

Chapter Forty Three

Wild Bill had a clear view of the surrounding mountains to his target Valley when his squadron arrived a few minutes early, but the ground fog prevented seeing any targets. So they circled, hoping the fog would blow away soon. Fuel was not an issue; they could linger for more than an hour.

"Stormy! Hold the circle. I'm going in for a look, think the fog is lifting."

"Roger that."

Wild Bill dove and came in from an unexpected north to south direction from the far north end of the Valley. The wind had almost cleared the fog, and he had a great view at 500 feet as he sliced down the Valley and pulled up amongst ground explosions and the site of a considerable smoking teepee.

"Stormy! Commence attack as planned. The fog has lifted, and the enemy's attacking!"

Flight A's three-plane section peeled off immediately and followed Wild Bill's flight path coming down from the North to take out artillery and supply units well behind the front lines.

Flight B's three-plane section was to take out the middle area of mortar, artillery, and headquarter units by going east to west so as not to conflict with flights A coming from the north and C coming up from the south.

Flight C, led by Stormy, had the toughest job. His six planes were coming in very low from the south to north and had to see the rag poles to know where the front lines of the ROK were, flying at 400 MPH.

Wild Bill flew Top with a full bomb load, watched, and listened. His radio filled with Stormy's men pointing out targets to fellow pilots and expressions of success at taking out something or other. He felt strange, detached. He started praying.

Stormy's Flight C, guided by the considerable smoke fire at the rear center of the ROK lines, were spread out and cleared the rag polls by one hundred feet. Flight C caught the advancing enemy infantry in the open with each plane's six machine guns on auto. They circled and found concentrations hiding. Napalm and bombs followed after continued circling and attacks.

It was the same with the other two flights. It was a rabbit hunt in a caged yard.

The enemy had no anti-aircraft, no enemy fighter planes, and the attack was a total surprise. It was a stunning victory.

Wild Bill came out of his funk when he realized it wasn't all on him and felt relieved. Deciding nothing more could be done here, he decided to give the Commies farther north something to think about, so he flew northwest toward Osan, now an enemy staging area.

Back on the ground, just before the air attack began and above the sound of incoming explosions, Rusty heard the roar of that distinctive engine, just above him. Then a great racket as planes passed right over his position with their machine guns blazing; the sound was deafening. That's when the enemy's shelling stopped.

The noise and detonations were now among the enemy. Rusty and all the men in the trenches on the five lines stood and watched as the American P-51's systematically weaved back and forth, raining death and horrible destruction with 500 lb. bombs and napalm.

Nobody had ever seen a tactical fighter squadron work a two-mile-wide by a three-mile-long Valley filled with advancing infantry almost fully exposed.

It lasted 30 minutes before the P-51's exhausted every round of ammunition they carried. Seeing the napalm hit concentrations of men was difficult to digest for many of the ROK soldiers until they remembered what these men had inflicted on their friends or family.

Rusty, nor any of his men had any such feelings. Not quite relishing the destruction, they felt payback was due. Much like the enemy they fought before, whether diehard Nazi's or Japanese troops, they'd come to hate these invaders. This enemy marched to a different code, showed no remorse, and killed indiscriminately.

Rusty broke the hush of the battlefield when he jumped up out of his trench and yelled, "Charge!" to his fire brigade, who then rose to follow him out through the ROK center defense line, into the center of the Valley, charging the enemy, alone.

It was purely an unplanned, emotional event. There had been no discussion with Red or Tully. But they too had gotten caught up in the ferocity of the air attack and the incredible devastation they witnessed.

Immediately separating into three fire teams in a tight V formation, they charged toward the first known enemy position about 70 yards dead ahead.

Foxy didn't follow. Instead, he turned to the ROK sergeant next to him and started yelling at him. "Get your men out and charge!"

It took a moment, but then the sergeant realized what was happening and obeyed Foxy. He jumped out and yelled at his men to follow him. The rest of the ROK troops, all around, still in their positions, witnessing these few American soldiers charging up the Valley, now also seeing their centerline start to advance, got inspired as well and joined the attack.

Running full out, leaping over rocks and across ravines, weaving among large numbers of enemy bodies, Rusty, at the head of the V formation, was 30 yards away from a loose grouping of boulders, brush, and foxholes. He could see a group of enemy soldiers, but they hadn't moved much nor fired a shot at them.

Joe was just to Rusty's right and wondered why he was still alive. He wasn't going to wait for an order; he opened fire with his Tommy without breaking stride.

The rest of Rusty's team must have had the same thought at the same time. All fired as they kept charging forward.

No return fire. Those of the enemy who could, ran. The air attack killed most of the enemy, but those still alive were in a trance-like state.

Tully's team on the left flank dropped to the ground as soon as the firing began. Moose deployed his BAR and started firing.

Sniper Dean found a boulder and commenced at what he did best. As he later described it, "A real good Turkey shoot."

On the right side, Red's team also dropped at the sound of the first gunfire. *One* and *Three* had become quite expert at the newly acquired Japanese "Knee Mortar" weapon and commenced to fire into the enemy's rear positions.

The enemy ran or stayed and died.

The ROK forces finally caught up with Rusty's team and kept ongoing. Foxy stayed along with a ROK sergeant and his men as they charged the next enemy stronghold. The farther away from the ROK lines they ran, Foxy realized that was where the enemy received most of the concentrated air attacks. When they reached this stronghold, they saw nothing but dead or dying soldiers. A napalm strike had hit the left side of this long shallow trench. Many bodies were still on fire; some were half burnt and still alive.

Foxy found a young soldier at the other end of the line, alive but in total shock, huddled with arms held tightly across his chest and shaking like a leaf in a storm. He pulled the kid up, turned to grab his canteen to give him a drink of water but heard a loud shot right behind him. The kid slumped in the mud with a bullet hole in his forehead. The ROK sergeant he had joined stood there and smiled at Foxy and said, "No prisoners!" Then he proceeded down the trench with his pistol, shooting all the enemy still alive or wounded.

Foxy turned away and headed back. He couldn't participate in further butchery. He hated these guys too, but still, he tried to justify, but all he could see was that scared kids face. He'd fought in Europe in the War and didn't experience the "No Prisoner" horror that many who fought the Japanese told him they experienced. But he had seen what horrors these Commies are capable of inflicting. When does it stop?

The North Korean's had never experienced a focused tactical air attack. They'd not dug in correctly, and for the first time, they suffered a napalm attack. Seeing your comrades running around on fire, screaming, being burnt alive, is devastating. The Germans and Japanese both used it against us, as we did against them in the big war. Americans knew its effects, and now the North Koreans knew it too.

Now gathered around the first captured enemy position, the adrenalin rush had long gone, Rusty's men sat back. They were exhausted.

"Don't ever do that again!" Said Red, upset.

Rusty just rolled his head to him. "Can't promise that."

"One great fucking call!" Said Tully, showing his Ranger attitude. "Wish we had talked about it first, though."

Rusty nodded. "Not a democracy here, Tully, it just hit me. I figured they were messed up by that attack. I saw a 500 lbs. bomb hit behind that line. The concussion effect of that kind of detonation is devastating. So I guessed."

He looked around to all his men.

"Glad you all followed me!"

Arron raised his head, "Can't speak for the rest of the men, Rusty, but I'll follow you anywhere."

Up in the sky.

Wild Bill continued towards Osan. High clouds, no rain, and a friendly breeze. Ideal conditions, he thought.

He flew to about 10 miles south of Osan to the Main Highway and turned to follow it north, hoping to catch a truck convoy. He had a full bomb load and wasn't going to waste it.

Cruising at 500 feet, Wild Bill felt like a God with *Just Due* as his instrument of vengeance. It didn't take long for him to find a target as a ten truck convoy came into view. He nosed down and fired his six 50 caliber machine guns starting at the first truck and continued the destruction up the convoy to the last one. He continued to fly north.

Approaching Osan, he saw vehicles hiding in a cluster of trees off the highway. He zoomed in and dropped his two five hundred pound bombs among trucks towing artillery and assorted other vehicles. He did a quick turn, came back at them from the north, and dropped his center mount napalm canister at 300 feet.

Pulling up, he yelled. "Burn you heathen Commies!"

Then he felt his plane shutter. He pulled left while still climbing and looked back to see if an enemy plane had caught him. There was no plane. He sighed in relief. But the reprieve was short, realizing ground fire hit him.

He kept climbing, still had full total control of *Just Due*. The gauges seemed all okay as he leveled off at 3000 feet, just under the clouds. He headed home with less than a 30 minute ETA.

A few minutes later, the plane suddenly took a violent roll to the right and dropped 300 feet before he was able, with much force, to correct the roll and halt the descent by overcompensating.

So my tail got hit, Wild Bill thought. Certainly the elevator, and part of the horizontal. Shit! How bad? Can it hold? Can I make it back? He talked to his plane, "*Just Due*! You're a man! Don't let this shit get in our way of doing what we're ordained to do. Get us home!"

He grabbed his mike and tried to reach Stormy, no go. Raised Billy at the base on his next try, told him his situation.

"Got it, boss, you'll make it. He's a sturdy bastard. Stormy's squadron all returned and are clear of the runway. See you in a few."

Heartened by the encouragement, he became lightheaded and began to sing an English Pub song he learned when he flew out of England on bomber escort duty.

Five minutes out from the field, *Just Due* started shaking violently and moving crazily, side to side and then up then down. Wild Bill had all he could do to hold on to the stick. He didn't want to move it too much for fear something would come apart. He felt that his warrior was in the throes of death.

He coaxed him, "Only a bit more! I know you can do it!"

He called the field again and got Billy, who was operating the radio like a puppy anxiously awaiting the return of his master.

"Got serious shit here, Billy. Very little control. Think he may break up, but we're almost there. Can't turn, so I'm coming in from the North, got just enough altitude to clear the mountain, then I'm coming in dead stick."

"Captain! Listen to me, bailout! This could go very badly. I don't want to lose you."

"Thanks, Billy. But trust in the Lord, I've not yet finished my work. Over."

The only outside speaker from the shed was left on, so the whole field heard the transmission.

Stormy and the entire squadron gathered to the side of the field. Billy and Arnie stood just outside the radio shed. A maintenance crew loaded a truck with the only two fire extinguisher canisters on the airfield along with heavy tools in case they had to cut him out. There was no ambulance or medical personnel on the base.

Everyone watched as Wild Bill barely cleared the north mountain and came straight toward the airfield. Flaps came down, wheels were down, and speed dropped immediately. The effect was dramatic.

Just Due shook and shuddered, wildly weaving and descending way too fast.

Wild Bill cut the engine and hoped he could maintain control and be able to pull up in time. He figured it was his only chance.

Billy watched the approach in horrified awe. He, a man of little connection to humanity, felt a deep-down feeling emerge that he'd never experienced before. He started crying.

Arnie, right next to Billy, although not a religious man, fell to his knees and started praying. He couldn't watch.

Wild Bill slid his canopy open as he descended, didn't want to be trapped. The wind blew in refreshing air for him. He thought of his death. How quickly the mind works at the near moment, as he looked back and wondered if it was enough.

He gave up on the thought and focused on the now. His plane was almost out of control, yet it flew.

A bit too steep in his approach, wobbling and coming in too fast, he cleared the north hanger by ten feet and hit mid runway hard and bounced. The entire tail end of his plane fell off at the bounce. The rest of the plane skidded and fishtailed off the end of the runway.

Late that afternoon, an unusual flight flew in, known only by Stormy. He made a ruse to keep Wild Bill and his grounds crew all together in their Hanger A to start planning for their next mission.

It was 1700 – (5:00 pm), when Stormy's Air Force squadron, pilots, and all service personnel silently entered Hanger B, adjacent to Wild Bill's Hanger A.

Lines of tables with chairs were each set with a bottle of Whiskey and Scotch. All first-class, but no ice. The men settled in; they were grateful but wondered what horrible mission must be next.

Five minutes later, Stormy escorted a surprised Wild Bill, Billy, and Arnie into the structure and brought them to the table of honor, at the head of the facility; they stood facing the men.

"What is this?" Wild Bill asked Stormy.

"Shut up! It's a much-needed soul replenishing for you. I only wish it could release your daemons."

"Attention!" Yelled Stormy, as Colonel Nelson and Master Sergeant Nick Beloit came in from the hanger entrance, marched down the center, and reached the group. They saluted.

Nelson grabbed Wild Bill in an arm embrace like long lost brothers and whispered in his ear, "Glad you made it you crazy fucker!"

Wild Bill, filled with emotion, was uncharacteristically speechless.

Nelson introduced Nick to Wild Bill with a comment that they'll be playing more together in the future. Nelson turned to all, still standing at attention in the hanger.

He saluted them, "Please sit and resume celebrating." They all knew what that meant.

Nelson walked back to the table and grabbed a glass of Scotch that Nick had poured for him and, still standing, took a gulp. Looking around, he thought most of the men had had a swig or two, so he grabbed a knife from the table and banged his glass.

The seventy men or so in the hanger got quiet.

"You didn't think you were going to get away without a speech, right?"

Lots of laughter.

"I'll be brief. Promise!"

More laughter.

"A man, much more capable than I, once said, 'Never was so much owed by so many to so few.' I think that applies here. Some may say that's over the top, but God knows we needed something over the top right now and goddamn it, you sure did deliver it today. So I raise my glass to one and all, to a great victory!"

Cheers, whistles, and clapping ensued.

Nelson raised his arms to quiet the men.

"I said I'd be brief but not that brief!"

Laughter.

"Besides, I'm told the steaks aren't ready yet!"

Again laughter.

"My boss, General Walker, and his boss, General MacArthur, followed this mission very closely and were profoundly impressed. Not only by its success but by its planning and leadership. So I'm here to not only honor you, the men who carried out this mission but to honor the men who made it happen."

Pausing a moment to a silent group,

"General MacArthur has authorized me to bestow his, and our Nation's gratitude on the two men who made this all work today.

"Colonel Malcolm Fredrick, please stand."

He continued.

"Air Force and Army usually don't get along well, but you, Colonel, an Air Force man now, was once an Army guy. You fought the Japanese as an Army pilot in the same way you fought today, helping the Army grunt in the trenches. You organized your squadron today in a masterful air attack and stopped a powerful enemy ground attack dead in its tracks. Your nickname, Stormy, certainly applies. For your efforts, General MacArthur, as Theater Commander, awards you the Distinguished Flying Cross."

As he placed the Medal on his uniform, a rousing chorus of cheers followed.

Nelson waived his arms for quiet, knowing the men were starting to get deep in the booze.

"And now, my next victim."

Laughter.

"Captain Stands, come forward." Turning to address the hall of men, Nelson continued.

"He is known as Wild Bill, for a reason. He and I go way back, and I'll attest to the Wild part of his name."

Some shouts.

"Captain Stands has a gift for bullshit that's beyond comprehension."

Yells and whistles.

"That's right. This man was able to convince my staff that, with a good squadron, something special could happen. My special operations man, Nick here, believed him and got the ball rolling."

Turning back to Wild Bill, Nelson said,

"For your efforts and foresight, planning and execution of this mission, and your intuitive attack on enemy ground traffic in the Osan area, Captain Stands, as a result of these actions, General Walker, Eighth Army Commander, has awarded you the Silver Star."

Clapping and whistles.

"And he should have gotten the Medal of Honor for that incredible landing!" Shouted someone.

Rousing laughter.

Colonel Nelson sat next to Wild Bill on his right and Nick on his left, as the steaks and potatoes came out.

"Damn! It's good to see you, Colonel." Said, Wild Bill.

Nelson looked back at him, "And you, my crazy Captain!"

During the ceremony, a lone P-51 landed and was escorted by Arnie to a secluded spot.

As their cargo plane left the runway to return to Japan with only Colonel Nelson and Master Sergeant Nick Beloit on board, Nelson turned to Nick.

"That was one hell of a risk you took, Nick. It's what I expected of you, and you came through. General MacArthur called General Walker about awarding those medals, but he knew the operation came from you, Nick."

"He wants you to take a battlefield commission to Captain. Walker said he didn't know if you would, but he would get back to him."

"I'm a grunt, Colonel. I've seen so much shit that I've concluded that it doesn't matter how many bars or stars you got, it's a matter of how effective you can be."

"So, Nick. Don't you think you'd be more effective as a Captain?"

"You picked me to lead this special unit, sir. Would being a Captain have made a difference in your picking me?"

"You'd make more money!"

"But I wouldn't fit in, you know, at the Officer's Club."

Chapter Forty Four

**Thursday, July 9, 1950 - Day Fifteen of the Invasion
Japan – Eighth Army Headquarters - Colonel Nelson's G-2
Conference Room – 0545 – (5:45 am)**

Arriving late last night from Korea, Colonel Nelson scheduled an early meeting for 0600- (6:00 am), NSOPU included.

The entire team got there early, ex Nelson. They'd read the after-action reports of the Central Valley fight that came in sporadically during the day and night.

Leyden's team monitored enemy communications continuously and picked up a nearby North Korean division's radio frequencies that were attacking General Dean's 34th Battalion. Also, late last night, Rusty's team reestablished contact and reported on the day's events, prompting Nick to make some significant decisions. He had his entire NSOPU team work through the night to address these new developments. Colonel Nelson was unaware of these events as he entered.

When Nelson opened the door, the smell of fresh coffee beckoned, but the sight of his entire team around the big table gave off a chilly vibe.

"What the hell! Did we surrender?" Asked a grumpy and tired Nelson.

Nick looked up at him, "Boss, we're all a little tired is all."

After Nelson got his coffee and had a few sips, he sat to a quiet room.

"Didn't sleep much? That doesn't sound good."

"But before I hear bad news, I want to begin with some praise, tell you how much you contributed to this victory yesterday. Yes, it's only a battle. But it's the first we won. It was a defensive victory but one we badly needed. It showed that the South Koreans would fight and fight hard for their country."

Taking another swig from his coffee cup, he continued.

"Balls! Initiative! That's what won this battle! Many men had both at this table, but none more than Nick. Who, without him, this battle wouldn't have happened."

Nick got red-faced.

"He has already turned down a battlefield commission to Captain, authorized by General MacArthur, for his leadership on this mission."

"Master Sergeant Nick Beloit, please rise and come front and center."

Nelson met him at the back of the room, facing the table.

"Nick's our grunt, maybe the most famous of them all. He can turn down a commission, but he can't turn down a medal."

At that, the entire table stood, and Colonel Nelson continued.

"Yes! Thank you. Recognizing hard work among your peers is necessary. So, by order of the Field Commander of all Forces in Korea, General MacArthur, I am honored to award you, Master Sergeant Nicolas Beloit, the Silver Star for your extraordinary efforts in organizing and coordinating the successful Battle of the Central Valley, Korea."

Everyone Clapped.

Now back at his seat when the regular meeting began, Nick went deep into his memory. He never felt like a hero. This event, this Medal, brought up old wounds, not his, but of his comrades doing extraordinary things that were not recognized in the jungle, charging a Japanese pillbox or rescuing a wounded guy, men dying beside him. He bent his head and lost it. Tears rolled down his cheeks.

"Let's take a break." Said Nelson.

Everyone left the room except Nick and Nelson.

"You okay, Nick?"

"Yeah, just had some flashbacks."

"I know about those, Nick. I have them. Sometimes I wake up in the middle of the night, screaming and drenched in sweat. When I came home after the War, my wife would have to jump on me to stop my thrashing. But it hasn't stopped." Pausing. "They'll probably never stop."

Nelson continued, "We've seen many horrors, and we'll see more. Most men who fight deserve a medal. The unsung warriors who died doing great deeds are too numerous even to comprehend. But you, Nick, are a true hero and deserved more then you got. You're alive and survived, but they didn't."

"Chance, fate, destiny! A damn crapshoot that you didn't die when you stepped on that mine. Luckily you only lost your foot. But maybe your survival was because your foxhole buddy was the General in charge of the whole goddamn operation."

"I'd start calling you Lucky, but I'd always think of that dog joke, so I'll keep it to Nick. You're alive and vital, and those past friends aren't, through no fault of yours. Feeling guilty or unworthy has no place in your lexicon. Nick, you are a true light. I order you to forget the past."

They both laughed at that.

The team came back and resettled back at the table.

Nelson addressed the table. "Now for the bad news! Please fill me in."

Nelson's deputy G-2 of Eighth Army, Major Hank Jarvis, started.

"Yesterday, General MacArthur ordered the dismantling of the 7th Division of all trained officers and men, and sending them to Korea as replacements."

Nelson nodded, "Good move. We need the men, and the 7th was not a fighting unit."

Hank Jarvis continued. "The 34th Infantry Regiment of the 24th Infantry's Division just suffered a horrible defeat on the West Coast Highway at the town of Chonan. Outflanked, they suffered severe losses before being forced to withdraw, but they're still fighting."

LT Larry Cole went next. "The 24th Division is still not fully deployed. The next Regiment up, the 21st, is desperately needed to relieve the 34th before they get slaughtered, but they're only now getting ready to board transport ships for Pusan. General Dean's last Regiment, the 19th, is still being assembled here on our base."

Colonel Nelson shook his head, "The enemy is rolling toward Taejon, the next enemy target. We've got to get General Dean's forces more help."

Major Jarvis responded with a "Working on that, Colonel."

Nick spoke next. "I think our plans for landing the 1st Cavalry Division on the East Coast above Pusan got approved. If so, we got a chance of not being humiliated, defeated, and kicked out of Korea."

Major Hank Jarvis spoke up. "As deputy G-2, I will say that we are at the nexus of events. It looks bleak, but some positive measures are happening. As Nick said, I think the landing of the 1st Calvary Division will be approved and help immensely to shore up our eastern defense of Pusan."

"Should all this be approved, when are they projected to land?" Asked Nelson.

Nick took the question. "That's complicated, boss. Some LST's have arrived, but we still lack adequate sealift. To overcome this, we will lease Japanese cargo ships and barges, and the Navy has offered many of their ships to ferry supplies. So, if we get an okay to go today, it may take a week before the first landings."

"Will the landing be opposed?"

"Can't answer that. Right now, the South Koreans are fighting a furious delaying action on the east coast. How long that will last is anybody's guess. A week is a long time."

"Okay. What can we do to help the 24th Division?"

"Sir." Lt Larry Cole started. "Advanced elements of the 25th Division will start landing in Pusan just as the 19th Regiment clears the area late tomorrow. It will take a week before the rest of the division will be fully ashore. They have a full battalion of light tanks, the M24's."

"That's all the armor they got?' Asked a disillusioned Nelson.

"Sir, it's the only armor we will have in Korea for some time."

The M-24, designed to be a scout, was a light tank for WW2 operations against German lightly held positions. Possessing a 75 mm gun, it was formidable against lightly armored vehicles. However, it was no match against the Russian built T-34, the best medium tank built in WW2.

"I'm talking about now, goddamn it! Not a week from now! Do we have anything?" An angry Nelson asked the table.

Nick's deputy at NSOPU, Captain Sam Haran, looked over to Nick, "Tell him, Nick."

Nelson glared at Nick. "Tell me what?"

Nick was quiet for a moment as he gathered his thoughts.

"Sir, I've been given a job with extraordinary powers, authorized by the Theater Commander himself and delegated to me by you. I'm not sure MacArthur or anyone else realized the extent of the authority I was authorized. It took me a while to realize the scope of it."

"And you're done a great job; I just gave you a medal for it." Said Nelson.

"And I guess that's why I got this job. I get thing things done."

"I'm waiting, Nick, drop the hammer."

"As a grunt, I only wanted clear and concise orders that were well thought out by reliable and responsible superiors. Never got those, so I improvised."

Nick paused.

"So here I am, with explicit orders to stop the North Korean advance using the USOPU special operations orders, although somewhat limited in scope, it's an interpreted order."

"Get to the god damned point!" A frustrated Nelson barked.

"General Dean is in command of all forces in Korea. But his 24th Division is being chewed to bits, and his staff is incapable of coordinating anything. General MacArthur's team is trying to run the war from Japan and not doing well. And then there's us, Eighth Army, caught in between all this bullshit with General Walker not in command yet, but involved, because of our logistics nightmare."

"And then there's me."

"Jesus Christ, Nick. I'm not sure if I should puke or applaud, please tell me what you've done?" A very anxious Nelson asked.

"I stepped in, sir. My staff and I took charge. Sam did most of the work. We have run the entire deployment and logistics effort to Korea for a while. We've coordinated with all commands, but we've issued orders, sometimes overriding superior's orders."

"As to your last question about helping the 24th Division. I canceled an order out of General MacArthur's staff regarding the transport of 2,000 trained officers and men stripped from the 7th Division. They were to go by boat. It would have been too late to help. I diverted air supply transport from Japan to Pusan to fly these troops into Taejon, so they can immediately join the 24th Division's, 21st Regiment. They start landing early today."

"Jesus! So you just pissed off a lot of McArthur's staff. Is that it, Nick?"

"No, Sir. I grabbed an advanced element of the Army's 187th Airborne Infantry Regiment that just landed in Japan and ordered an immediate parachute drop around Taejon. It is the focus of our delaying defense. Their 3rd battalion will drop late today."

With an amazed look, Colonel Nelson sat back in his seat. Silent for more than a few moments, he finally spoke.

"How the hell did you organize this? Who knows? And where are all the transports coming from?"

Not cowered by his boss's somewhat belligerent questions, Nick squared off at him.

"I have a mandate with high authority, and I have Sam, the most fabulous planner on the planet. And he has a great staff. As to who knows? The people on the ground were all contacted personally. Confirming communications also were sent to all commands."

Looking over to his deputy, Sam, for some help, he got a turned head, so Nick continued.

"I'm afraid that the transport issue may cause some negative feedback. I stepped on a lot of toes diverting *all* small transports in Japan for these missions."

"What do you mean by **small** transports?"

"All available C-47s and a whole Group of the new C-119 'Flying Boxcars' that just arrived in Japan.

"How many of the Boxcars did you take?"

"All 40 of them."

Colonel Nelson's blank face finally broke into a smile.

"Did you manage to get any tanks on those planes?"

A relived Nick, "No, sir, but maybe we can after we drop the airborne unit."

Nelson nodded and leaned back in his chair, looked up at the ceiling then back at Nick.

"A shit storm is about to erupt, and I'm the point man. Nick. You continue stepping on toes, kicking ass, and getting the job done. I've got your back!"

The conference door opened, a harried captain stuck his head in and called out. "Colonel Nelson, sir. General Walker requests your immediate presence. Could you please follow me?"

As Nelson rose, he addressed the table. "It begins. Carry on."

Chapter Forty Five

**Thursday, July 9, 1950 - Day Fifteen of the Invasion
Korea – Taejon Airfield – Ten Miles from Hill 102 – 0700 –
(7:00 am)**

Wild Bill rose early, 5 am. He was distressed at the loss of his beloved *Just Due*, knew he wasn't flying on a critical mission today; he was emotionally down. He prayed to the gods of war for guidance and accepted their judgment, but didn't like it.

Stormy was waiting for him at the coffee table.

"Grab a cup, Wild Bill, and follow me." They left the hanger into the morning dark and turned right.

Arnie was sitting in a truck not far away. When he saw the two men make the turn, he turned on the truck headlights, which lit up a covered plane directly in their path.

The P-51 was slightly angled facing the two men, with a covering over the front of the plane.

Then Billy came out of the dark.

Stormy turned to Captain Stands. "I couldn't think of you *not* continuing to lead this next mission with me."

Stormy then nodded to Billy.

Billy pulled the shroud off the front, revealing the same clothed man carrying the avenging scythe as was on *Just Due*, but now named *Just Due 2*.

Wild Bill went rigid in disbelief. He looked up to the night sky and whispered, "Thank you!"

Then he immediately grabbed Stormy. "I knew you were sent here for a purpose, and I thank you. You're a good man, and now you are my friend forever."

"Wild Bill! If ever a man deserved a good thing in his life, it is you. I consider it an honor to be your friend."

Arnie came over to be close to Billy near the plane and said to him, "Do you think he likes my art, Billy?" Billy was feeling emotional again. He grabbed Arnie around the shoulder and said, "Arnie! How could he not like your art? It's beautiful."

Stormy spoke loudly to Wild Bill so Billy and Arnie could hear.

"I enlisted your crew in this surprise. Billy and Arnie worked all night to get your new man ready for today."

Turning to them, his eyes misty, Wild Bill said, "Thank you." It was all he could say.

Stormy, Colonel Malcolm Fredrick, commander of the 7th Fighter Squadron, who had just completed a historic mission yesterday, sat on a crate at the very back of the hanger, next to Captain Stands, his current boss.

They were waiting. The entire base personnel had assembled in the hanger for an important announcement.

Off from the side, General Dean came forward to the sitting officers, who immediately stood to attention and saluted.

"Attention!" Yelled Wild Bill to the men in the hanger.

"At ease." Said the General as he entered.

He presented himself in full combat gear and holstered sidearm. His ruffled and dirty BDUs paid tribute to his time on the line. Removing his helmet, he stood facing over one hundred men in the hanger.

"I'm General Dean, commanding officer of the 25TH Infantry Division and commander of all forces in Korea."

Pausing, he stepped aside to look at Captain Stands and Colonel Fredrick, he then said.

"Your leaders here and you did a fantastic job yesterday. I need you to do that often."

Now pacing, the General continued.

"We're getting help today, and I need everybody to do their best. We're making a determined stand north of Taejon. We must hold out for as long as we can. Thank you for your effort."

General Dean stepped back as Wild Bill moved forward.

"General Dean's division has sacrificed his men to delay the enemy, and now it's our turn to help. Planes will be landing shortly with replacement troops. You 7th Squadron ground crews need to move this along. I know it's not your job, but as you've noticed, this base is a shit hole!"

Laughs from the hanger.

Serious now and standing still. "Maybe you got what General Dean implied just now, but I'll be blunter. We're about to be overrun by these Commies. It's only a matter of when. **When** that happens is in our hands! Do your best to make it a costly **when** for these bastards!"

The hanger was silent. Pausing again, the Captain continued.

"In about an hour, four thousand men will start landing. God willing, they'll have artillery. General Dean has his team and transport ready to move them out. Later today, an airborne battalion will parachute into our area, and other planes will start landing with their supporting heavy weapons and ammo. To all of you in the ground crew, God bless you for your efforts today because it's going to be a bitch of a day!"

Some chuckles.

Pacing now, Wild Bill continued.

"Do not disappoint General Dean or Stormy, or your conscious. Remember that our God is on our side!"

The large hanger was silent.

Stormy stood next.

"I'm proud to be here at this critical point. I'm counting on you to continue to perform to the excellence that you have demonstrated. Pilots and ground crew of the 7th Squadron are the best of the best. Prepare to fly out of here in 30 minutes to destroy enemy traffic on the main highway. Are there any questions?"

A pilot hand raised at the front row.

"Colonel, sir. Reports indicate heavy civilian refugees intermixed among North Korean troops and armor on the highway. How are we to deal with this?"

Stormy sighed.

"A difficult question. But it's a matter of survival. Ours, to be exact. If we don't slow the advance, we die. The North Korean invaders caused this issue; I suggest any morality question rests on their shoulders."

"Did I answer your question?"

"Yes, sir."

Stormy met Wild Bill outside the hanger as his men proceeded to their planes.

"This could be a major fuck up if we interfere with the troop landings when we return to rearm and refuel." Said Stormy.

Wild Bill looked at him. "So we won't cause a fuck up! Troops on the ground come first, got it? Make sure you stagger your return and don't go hell bent for leather on your first run. You need to circle and be a vulture, pick and choose and take your time. We need to be here tomorrow; then, you'll have free reign."

Stormy nodded and walked off toward his plane.

Wild Bill watched the 7th fly out and wondered if this was going to be a major disaster.

Walking to *Just Due 2*, he reminded himself of the ingenuity of man and how, believing in a higher power, and oneself, things usually worked out. He said a silent prayer that this would be so and introduced himself to *Just Due 2*.

Chapter Forty Six

Thursday, July 9, 1950 - Day Fifteen of the Invasion
Japan – Eighth Army Headquarters
General Walker's office – 0800 – (8:00 am)

As Colonel Nelson entered the general's office, he sensed something different, a coldness he hadn't felt before.

Without returning his salute, General Walker asked him to sit.

"You've disrespected me, Colonel, and I'm pissed."

Nelson looked incredulous. "I'd never do that, sir! What are you talking about?"

"These operations! The scheduled 1st Calvary Division landing, rescheduling replacements to the 24th division from boat to air, the diversion, and parachute drop of an Airborne Infantry Regiment into Taejon. These operations have diverted all air supplies from Pusan!"

"All Sea support was redirected to the 1st Calvary landing! Nothing is flowing into Pusan! Nothing!"

His face was getting red.

"Everybody is up my butt, even MacArthur. I told you Pusan is our Alamo! What are you doing, Colonel?"

"I'm sorry you're not in full command of Korea yet, General. But the current structure is mucked up with many hands in the pie. Things are moving too slow, and our enemy is moving very fast."

Catching his breath, Nelson kept going.

"Isn't that why I was given this authority under NSOPU? It's an emergency measure that authorizes broad initiatives, which I have taken. Because, if I hadn't, your Alamo would be overrun in a week." Pausing again, "and General, I still can't guarantee that these efforts will be enough."

General Walker sat back in his chair, a blank look on his face.

An angry Colonel Nelson proceeded.

"General, I have no idea who is running this show, but from what I can see, it's a collection of ill-informed World War Two commanders that still think we have superior forces and are making independent decisions without any coordination."

"Be careful, Colonel. Are you finished?"

"No, sir. My group and our secret equipment are reading the enemy's communications in the field. They are excited about defeating us at every turn and are increasing their efforts. They've captured more than three-quarters of South Korea. Total victory, they feel, is within their grasp."

"That little Central Valley setback of theirs may have delayed them a day or two and probably cost them a regiment or more. So what! They have 80,000 men and tanks a mere 15 or 20 miles from Taejon, barreling their way down the highway. After taking Taejon, which they will, it's just a hundred miles to the new capital of Taegu, the most critical point of your northern defense line. It's the anchor for your entire defense of Pusan, just 50 miles from the harbor. We don't have much to stop them, sir."

"That's why I did what I did, sir."

"Was it you or your man in charge who ordered all this?"

"General, I'm commander of this unit, and as such, I will take full responsibility for its actions, should shit come raining down."

"As will I, Colonel. We are linked, as you know. It seems communications is always about a day or two behind events, maybe longer when crisis upon crisis piles up. Stuff happens in the heat of events. That's what I'll tell MacArthur, and if anyone persists, I'll remind them of their orders from NSOPU."

The general seemed to have blown off his steam and sat back in his chair.

"Can you do more, Colonel?"

"It's hard to believe that a master sergeant has done so much. He seems to have a way of knowing what to do next. I'm hopeful, General."

"Thanks for being honest with me, Jim. Sorry for being so irritable with you at first. It's getting pretty hairy out there, and I overreacted. It's just frustration, a fault I have. Continue your good work, but communicate with my staff more often as it looks like the Eighth Army will take over Korea in a few days."

"That is fantastic news! About time for you, General!"

Chapter Forty Seven

**Thursday, July 9, 1950 - Day Fifteen of the Invasion
Korea – Leyden's Spy Team on Hill 102 Ten Miles North of
Taejon -0900 – (9:00 am)**

The sound of planes passing near was heartening, going northeast. Toward the enemy, not far away.

"What's the feedback, Phil?" Asked Staff Sergeant Leyden. Greg was cranking on the portable charger. Phil was translating the incoming code onto paper. It was a lengthy message; in the end, he turned to Leyden.

"It sounds like the enemy took a hell of a beating in the Central Valley and are consolidating there. They'll be reinforced with another division shortly. Other intercepts confirm an enemy victory and capture of a town held by the 34th Infantry Regiment at Chonan, north of here on the Coast Highway. The 34th is falling back and intends to make a stand a few miles north of this hill."

Leyden sat back against a rock, on top of this hill, looking out over this valley, surrounded by mountain peaks for as far as he could see on this rare bright morning and wondered how much American blood would be spilled here in these desolate hills and valleys. An experienced infantryman, one that fought the Japs in the jungles, knew that mechanized warfare would soon become less critical here. It didn't work in the quagmire of the Islands, and it won't work here in the mountains of Korea. The foot soldier would do the heavy lifting.

Enemy tanks were easy targets on this highway if one had the right weapons, he thought. Not a religious man, none the less, he'd recently taken up praying and did so just now so that America would quickly bring these killing tools to bear. Then he felt confident that they would, but didn't know why. Events were counterintuitive to his belief, and so it was a matter of time. He'd seen terrible situations and knew awful things could change to favorable conditions. That was a comforting thought that he hung his hat on.

A flash roared through his mind about his whole experience here since his friend, Nick, called him into this strange hellhole of Korea. Did he know how weird it might all unfold? Did he know how it might end? Damn, he thought, he's smart, but I don't think Nick is God. But maybe he's got relatives up there. Leyden smiled at that because he remembered him being blown-up on that mine, thinking he was dead already, and only God could raise him.

Phil's yell got him out of his thoughts.

"Tom! Got an urgent incoming for you! Come quick!"

"It's from Nick."

Phil translated the code on paper as Greg continued to crank the portable generator. When finished, he acknowledged receipt, signed off. He turned to Leyden and read the message.

"Your team is now the central focus of our defense of Taejon; we rely on your tactical feedback for an effective defense. Your position is critical and cannot be replicated, and cannot be abandoned. You will be reinforced, details to follow. But I can't emphasize enough how critical and secret your equipment is and that it cannot be compromised at all costs. Counting on you, Tom. Nick."

Tom had to sit back and digest this message. His head was swirling. Is this our last stand? I got shit here with only Phil, Greg, J P, George, and me. Five men on a hilltop. Reinforced! By whom?

His men were looking at him. He saw fear in their eyes and knew he had to say something, but didn't know what. Leyden got up and decided to wing it.

"I don't know about you guys, but I like being the center of attention." He smiled, "My friend, Nick, has never steered me or us wrong, so far. So I trust him, as should you. We five here, on this fucking no-name hill they call 102, are a vital part of this whole battle for Korea."

J P was so upset he interrupted. "What about that part about the secret equipment, you know, the part about 'at all costs'?"

"Are you impaired, J P. We have in our possession the most secret equipment of our time. Have you not been here? The answer to your unasked question is YES. We will die to protect it from falling into the enemy's hands."

J P was afraid of a lot of things and complained intensely about most everything. He looked back at Leyden; his comment had hit home.

Moments of truth are rare. It comes inexplicitly from the soul, and J P's came from his.

"I don't want to die, Tom! It's bullshit! To save this country?"

Against his natural tendency to attack weakness, Tom reflected a moment.

"None of us want to die, J P. It's not preordained. Think back; we've all been through really tough situations. It's a wonder any of us are still here today. So, as my drunken Dad would often say to me after I'd got beaten up after school, 'buck up asshole, it only gets worse.'"

Greg, being the most level-headed of the group, reacted.

"Damn it, and you were doing so well until that last bit."

"Let me be clear. We are in the center of a hurricane. I'm not here to gloss over anything. But I'm also saying we have help coming, and I don't want you to lose hope. Without hope, we got nothing."

Leyden sat back and wondered if, except for his Dad's story, any of his other bullshit worked.

Chapter Forty Eight

**Thursday, July 9, 1950 - Day Fifteen of the Invasion
Korea – Rusty's Team on the Move – Mid-Morning**

In anticipation of a significant counter-attack after their success yesterday, Rusty and the South Korean forces had regrouped back to their start positions. Scouts sent out indicated there was no enemy build-up, and in fact, the North Koreans pulled their units much further back.

With this information, all forces withdrew by late afternoon to the small village a few miles south.

As soon as they got settled, Rusty sent Frenchy and Tracker plus a squad of ROK back to their communication place, to deliver a message, and get new orders.

Around 0200 (2:00 am) on Friday, July 10, Tracker returned to the village and woke Rusty, he had orders from NSOPU, Colonel Nelson's secret unit.

Rusty read the brief decoded message. Ordered to head toward Taejon and set up a defense about 10 miles north of the city, on some hill named 102 on somebody's map.

The orders ended with, "Your arrival is Urgent and Critical. Nick."

Rusty looked at Tracker and asked, "Did Frenchy see this message?"

`

Tracker smiled, "White French men are brilliant. Yes, boss. He understood, organized the dismantling of the camp. They're about an hour behind me."

They needed to leave at first light.

Rusty then woke Foxy and C J to discuss the new orders and the need to get this South Korean commander of the Central Valley troops to join them.

They finally just decided to wake him and ask him to join forces with them to defend Taejon. The purpose of which was to delay the enemy, and then start a gradual fighting withdrawal toward the new capital of Taegu.

After a brief explanation by C J, the ROK commander broadly smiled and, with enthusiasm, immediately agreed.

They left at dawn, Rusty's team at the head of about a 2,000 man South Korean force, remnants of the 3,500 men that started the defense in the Central Valley.

C J, Joe, and Tracker were on point. Nobody knew this track southeast, but there were trails, and Tracker had an internal compass that kept him going through hills, down ravines, and across streams.

By midday, hot and tired, but making decent progress, Tracker, in the lead, suddenly stopped. C J, just behind him, almost bumped into him. Joe, at the rear, heard the sound as soon as Tracker and C J went still. But it was too late.

"I got twenty men with guns on you! So don't move a fucking muscle." Shouted an American. "Speak up, or you're dead!"

Tracker recovered first. He yelled.

"You must have a true American Indian warlord with you to get the drop on me."

There was silence for a moment.

"Stand and come forward. Who are you?"

He stood, weapon down. "My name is Tracker, famous among my Tribe from the lands you took from my people. You call it Michigan."

Joe, kneeling but five feet behind Tracker, burst into laughter and yelled, "Will you ever get over it, Tracker!"

The men in cover started laughing and came out with guns at the ready, just in case.

Joe grabbed C J and moved him close to him as they followed Tracker into a small clearing, he worried they might shoot him because he was Korean.

But C J was recognized.

"I think we met at Osan," said First Sergeant 'Whitey' Dillon. "Where's your boss?"

It was C J he was talking to, and he answered, recognizing Whitey.

"Good memory, Sergeant. Glad you made it out of there. Rusty is behind us. How about your colonel?"

They came together in the clearing. Now clearly seeing the desperate condition of Whitey's men, Joe was the first to take his canteen out and give it to the closest man. C J and Tracker did the same.

The men passed the canteens around, making sure all 20 had at least a gulp. They were also starving. But the point team traveled light and had no provisions to give. They did have cigarettes, which they passed around.

Settled and sitting, Joe thought he'd break the silence that had descended like a dark cloud.

"So, Tracker, you led us into a trap. I want to know what happened to your superior Indian skills. You didn't sniff out these stinking bunch of GI's?"

Tracker stared at Joe. "Not sure what happened; think you were too close to me; they smell just like you."

It broke the gloom.

"Don't know where Colonel Smith is?" First Sergeant Whitey Dillon said, answering C J's earlier question. "When the shit came down on that ridge at Osan, I lost contact with my colonel. When we retreated from the line, I stopped at the CP to take him with us, but it was empty. I wanted to search for him but knew I couldn't. Just barely managed to get a few of my platoon out of there, then took my men into the rice paddies and then the hills. I picked up a bunch more men along the way. Been fumbling around heading southeast ever since. Four days now, I think."

"We got a big crew behind us," Said Joe, "Lots of provisions and medical care; maybe a half-hour out. You got any more men about?"

"Yeah. Fifty or so, in bad shape, not far from here. I don't even know where here is? Do you?"

"I'll defer that answer to my most trusted Indian scout."

Tracker was upset with himself on his lapse and wondered why. It was a first for him. Could have been his end, as well as his team members. Maybe, he thought, it was the relentless pressure, he just had to let it go.

"Joe! You are such a pale-faced asshole at times. But I do respect that you know who to turn to for correct information. So, with my superior skills, I will tell you, First Sergeant, that we are about eight miles from our destination, which is then about ten miles north of Taejon."

Earlier that morning, at Taejon airfield, excitement reigned. The initial 10 of the new C-119 'Flying Boxcars" started landing. The planes had the grounds crew spellbound, having never seen this new plane with its carrying capacity and odd shape. When the first rear door dropped, and a jeep rolled out with a 75mm recoilless rifle mounted in its center, the grounds crew went wild and started cheering. It was ready for battle, and it looked lethal because it was.

They loved the 11-foot long cannon mounted on it.

The thirty soldiers aboard were awed by the ferocity of the grounds crew as they rushed aboard to unload the ammunition boxes. They had to get out of their way to deplane.

These soldiers were replacements, stripped out of their 7th Division units. Some were veterans, but all had received extensive combat training, and they were pissed. Besides losing unit cohesion and being separated from their friends, they hadn't been told much except to pack heavy and be ready for immediate combat.

The 7th Division men were also frustrated seeing these jeeps because they weren't theirs; they belonged to an airborne outfit. The paratroopers crewing the jeeps told them that their Battalion was being airdropped later that day. The 7th Division guys loved these fearsome looking weapons and wished they had them.

Before these men landed in Korea in record time, a behind the scenes logistics miracle of sorts took place. Something happened when grounds crews in Japan received emergency orders from a new unknown command structure, NSOPU, with Theater Wide authority, and signed by a Master Sergeant, a man named Nick Beloit. They felt somehow empowered and emboldened.

Usually, orders were precise, put together by men and officers who had little idea of how logistics should work but were more interested in paperwork and CYA. But these orders relied on how they were to be interpreted, as they were meant to be, somewhat vague in how to do it, but just do it — for many, it was a first.

The men behind the scenes were motivated to do their thing yet rarely had the freedom to do it. And now, ranks talked across ranks and services spoke to each other. After all, most things get done below officer status, and now they didn't have to wait for paperwork. They collectively thought, if a Master Sergeant can issue these kinds of orders, well shit, we may win this war yet, if we sergeants all band together.

And so they did. Reshuffling plane loadings to maximize efficiencies and putting jeeps and artillery on C-119's instead of C-47's. It made a difference.

Chapter Forty Nine

Thursday, July 9, 1950 - Day Fifteen of the Invasion Korea – Leyden's spy team on Hill 102 Ten Miles north of Taejon - Mid-Afternoon

Earlier, Leyden's team received a message from NSOPU concerning the imminent arrival of Rusty's men sometime that day.

Rusty had never confirmed to Colonel Nelson that the ROK troops of the Central Valley would join his command.

So the sudden appearance of hundreds of soldiers coming out of the low canopy of trees and bushes from the east below, less than a quarter of a mile away, freaked out the Leyden team. There was no question of firing on them, five against hundreds?

But then Leyden, lying flat on the ground, trained his binoculars on them and saw their tattered uniforms and how disheveled they looked. Yeah, he said, must be our guys. He then rolled over on his back, looked up to the clouds, and let out a big sigh. "Thank you! Whoever you are."

The new arrivals spread around the north side of the hill, along lower ridges, setting up defensive positions. Marty directed the wounded to the south side, and with the ROK's medical team, started setting up an area to begin their work.

"So, you're my piece of shit reinforcement?" Said Leyden to Rusty in greeting at the top.

"What'd you expect? Girls and beer or the 5th Marines. Sorry! But this is it, buddy. But glad you're still around and hope you're still transmitting. And oh, you should be glad you at least got a few new friends."

Changing his demeanor, Leyden smiled, "Glad you made it too, Rusty. But fuck all if that's all you got! Because *a few new friends* ain't even near enough!"

Ranger Tully came up behind Leyden and slapped his back. "You must have major pull, asshole! Hanging out on a hill behind the action while we lowly men are out fighting at the front."

Leyden did a sharp turn to Tully, ready to rip his head off at the slight, but then saw a big grin. He deflated.

"Good to see you, Tully." Turning back to Rusty, "Sorry! Didn't mean to disrespect you, I'm just frustrated. It's good that you all survived, and we're together again. I'm sure glad you're here."

A few minutes later, Red called Tracker, Mario, Snake, and Joe together and sat on a hilltop edge that overlooked the three-mile long north valley.

"I need you to do some serious scouting, not killing."

Mario frowned.

"After scouting, Mario, I'm pretty sure your needs will be satisfied."

"Good! Been to many days."

"We came in from a roundabout route from the northeast. Find out what's in front of us in this valley and along the eastern edge along the deep forest that butts up to the ridge."

"What about that ridge?" Asked Snake.

"GI's just moved into it, falling back from up the road, think they're making a stand. We're next. Find out how the Commies can get at us. That's your mission."

The men nodded.

"You know what I'm looking for, spots where we can set up a good ambush or locations where you think they'll set up mortars, and of course, estimates of their best line of attack."

"Any bad guys out there?" Asked Joe.

"All I know is that our guys are on that far ridge about to get their asses kicked. God only knows what's in that valley. Might be good guys running. Shit, we just skirted it getting here!"

"Can we scout the ridge, maybe make contact with the 34th ?" Asked Mario.

"I don't want you getting killed by our own guys up there, but yeah, if you think it's okay, go for it. We need intel."

"Do we take any scalps if we meet any bad guys?" Asked Tracker.

"You're such an asshole! Just don't bring them back." Pausing, "Okay, Mario and Snake scout northeast on that edge. Joe, you're stuck with Tracker at the center."

"I'll be especially alert!" Said Joe.

"White men know nothing!" Said Tracker, as he rose to get his gear.

A while later, an out of breath Marty, approached Rusty.

"Any news of somebody coming? I got 60 plus seriously wounded that will die unless I can get them to a proper medical unit quickly. Can't you call Colonel Nelson?"

"Why are you breathing so hard?"

"I'm upset about these men and pretty much almost ran up this hill."

"Sit down, Marty." Rusty then turned to Leyden, "You got any info on what's coming?"

"Nothing specific, but I think major shit's going to happen around this hill. And I sure hope whatever it is, happens real soon. As I said, we need a lot more friends."

"Jesus Christ! Are you not hooked up to command, Leyden? Why don't you know?"

Leyden looked at Rusty with defiant eyes.

"Because I'm only a listening post! They don't tell me shit!"

"Larry!" Rusty cried out. His communications expert came running.

"Immediately set up and contact Colonel Nelson. Tell him we're at our objective. Further, tell him we need immediate medical transfer for over 100 severely wounded. Tell him we need reinforcements to hold this position. Ask for an approximate time of arrival. Got it?"

"Equipment's set shouldn't take too long." He went off.

Arron found a cooking area and made coffee. He somehow intuited that he shouldn't do his usual step & fetch it routine and just served to the solemn group of leaders settling in at the top of Hill 102.

Runners were coming in, relaying messages. Everybody was anxious about their new surroundings. A muted drumbeat of explosions started coming from the north that added to the tension.

After the first sip of coffee, "Damn special! Arron, thanks." Said Rusty and turned to Leyden. "What have you learned so far on this hill?"

It was a fascinating moment. Men who were mostly of equal rank, who had fought side by side, plus a South Korean commander of a significant force, all had acknowledged that Rusty, a First Sergeant, was their leader.

"So that would be Staff Sergeant Leyden, First Sergeant." Visibly upset at being put on the spot.

"I have learned that a determined superior force could overcome anything, particularly a small band of under-armed defenders."

"So, you're not a history buff?" Asked Rusty.

"My history lessons started on the streets of New York and ended on a godforsaken island in the Pacific. What's your point?"

"Remember the Alamo? How about the Battle of the Bulge? Both had low odds of success against them, yet delayed an enemy's superior force long enough for both to be defeated."

"Didn't like how that Alamo fight turned out."

"Are you afraid, Leyden?"

"Let's get this straight, Rusty." Leyden paused a moment. "I ain't ever been afraid of dying, if that's what you mean. But I'm sure as shit afraid of letting my men down."

Rusty nodded.

"Look north." Leyden said, "At the end of this valley, you'll see low ridges rising into higher hills, it's all rough terrain that flows through this valley. Only a few miles away. That's where General Dean's 24th Divisions' 34th Infantry Regiment is making a stand right now. They got there just after we set up here. They're just starting to get hammered. I give them a day, maybe two, and they'll be overwhelmed. Then the Commies will take their positions and move up their artillery and pulverize this position. And just like you, their infantry will crawl through this valley and attack this hill like ants in a sugar bowl."

It was a somber assessment for all in the circle.

A smiling Larry came running and interrupted the gloomy group.

"Good news! Within the next few hours, a regiment will be arriving. They'll have transport to take the wounded out."

First Sergeant Whitey Dillon, sitting at the edge of the group, let out a whoop! "Damn, that's good news!"

Standing up, he looked around at the group. "It's time for me to leave. I've got to help my men get ready to be taken out of here. Can't say I'll miss the upcoming fight, but I sure hope you all give'em hell and live to tell about it." Saluting the group, he said. "Good luck." Then turned and left.

Somewhat later, a subtle hum got their attention. It quickly grew in intensity from above. Most of the men knew that powerful hum — the sound of many planes approaching.

Seen now as only specs in the sky, Red called out. "Can't be bombers! They're too low and too slow."

Rusty and Tully looked at each other and smiled, pretty sure they knew what was coming.

Tully said it first.

"Damn, if it's not an airdrop! Airborne? Hoorah!"

Parachute's billowed as the wave of the first two planes approached Hill 102. Every man on the hilltop stood, transfixed at the sight of C-47's as they flew over. The number of billowing chutes growing ever larger.

The South Korean soldiers around the hill were watching this magnificent sight; something few had ever seen. They were silent, spellbound. Inwardly, most shivered at the thought of jumping out of a plane, knew that these men must be special. Then a realization hit them. These American soldiers were coming to help *them*.

"America! America!" Came a spontaneous shout from them from all around the perimeter, seeing hope floating down from the sky.

Paratroopers started landing.

Rusty was mesmerized at the sight of all those men hanging by their parachutes floating into an unknown world. He had jumped twice, on secret missions for Colonel Nelson in WW2 in France. The colonel was a major then. Yeah, he remembered the jumps and the operations. They were ugly thoughts, and he quickly swept them away.

Tully was excited, remembering his first and last Ranger jump into combat in Belgium with his battalion. A grand victory after a fierce fight.

The trooper hit hard near the edge of the hilltop and rolled. Tully watched the paratrooper expertly gather in his chute, unhook it and stuff it a small satchel.

As he approached this trooper, Tully yelled to him, "You okay, buddy?"

"Fucking mountains! Rocks suck! Yeah! Okay! Airborne yell and bitch, but I'm happy to drop in and save your ass today. Names Riley. That's First Sergeant Dan Riley."

"Welcome to Korea, Riley. Ranger First Sergeant Tully at your service. And oh, you'll not be saving anybody's ass today. Though, you might in a day or two."

"Any other guys land up here? Where's your officer?"

"A shit load of your men are landing all around this hill, but you're the first to capture it. We've got no officer here; hope you bought one."

A little later, a three man contingent showed up. They were led to the hilltop leader group.

The colonel stood somewhat awkwardly in front of the eight men.

"I'm Colonel Jeff Daniels, commander of the 3rd Battalion, 187th Airborne Infantry Regiment. Who's in charge here?"

"I am, Colonel." Rusty stepped forward. "First Sergeant Rusty Fabiano, Eighth Army, Special Operations Group, sir. I am first among equals in this group."

"What the hell! What happened to your officer?"

"Guess you haven't received a whole lot of information, sir. If you don't mind my asking, what are your orders here?"

"Who the fuck are you asking me what MY orders are, Sergeant! What is going on here?"

"Sir, we need to talk, can we please sit?" Rusty then yelled over to Arron. "Please get the Colonel and his men some coffee."

They joined the circle, Rusty introduced each man and told the colonel that they've been fighting the enemy non-stop since the invasion and finally, that they possessed Top Secret communication and spying equipment.

Colonel Daniels drew back at that last piece of information, not sure he believed it.

Rusty saw the reaction, ignored it, and went on.

"I'm sorry you jumped into a pile of crap without knowing what you're in for, Colonel. But major shit is happening very fast at our front. North Korean forces are attacking General Dean's 34th Regiment on that north ridge, about three miles from here. They'll fall back here in a day or two or perhaps they'll be overrun."

"We here are the last major line of defense for Taejon. I guess we aim to make a stand of sorts, mostly trying to slow this enemy's advance. I just got here myself. Didn't know you were coming, but you're sure welcome."

A more subdued colonel answered.

"My orders are to link up with all forces around this hill and form a defense to slow the North Koreans. How many men do you have here Sergeant?"

"We're all sergeants in this group here, Colonel, so please call me Rusty. We have about 75 American and 2000 or so ROK soldiers commanded by, well, we don't know his name or status, but a fighting commander of these troops. That's it around Hill 102. Plus a few machine guns, fewer mortars, and sparse ammunition."

"What's coming at us?'

"As best as we can tell, sir, at least five divisions heading down this road, 50,000 men with tanks and artillery."

"Damn!"

Larry interrupted. "Got a message, Rusty!"

"Excuse me, Colonel, maybe I'll have good news when I get back."

Red came over to the colonel, sat, reintroduced himself and asked, "Have you sent out scouts?"

"Of course! Both sides of the highway to that ridge."

Red chatted with him for a while, filling in some details about their experiences. Then after a pause, he asked, "Colonel, please answer this honestly, as one vet to another. Are your men good? Can they fight hard?"

The colonel knew a fellow combat man when he met one and didn't hesitate to answer an impertinent question from a sergeant, who acted as an officer, as did Rusty. He realized he'd jumped into a lousy combat situation, but felt somehow confident.

"They're pretty good, Red. Maybe 70% are lifers that chose to stay in after the war and were either in the Airborne or other special services that volunteered. The rest are combat experienced. I worked them all hard, especially dropping behind enemy lines and setting up ambushes. We're well versed in stealth operations and especially outstanding in hand to hand combat.

Red smiled, "That's good news, Colonel. These bastards you're going to meet are tough fighters; you'll need all the tricks you can conjure up."

Rusty read the translated message from Larry. At first, he was stunned, which turned to anger; then he thought it through and made a decision.

"Larry! Say nothing of this to anyone." Worried now as to how this new information would be shared, he rejoined the group.

"So, I have good news." Said a subdued Rusty. "General Dean's 21stInfrantry Regiment should be here momentarily.

They will also have replacements from the 7th Division, some 2,000 combat-trained men. The 21st will also have some artillery."

"Is there more?" Asked a very observant Tully.

"We'll talk about that later."

"Who's in charge of this overall operation?" Asked Colonel Daniels.

Rusty scratched his head.

"As far as I know, it's General Dean as overall commander of all Korean forces. But for our purposes here, we haven't heard from him. So we take our orders from the next level UP."

"Okay, I'm convinced you got some major juice, from where?"

Rusty wasn't apologetic when he said, General MacArthur. Yeah, he made a slight lie, but Rusty realized he had to get this colonel on board.

"So, First Sergeant Rusty Fabiano, are you telling me that you are in command of our forces here, at this hill, and of all of my troops surrounding it?"

"Yes, Colonel. Please don't make this an ego thing. Based on the last communication from my boss, my orders come from the same source that ordered your unit deployed here. Right now, the command function is fungible. Not bragging, Colonel, but my men and I are good at what we do, no reflection on you, sir.

"But let me be clear, Colonel." Rusty continued. "Nobody in the real Army likes your airborne elite status. So you may be sacrificed, maybe here. Let me tell you my thoughts."

"Never had a deep discussion with a First Sergeant before, so I'm game."

"You strike me as a practical man." Said Rusty. "As infantry, your paratroopers are wasted. Your purpose is to fuck up the enemy behind their lines. Red tells me you and your men are ready. Well, we need to start thinking about that now."

Pausing, he continued.

"Think attack. But we'll wait to hear from your scouts and mine when they report back. Then let's see what news is coming down from the God message. Then we'll talk."

"The God message?" Asked the Colonel.

"That's our Secret communication equipment. That's all I can say about it."

Colonel Daniels nodded. "I'm open to any plan! Because the only plan I received as orders, was no plan at all. Dig in and defend this hill? Well, that hasn't worked so far. I'll be dammed if I'll let my men sit on their asses on this hill and get their brains blown out. So I'm on board with anything that gets my men out of a fucking foxhole before they're shelled into a mass of mush."

Rusty nodded.

"Sir, I respect your concern for what's coming. We'll formulate a definitive plan when we have more information."

Looking worried, Rusty looked back at the colonel.

"Of immediate concern is the arrival of the 21st Regiment, for I fear your command will be taken over by them. I don't know that they even know that your unit is here. I'm not even sure they're in touch with General Dean's HQ."

"Colonel, knowing how this Army operates, and so you don't get compromised, I strongly suggest you move your battalion to the northeast base of this hill. Move your men in with the South Koreans, and tell your units to only take orders from you."

"Jesus, Rusty, I've got to communicate to my last unit coming up here."

"Another unit? What the hell are you talking about?"

"I've got a light artillery company coming up from the airfield at Taejon, probably tagging along with the 21st. I better get hold of them and make sure they don't get shanghaied."

"What kind of light artillery, Colonel?" Asked Rusty.

"Jeep mounted recoilless rifles, 75mm mounted cannons, to be precise. We've been training on them since the unit started."

"Damn! That is great news. How many?"

"Twenty-two jeeps, eighteen cannons."

Tully was beside himself. "As I said, I love the Airborne!"

Chapter Fifty

**Thursday, July 9, 1950 - Day Fifteen of the Invasion
Korea – Taejon Airfield - Mid-Afternoon**

From five separate airfields in Japan, planes got loaded by orders not seen before. Get everything there and get them there now! So planes carrying only soldiers were mixed in with flights loaded with supplies or ammo, and everything else an Army needs.

The small airfield at Taejon was a third world facility that became a focal point in the Korean War with just a radio shack for communications.

The planes arriving were anything but coordinated.

What started as a unit, in a flight of five planes, arrived at the same time over Taejon, but then they were ordered into a stack of circling planes without any order, to wait their turn to land. When they finally did, they found that different unit planes had landed before them and had left the airfield, thus losing immediate unit cohesion as the troops got on trucks for transport to the front.

It set the stage for the lack of order and confusion when they reached their final destination at Hill 102. The field was inadequate to allow for any lingering transport planes, so they were quickly unloaded and turned to fly out. The loading of the trucks depended on the order in which the aircraft landed, first in first out. The men and supplies piled into waiting transport.

Long lines of trucks waited just outside the airfield for their turn to drive up to the arriving planes and load up with incoming troops and or supplies, then race out to join the convoy heading north.

The convoy carrying the 21st Infantry also carried the 7th Division replacements intermingled among the trucks in no discernable order and further mixed in with supply trucks, ammo carriers, and many other vehicles.

The convoy started arriving at Hill 102 around four that afternoon. It was a sight. On the narrow highway at the base of Hill 102, sorting out what went where became an Olympic sport.

The 21st Regimental commander, Colonel Bob Doller, was an old-school man, a tank brigade commander in the last war. He accepted a demotion in status to lead an infantry regiment in peacetime Japan.

It was more a political appointment than his accomplishments warranted because he was not well regarded among his peers.

Brave but stubborn, he was a leader with little tact. His motto was 'attack,' and keep attacking. Hs unit encountered one horrible 'tank to tank' battle where luck played more in his victory than his leadership. He was a warrior more in his mind than in reality.

Overwhelming firepower and resources worked back then. But deficiency skills in organizing became apparent in a few of Colonel Doller's last engagements where high unit losses raised eyebrows and started negative whispers. His total lack of any basic understanding of defensive strategy was a known fact among those who knew him and of him. Widely known among his peers was that his old schoolboy chums from the Point and the Pentagon kept him in the service, despite his failings and got him the cushy occupation duty in Japan.

He never tried to learn how infantry tactics were different from Amour, nor did he try to acquire any defensive tactics of any sort. He had mentally checked out of the war in 1945 and never thought he would need his mind again to fight.

He was a lost soul in this new war and unfamiliar country, as was his staff, who were without any combat experience.

Colonel Doller's orders from General Dean were simple. Form a blocking position along the main highway to Taejon around Hill 102, assimilate the retreating 34th Regiment and put up a stout defense.

General Dean never received any information about the rapidly changing events around Hill 102, nothing about Colonel Nelson's involvement, NSOPU's new orders, Rusty, or the airborne drop; he got nothing. All this information was TOP SECRET, even under code, it had to be communicated to him personally in his presence, but he couldn't be located.

His love of his troops caused this problem as he frequently left his headquarters, out adjusting positions, inspecting, encouraging, and making sure his men knew their commander was concerned about them. His HQ staff often had no idea where he was.

General Dean didn't know his 21st Regimental Commander well; actually, he didn't know him at all. Colonel Doller was foisted on him from afar. Doller was a decorated colonel that led the charge in the last war, so he gave him a wide birth, with friends like he had you didn't want to piss anybody off. After all, it was peacetime. He often said, "Next to politicians, the Army is one of the last bastions of pettiness, jealousy, and animosity."

When the advanced unit of the 21st Regiment arrived at the southern base of Hill 102, they encountered a much-disheveled group of soldiers attending many wounded on the ground. The young, newly minted recon lieutenant of the 21st left his jeep and walked over to them. He'd never experienced war nor its graphic effects, and here it was all laid out for him, in filth and bloody bandages, lost limbs, young men just like him all cut to shit. He almost puked.

He saw a ragtag looking G I approaching with a First Sergeant's patch on one sleeve, no sleeve on the other arm.

"Jesus!" The LT said to the soldier. "Are these your men?"

First Sergeant Whitey Dillon just stared at him for a few seconds and finally said..."Yeah, mostly. Got some South Korean troops mixed in."

Seeing the jeep pull up from way back in the area, Marty started his run at that moment, yelling and screaming along the way to all, "You're all saved! Hospital next."

Marty reached the lieutenant.

"Your timing couldn't be better, sir!"

"It sure as hell looks that way. Who are you? And who are these men?"

"I don't have time to tell you a lot, but I'll tell you I'm a combat medic, been here since the invasion and these brave wounded men, South Koreans included, have been fighting since Osan with Colonel Smith and they need to get the hell out of here!"

The Lt called his captain, who called his battalion commander, who issued orders to immediately evacuate all wounded around Hill 102 and transport them to Taejon.

As the advance units pulled in deeper to the front of Hill 102, they became aware of some of the unexpected company they were joining. Colonel Doller thought the men around the hill were mostly South Korean stragglers or a few American survivors from the previous defeats. He had no interest in them and proceeded to direct his men to set up defensive positions on both sides of the highway and along the base of the hill.

A volunteer from Colonel Doller's staff took a jeep up to the north ridge to try to make contact with the 34th but never came back. Additional scouts left on foot.

The most significant problem of them all, caused by this loading chaos at the airfield, emerged immediately upon arrival of the 21st when the regiment unit communication vehicle had not yet arrived. Things became further mucked up when it became apparent that the signal corps units were loaded among the trucks in a haphazard pattern, a catch as catch can type of thing, not unit-centric.

Combat units were not connected to their command structure until hard lines of the signal corps are connected, and that was going to take a while. Portables were available but were problematic because they either didn't work or frequency settings had not been established or were set wrong.

Twenty minutes into the arrival of the 21st Infantry, no communications had been attempted by the newcomers to anyone stationed on top of the hill.

Chapter Fifty One

Thursday, July 9, 1950 - Day Fifteen of the Invasion
Korea – At the Base of Hill 102 – Around the Same Time

Colonel Drew Haskins was commander of the 32nd Infantry Regiment of the 7th Division. The Division had a well-deserved tainted name for being ill-prepared and lacking in discipline, but it was not his doing, and he was anything but that type of leader.

He'd been with the 7th Division since '42 as a captain, then a major. Had many decorations and was wounded twice. He cut his teeth at Makin Island in '43, then went on to battles on Saipan and then Okinawa, where he was promoted to colonel.

Haskins was a fighter, a good tactician, and a great teacher. He trained his men as best he could in the peacetime atmosphere. Considered fair, he was respected by his men and liked.

When it became clear that the peacetime leadership of the 7th Division had become a political club, he kept his mouth shut. The stuffing of incompetent officers within its ranks became a widely known fact. Limited training schedules over the years to save money coupled with sheer laziness of officers and instructors produced an ill-equipped fighting division that was recognized by senior command officers, which finely led to the decision to take it apart.

7th Division's orders were to strip out all combat-experienced trained men and assign them as replacement soldiers in the Korean Emergency Act. Then attach them to General Dean's 24th Division, under direct orders from God himself, General MacArthur.

Officers of the 7th above the rank of Captain were not going with the replacements.

When Colonel Haskins learned that these replacements would be sent directly to the front and absorbed by Colonel Doller's 21st Regiment, the first thing he said out loud, to nobody in particular, "My men will be slaughtered!" He knew this man.

He then made a decision.

He ignored orders and hid in with a few of his regimental staff officers and non-coms. He was the only senior officer from the division that went with the replacements.

When his truck finally arrived and pulled to the side of the narrow highway, MP's were screaming at them to hustle, so they quickly dismounted. Others, in front and behind, did the same. They assembled at the side of the road. Men of the 21ST moved forward. Supply trucks kept going. His group of 7th replacements were finally directed to go across the highway and wait in a field.

Colonel Haskins started thinking about the situation and Colonel Doller. Why weren't they assimilated into the 21st in Japan or here at the airport? Has it all been so rushed?

And why aren't we being assigned to the front now? Or at least have somebody here to tell us what's going on?

It was turning out to be a significant FUBAR if he'd ever seen one, and he'd seen plenty.

More men kept coming into the field. Nobody from the 21st came over. Haskins was pissed.

Standing there, watching the stupidity around him, it finally came to him. Somebody screwed up, really bad, and if he didn't do something about it, many would die.

He had thought about this as the exact reason for disobeying orders and his being here. Everything on the line, right here, my men and my life.

It had been a while since he faced this kind of moment when you knowingly place your life in harm's way. Real-life potential death that you've seen close up and experienced in a visceral, horrifying way. Most humans barely survive the trauma of the first event. Haskins campaigns through the Pacific, and finally, Okinawa was hard for a human to understand or even imagine. It was miraculous that he survived the brutality of those terrible battles, but he did. He tried hard to maintain his men's sanity and humanity, and his own. Seeing your friends die because the Japanese soldier would not surrender. They were fanatical and often fought to the last man because Okinawa was considered part of Japan and the last defense of the homeland.

The memories all came back in a rush. Only five years ago. Colonel Haskins looked around him and felt like he was right back in the worst of Okinawa, where bad leadership caused horrific death.

FUBAR! He'd seen enough and acted.

He found a captain, two lieutenants, and four sergeants and ordered them to start organizing the men in the open field into platoon units.

Haskins wondered if anyone from the 21st would start to notice the large force building up in the open field getting organized. He decided not to care.

A commanding leader, Colonel Haskins, quickly sorted his men into semi-structured units. It happened on the fly, platoons run by sergeants, some companies led by captains and some by lieutenants, and before long, they were more or less organized.

Since he had no communication equipment, the colonel set up an early system of runners between units and organized a small command staff.

Intuiting that Doller's Command Post would be on top of the hill, he sent his trusted regiment's Top, First Sergeant 'Pug' Puggliessi to find the colonel. He instructed him to inform the Colonel that he wanted his newly formed units to tie into a defensive plan, should one be available, but that he was immediately vacating the chaos around Hill 102 and heading due west.

Further, he was to tell Colonel Doller that he had no communication equipment or heavy weapons. Finally, he was to stay and direct any runner or any communication back from the colonel.

Colonel Haskins then led his reconstituted 7th Division, now a regiment-sized unit, off into the rolling hills heading west along a dirt road. Not waiting for any help from Colonel Doller, he left the division's best group of thieves behind to scour for needed equipment; food, radio communication gear, ammunition, heavy weapons, and of course, a truck or two to haul it away.

Haskins figured he'd be court marshaled sometime down the road if he survived, but didn't much care at this point.

Pug made his way up the west side of the hill, avoiding soldiers to the north and south, and although steeper, he figured the quicker in, the quicker out. He was a practical Chicago street survivor who also managed to survive two serious campaigns in the Pacific with but one minor wound, but two bronze stars for extraordinary bravery.

As he crested the top on his knees, he was winded, and was greeted by a guy with a big .45 1911 Army issue automatic pistol pointed at his face.

"Hi!" He nervously said. "Not invading, just want to visit."

The big guy bellowed a big belly laugh and dropped the gun to his side.

"Well then! You're welcome to come forward as long as you say who you are."

He did and then said his unit.

Red was quiet for a moment. "You're with the 7th Division? Are they here?"

"No. Who are you? I'm looking for Colonel Doller, isn't he here?"

Red shook his head. "Follow me, you got some explaining to do, Pug."

Red briefly filled Pug in on who was in charge so as to save time.

"Who sent you up here?" Asked Rusty.

"Colonel Haskins, sir, commander, 32nd Infantry Regiment, 7th Division, my boss."

"I thought only replacements were coming, not a full regiment?"

"The regiment is not here, only replacements. My colonel is not even supposed to be here. He's furious about all this replacement shit, felt the politics of the War Department fucked his Division. Anyways, he knows this guy, the 21st colonel, thinks he's an idiot. He was hoping to save his men from being killed."

Rusty and the men smiled at this. "We know this colonel as well." Said Rusty. "Were you to report in?"

"Yes, sir. He thought Colonel Doller would be up here. I'm to tell him that my colonel has taken command of the 7th Division replacements as a unit and was marching west to add to the defense of Hill 102. He further requested communications equipment, heavy weapons, and ammunition."

"Your colonel has some balls, Pug!" Said Red

Pug nodded his head with a smile. "He's got big ones! Been with him since Saipan, and I can attest to that."

"Well, that's good because that attitude is going to come in handy pretty damn soon." Said Colonel Daniels.

"No offense to anybody here, particularly you, Colonel, but a First Sergeant named Rusty seems to be in charge. Am I wrong?" Asked a confused Pug.

Colonel Daniels laughed, which startled Pug.

Rusty leaned in, "I can see why Colonel Haskins has confidence in you, just as my boss has confidence in me. I'll keep the answer to your question very brief because we don't have much time. Yes! I am the de facto leader of this operation around Hill 102 by orders that supersede General Dean's, with some restrictions."

"What are they?" Asked Pug, awed, but weary.

"Neither my boss nor I can take control of Colonel Doller's regiment without General Dean's approval. But we can't locate him."

Pug looked over at Colonel Daniels for conformation, who said, "Son, I'm just as dumbstruck as you. But Rusty is surely in charge, and I'm following his orders."

"Damn!" Was all he could say, then asked, "What do you want me to tell Colonel Haskins?"

"Tell him we're working on a plan, and he'll be part of it. I can't tell him how, but we know what the enemy is going to do next, and he should be prepared to move on my orders."

"We'll give you a long range radio preset to our frequency, complements of our airborne friends. Under no circumstances are you to encounter any of Colonel Doller's men. Can you do this?"

"Yes. I'm very good at avoiding trouble."

Rusty laughed. "Pug! You're here on Hill 102! So you didn't do a very good job on that score, my friend."

Pug strapped on the new advanced portable radio on his back, pocketed extra batteries for it, then stashed a detailed map of a large western quadrant of Hill 102 in his jacket, all compliments of Colonel Daniels.

As he was leaving, Pug turned, "Damn! A first sergeant commanding a battle!" With a big smile, he was off and laughed as he went over the hill.

Chapter Fifty Two

Thursday, July 9, 1950 - Day Fifteen of the Invasion Korea – Hill 102 – Ten Miles north of Taejon – Late Afternoon

The 187th Airborne Jeep Light Artillery Company could have parachuted in with their battalion, but clearer thinking prevailed and concluded that terrain around the hill was too rough, and an airfield was nearby.

Jeep artillery was relatively new and perfectly fitted to quick-reaction forces like the airborne. This weapon saw some action at the end of WW 2, and the Army recognized its usefulness, and built on its potential by organizing them into complete company-sized units.

The 187th was one such unit and was formed in 1948 from remnants of the disbanded airborne divisions after the war when more enlightened generals realized that airborne forces were here to stay. It, and Colonel Jeff Daniels 3rd Battalion of the 187th Airborne Regiment had trained together ever since.

A lethal weapon, the 75mm recoilless rifle mounted on a jeep, could fire a 'Heat' round that could penetrate 4 inches of armor plate, powerful enough to knock out any tank in the world. Besides its power, it had range, 7,000 yards. So it could hide at a distance and kill from afar. A conventional 'HE' (high explosive) round was also available for anti-personal and similar artillery use.

They followed at the back end of the 21ˢᵗ Regiment's truck convoy, arriving at the south side of Hill 102 late in the day. It had been a slow, dusty, and hot journey. Captain Les Baker, Commander, was in a foul mood when he pulled the unit off the highway to wait. Part of the reason was that he felt uneasy about orders he had received earlier, in route to the hill. The radio communications from his boss, Colonel Daniels went like this;

"Les! Under no circumstances are you to take any orders unless I give them!" A pause. "The 21ˢᵗ may try to hijack your company. You are not to allow this. Proceed to the south side of the hill and await my orders."

Captain Baker sat on the side of the highway for a long while, activity all around. The dull sounds of artillery explosions out of the north, echoing through the valley created unease. He watched as clouds rolled in with gratitude, as they brought some relief from the heat. When the clouds settled over the hilltops surrounding this valley, he wondered about the conflicting duty he now faced. Never before had anything like this happened to him.

He decided not to dwell on the issue because he trusted his colonel.

So here he was, waiting at some godforsaken hill that nobody in history will ever remember.

He thought of his men lined up behind him, four soldiers per jeep, all experts at their jobs, sitting and sweating, knowing this was going down to the wire. Airborne or not, they were scared. Action was coming and coming soon.

A young major soon came over to his jeep and told him that he was with General Dean's 24th Division's 21st Regiment, and a member of Colonel Doller's staff, who sent him to find out about this unit.

"You're Airborne?" Said the surprised Major.

"There seems to be some of you around here, and we don't know anything about it. Your unit looks like it could help us out here defending this highway. Please come with me, Captain, to talk to my colonel so we can coordinate this fight."

Captain Les Baker was a Bronx boy, all of 27 years old and a decorated combat veteran of the 101st Airborne Division in the Big War. And he had his orders.

Realizing that this major was his age and had never seen a battlefield, let alone a fistfight, he figured this guy had no idea what was going on around this hill, so he decided to go street smart bullshit.

"Major! I think you're confused and maybe ill-informed. But I've been ordered here by a higher power than you, sir. So unless you have orders from *MY* colonel or higher, I'm not moving. So Major, please go away! I'm asking nicely."

The major was taken aback. "Jesus, Captain, we're about to engage a superior enemy, and we need your support and coordination. Please come and report to my regiment's commander."

Captain Baker got out of the jeep and came within a foot of the major. "Please leave, Major."

"Are you threatening me, Captain?"

"No, sir! I just wanted to express my displeasure at the major's demeanor when confronted with overriding orders, when the major, of superior rank, should have known better, *sir.*"

He did have a smirk when he said it.

"You asshole!" Said the major, as he lifted his right arm to deliver a roundhouse to this insulting lesser ranked officer. He had no idea who he was assaulting and paid the price. Airborne had a rule. Attack me, you suffer.

After lifting the embarrassed major off the ground, the captain continued to hold him tight, focusing on his eyes. "Sir! I'm glad you didn't hurt yourself when you tripped. It can be dangerous out here. I suggest you go someplace safe because the next time you might not be so lucky."

The rain began slowly, light, but steady. The Korean's all knew it was going to be something. American's were only beginning to learn about the local weather and the Monsoon season.

Soon after this incident and well after Pug had left to rejoin Colonel Haskins, the men at the top of Hill 102 came to some decisions.

Colonel Daniels called Captain Baker.

The 187th Light Artillery Company got their orders and was on the move. Twenty-two vehicles and eighty-eight men turned around on the highway and headed south for a half a mile, then made a right onto a dirt road heading west into rough country of steep hills and narrow potholed, dirt roads.

As they progressed, the rain fell harder, and the road became steeper with sharp zigzagging turns. Dangerous rock outcroppings and water ravines were racing across, digging ever deeper trenches to bump across, it was slow going.

About a mile or so in, Captain Baker came to a bend, with a level clearing and a view, so he stopped.

Even with the heavy rain, he could see the highway north up the valley to almost the ridge.

Baker exited into the pouring rain and proceeded to the jeep behind him.

"First Sergeant!" He called to the man sitting at the door. He came out and stood in front of his captain, in the pouring rain.

"Your 3rd Platoon is to set up here and defend Hill 102 and this highway. Spread your men anywhere around here that gives cover. Sure as shit, you're going to get hell coming in. Enemy tanks are going to come right down that highway. You're going to take them out!"

The veteran sergeant stood in the rain and smiled, "Do my best, sir!" Then saluted. "Captain! Been proud to serve with you." He quickly turned to position his jeeps. He didn't think he'd ever see his captain again.

Les watched him walk away for a few seconds, understanding his meaning. Then he got back in his jeep and waved to his driver to go. He had his orders but thought about his best non-com and friend.

The going remained slow for quite a while as the terrain was tough. Then it seemed to settle into many more miles of a twisting pattern on a very narrow mud road, of up and down driving. The heavy rain made visibility difficult but manageable. Although it was late, the summer sun had still not set, so it was still light through the dark clouds.

They were surprised when they crested a hill and popped up on a flat plain, proceeded about a mile to a sharp bend in the road, and ran into serious men with weapons pointed at them.

A young lieutenant approached.

"Nice day for a ride in the country, Captain! Welcome to 7th Division left-overs western headquarters."

"I was starting to think we were lost. You the rear guard?"

"Yes, sir. Good thing Colonel Haskins told us you were coming; had a run-in with a North Korean scout team already. We're on high alert. If I can squeeze in the back, I'll take you to our CP. It's about a mile or so up the path on the right."

A short time later, they passed a duce and a half without its canvas cargo cover parked way off behind a group of big rocks. "Why is that truck there?" Asked Baker.

"Oh." Said the lieutenant, "Before we left, we needed to borrow needed equipment from the 21st, so we left behind a few guys to gather it up. Then they borrowed the truck. Good thing too, that canvas cargo cover is now our CP tent."

Chapter Fifty Three

**Thursday, July 9, 1950   Day Fifteen of the Invasion
Korea – On top of Hill 102 – Early Evening**

The bright early morning became cloudy by midafternoon, then turned dark and finally led to a deluge by late afternoon. It was, after all, monsoon season. Beautiful days were rare. It doesn't rain all the time, but it usually threatens most every day with low clouds with days filled with high humidity, even in the higher elevations.

Under a makeshift shelter, with the faint sound of explosions miles away, echoing down the valley as a backdrop, the leaders on Hill 102 sat.

Rusty stood. "So you all know how fucked up our command structure is right now. Colonel Doller can't coordinate a goddamned defense of this hill!" He was furious, red-faced. "Well, that's what Eighth Army is NOT about! So let's get to it!"

Everybody's nerves were raw, and they were all pissed.

Earlier, when it became apparent that nobody was in charge and those that thought they were, had no idea what they were doing, Rusty sent off an SOS message to Nick at NSOPU at Colonel Nelson's unit, detailing the FUBAR unfolding and requesting advice. He also adamantly refused their prior collective order to withdraw his Post team, which he had not shared with anybody.

As the meeting continued after Rusty's heated beginning, Ranger Tully angrily asked, "Where's General Dean?"

Still standing, Rusty calmed himself. "Doesn't matter, Tully, not sure his presence at this point would make a difference. General Dean was dealt an aces and eights hand when he arrived here. He never had a chance."

"But here we are."

Airborne Colonel Daniels spoke up. "I still feel weird being organized by a bunch of sergeants, but you guys seem to be the only ones that know what the hell is going on here, and I respect the fact that you have major command connections. Besides, your advice to move my battalion to this hill's front was most prescient as the newly arrived 21st Regiment's Colonel wanted to spread out my men along the highway. I told him I had my orders. I don't think this man has any idea of defensive tactics. So I'm all in."

Rusty, still standing, responded.

"Thank you, Colonel, for your trust in my team and me. Your men will play a pivotal role in what's coming. So your belief is vital.

"Are you all hearing that noise up north? That's General Dean's 34th Infantry Regiment getting pulverized by enemy artillery. I don't intend to experience that same fate. I've been here before and, although we have a few standout tacticians, like our Ranger Tully, few compare to Red, my right-hand man. A uniquely talented man and a brilliant tactician. I have trusted him with my life, and he's not failed me yet. Hear him out."

He nodded to Red, who stood as Rusty sat.

"I ain't Jesus!"

The tense gathering was still anxious as nobody laughed.

"None of our scouts have returned yet, so we don't have a detailed tactical situation plan. But what we do know is what the enemy's strategic plan is."

That got everybody's attention.

"The North Korean's have moved a division to the west and another further east to bypass our 34th Regiments defensive line and try to envelop their and our hill positions. They want to capture or destroy all defenses in or around Taejon."

"How do you know this?" Asked a troubled Airborne Colonel.

Rusty looked at them. "Because we got God's ears here, and that's all I can say."

The noise of the rain intensified the silence of the men under cover of the tent.

During this whole confab, C J had been quietly translating everything to the South Korean Valley Commander, who'd been quiet.

He'd witnessed America's help in saving his men in the valley and watched the American men jumping out of planes and thousands of soldiers moving in from trucks into positions to stop his enemies.

At the end of C J's last translation, he stood.

Still standing, Red didn't know what to do when the ROK commander stood, so he sat down.

In Korean, he spoke; C J immediately stood next to him and translated.

"Thank you for coming to help us! It's an important battle coming here, but it is only a small fight in a much bigger war that only you can win. My men and I are not stupid. Without your help, we'd be all dead in the valley. We'll never be able to save our country without America. So we must prove to you that we are worthy of your support. If you approve, I will lead my men to intercept the Eastern North Korean Division. It's probably the same unit that attacked us in the valley." He nodded to C J and sat down.

Rusty got up. "Thank you, Commander. We don't have a lot of time, but the good news is that this rain will slow their troop movements. Red hasn't finished his assessment of an overall plan, so I want him to give you his thoughts. Go, Red."

"We have the advantage here!"

"Oh shit!" Said a disbelieving Tully.

"I know you think I'm crazy, but hear me out." Red shifted his stance.

"First: we know precisely what these divisions and their battalions are planning to do next. I can't tell you how we know, but we do. Second: the North Koreans think we are defeated and that we have no fight left in us. Third: they don't know that more than two Regiments have reinforced us. I suspect they saw the parachute jump, so they're aware some support showed up but nothing that would cause them concern. But they think they have overwhelming manpower and tactical advantage, and defeating us will be pretty straightforward.

Pausing now to collect his thoughts, he continued.

"What *we* have is a bold plan and tactical surprise. The Commies will never expect us to attack, and that's what we will do against that ridge, right after the 34th Regiment abandons it or is about to. We will do it at night in a stealth attack. Our force will consist of Rusty's team and the entire Airborne Battalion."

"Also, Colonel Daniels has ordered his Light Artillery Jeep Company West to reinforce Colonel Haskins 7th Division's replacement unit and will prepare to ambush that North Korean Armored Division coming his way. I think our South Korean Valley Commander has the right idea about moving to ambush that Eastern North Korean Division that is trying to outflank us. We should coordinate with him and give him support."

Red stopped and looked at the silent men.

"Damn!" Said Colonel Daniels.

"Oh! I like this, Red." Said Tully.

After the translation, the South Korean commander nodded his understanding and smiled.

Chapter Fifty Four

The listening posts around the hill had been alerted to be aware of friendly scouts or other friendly retreating 34th soldiers that may filter into their lines. But that was a difficult task. The hard rain precluded any soft noise, and every post was jumpy and on high alert. The explosions in the north kept everything real for the men in the valley and around Hill 102.

All of the South Korean soldiers out front on the edge of the hill were no strangers to the cunning of the North Korean Special Forces. They usually preceded a night attack by infiltrating defensive lines and brutally slitting the throats of all who were not alert.

Everyone was jittery.

Some men from the 34th did filter down the highway carrying wounded buddies. Most were in shock. Others came by way of the valley. The terrible rain made it almost impossible to identify approaching soldiers until they were very close.

Under these extremely stressful circumstances, some Americans were shot by ROK soldiers in the valley.

`

Being near his men and responding to the gunfire, the South Korean commander came to walk among his troops at the very front, to reassure his men, telling them not to be trigger happy. "Please don't kill Americans! We do not expect an attack tonight."

Later, the ROK commander made his way back to the hilltop and sat under the small tent by himself. A few minutes later, Foxy came along and sat near him. "Can't sleep, sir?" Foxy asked in Korean.

"Were you born here?" He replied.

"I was born in Chicago, America. My mother is from here, and my grandmother still lives here." Hesitating. "I hope she still lives."

"Where is your grandma?"

"She lives in Seoul, but I warned her to get out before the invasion. I don't know if she did or not. I hope she did. If so, she's with a relative near Pusan."

"Have good thoughts; she is there. I've never been to America, do you like it."

"It's a strange and wondrous place, like nothing else in the world. It has its good and bad like everywhere, but it's unique, difficult to describe."

"I've only met a few Americans. They are different. I like what I see so far."

"Even though I'm half Korean, I'm an American, as are the Black and Hispanic soldiers you see around the hill and oh, yeah, Japanese, Chinese… well, people from every part of the world that have come to live in my country."

"I can't imagine that. How does everyone get along?"

"Sometimes they don't, but mostly they do."

"Do you trust your leader, Rusty?"

"Completely. He's a good man, smart and has a heart."

"That's how I feel about him."

Foxy thought about this guy, how well he spoke, his insightful questions, and concern for his grandma. He's well educated. I think he's more then what we think he is. Why does his men follow him but won't speak of him? He doesn't have any rank designation on his uniform; why? Why doesn't he say who he is? Foxy concluded that this man was something special, a leader, and in hiding. Yes, he thought, the only explanation for his actions.

The scout team of Joe and Tracker made their way back into the hilltop tent, miserably wet, muddy, and somewhat upset as Joe reported to Red.

"The mission you sent us on is detailed and mapped for all attack routes and potential mortar positions. We got close to that pass, 34th Regiment trucks lined up off-road on both sides, some burning, but most looked workable. Heavy artillery fire all around that pass drove us off. Don't know how our guys up there are holding on."

Later, Snake and Mario reported a little later that their recon up the Eastern edge was productive. They found deep forests at the northern side of the valley that looked impenetrable, but by exploring deeper, they found a path farther in that led to a blind spot with access to the very end of the ridge.

Moving onto the ridge from there, they made brief contact with a wounded sergeant from the 34th. He didn't know much except that they were preparing to withdraw soon, maybe tomorrow, but he didn't know. They told this sergeant that Hill

102 was now heavily defended; that the route for a withdrawal down the highway was open. Mario recalled his last words before they left, "My colonel is a fighter and won't give up this ridge easily."

The tarp on the improvised CP of Hill 102 kept them dry, but the sound of the rain was furious. Colonel Daniels had come equipped with so many maps it had become a joke, but a welcome one, because everyone else had zero, not even a drawing, of anything south of the capital of Seoul.

A detailed aerial map of their area was laid out on an empty crate for all to see.

Earlier, they spent a lot of time talking to the scouts, questioning them as to the maps and their impressions.

Mario's probing and report stood out, especially his answer to a critical question.

"Yes, the eastern edge of the valley has access to a blind spot on to the ridge."

A continuous feed from CIA Japan, translated from Staff Sergeant Leyden's team intercepts about enemy movements soon prompted questions and affected their tactical decisions. Since they had no contact with General Dean's 34th Infantry Regiment, the only information they could gather about what was going on at the ridge just a few miles north of Hill 102 was from enemy intercepted transmissions.

The secret equipment developed by the CIA to capture radio frequency transmissions used to decipher enemy communications in the field, between individual units, was impossible until the CIA broke the North Korean military code right before they invaded South Korea.

The CIA quickly assembled teams of analysts to translate the coded messages. The North Koreans used wireless transmission to communicate from headquarters down to battalion level, opting to mostly use hardline or runners from battalion down through company and below.

All transmissions from different North Korean units used a unique radio frequency. As the days progressed and more enemy divisions came within range of being intercepted by this equipment, the CIA became overwhelmed. They quickly responded by adding more critical personnel.

Then a master sergeant asked a simple question. Why can't we transmit this tactical information we collect back to our commanders in the field?

Realizing the incredible potential this could give our field commanders, if they could get this information in a timely fashion, the CIA ramped up their efforts in a herculean effort.

It was a daunting task.

All frequencies could be captured within a 10 to 15-mile radius of this secret equipment; each North Korean division would generally have upwards of 15 different radio frequencies. If there were six Divisions within range as there were around Hill 102, then 90 radio frequencies would be intercepted.

On the back end, it required that the CIA find out which ones were significant enough to monitor until they had enough human resources to monitor all the frequencies.

But that was only half of the equation. Making sense of it and getting that information back to a field commander who could use the data was the key.

And that's what the CIA figured out. With an unlimited budget and an answer to how we might not get kicked out of Korea. All thanks to Master Sergeant Nick Beloit, asking a simple question many days ago.

When the 21st Regiment started showing up, Rusty had ordered his team's expert electronics guy, Larry, and two of his best thieves, Arron and Foxy, to go down the hill and steal some of the portable radio equipment, since they had none. He knew that these 21st guys were not going to share.

It was the right decision, and they were successful in stealing eight radios and extra batteries.

Before finally closing his eyes, Rusty rested under the shelter, trying to comprehend the enormity of events unfolding around him. Then he tried to focus. Rusty thought it was beyond odd that nobody from the 21st came up to see what they were defending nor to see what this hilltop had to offer as an observation post. He was disgusted at the poor tactical showing below and lack of any military sense on their own unit's deployment. Rusty became even more distrustful of Colonel Doller and his decisions concerning his 21st Regiment. He thought him incompetent.

Just as dawn was breaking, the command group reconvened under the tarp in the continuous downpour.

Larry had handled the communication equipment all night with Moose on the foot pedal electric generator. He had new information that had come in earlier and came to the group.

"This came in about an hour ago. I didn't wake anyone because I thought you all could use a little more rest. It's feedback from intercepts of units fighting our guys, says that the 34th is putting up a staunch defense and that the rain is hindering the enemy's envelopment plans."

Red looked around at the group, "We need more information, but delaying the enemy is a good thing."

Leaning against the wall of a trench on top of Hill 102, Joe and sniper Dean tried to figure out how to keep their boots from being overwhelmed by the buildup of water. They started laughing.

"Just like old times." Said Joe.

"Yeah, I forgot just how much I missed them again." Said a snarky Dean. "At least you were warm in the Pacific."

Joe scowled. "Jesus! You are misinformed, my friend. Yeah, I had a one hot jungle fight. It was short, terrible, and a prelude of what was to come. And then there was Okinawa; a harsh but beautiful place; mountains, rivers, a lot like here. Temps varied from the valley areas of 80 or so to the high ridges of around 40. And yes, I had tropical gear. I froze my ass off. So fuck you with that European cold weather bullshit."

They laughed and then got out of their trench to find some coffee. Arron had set up a little tent over a cooking fire in his particular way, coffee brewing. The command group had taken their coffee earlier; stragglers like themselves were showing up at random. It continually amazed Joe that Arron had enough coffee and enough food for all. Usually, the food was good, but the coffee! It was always heavenly.

After a few sips, Joe got serious. "Today might bring us some bad shit, Dean. You think we're ready?"

"Ready? I think you and I are ready for just about anything. As to the rest of what's going on, I haven't a clue."

"Hope for the best and plan for the worst is my motto. Hell! I've been in more crap here in less than three weeks then I saw in two years of fighting in Europe."

"So, let me ask you a question, Joe. Have you ever been around a more shit kickin' outfit in your life?"

Joe laughed. "Got me there!"

Chapter Fifty Five

**Friday, July 10, 1950 - Day Sixteen of the Invasion
Korea – On Hill 102 – Just after Dawn**

The downpour was continuous and showed no letup. Larry busted into the command group under the tent with a new message. From CIA HQ in Japan, he said. It relayed the latest enemy movement. Rusty read Larry's translation and went to the map on the crate box in their center and then addressed the group.

"We now have a clearer picture of their line of attack. Not too different from what we expected, just a bit more powerful."

Red raised his head, and with a squint in his eyes, he asked. "Just how much more powerful?"

"Well, it's a relative term, Red." Rusty nodded to his best defensive tactician. "It all depends on how you look at it?"

Tully looked at Foxy and then at their paratrooper colonel to see if they bought this bullshit. Their faces said it all.

"Don't spin this, Rusty!" Said Red. "It's bad, isn't it? So get on with it!"

"You're a pain in the ass Red, but you're right in one respect. The enemy just added another division to swing to the west with multiple developmental orders. They want to outflank the 34th Infantry's retreat and crush this mountain bastion in a two-pronged assault from the west and the south with these forces. That's about 20,000 men at CIA's best guess."

Red, being Red, said. "So that's in the west. They have to break up their formations to achieve all their goals. Even with the added force, that road out west of us sucks, it's narrow, and the terrain favors the defense. This rain will bog them down. What else have you've not told us?"

Rusty stood tall with his head hitting the top of the tent, the rain careening off the sides. He had to speak loud.

"You're special, Red. These commie assholes have made it a point to kill us all here! I think they're overconfident. But yeah, there's more. They're moving another division to the east to do another envelopment maneuver to this mountain, with another added element to go straight on to Taejon."

C J translated the message into the ROK's Commander's ear, who then rose and spoke forcefully. C J started to interpret to the command group

"My command will meet this eastward movement!"

"Damn! I like this guy." Said Tully. "What the hell's his name?"

To the surprise of everyone, no one knew. C J was embarrassed and asked the ROK commander.

The ROK commander, still standing, answered, with C J translating.

"My name is Choe U, General of the Republic of Korea's 1st Infantry Division. Unlike many of my peers, I have many years of combat experience. I was a Korean major general in the Japanese Army that fought against these communist bastards in China. I want a free Korea. My men and I have fought this invasion from the border to here. I have lost a good deal of my men, but since you Americans came in, everything's changed. Our spirits have revived. We now think we have a chance! But it's on us to play a major role in this fight for our country."

The silence at the end of General Chou U's speech was overwhelmed by the monsoon rain hammering on their tent, water now flowing around their boots.

Rusty got up and went to the ROK general, saluted him, then grabbed his shoulders. At first, he was tense; then Chou U relaxed, knew what it meant, then grabbed Rusty's shoulders with quick recognition.

Facing him, Rusty asked, "General, is this all that's left of your division?"

Translating the response, C J said, "What I have here are remnants of two regiments. My third regiment was sent into the mountains, farther east of here, on the east side of the Central Valley. I lost contact with them some time ago."

"Do you think you could link up with them?"

"I don't have communication equipment to do that, nor do I know if they do either."

"Maybe we could find out." Said Rusty.

"Larry!" He came quickly. "Contact Colonel Nelson, see if he has any contact with South Korean 1st Division forces in or around the Central Valley. Make that any ROK forces in that area."

"Got it." He went off.

"General, please wait until we receive word back from my command."

Red stood up. "I think we need to act boldly and take advantage of the gifts we've been given. This bad weather, the enemy's troop movements, and the determined resistance of our guys on the ridge. These gifts won't last long; we need to act now!"

The group nodded, and Rusty said, "Okay, Red, tell us what you have in mind."

"I said it before; we support Colonel Haskin's 7th Division's unit in the west to ambush the North's units driving down that narrow road and blocking them from turning our flank. We send General Chou U's force to intercept the eastern forces trying to do the same thing. Hopefully, he can hook up with additional ROK forces in the area."

Pausing, Red saw the intensity in the men's faces.

"We and Colonel Daniels men will attack the ridge and relieve the 34th, then break up the North's advance down the highway. We should do all this early tonight."

But for the rain, there was silence.

Finally, Rusty said, "I don't see another choice. We either do something that gives us a chance to delay them, and maybe get our asses out of here alive, or we wait here to get slaughtered."

Colonel Daniels stood up and said, "Rusty, I suggest my battalion number two get with Red and your men to plan our assault on the Ridge."

"Let's start now." Said Rusty.

It was late morning when the shout came. "Colonel!" His com man interrupted the group. "Got listening post # 1 on the line, they're just off the highway, mile and a half out, says it's important." He handed him the phone from his backpack unit.

"Colonel Daniels." Listening for a few moments. "Can they make it back here?" A pause. "Ask him if this is the start of a general withdrawal." A pause. "Wait. Ask him how far out their perimeter is now." A pause. "No, hold your position, and stay sharp. Good job, corporal!"

"Damn!" Said the colonel, as he looked around the group.

"Two wounded were questioned walking down the highway. One was in pretty bad shape and was being carried by the other guy who had a bad arm wound. Their captain was KIA. The LT that took over command of their company just ordered all wounded off of the Ridge. Severely wounded are being loaded onto the few vehicles they have left."

Rusty watched Colonel Daniels digest his thoughts. Everybody in the group stayed silent.

"He's a private, the soldier carrying his sergeant and is not aware of any general withdrawal orders, but he expressed how fucked up his company was, and how few of his men were left. My guy thinks he was in partial shock. He was on the perimeter when he was wounded early this morning and thinks he was about a half-mile out, maybe a mile at most. He wasn't positive because they kept falling back through the night."

"Oh, my guy said he spotted a few more soldiers walking down toward him."

Colonel Daniels looked around at the group. "This is bad! Somebody in the 34th fucked up. I think they waited too long.

They're about to be overrun." He shook his head, thinking of the loss of their men.

Rusty was thinking of something else.

"Colonel!" Rusty snapped. Daniels mind came to full attention.

"Get Colonel Doller on the line. You met him. Tell him the ridge is about to be overrun. They need supporting fire from his artillery. We now know the 34th perimeter is one mile or less from the ridge. That's a minimum of five miles from that battery of 105s, of Doller. Those guns have a seven-mile range. Tell him to order his guns to open fire at maximum range and slowly walk it back two miles. Those guns are very accurate. It might break up the attack and maybe give the 34th more time to retreat in some order."

Red chimed in. "And give us some cover for our little excursion!"

The overheard phone conversation between the colonels was heated for a while until Colonel Daniels pointed out that the North Koreans would soon be at Colonel Doller's front door and that the more 34th infantrymen he could save would soon be fighting alongside his 21st Regiment.

Within minutes, the six-gun battery commenced firing. They had amassed a large stockpile of shells, so they were in rapid-fire mode. The booms of their cannons firing were exhilarating to all on the hilltop.

At the same time, Rusty sent Tully, with Moose as his escort, down the hill to inform Colonel Doller of the significant change in the defensive situation developing around Hill 102.

They weren't greeted well at the 21st CP entrance. Moose stayed outside. Tully, being his Ranger self, barged into the 21st

Command Post's inner tent. A startled Colonel Doller rose behind his improvised desk. Indignant, "Who are you?"

Tully was not short of words. "I've come to save your reputation, Colonel."

"What the hell are you talking about? Tell me who sent you?"

After a few heated words and a brief about who he and his team were and their command structure, Colonel Doller listened to the tactical dispositions taking place.

Colonel Doller was stunned. "So, let me see if I got this right. An Army first sergeant has ordered an Airborne Battalion to leave its assigned defensive position to stage an attack against an overwhelming enemy force. In addition, he's allowed a substantial ROK force to abandon **its** defensive position to attack a similar superior enemy force somewhere in the east. Did I get this right so far, First Sergeant Tully?"

"Yes, sir. So far, so good. His name is Rusty, sir." Tully was pissed at this asshole and was trying to contain himself.

"And then this Sergeant Rusty took control of my 7th Division replacements and sent them off on another offensive mission. That leaves me here with my regiment alone. I should have you and this Rusty shot for insubordination."

That was it for Tully. A Ranger could only take so much horse shit. "Colonel! Usually, I would address an officer that I disagreed with, with the praise 'with all due respect,' but I won't here, because I don't. My opening comment when I came here was that 'I've come to save your reputation,' but it's clear I can't."

Pausing to constrain himself, Tully continued.

"I know your orders, Colonel, and they did not include the ROK force that First Sergeant Rusty brought in, nor did they include the Airborne Battalion that our Eighth Army boss ordered deployed. As to the 7th Division replacements, well, I think you need to look into how you handled that. They certainly have a colonel that knows how to organize, and by my guess, knows how to fight."

Colonel Doller face was blood-red, about ready to explode, but he was now scared.

"Let me leave you with one name, should you want to go up the chain of command. Master Sergeant Nick Beloit. A big deal in Eighth Army and a friend of General MacArthur."

"And, oh, if you want to coordinate your defense here, have your staff contact us. We're at the hilltop now, but we'll be moving very soon, before the enemy starts shelling the shit out of this location."

Pausing, Tully looked into the stunned face of the very angry Colonel Doller and said, "Thank you for listening to Colonel Daniels, it will help."

Before any response, Tully turned and left.

Outside, Moose asked, "So, how did it go?"

Tully turned to Moose as they walked away. "Remember that bridge we blew up with all those North Koreans marching across, where we killed many but it didn't stop the advance. Well, it seemed like that, just a short term high."

Late that afternoon, at the hilltop CP, Larry came into the group. "Message just received, Rusty." He read his note. "Confirm ROK forces eastern Central Valley, approximately 15 miles due east from your position. Elements of 1st and 5th ROK Divisions are heavily engaged with the enemy."

After C J translated, General Choe U rose. Got ramrod straight and saluted the group and said thanks, turned, and left.

Red got up, "C J, follow me." Away from the group, Red told C J, "Tell General Choe U that he is crucial to the defense of Taejon and his tactical attack is important to delay the enemy. But his troops must survive and fall back. Remind him that this is early in the war, and America is here to stay. And C J, ask him if he has communications to us? If not, get him one of those new radios that we stole."

C J stopped. Made a decision he'd been thinking about for a while. "Red, it's time I fought alongside my own Army. I'm going with General Chou U. I'll convey your message, and I'll take a radio. Thank you. It's been an honor to serve with you, Rusty and the rest of the men. Please tell them so."

Colonel Doller was not an idiot. Now having been forewarned of the massive change about to take place in his front defensive line, he started issuing orders. He also ordered that a communication link be setup to Rusty's command.

"Colonel Daniels, are your teams ready?" Asked Rusty.

"Nevermore than now!" Said the colonel to the first sergeant.

"I think we should leave shortly."

Rusty started issuing orders.

"Larry, come with me." They went to the secret equipment.

"Get a setup going to Colonel Nelson." Moose was standing by at the portable electric generator. "Larry, I'm going to dictate a detailed message about what we intend to do here.

"After I finish, wait for an acknowledgment, then pack up. Then you and C J's *One* are getting your asses out of here. We'll meet you in Taejon tomorrow or the next day. Can't gamble on getting this equipment captured or destroyed."

After finishing with Larry, Rusty found Staff Sergeant Tom Leyden.

"Leyden! Your team is out of here as of now. You're going somewhere south of Taejon, where you can continue to help us. I don't want you captured or killed here. Confirm you're leaving to Colonel Nelson. Gather your equipment. You've got ten minutes. No discussions!"

"Goddamn it!" Said Leyden. "You have all the fun." Then with a smile, "Good luck, Rusty."

Turning quickly, Rusty left to find Red. "Red!" He called out.

He was nearby.

"Are our teams ready?"

"Sometimes, I think you're crazier than me, Rusty. But yeah, they're ready."

"Good. Let's get our plan into action!"

The paratroopers left their defensive positions and headed out, guided by Rusty's scouts.

Chapter Fifty Six

**Friday, July 10, 1950 - Day Sixteen of the Invasion
Korea – Around Hill 102 – Early Evening**

The monsoon's rain was constant, providing excellent cover for the five columns advancing on the 34th Regiment's ridge positions.

The paths through the valley were mapped out yesterday. Concealment wasn't an issue as the rain was so fierce, visibility was down to yards. But the going was rough, ravines and fast-flowing water hampered rapid movement. The canopy was sparse except on the eastern fringe. On the right or east section, the north valley ended at a high mountain that tied into the ridge.

As the columns got close, enemy artillery suddenly stopped shelling the 34th Infantry's positions along the ridge. That was a bad sign for its defenders. It was a sure indication of an imminent frontal assault. Detonations from Colonel Doller's artillery could be heard to the rear of the 34th position.

Rusty's column started up the high slope in the middle of the ridge and spread out under its overhang. Well down from the top and out of sight, they realized that none of the 34th men on top could easily exit down this slope into the Valley. Too many outcroppings and steep drops. Suitable for their cover but awful for escaping.

Rusty's assassin teams and Colonel Daniels handpicked best operators took their positions all along the ridge, just below the top.

At first, it began slowly, in twos and threes climbing down from the top, some coming along the highway through the narrow pass in the ridge as the abandonment of the ridge by the 34th Infantry began. They were mostly wounded, and it was orderly. The severely wounded were helped on remaining vehicles and started leaving when they were full.

Then, all of a sudden, there was a surge. Soldiers were running, trying to get on any vehicle moving or giving up hope for a ride, continuing to run down the road. Men scurried over the top all along the ridge; some fell into Rusty's men lying still on the slopes, others slid down, more still came falling or tumbling to the bottom, banging into rocks on the way down. It was an unholy site, if one could see through the heavy rain.

The 34th had been attacked and bombed for too long. They'd had it, and they cracked. They were now a panicked mob.

Rusty moved close to the highway, under the ridge where he saw and heard the panic of the 34th. Not sure who he wanted to kill first, the Washington politicians who gutted the Army or the leadership of the Army that allowed it to happen. Mulling it over for a few seconds, he decided that since he was here, it should be these communist bastards.

Before too long, the cheers of the North Koreans echoed across the captured ridge. The staunch defense of the 34th had taken its toll on the enemy, so there were scores to be settled.

Screams reflected the bloodlust that soon enveloped the area as the enemy found and killed wounded or surrendered captives. Any American soldier found alive on the ridge was quickly murdered.

The Communist North Korean commanders were so pleased with their troop's victory that they became overconfident. It filtered down to the front line units because they didn't pursue the 34th off of the ridge. They felt that they could wait until tomorrow.

It was something anticipated by Red and Rusty and guided by their intelligence communications capability and the horrible weather. However, they didn't expect the collapse of the 34th and subsequent butchery.

The stealth teams were now in place, just below and around the long ridge. The teams waited patiently for orders. They wanted the enemy to expend their energy and rejoice at their victory.

Chapter Fifty Seven

**Friday, July 10, 1950 - Day Sixteen of the Invasion
Korea – Colonel Haskins 7th Division Replacement Unit CP
– Early Evening**

The ridgeline was located about seven miles west of Hill 102 in the low foothills below a small mountain range to the north and a broad flat valley to its west that met another mountain range. The valley ran north and south, with the northern area becoming rolling hills.

The ridge possessed a strategic command of the road that allowed a way to bypass the main highway to go south, primative as it was.

"I surely do welcome the Airborne, Captain Baker, with cannons, no less! How many did you bring?"

"Thanks, Colonel. A lot less then you'd like, I'm afraid. Got 12 jeep mounted 75mm recoilless rifles with both heat and high explosive shells and 2 jeeps with 50 caliber machine guns."

"It's sure better then what I have, but your right, not much against an armored division. So, I guess you need to make every shot count."

Yes, sir, that's my intention. What do you have, Colonel?

"So, you haven't been briefed?"

"I was just told to get here ASAP and support a bunch of courageous soldiers."

"That was kind. Who's your boss?"

"Colonel Jeff Daniels, 3rd Battalion, 187th Airborne Regiment, sir."

"I've only spoken to a First Sergeant, Rusty. Impressive guy. Did you meet him?"

"No, sir."

"To answer your earlier question, I've got about 2,000 men, armed almost 100% with rifles, M-1s and carbines, all trained soldiers. Most have seen combat. I've got one 60mm mortar, six bazookas, six 30 caliber machine guns, and a good deal of ammunition. All thanks to my thieving hustlers and the truck they borrowed."

"Jesus Christ!"

"Yeah! I sure hope he shows up, because what we have *is* pitiful."

Colonel Haskins led the captain over to a flat dry dirt area under the stolen truck tarp that served as a shelter for his CP. He showed him a basic layout of the valley and the positions of his men.

"Can't see shit out there right now with this rain, so this will have to do for now."

The Colonel bent on one knee and pointed to the rough dirt drawing.

"We're here, on the northern edge of this flat ridgeline that runs south for about 5 miles, then ends at a much broader open plain. We occupy a little over a mile of it, starting from the base of that mountain, north of us.

"This ridge is about 200 feet high off of the valley that stretches almost 3 miles across. There's a dirt road through this valley that passes within 1500 yards in front of our position.

It's primitive and in bad shape with these rains, heavily rutted and muddy, but it's wide. There is no cover between this ridge and that road, just low bushes and grass. From the road to the west side of the valley are rice patties, right up to the foothills on the far side."

Kneeling next to him, Captain Baker commented, "Damn! Kinda reminds me of a battle I studied at the Point, about the slaughter of the British Army when they were retreating from Kabul, Afghanistan, in, I forget what year."

"Good memory, Captain. It was 1842. Yeah, similar in some ways, they were marching through mountain passes of the Hindu Krush, with no cover. I hope we achieve the same result as those warlords."

"What's the point of them coming down this valley?"

"Well, I'm pretty sure they want to outflank Hill 102. That road you came here on, had you gone farther along, it would have come around a bend heading south and slowing dropped down to that road in front of us, about two miles further south of our position. They'd use that entrance to retrace your journey here and come out right behind Hill 102 and kill your friends."

"The other thought would be for them to split their forces and have one column continue on and swing southeast toward Taejon, their main objective, less than 10 miles or so away and encircle the city."

"How do you know all this?"

"That First Sergeant Rusty I asked you about earlier. Said he has ears on the enemy. I believe him."

Chapter Fifty Eight

**Friday, July 10, 1950 - Day Sixteen of the Invasion
Japan – Eighth Army Headquarters - Colonel Nelson's G-2
Conference Room – Early Evening**

Colonel Nelson called for a meeting with his G- 2 Intelligence group and NSOPU team leaders. Not an uncommon thing over the last many days, but they had all gotten together already earlier that same day, so they all thought that something had happened, and maybe another crisis was brewing, with another threat, felt that they didn't need more of the same.

After assembling, they all sat around the large oak table in the conference room.

"You all have read the transcript of Rusty's last message that came in earlier. I need your assessment of his plans." Colonel Nelson then leaned back in his seat with a somber look on his face.

Master Sergeant Nick Beloit, head of NSOPU, spoke first.

"The man should be a general, boss. I mean, to come up with a plan like this is beyond brilliant."

"Just to be clear, Nick, I know each of these men. This plan has Rusty's number one, Red, all over it. So you like his plan?"

Nick didn't back down. "Rusty's the leader, and he approved it, so it's his plan, and yes, I love it. It'll buy us another day or more. Show the enemy we've got some spunk.

`

Maybe get them to hesitate, think a little more cautiously and maybe hurt them right now."

"I wish I was as optimistic as Nick." Said Lt Larry Cole, from the Colonel's G-2 team. "On the surface, it appears well planned, but I don't see an exit strategy. How do they disengage and get the hell out of there?"

"Good point, Larry." Said Major Hank Jarvis, Larry's boss and Deputy Director of G-2 operations. "Though you forget one thing. Rusty and his men are resourceful, they are genius in fact, at getting out of impossible situations. I trust they'll come up with something and avoid disaster. I like this bold move. I'm in full agreement with Nick on its potential."

"Any other opinion?" Asked the Colonel.

No one spoke.

"Okay, let's talk about Taejon. What's the tactical situation?"

"I'm watching that very closely." Said Nick.

"The weather in the whole region is socked in with heavy rain. Nobody can predict when it will clear. The airfield was cleared yesterday with all planes, and most crew service support personnel relocated to the capital at Taegu, 100 miles to the southeast. Oh, except our favorite Special Operations fighter pilot, Captain Stands. Wild Bill refused to leave. He thought he, and his baby Mustang, *Just Due 2*, might be needed at the last minute. No sense arguing with him, so I didn't."

Colonel Nelson nodded. "Crazy son of a bitch. Proud of him."

Nick continued. "As to the rest of Taejon, the civilians have mostly evacuated or are in the process. We're in contact with General Dean's remaining Divisions' 19th Regiment, which has taken up defensive positions around and in the town. They're at half strength and only have around 1,300 men plus a battalion of 105mm howitzers and some light armored vehicles, like half-tracks and scout cars. We think General Dean is with them but can't confirm that."

"Odd, damn odd." Said Nelson.

"Very." Said Nick. "Some brighter news. We've got Company A of the 1st Cavalry Division's medium tank battalion on its way and should arrive in Taejon late tonight."

"Sherman's! That should stop those T-34's." Yelled LT Cole.

Nick looked over to him. "I hate to burst your bubble, Larry, but there was a mistake made when General McArthur ordered that unit to Korea. That units medium tanks were replaced by the light tank M-24 Chaffee because the Japanese roads would not support the heavier medium tank. So their light armor and their small 75mm cannon will be no match for the North Korean T-34's. But still, somethings better than nothing."

Unfamiliar with armor formations, LT Cole asked, "How many in a company?"

"Usually, they have three platoons of three tanks each plus a command tank, but who knows how many they have?" Answered Nick.

"Can we bring in anything else?" Asked a somber Nelson.

Nick deadpanned a look at Colonel Nelson. "I got nothing to help for many days, boss. The 25th Division just started disembarking at Pusan yesterday, and it's going slow. Its 150 miles away. The 1st Cavalry Division is on schedule to make its amphibious landing tomorrow sometime; we still don't know if enemy resistance will meet it. But it's far away on the West Coast, and it will take a few days before it can get in position to be of any help at Taejon."

"Well, let's hope the weather clears. Maybe our flyboys can help?" Colonel Nelson ended the meeting.

Chapter Fifty Nine

Friday, July 10, 1950 - Day Sixteen of the Invasion
Korea – Beneath the Ridge of the Recently Captured 34th
Regiments Position – Late Evening

A few hours earlier, from well behind the ridge, North Korean long-range artillery had commenced counter-battery firing on and around Hill 102. The shelling was severe and continuous.

Under the ridge overhang, Foxy was paired with Arron to lead their airborne column. They also had ten assassins from the 187th who would accompany them when they were to lead the stealth main assault.

Foxy turned to Arron and whispered, "Those are big rounds hitting back on our hill, think they're the same guns that clobbered us at the Post." Arron nodded. "Think you're right. Colonel Nelson told us, but I forget what they were."

"Russian! A big gun, but I forgot the details. I was trying to figure out how far back it might be."

"Jesus, Foxy. Don't get all ambitious on me now. We'll be lucky to get 1,000 yards into their lines. Forget about a few miles."

"Maybe Rusty will do one of those crazy charges again?"

"Oh, shit! Don't say that."

Rusty's team and the rest of the paratroopers waited along the underbelly of the ridge, wondering if the enemy was planning a full-scale attack on Hill 102. Rusty didn't think so but wasn't convinced.

He wanted to wait a little bit to make sure. The rain still poured, as time passed, he became positive the enemy wouldn't attack now. Rusty figured the artillery barrage would probably hammer away all night to soften up defenses for tomorrow's attack.

Rusty leaned over to whisper to Red. "It's time to send our scouts out. First, I need a sitrep. No action, I want to know what we're facing."

Prearranged along the ridge, Red had placed his best assassin scout teams among the airborne units. They all had hand-portable radios. Red called only the two he most trusted, gave them instructions. Told them that he wanted them back in thirty minutes.

They made their way up to the top of the ridge and slithered over.

Mario and Snake had the left-center, the area closer to the highway. Tracker and Joe proceeded closer to the mountain end. Over the top, they crawled for a while without encountering anyone near the edge. Visibility was poor, and the harsh sound of rain pounding on rock and mud precluded early warning of any near encounter. Both teams wondered what they could accomplish.

Farther in, Mario came to the edge of a long trench filled with water, and as he got closer, he realized it was also filled with bodies; dead Americans. Together, they had to step in and cross to the other side to continue. Snake felt bad, Mario got angry.

Yells and shouts focused their direction, and they continued forward and found a large grouping of tents, cooking fires going inside where men were laughing and shouting. There were no guards.

Mario checked his watch, signaled to Snake that it was time to head back.

Tracker and Joe went deep into the enemy lines. They bypassed a series of tents until they got to what appeared to be the heart of the 34th Regiments' main defensive location on the plateau. The area had foxholes everywhere, now empty of live humans, just filled with water and bodies.

Joe whispered to Tracker, "Where the hell are all the soldiers? Those in the tents we passed weren't that many. I don't get it."

"Maybe they're afraid we'll start shelling the ridge, and they pulled back some."

"Maybe? Said a doubtful Joe. "I'll leave that up to Rusty to decide, but it's time to go."

After Joe and Tracker reported back to Rusty, he was puzzled by the reports. Turning to Red by his side, he related the scout's messages and asked his opinion.

"So, Mario has lots of tents closer to the road, and Joe found only a few. Mario didn't go too far into the position, and we don't know what's beyond the highway through the pass. Kinda blind here, Rusty. But from a tactical angle, I think we should funnel most of our troops through that sparsely held eastern edge and go deeper into their position, then come at them from the flank, maybe somewhat from behind. I think we should hold back a small force, maybe 100 men near our position by the highway here until our main force is fully engaged, then we'll attack the enemy in the rear, as they will have organized and turned to the east and rear."

"I like it, Red, with one addition. I want to maintain silence for as long as possible, so let's have all of the assassin teams lead the men in and start them sweeping east when all the men are in position."

Red got on the radio issuing orders. Finishing, he then called Colonel Doller's CP, told him that they were about to commence their attack and for him to cancel his artillery barrage in precisely 30 minutes. Red checked his watch.

Rusty told Red he wanted Tully to lead the assassins. Tracker volunteered to go with Joe and Arron and follow Tully in. Rusty gave his okay.

It took 15 minutes for the special operators to assemble on the far right side of the ridge. The rest of the soldiers slowly shifted over and tightened up. Colonel Daniels ordered two platoons to move near Rusty and told the two lieutenants that Rusty was the boss. Colonel Daniels was leading the main attack from the east.

With Tully at the center, Tracker on his left, Joe and Arron on his right, they huddled under the top edge waiting for the go from Colonel Daniels. Twenty special airborne operators were behind them. All had Tommy guns slung around their backs and an eight-inch knife in hand.

They'd all shed any non-essential gear at Hill 102, including their rain slickers, because stealth was paramount, and ease of movement was a life or death moment. So they were soaked to the bone.

Mentally preparing for the unknown, each man said his private prayers. Some, like Tully, just wanted it to start.

Tracker whispered to his Spirit to guide him in his killing. He took out his tomahawk.

Tully unsheathe his Bowie knife.

Arron took out his special knife; he carried two. This one was his Fairbairn. He got it from a dead SAS British guy, Bernard, a friend, with whom he was on a special operations mission in the mountains of the Balkans in the WAR. A fierce weapon, the Fairbairn had a seven-inch double-edged blade. A sleek dagger. It would cut through anything with ease except metal. That would take a bit longer. He called it his *Bernie*, in deference to his fallen friend.

Joe had two silent killing tools, his combat knife, and his favorite, from his Brooklyn days, an 8-inch ice pick. He was an expert with both.

Colonel Daniels got the call from Red. Everyone was in place. Go!

Tully and his three men slid over first, each, three feet apart. Arron, on the far right, immediately crawled within a few inches of the back of a pair of combat boots. Slowly standing up, the guard was watching flashes of exploding artillery shells in his rear, Arron quickly slit his throat and lowered him to the ground. He now proceeded in a slow duck walk.

The twenty assassins came up and followed the lead of the four men and spread out.

Tully's lead team came across a few wandering soldiers and sentries as they moved deeper into the enemy's lines until they came to a cluster of tents. There they waited for the rest of their airborne help to catch up.

Colonel Daniels rechecked his watch. Five minutes was finally up since the assassin teams left. Time to go, he signaled his two lead scouts, and the main column started their advance, two men abreast along the eastern edge. They moved quickly, as their objective was to get as far into the enemy's rear as possible before the shooting started.

The 187th was designed to be a light, fast-moving, behind the lines type of unit and had trained relentlessly for just this kind of operation. Although classified as light infantry, they carried some sting. The three companies that made up the battalion had what they considered, a heavy weapons component. Each company had a 30 caliber machine gun with a four-man crew (shooter, loader, and two ammo carriers), a bazooka with a four-man crew (shooter, loader, and two ammo carriers) and a light 60mm mortar team of five men (gunner, loader and three ammo carriers).

Colonel Daniels and Rusty thought all three mortar teams and the three machine gun crews should go with the main body of troops. The three bazooka units would stay near Rusty since he was closer to the road and more likely to encounter armored vehicles.

Red told Mario and Snake to get ready. He wanted them to clear any sentries that might be nearby before they went into action. He checked his watch, assumed that it might take 15 minutes or so from Tully's start before something happened. Only 10 minutes had passed, so he decided to wait two more minutes.

Rusty had a last-minute idea, so he turned to Red. "How about taking half of our men to attack through the highway pass then filter toward the front of the ridge?"

"I'd say it's risky. Don't know what's on the road, tanks, half-tracks, shit, anything! But I like it. Once it starts up there, the enemy's attention will be diverted from the pass."

"OK. Get Foxy to lead that group, tell him to get in position now, but hold his attack until we're fully engaged up here. Make sure he brings the bazookA-Teams with him."

Red moved, told Mario and Snake to go, then found Foxy.

Foxy quickly got the airborne LT next to him while he moved his platoon down to the road towards the pass.

Tully's advance stealth teams started killing. Bull rushing into the celebrating enemy in their tents, the assassins caught them off-guard, with no weapons near. The six or eight soldiers in each tent were quickly silenced with nothing more than a grunt or a muffled scream.

The teams kept moving west, from tent to tent, wondering how long they could keep this up.

Colonel Daniels left Company B's gunnery sergeant (universally known as Gunny) in charge of the three mortar crew's midway into the plateau, behind the first tents Tully's men had ambushed. They spread out and set up quickly. "Keep those muzzles covered and fuses dry!" The sergeant unnecessarily said to each team. The men were well trained and knew that if either got wet, it could cause a no fire or worst yet, a short round.

Each of the five crew members carried specially made ammunition carrier backpacks that held 12 rounds of the 3 lb. shells. Also, two of the men wore an extra pack that clipped on to the main pack that contained six additional rounds.

Seventy-two shells per crew Gunny thought, I've got to space out the salvos.

"Listen up!" Said Gunny to the gathered gunners from each crew. "We think the bulk of resistance will be near the road just north of this ridge. So we will concentrate our fire there until we get better Intel. When the shooting starts, I'll give you the order to fire. I may hold off for a bit, so don't jump the gun. Wait for my orders. Set your range for 1200 yards and slightly right of this ridge. I want 3 round volleys every 50 yards as you walk it forward. Don't stop until I say. That clear?"

"Yeah, Gunny!"

Colonel Daniels's main force, numbering close to 300 men, were spread out north of the ridge in a relatively flat rocky plain. He left almost 100 men up on the ridge plateau to trail Tully's killing teams.

All set and ready but nervous, the colonel wondered why there was no shooting yet. Were they walking into a trap?

A fluke. When Tully burst into the next tent, Arron split to the left and stabbed the closest guy, Tracker and Joe went right and got two. An officer on the far right had just finished cleaning his pistol, hesitated for a second, then raised the gun and fired into Arron, knocking him sideways and onto the soldier he had just killed. Tully reacted swiftly, hurling his Bowie knife into the officer's chest, knocking him back and involuntarily, he squeezed the pistol's trigger, firing the gun in the air. Dispatching the remaining enemy, Tully went to Arron.

"Jesus Christ, Arron!" As he turned him to see his wound. "You okay?"

He looked at Tully with wide eyes, "No! That motherfucker shot me! Hurts like hell."

Joe slipped out of the tent as soon as Tully went over to Arron, worried the two shots might alert the next tent only ten feet away or somebody walking near.

Tracker came over. "Let me see." He removed Arron's combat belt, lifted his shirt where blood was pouring, mixed with the water from his soaking clothing. "Spirit is with you, Arron! Bullet took an inch out of your scrawny side. It's more than a flesh wound, and it does look like shit."

"Fuck you, you Indian Medicine man, patch me up, will you and make it quick. Think we might have some trouble coming. And oh, anyone got a pain pill?"

Tully ended that discussion. "That's a bad wound, Arron. It needs to be stitched and treated so you don't get an infection. The pain has got to be fierce; Tracker, give him a syrette."

Tracker bandaged the wound and gave him a shot of morphine. Tully went out and met Joe.

"Anything?"

"Two guys came out of that tent." Joe pointed. "Stood around for about a minute, then went back in."

Tully heard the explosions far away from the 21st artillery barrage and wondered if that was enough noise to cover the gunshots, he had doubts. The detonations were pretty muted.

"Keep watching, got to get Arron some help." Tully walked back a few yards passed their tent and found the trailing airborne guys crouched low. He found the unit's LT and had him order two of his men to take Arron back to Marty, their combat medic, who had set up a station behind the mortar teams.

Tully knelt next to Joe as he watched the two men carry Arron away from the tent. Tracker came out to join them.

"Do we keep going?" Asked Tracker.

The question went unanswered as six soldiers came out of the next tent with rifles at the ready.

Joe had his Tommy gun waiting as the last man emerged from the tent and turned toward them. Joe opened fire with a long burst, hitting all six in the four-second torrent of bullets.

That signaled all the fellow assassins and the trailing airborne forces to abandon their stealth movements and commence their armed assault. Tully's team hit the deck firing on the next nearest tent and waited for their airborne support to catch up to them.

Chapter Sixty

Friday, July 10, 1950 - Day Sixteen of the Invasion Korea – On and Around the North Korean Held Ridge – Same Time

Like an anthill that had been stepped on, enemy troops poured out of their tents and foxholes. Shouts of alert were loud even amidst gunfire. But many of the enemy soldiers were disoriented and didn't know the direction of the danger; panicked troops fired in all directions at perceived enemies. That soon became moot on the ridge when the full force of the charging line of airborne soldiers, all firing Tommy guns, slammed into this disorganized, unprotected mass.

Bugles sounded throughout the ridge and flat area to the north as the North Koreans started to rally. As the intensity of the initial action on top of the ridge increased, Colonel Daniels ordered the main force to move forward. Splitting his men into three tight V formations, they moved quickly and at first silently, through the rain, across the rough flat land.

Initially, they too met disorganized, unsuspecting groups of soldiers, standing uncovered in the open, preparing to move to the action taking place on the ridge. Easy stealth kills encouraged quicker movement. Each airborne soldier knew that speed was the key to survival on this potential suicide mission, so they kept moving as fast as they could over the bad terrain with limited visibility. If they got stuck and had to dig in, they'd probably die.

Gunny felt the tempo of the battle was reaching a point where more aggressive action would help the attack. So he blew his whistle for a steady three-seconds to alert his three mortar teams that they were to prepare to fire on the next whistle signal. Already on standby, they were ready when Gunny gave his order thirty seconds later.

Whomp! Whomp! Whomp! The three mortars fired their first salvo. The gunners then made a slight range adjustment, adding a few yards forward, then the loaders dropped another round into the tubes. Whomp!

Rusty felt he had waited long enough, "Red, I think it's time for us." It was like a question, but he just really wanted confirmation on a made decision, and Red gave it to him, with a nod. They moved up to the edge and signaled to the men on each side to come. They climbed onto the ridge, moved forward about 10 yards, found Mario and Snake next to a dead sentry, and waited for the airborne platoon to catch up.

Hearing intense gunfire to their right, Rusty ordered a careful advance straight ahead. That paid off quickly. A massed company formation came jogging across their front, heading toward the substantial gunfire in the east.

Rusty and his men froze. The enemy didn't see them.

"Open fire!" Rusty yelled. Thirty plus Thomson submachine guns opened fire at point-blank range. The 45 caliber bullets tore into the enemy, knocking them down like a giant sledgehammer sweeping along the outer edges of the mass formation. The airborne platoon had trained for something like this, so when the first magazines of their Tommy's were being changed out, six preselected men would switch to throwing hand-grenades.

After several magazines were spent and 24 hand grenades had detonated among them, Rusty ordered a continuation of their advance. They stepped through the bodies; some men found survivors, and sporadic gunshots ensued as they moved forward. Firing off to their right on the ridge started to taper off rapidly. Rusty felt that the fighting on the ridge was just about over.

Mortar explosions and heavy gunfire started just north of them. Rusty knew it was Colonel Daniels's main force. By the volume of noise the firefight was making, he thought they were starting to meet significant resistance. He kept his men moving forward.

Foxy huddled with Frenchy, Moose, and the airborne LT on the side of the highway just south of the entrance to the small Pass at the base of the ridge. Not knowing what to expect, he was anxious. Rusty ordered him to wait until the other teams were fully engaged before starting his assault, hoping to catch the enemy diverted and attacking in their rear.

Foxy spoke to the three men.

"Lieutenant, I'll lead with my guys. I want you to take a squad and follow me on the right side of this pass. Order another squad to enter on the left side and the last squad to trail in the middle. I want a bazookA-Team with each."

"Got it!"

"Foxy, let me go first." Said Frenchy. "I look more Korean then you with your six-foot frame; if I'm challenged, maybe I can fake them out first, just like I did on that bridge, way back when."

"You're funny, you know. We're in the middle of a goddamned major battle, and you want to go subtle. Forget it! Now follow me."

Foxy edged along the road next to the highly sloped ridge and entered the pass. Visibility was about 20 yards, seemed to be improving slightly as the rain slowed from a torrent to just very heavy. The airborne soldiers scrambled into their following positions. Exiting the Pass, Foxy halted and took in the surroundings.

The noise to his right on the rear of the open plain was intense. Machine gun fire, volleys of rifle and submachine gun chattering, mortar shells exploding, and bugles blowing added a bizarre mixture to a hellish battle raging. Adding another layer to the drama, artillery from the 21st was still firing into the enemy's rear.

Vehicle sounds from up the road got his attention. Old diesel trucks, he thought, but couldn't see them.

"Frenchy! Get the airborne bazooka A-Teams to the front. Now!"

As the airborne soldiers came up, Moose, lying prone in the road near Foxy, suddenly opened fire with his BAR (Browning automatic rifle). Foxy dived to the ground and brought his Thompson to bear on the just appearing North Korean soldiers.

The enemy hadn't seen them and had been just rushing down the road to guard the pass when they burst into view. Moose didn't care when they suddenly appeared, nor did Foxy, when he opened fire as well.

The rest of the men reacted quickly, spread out, and dove to the ground, and opened fire. The enemy front line immediately fell dead from Moose's 20 round burst. The soldiers directly behind them turned to retreat but ran into their men, and then they died by the combined volley of Foxy, Moose's second magazine, and the newly joined airborne troopers.

They kept firing into the panicked formation until Foxy couldn't see any more soldiers and yelled for them to stop shooting and advance up the road.

Foxy grabbed the airborne LT, "I heard trucks not far up the road. I want your bazooka guys to set up here and fire blind up the road. Fire slightly left and right and one straight up the middle. Do it now!"

Rushing forward, the bazookA-Teams caught up with their advancing unit. Foxy called for a defensive line while they quickly loaded their rockets and fired blind, up the road, into the rain.

The rockets had barely left their tubes when a tremendous volume of rifle fire burst at them from straight ahead. Four of the bazooka men immediately fell back, many prone airborne soldiers were struck in the head and slumped dead. Return fire was immediate, firing blindly into the rain. Some very brave knelt as they threw grenades. Two flashes of bright light not far up the road told Foxy that those bazooka rockets had hit something substantial.

Foxy didn't know what to do. They were pinned down, taking casualties, and he had no plan but to keep firing. He then got hopeful as the volume of the enemy's gunfire slowly diminished. Then a series of explosions suddenly ripped through his rear.

"Mortars! Got to move!" Yelled the LT to Foxy, jerking him into action.

"Get your men off the road into the flats in front of the ridge!" Foxy yelled back as he got up and started running. Moose followed with the rest of the soldiers. Some fell as they ran; others dragged their wounded buddies.

Frenchy had another idea as he slipped across the road in the opposite direction. He came to the bodies of the fallen bazooka men, used them for cover, and crawled through their blood mixed with the rain. Brave fuckers, he thought, kneeling in the open like that to take a shot. Or just damned stupid!

Stupid led him to think about what he was doing, as he kept moving to get off the road. Mortar explosions at his rear were getting dangerously close. The sound of bullets zinging past his head spurred him on and increased his assessment of the spur of the moment decision to do a Ranger thing, which means crazy. I am a Ranger! He said to himself, so I can't help myself.

Off the road and out of immediate danger, Frenchy found the steep base of the mountain on the west side of the pass and flatland area. Doing a slow climb and crawling along and over boulders, he reached a rough rock ledge about 20 feet off the ground and started heading north, following the highway a mere 10 yards away.

Threading along the tight, uneven ledge, he suddenly stepped under a streaming waterfall that almost swept him over the side but for his grip on a big root. Although already soaked, the cold mountain water was a jolt that caused him to shake. Fear, adrenaline overload, just being wet and cold, he didn't know why. So he started to laugh.

Chapter Sixty One

Friday, July 10, 1950 - Day Sixteen of the Invasion Korea – On and Around the North Korean Held Ridge – Same Time

When Foxy fell headfirst into the water-filled shell crater, he cursed the muddy hole but then realized how relieved he felt that he was out of the direct fire. It was a big space, indicative of the heavy artillery the enemy used against the 34th Infantry.

Quite a few men joined him, including the airborne LT who, right after he jumped in, turned to his shadow, his radioman, "Get me the mortars!"

Switching to a preselected frequency on the internal battalion network, he clicked the send on the handheld. "Mortar, mortar! Lieutenant Manson needs fire support!"

"Mortar! Gunny!"

Passing the phone to the LT, "Gunny!"

"I need help, Gunny. I'm 25 yards north of the highway pass and 20 yards east of the highway, right in front of the ridge. There's a large enemy concentration on the highway due west and north of me on the highway. Can you lay it on them?"

Pausing a few seconds to visualize his location, "I'll be shooting in the dark, and that's max range, so I'll need some help from you. Hold one!" Gunny turned to the closest mortar team. "Beaver! New fire order! Max range, left 50, fire one!"

"Got one inbound, Lieutenant. Give me feedback!"

He saw the flash but no noise. "Gunny! You got the range but too far north, adjust south 100."

An explosion flashed right on the road. "That's it! Gunny lay it on, then walk it north. You saved our ass! Thanks."

Foxy watched the bright flashes of mortar shells hit every 6 seconds. His ears rung, and his body vibrated from the proximity of destruction. Watching the clustered ranks of the enemy disintegrate within each detonation caused him mixed feelings but didn't dwell on them but for a few seconds.

With all of Foxy's men focusing on the west side of the road, they didn't see the enemy charging them from the north. The enemy didn't know they were there either until visibility through the rain allowed.

The momentum of the first wave stumbled, fell, or jumped into the outer airborne positions. Some shooting by the enemy alerted the rest of the rear American soldiers, but it was mostly hand to hand fighting for those first attacked.

Moose had just reloaded the fourth of his BAR ammo boxes, each containing 20 rounds of 30 caliber cartridges; he carried six boxes on his belt. At the sound of close-in gunfire and Foxy screaming in his ear, Moose swung his automatic rifle to the firing and started shooting. Aware that friends were being overrun, the rest of the airborne didn't toss any grenades, just fired their Thomson's at the charging hoard.

Corporal Dan McKinley had been in this airborne battalion for just six months. Having just graduated from jump school at the age of 20, he felt like he belonged to something special because his growing up was anything but special. Big and physically tough, Dan always had to reassure himself of his self-worth, a product of his abusive parents. The Army and then the Airborne reinforced his confidence and showed him another path.

Ten feet behind his friend's foxhole at the very edge of the front line, he saw the rush of the enemy moments before they overtook his buddy's position. Like a camera in slow motion in his mind, the picture show played out. Rigid at the sight of his friend's death, his mind went blank.

Screaming soldiers ran at him with their Russian made rifles thrust out in their hands, holding 17" long bayonet blades on their tips. He stood, cursing them as he fired, killing many until Dan ran out of ammo and then fought with his combat knife, killing a few more until he was shot in the head by an enemy officer.

Foxy, Moose, Lieutenant Manson, and a few others who were in the crater 30 feet back from Corporal McKinley's position, fired continuously as the enemy rolled over their forward positions.

Foxy felt weird watching the attack. His thoughts were at odds with his reality. He wasn't afraid. Why weren't they shooting much? Foxy thought it odd; they're just charging and dying in prodigious numbers. Yet, they still kept coming. It was just like Joe said about how the Japanese made their banzai attacks until they were all dead.

Foxy realized he was going to die. They were about to be overrun in seconds.

Then a big bang and a bat hit him. Foxy felt like he levitated. Then he heard a sudden high volume of shooting around him, then explosions flashed, as many grenades went off in some crazy sequence that seemed to last for a while.

Dizzy and confused, he felt himself to see if he was wounded but discovered no blood.

Foxy slowly moved and kneeled, looked out of the shell hole but saw nothing but smoke and bodies. He couldn't hear a sound; figured he lost his hearing. Still confused, he turned to find Moose but saw many bodies instead. No, that's not accurate. He saw many parts of what were once whole humans. He thought he was hallucinating, having a hard time focusing, and then something grabbed him.

"Foxy! Can you hear me?" Rusty was yelling at him, distraught.

He didn't hear anything as black surrounded him.

"No!" Said Red, as he knelt next to him. "He's still breathing! Got to get him to Marty!"

"Slow down, Red." Said Rusty, "We need to check him out first."

Red was adamant. "I'll take him to Marty."

Mario and Snake, knelling next to Red and Rusty, were of a different mind. Mario spoke out.

"He looks bad, but it looks superficial, no hard bleeding, he's in shock. I'll bandage him up and stay with him. Marty's got enough things on his plate, and besides, I think you got more important shit to do."

Red snapped his head back and thought, it took a Ranger, an outsider to his immediate family, to remind him of his primary duty.

Mario said to a hesitating Red. "Don't get your judgment screwed up because you lost some men. You have more men to save."

"Thanks, Mario. Take care of him; he's in your charge, don't fuck up!" He and Rusty hurried away.

Mario, always watching, "Let's check him out for shrapnel damage!"

Snake turned Foxy; the rain made the blood trails more noticeable. "Shit!" Said, Mario.

"What?"

"Piece of something sticking out of his back. It's just oozing blood; we've got to take it out."

Snake stared at him. "There's No *WE* about that, Mario! You got that job."

As midnight approached, the rain lightened. Although substantial, it no longer was white-out conditions. The battlefield had settled into minor skirmishes in the open field with continuous explosions a few miles to the north. Two trucks were burning on the highway near the pass, and two more looked damaged and disabled further north.

Rusty hung up his field phone and turned to Red. "Colonel Daniels reports the enemy has mostly withdrawn. He's cleaning up pockets and has begun evacuating his wounded as well as some of his troops. He says it'll take about half an hour to reposition behind the ridge. He urges us to hurry and do the same, thinks they'll start a fierce artillery barrage soon."

The ultimate tactical oracle in Rusty's life, Red, spoke, "Tully's team swept the mid-ridge and teamed up with Colonel Daniels as planned, and were successful, they are now withdrawing, as should we."

Red continued. "He's right. We broke up their attack, so let's vamoose."

Rusty nodded, told Red to signal withdrawal.

A grizzled airborne first sergeant came up to Rusty. "My platoon LT is in that crater, and I'm taking his body back with me. I know your orders about wounded only, so I hope you don't give me any shit. He was a good friend and a great officer."

"No, First Sergeant, I'm proud of you for caring; only wished I'd known him."

Moved by the encounter, Rusty looked back at the crater where the LT's body was being removed by his first sergeant and two of his men. Mario and Snake were there jerry-rigging a stretcher for Foxy out of long Russian rifles with their bayonets attached. They attached two combat belts fixed width-wise to hold the rubberized slicker in the center to make a perfect stretcher, as long as the guy holding the bayonet end either had a pair of welders gloves on or some other protection from the razor-sharp edges.

Lying next to them was Moose's remains. Mario's thoughts raced from anger to sorrow to dreading telling his Ranger boss and friend, Tully.

And then it hit him. "Where's Frenchy!"

His brain was still a bit scrambled after the mortars exploded around the trucks that he was parallel too, just 20 yards away. Not remembering if he had been knocked out or not, Frenchy had moved on.

Forgetting why he was going forward alone and what his mission was, he decided to lie next to a boulder. Inspired by the diminishing rain and reduced battle activity, he stirred, wondering where the hell he ended up.

Frenchy looked out on the burning trucks: he was midway between the disabled vehicles and the elbow of the highway about a mile away. For the first time since he'd been crawling along this elevated ridge, he could finally see his surroundings.

"What the hell!" He softly spoke. Bodies! Lots of dead lay on the irregular plain in his vision. He saw men running back toward the ridge, some carrying wounded. He assumed they were the airborne guys. "What the fuck did I miss?" He said out loud.

His thoughts were interrupted by the hissing sound of incoming, followed within seconds by multiple explosions on the open plain among the soldiers withdrawing, followed quickly by a massive barrage impacting on the ridge.

"Oh, fuck!" Frenchy yelled. He felt helpless as he watched his comrades die. Trying to focus on what he could do, he scanned north. Yeah, that's what I thought, as he watched mechanized vehicles come around the elbow on the highway. They were coming fast, led by old captured WW 2 German half-tracks that the Russians donated to their North Korean friends, still considered one of the best mechanized assault vehicles ever made.

Wanting to run back, Frenchy paused. I'm in a unique spot here, he thought. If I stay, I'll probably die, but that was a lesser concern then what good can I do? Never a doubt about his safety, he now remembered why he crossed that road by himself and crawled along the ledge.

"Yeah! I remember now." Frenchy said aloud. "I'm a crazy Ranger!" He grew angrier at seeing the armored vehicles coming down the main road toward him.

Behind him, he felt a presence. The hair on the back of his neck went viral. Then he heard a whisper. "You fucking crazy Ranger, I got your back."

"Holy shit! Dean!! You scared me! What the fuck are you doing here?"

"Not sure. But I did see you scurry off when everybody went to the other side when shit happened. But after, I figured you were alone and might need some help, so I came looking. Glad I did, as I think our northern friends have an idea about busting this little party we had at their expense."

Frenchy was incredulous. "I've known you for more than three years and have never heard you speak more than a sentence at one time. Is this an omen?"

"Contra, my upstate New York friend. I get wordy when I'm not sure what to do. I get quiet when it's time to kill. So, I'm hoping you got a plan, but if not, I'm happy with taking out a bunch of these maniacs, and should it be necessary, I'm with someone who I share the honor of dying with." Sniper Dean then looked at Frenchy with a slight parse of a smile.

"How many grenade's you got?" Asked Frenchy, with a half-smile.

Everybody dove to the ground or into the nearest hole or crevice at the first sound of incoming. Exposure meant death. The withdrawing soldiers knew that the first wave of shells was just the appetizer for the forthcoming entre of a supremely pissed-off enemy. They moved off the field as quickly as they could.

At the onset of the mortar attack, Rusty first heard and then saw the mechanized vehicles enter the highway about two miles away. Red's head snapped at the clanking of treads on the half-tracks.

Rusty ran to the airborne sergeant's team, taking their LT's body off the field.

"Stop!" He yelled as they were running to get away from the shelling.

They dropped to their knees as Rusty caught up.

Out of breath and anxious about the nearby explosions, Rusty grabbed the sergeant.

"I need you, First Sergeant! Your platoon had all of the bazookas in your battalion, and I need them. Now!"

At first, bewildered, the stupor of the loss of his leader and close friend had left him dazed, but the explosions shook him up, and with Rusty yelling in his face, he got out of his trance. He also heard that awful sound that strikes terror in any infantryman, the clanking of metal tracks created by armor, whether in be tanks or half-tracks, it didn't matter.

Turning to the two men helping him, "Take LT back to the hill." Then to Rusty, he said, "Follow me." As they ran to the highway pass, he yelled back to him. "They got fucked up, the bazooka guys. I pulled the survivors back after they recovered their equipment. They're back in the highway pass."

Bright flashes of explosions lit up the night.

After gathering his troops at the pass, Rusty made his way north along the highway with the remainder of Foxy's airborne unit, led by its first sergeant with the battalion's three replacement bazookA-Teams trailing.

Moving forward along the west side of the road, close up to the edge of the mountain, Rusty knew that armor wouldn't attempt to go it alone. That would be stupid, except if you're really pissed and acted stupidly.

If he guessed wrong right now about that stupid thing, he was probably going to die. With his airborne radio guy following him like a puppy with Red at his side, he paused.

"They stopped shelling, Red. Hear those tracks? Those are tanks! Can't see them, but I think they're swinging out off the road onto the flats to bypass the truck wreckage."

He pulled his radioman close, "Get Colonel Daniels!"

Shortly connected, Rusty started, "I need your mortars, Colonel. They've got tanks coming down the highway. Think they're off somewhat into the flat. I'm almost in their face, but I need support. A flare and a few rounds should do. Can you help?"

Without a pause, "We're set up behind where we first started at the plateau. Got your back, Rusty! I'm right here with my mortar man." After a brief pause, "Gunny's got no idea where you are, so he's sending out a star shell and one round. Report back."

The burst of the brilliant star shell was off to the right but still illuminated the highway and part of the open field. The explosion of the round was enough for Rusty to call an adjustment for a concentration of fire from the mortars, even though he was very close, he gambled a bit on this, hoped his instincts were right.

Rusty knew that this mortar fire wouldn't take out the tanks, but it would kill any flanking infantry or any other non-tank vehicle and maybe give the bazookA-Teams a chance.

After rethinking their original plan, which included certain death, Frenchy and Dean had slipped back along the narrow pathway until they were just north of the still-burning tires on the destroyed enemy trucks.

"I like this spot." Whispered Dean to Frenchy.

Kneeling behind a four-foot boulder, Frenchy felt the same, "Me too!"

"Look here!" Pulling Frenchy up so he could see beyond the big rock.

In the dim light cast by the glow of the burning tires, they saw the lead half-tracks just north of the destroyed trucks, not moving, with infantry piling out. Nearby, just off to the right, a T-34 tank was slowly moving up off the road to parallel the half-tracks position. They couldn't see any farther out but heard other tank noises beyond.

Dean took out his rain pouch and set up his sniper rifles scope tent over his firing spot. He felt rushed; he wanted that tank commander.

About set, he turned to Frenchy. "Start hurling those grenades as soon as I fire. I'll try to get the half-track commander next, and then we'll crawl out of here."

"Qui!"

Dean almost laughed out loud. "Love fighting with you! You're an asshole just like me."

As Dean focused his scope on the head of the tank driver and fired, the sky lit up. A bright mortar Star shell burst off to the right over the open field. Frenchy took the clue at Dean's rifle shot to pull and throw his first grenade. Then a mortar round exploded about 70 yards due east from them, just as Frenchy's grenade went off.

Although stunned for an instant, both knew what this meant; they were now at the spear. Frenchy grabbed the next grenade as Dean fixed on his next shot, now illuminated by the fading flare. The tank commander next to the one he just took out was oblivious to his comrade's fate. It was a clear shot that scored. Dean then pivoted to the other tank at the far right, but the Star flair died just as explosions started to impact his entire area.

Grabbing Frenchy by his harness, "Got to go now!" Dean pulled him pretty far along the narrow pathway as mortar shells impacted near their just vacated position.

"Stop dragging me! Are those ours?"

"Not sure. Think it's both." Dean let go and stopped to catch his breath. "We need to get back to the ridge pass."

"But that's where most of the big shells are falling!"

"Start praying and hope for the best, my French buddy."

Explosions filled their ears and lighted the way as they scurried along the ridgeline pathway.

Watching the corrected mortar rounds hit where he directed, Rusty suddenly realized he figured this all wrong. In the blink of an eye, he understood the determination of this enemy. The enemy tanks pulling out from the road and infantry coming out of that north funnel were like roaches smelling sugar. He knew his stop-gap bazooka A-Team effort was a suicide mission.

"Back! Retreat!" Rusty yelled to the men. Grabbing his radioman on the run, he hooked up with Colonel Daniels.

"They're coming, Colonel, and they're pissed. Get all your men back to the Hill and get ready for awful!"

Then the enemy artillery shells started exploding on the ridge and beyond.

Chapter Sixty Two

**Friday, July 10, 1950 - Day Sixteen of the Invasion
Korea – Ten Miles West of Hill 102 at Colonel Drew
Haskins 7th Replacement's Division Position – Late Evening**

Heavy clouds finally stopped dropping the white rain and moved on to a constant drizzle to maintain the complete wetness on everything and everyone. It was so black it was as if someone pitched a heavy cloak over the earth.

The almost 2,000 men spread out along this plateau pondered their faith. They faced the only road the enemy could use to outflank the troops on Hill 102 and then capture Taejon. Despite having slickers, most men were soaked to the bone. Having had no hot food for two days and not a dry smoke in too long, the men were angry, on edge, and just plain tired.

The far distant sounds of war echoing through the mountains added to the strain, especially for the veterans who had a sense of what was coming. It was a long time ago, but the ugly memories now seemed fresh. Most were scared.

"It's going to fall mostly on you, Captain. Are you and your men ready?" Asked Colonel Haskins to Captain Les Baker.

"If you're asking will my men stand and fight? Well, that's easy. My question to you, sir, will yours?"

Both were sitting in the command jeep, positioned in the center of their position, back on the plateau. The jeep had full communications to all of the other 14 jeeps that had been strategically placed; 12 with 75 mm recoilless rifles and two command platoon jeeps with 50 caliber machine guns.

"I think we're going to find out if everybody fights pretty soon, Captain."

The scouts positioned far up the valley ran as fast as they could to the first position, where the 2nd platoon commander jeep reported the sighting of an enemy armored column entering the road heading south with lights on and moving fast.

Captain Baker, all of 27 years, had experienced much in his young life. Just six years ago, fresh out of the Point and completing his Airborne training, led a brand new light artillery jeep unit, with a 75 mm recoilless rifle affixed, into Germany. He encountered a Panzer attack, his platoon stood its ground and proceeded to wipe out the attack, saving countless lives, but with much loss to his outfit. He received a Silver Star for his courage and determination.

"Colonel, I'm calling the alert now. Are we good?"

"Yes, Captain. We engage as planned. You have tactical command."

Switching to the command network, Captain Baker started. "Alert, alert! Plan A in motion. Mechanized units are entering the kill zone. Remember! Tanks first."

Already in position, both platoon leaders acknowledged the call.

First Platoon Sergeant Angelo Menotti felt a shiver go through his body at the captain's call. Within minutes he was the one who would start this fight. Maybe dying here was destiny, though Angelo was a devout Catholic and didn't believe in predestination, but still? Stupid stuff came to mind, like why am I still a virgin at 21? And why am I fighting and maybe going to die in this unknown country? Snapping out of these thoughts, the focus became his men in this jeep and his platoon. My family, he finally said to himself.

Positioned at the end of the mile-long kill zone, Angelo's command jeep lay just off the dirt road. Not knowing if the enemy would be fully mechanized or combo with infantry or if they would be dark or with lights, he was tasked to light up the convoy and stop any forward progress on the road, thus setting the kill zone.

After much training and excellent natural tactical abilities, Angelo had positioned his kill jeeps along a long line, with the closest about 50 yards away. As with all the jeeps, they had little natural cover. They were vulnerable, exposed on the plateau, with only darkness, rain, and surprise as their main hope of survival.

But he had extra protection with him. Colonel Haskins positioned 200 of his troops around this blocking point and in front of Angelo's jeeps.

Angelo watched as the column advanced down the road. He was amazed that the vehicles' low lights were on. They were moving fast; he figured maybe 15 MPH.

His radio clicked, "Angelo! No need to light your position! Move your jeep to safety. That's an order!" Said Captain Baker.

With the enemy convoy halfway down the road, Angelo turned to his driver, "Get us out of here to our next position!"

The relief in the jeep by all four men was not discernable, but if someone had taken a blood pressure reading of the men, it would have registered a noticeable drop. They pulled up to higher ground on the plateau and got the 50 caliber machine gun aimed toward the road.

The vehicles approached his blocking position. From the plateau, less than a mile off the road, the dim lights clearly illuminated each vehicle with optics. Angelo focused on the lead machines through his binoculars. Those big nasty old German half-tracks, the first three. Then two Russian tanks followed by three big covered trucks. He stopped looking and focused on his job.

Angelo grabbed his mike, switched to his platoon frequency. "Unit One, take out the first vehicle as planned, then shift to tanks, then back to the front next two half-tracks. Commence one minute. All units! Tanks are first, wait for sparks. On my order in 10 seconds."

Corporal Steven Kaminski, known as Ski, commanded his four-man recoilless rifle jeep Unit One, sat in the gunner's seat, staring through his gun firing, sighting optics at the enemy column. Ski yelled to his crew, "The first five are Heat, next five are HE."

Like a professional hunter with a high powered telescopic scope, Ski adjusted his aim to pinpoint the crosshairs onto his target spot.

They were a well-trained unit that could fire, reload, and fire again in 30 seconds. They knew they'd have to be fast to survive this kind of action against front line main battle tanks they were attacking from an unprotected position. Each shot from their 75mm rifled cannon was like a flair that ignited their location. Exposing your area when firing was the only drawback to the recoilless rifle, but a major one.

Angelo came on the net. "Open fire! Kill'em!"

Ski tracked the lead half-track and aimed just behind the enclosed driver's position, in front of the troop compartment and fired. The jeep hardly moved, but the blast was loud, like an enormous rifle crack, followed by the hiss of a massive smoke cloud of escaping gasses.

As the round destroyed the half-track, Ski quickly shifted his gun to his next target, a tank, still moving. He fired. The tank exploded. Next, he thought, as he swung his rifle to the next tank in line. That turret barrel was quickly turning and coming up to his position. He counted that the speed of his crew was as fast as he thought, or they were all going to die. He fired as the tank fired. The tank gun never got high enough. The round exploded harmlessly low into the plateau. His was a kill shot, blowing the turret five feet in the air, flames curling high, lighting the area.

In less than two minutes into the ambush, Captain Baker's 187th Airborne Jeep Light Artillery Company's 12 kill jeeps had destroyed all 25 T-34 Tanks and 8 half-tracks at their front, with no causalities.

They now turned their guns on the troop-carrying trucks and the soldiers piling out seeking cover. The burning tanks and half-tracks offered an almost daylight view of the long road.

All 2,000 of Colonel Haskins 7th Division replacements opened fire the moment they heard the first explosion at the front of the column. As the tanks started burning, sighting on the soldiers running from the trucks trying to find cover was easy.

The roar of the gunfire and explosions was continuous and deafening. It was as if a giant wood chipper was destroying a great tree.

Captain Baker watched the slaughter of the enemy with mixed emotions. Colonel Haskins was with him and felt something amiss with this new warrior. After a bit, the colonel put a hand on the young captain's shoulder. "Remember this, Les. Arrogance and stupidity lead to disaster. They didn't scout this road because they didn't expect we'd have any resources, and they were in a hurry. Most of all, don't forget that these communists have no morality, and they don't take prisoners."

Captain Les Baker looked at the colonel and nodded. "Thanks."

"I must tell you, Les." said the colonel, "I've never seen a better orchestrated attack plan executed as perfectly as yours. You and your men deserve medals. Should I survive this mess, I will make sure you get them. That was one hell of a great job, Captain!"

Chapter Sixty Three

**Saturday, July 11, 1950 - Day Seventeen of the Invasion
Korea – Behind Hill 102 at Colonel Doller's 21st Regimental
Headquarters bunker – After Midnight**

The pounding of artillery bursts and their vibrations were constant in the background of the HQ bunker, behind Hill 102, as the men gathered around a makeshift table, Colonel Doller on one side, flanked by his standing aides.

"So, First Sergeant "Rusty," thanks for causing this horrific artillery barrage as a direct result of your impulsive and unauthorized attack. I've lost all communications to General Dean's HQ, got only two artillery guns still alive, and have significant casualties."

Doller looked like he wanted to shoot someone, anyone, but focused on Rusty.

"Since you seem to have been in command of this renegade operation, what do you have to say?" Asked an almost snarling Colonel Doller.

Not at all intimidated, Rusty was standing next to Colonel Daniels, their uniforms soaked and muddy, he had a blank look on his face.

Rusty looked at him with cold eyes. "I guess at one time in your career, you were really fortunate, or you actually knew what you were doing. But your rank now far exceeds your capabilities. I fear for your men, and I question your judgment."

Colonel Doller leaned back on his crate. "You are an obnoxious piss ant, First Sergeant! Think you're somebody? Do you? Well, you're not! You're a fucking non-com! A nobody! How dare you speak to me this way? I've destroyed more enemy formations and earned more battle stars than you can even imagine in that puny brain of yours."

Doller abruptly stood up. "I've had enough! Arrest him!" He screamed.

As his two aides moved to un-holster their sidearm, Colonel Daniels was two moves ahead of them. Holding a .45 caliber Army 1911 automatic in their faces, they dropped their weapons before they could bring them up.

"Colonel Doller," said Colonel Daniels, "Despite you, our action bought us a day, maybe two. This First Sergeant Rusty, conceived this brilliant plan. You should thank him for giving you more time. Now it's up to you to gain another day. I understand you were a good leader once. I hope you can reach inside yourself and find that leader again."

Colonel Doller stared at him, dumbfounded at his action and his words.

"I'll have you court marshaled and thrown in jail, Daniels!"

Standing there with his 45 aimed at the two guards, Colonel Daniels took in the threat and insult of not mentioning his rank and smiled at Colonel Doller.

"I've not fought with lesser men than you, Doller. A first for me. But there is a great deal at issue here besides your ego. My unit, like yours, is charged with delaying this enemy's advance, I've done that. Since you have no fucking idea of how to do that, I will continually rely on a more superior tactical mind for my unit's survival. I feel sorry for your men, Doller. Should you survive this, I want you to think about all of the men that you have poorly led and that have died here. But I sincerely hope that you are one of them."

Moving behind Rusty to the exit, Colonel Daniels was still holding his weapon on the guards, "Doller!" He yelled back, still not addressing his rank, "Not sure I'm staying to see you die here, but I'd advise you to consider withdrawal of your regiment."

As they exited the bunker, Red was there. "Got stuff from the western front, Rusty."

They walked a little further back behind the hill to another bunker, also reasonably safe from the incoming shells hitting the Hill and its surrounding area.

They settled into the small space, a lone candle cast shadows on the dirt walls. Rusty was agitated, still angry with Colonel Doller and upset about his own losses; Moose dead, Arron and Foxy severely wounded and Frenchy and Dean MIA.

Red saw the angst in Rusty and his sad look. He grabbed the front of his shirt in front of Colonel Daniels and pushed him against the dirt wall.

"Get control, dam it! You're not finished here yet. Frenchy and Dean are not dead! Those fuckers know how to survive, you'll see!"

Red released him when he saw a glimmer in Rusty's eyes. Rusty relaxed against the dirt wall and looked at Red. "I knew you'd be my best number two."

It broke the tension in the bunker.

Red sat down. "Like I was saying, Colonel Haskins pulled off a great ambush, just like you hoped. Maybe killed two armored regiments on that western road."

Rusty looked at him, "Bullshit! You planned it and deserve the credit." Then he looked over to Colonel Daniels.

"Your jeep Company did this! Damn it all, Colonel. You should be the proudest man in this bunker. I hope you have lots of medals with you because your soldiers deserve them."

Colonel Daniels looked haggard and angry. "First Sergeant, if it weren't for you, none of this would have happened. But I lost a lot of men today on that ridge. A brilliant plan and a great tactical victory. But here we sit, back where we started, and I wonder what's next, and was it all worth the cost?"

Rusty lowered his head and pondered the question. His mind went into a tailspin. Was he responsible for all this death?

The bunker was intensely quiet for a spell as each man pondered the loss of friends, for what?

Red broke the silence with a question. "What's the status of your battalion, Colonel?"

"Best info so far is 43 confirmed dead, 80 or so wounded and five missing. All heavy weapons sections are operational, and communications are intact." Pausing for a second, "I lost one company commander, two LT's and two platoon sergeants, all friends."

Rusty snapped out of his thoughts at that word "friends" and leaned forward toward Red. "Where's Tully?"

Red saw Rusty's fearful eyes. "He's okay, boss. Back with Marty loading the wounded on trucks. Getting them the hell out of here."

Relieved, Rusty looked at Colonel Daniels. "I'm sorry for being distracted, Colonel. The loss of your friends reminded me of mine. It was a hard night for you; your battalion took a big hit, but goddamned if they didn't perform magnificently!"

Colonel Daniels did a double-take at the last remark, "If I didn't know any better, I'd thought I was being spoken to by General Montgomery himself, after the victory at El Ala Maim."

Rusty stared at him and then laughed. "It did, didn't it? Didn't mean it to be like that. It just popped into my head. An English major, on D-Day, said those exact words to me. He was at my company's flank at the end of a nightmarish day when we met at the back of the dunes. It was because I was crying about the loss of most of my friends and pretty much my entire battalion. And yes, the words were well earned, as we finally broke through. That's what I meant."

Rusty bowed his head at the harsh forgotten memory that suddenly reappeared, then stuffed it back into a dark recess in his mind.

Then Rusty said to Red and the colonel, and maybe he just needed to say and hear his own words.

"Nobody will ever remember this day except us. We did do a magnificent job! We caused serious harm to our enemy. Surprised them and stopped their advance for a day or two. That was our purpose, dam it! We will continually lose ground until we can build enough forces to defeat them. Our mission is to survive and keep delaying them until then."

The bunker only echoed the muted explosions from the enemy artillery barrage.

Colonel Daniels was first to speak.

"I was ordered here. My battalion can still fight, and my jeep artillery company is fully operational. Plus, let's not forget Colonel Haskin's 7th Division replacement men, we could make a hell of a stand here."

Rusty looked at him. "You're a dedicated man, Colonel, and you're right. But this is an indefensible position with few protected fighting positions and no cover at all from concentrated artillery shelling. Custer had a better chance on his puny hill then we have here. Why General Dean sent his last full regiment here is a mystery to me. Maybe it looks good on some map, but even that's hard to believe. Somebody just had no fucking idea how bad this terrain is to defend."

Rusty looked down then looked back into Colonel Daniels eyes, "This is suicide for no good reason. I know you're smarter than knowingly leading your men into a slaughterhouse. So don't be stubborn."

Colonel Daniels looked troubled, hesitated before he spoke. "I still have my orders, but they didn't come from General Dean. But I agree with your assessment; it would be a waste of good men. So, do you have another option?"

The shelling intensified and shook their bunker.

"I only have one plan now, Colonel, and that's to live to fight another day, which means not here. I can't believe General Dean would allow a whole Regiment of his 24th Division to be squandered after learning the fate of his 34th Regiment, which had a superior defensive position. No! I think he'd order his men to fall back to better defensive positions around Taejon. But communications are cut off, so Colonel Doller hasn't received these orders. But I'm not waiting."

Daniels nodded. "Since I seem to be taking orders from your boss, and your logic is clear, I'm with you. I'll contact my jeep company, tell them to stage a withdrawal to Taejon, and advise my captain to suggest Colonel Haskins join him, based on your advice, Rusty."

"Good! If Haskins balks, let me know."

Rusty then said, "It hurts me to say this, but I'm going back and try to talk some sense into Colonel Doller's head about withdrawing. At the very least, tell him we're all pulling out."

Chapter Sixty Four

Saturday, July 11, 1950 - Day Seventeen of the Invasion Japan – Eighth Army HQ, Colonel Nelson's Conference Room – After Midnight

"It's official." Said Colonel Nelson to his full team seated at the big oval table in his conference room.

"General MacArthur has announced that General Walker will take over command of all ground forces in Korea as of tomorrow, July 12th."

Knowing this was coming, it was a subdued celebration, but they still clapped.

Nelson continued. "Eighth Army is now fully in the fight. That means now, not tomorrow. Nobody is waiting. Among other pressing things, General Dean has lost contact with his 21st Infantry Regiment around Hill 102. Rusty initiated, some might say, a daring counter-attack that may still be going on. We haven't heard anything from our side and are totally in the dark about the enemy's reaction or intensions since Rusty ordered our listening post repositioned to Taejon. It's too far away to pick up any signals. Any suggestions?"

Major Hank Jarvis, G-2 Deputy of Eighth Army Intelligence under Colonel Nelson, spoke. "I've been in contact with General Dean's HQ in Taejon many times, got the runaround. He's not available, their working on defenses, etc. Bullshit! I think they lost it."

"Anybody suggest they send a recon squad up to reestablish contact with the 21st?" Asked Captain Sam Haran, Deputy Director of the secret NSOPU unit under Colonel Nelson, led by Master Sergeant Nick Beloit.

"I asked." Said Major Jarvis. "They said they got trucks of wounded from their 34th Infantry a few hours ago with word that the 21st was in position and holding. They felt they didn't need to check further. That was three hours ago."

"So." Said Master Sergeant Nick Beloit, "Assuming a few hours to assemble and drive to Taejon, these guys have no damn idea what the hell happened with Rusty's counter-attack or the disposition of the 21st. For all we know, the North Koreans are pouring through that gap running down the main highway about ready to surprise Taejon."

The room felt like someone sucked all the oxygen out of it.

"Do you believe that's possible?" Asked a concerned Colonel Nelson.

"Boss, what I believe is irrelevant. I'm a grunt, and I've seen unbelievable things. Men fuck up; things change, shit happens! My motto is *hope for the best and prepare for the worst*. Without information, we need to prepare for the worst."

LT Larry Cole sat at the table, racking his brain for some insight into this problem. Larry had a mind like few others, able to digest vast amounts of specific data, assemble it into a coherent construct, and then articulate its meaning. He was a vital member of the planning of all G -2 Eighth Army operations and a critical assist to previous secret actions.

He suddenly got ramrod straight in his chair. Everybody quickly looked at him.

"You okay, Cole?" Asked Colonel Nelson.

"Yes, sir. Just had a sudden revelation." Pausing to catch his breath and condense his thoughts, he continued.

"We've always thought of our secret CIA signal gathering equipment as a fixed land-based operation using the relay towers in place. But what if we could mount the equipment in a plane? I think the sending signal has a wide enough bandwidth to connect to the towers without being too precise."

Nick jumped out of his seat. "Holy Shit, Boss! You got to give this man a medal! I know just the plane and the man to fly it. I gotta go and make some calls!" Almost running on his new prosthesis foot, he got to the door and stopped, turned back. "Sam! Get hold of Leyden's team in Taejon and get them on alert to move out within the hour, equipment and all, on a truck." With that, he was out the door.

Nick had a way with his battery of assistants outside his office, two men and a woman, whom he favored best. Not only because she was good looking, but she took no shit from anybody and got through to whomever he needed. Ronnie was the best at getting it done.

They were all back at their desks within 30 minutes of his call, at 12:45 AM, after leaving but 5 hours ago. They looked like shit, and Nick knew he did too, but there they were, coffee from the never closed cafeteria in the facility, at their desks.

He quickly assigned Norm to CIA Japan Intercept HQ to wake them up and start asking questions about this new idea that was going operational within hours.

Donny was next. His job was to find the PBY that landed near Taejon and find out if it was flyable. A secondary mission was to locate another PBY if the first one was unavailable.

Ronnie had the most channeling job. Locate the wounded Navy Commander John Muzich, the pilot of the PBY plane that was sent on a successful secret mission to blow up the Han River railroad bridge and became, inadvertently, a participant.

Nick felt that except for Captain Stands, Muzich was the best-damned pilot he'd ever known.

Ronnie found him in 20 minutes.

Back at the conference room, Colonel Nelson sat, thinking, then got up and looked at the big wall map at the end of the room that focused on the roughly 200 miles from Taejon to Pusan. He thought again, as he had many times, a hundred miles from Taejon to the new capital of Taegu, then a hundred miles to Pusan. He'd seen this map in his dreams a few times and always woke up in a cold sweat. He felt that way now.

Nelson turned to his team at the table. "Taejon will fall, but goddamn it, we will not sacrifice General Dean's 24th Division! We need them!" He was shouting now. His face beat red. Then he swayed sideways and grabbed a chair.

Major Jarvis, Nelsons number two, rose quickly and grabbed the Colonel. "Sir! Are you all right?"

"No!" His eyes turned up and collapsed into Hank's arms.

Chapter Sixty Five

Saturday, July 11, 1950 - Day Seventeen of the Invasion Korea – North of Taejon – In the Central Valley – After Mid-night

General Choe U's 2,000 surviving men of South Korea's 1st Division left Rusty's command yesterday to intercept a significant North Korean force converging on elements of two depleted ROK Divisions defending the Central Valley, just north of Taejon.

The General showed his stuff, as he staged a successful ambush against superior forces. Then he linked up with his divisions' regiment and significant remnants of another division led by its General. General Choe U then took command of all ROK forces in the Valley and ordered them to fall back.

This other General was infuriated by his orders and refused, citing the fact that his division was numerically superior, and the fact that General Choe U had no authority over them. General Choe U then ordered a meeting of all senior grade officers. The group assembled behind a defensive line that was currently not threatened. Some were colonels, plenty of majors, and a bunch of captains, maybe thirty or so in all. They commanded all ROK forces in the broad Central Valley, perhaps 10,000 plus men.

`

General Choe U stood before them. There was no need to discuss his past actions, as they knew he was a warrior, fought bravely against the invasion, saved a lot of his men, but most importantly, just saved their collective ass by his ambush of a superior force that was about to attack them.

"Nobody likes to fallback." The General started. "I'd like to quote a famous US Army general that said during the WW2 Battle of the Bulge, 'Retreat? Hell! We're attacking to our rear.'"

That got a few laughs from a somber crowd.

"I'm here to tell you of my recent experience and a lesson I learned at Hill 102, that's not too far from here. America's airpower saved my regiment before I even got to that Hill, destroying two full enemy regiments before my eyes, in 30 minutes. I'll tell you it took a lot of Americans planning to do that. They were helped by a special American unit on the ground, in our trenches. These Americans then led the attack after the planes left."

Pausing to a transfixed group, the general continued.

"My regiment then followed this American unit to this Hill 102, on the main highway north of Taejon. A major American unit was fighting a holding action a few miles north when another American regiment showed up to defend this Hill. And then the most extraordinary thing happened. A fleet of planes came roaring overhead, and men started jumping out, parachutes billowing, hundreds of them! A whole battalion! It inspired me! They landed all around this Hill. American Airborne, I was told, the best fighting men in America's Army."

Standing tall in front of this diverse group of unit leaders that he just took command of, he smiled.

"America is here! They will not leave these brave men to die. America will come in great numbers to help us. But we must hold out, survive and delay and fight again. That is why we must 'Attack to the rear'!"

It started slowly, but the clapping built quickly as the officers expressed approval of their new leader and his orders. The General who had objected came forward, saluted Choe U, and shook his hand. More cheers, they were united, and they felt they had a purpose.

Together, they were a Division size unit of hardened veterans.

General Choe U set out plans to fall back.

Chapter Sixty Six

Saturday, July 11, 1950 - Day Seventeen of the Invasion Japan – Eighth Army HQ – NSOPU Secured Area, G -2 Intelligence Section – 0130 – (1:30 AM)

"Listen to me, you puke ass lieutenant, you make another crack like that and I'll have your balls for breakfast. Now go fucking wake up Commander Muzich! That's a direct order from General MacArthur himself! If he's not here in 10 minutes, so help me God, you will be a fucking corporal digging ditches in Alaska. Now go!"

Overhearing the one-way conversation just outside his door, Nick almost laughed. She was something that Ronnie. Colonel Nelson ran into her a little while ago when he went after an asshole colonel who was causing a problem. Ronnie was his secretary and helped Nelson get rid of him. She immediately became a marked person in that section, so Nelson transferred her into his expanding area and assigned her to Nick's secret unit.

She was worth her weight in gold. And besides, she was cute.

Nick rarely thought of potential companionship after he lost his foot to that Japanese mine, but since receiving his prosthetic, and being able to walk normal, he started to think differently. He liked Ronnie.

"Hello! Is this Commander Muzich?" Pause. "One moment, sir, I'll connect you."

Nick picked up the line. "First off, I'm sorry to fuck up your night. Secondly, I hope your arm is healing, and you're feeling well. Lastly, I hope you're bored and need some excitement."

"Who the fuck are you?" Asked a drowsy Muzich.

"I'm the guy who ordered you to pick up Tech Sergeant Leyden's team in Pusan and drop them near the Han River bridges. Hell of a job, by the way."

"Holy shit!" There was a long pause. "Leyden mentioned a friend of his, Nick, I think. Are you he?"

"Tom Leyden and I go way back, so yes, I'm Nick."

"What do you need me for, Nick?"

"Commander, I need you to be frank with me. I wasn't just asking those questions because I'm concerned, I'm asking because I have a mission. I need a reliable leader to pilot a PBY for Intelligence gathering, flying over enemy space in bad weather just above mountain peaks."

"So you need lots of hang time like a PBY can give. Fly circles for 8 hours or more."

"You got it, sir."

Muzich was no stranger to dangerous missions and proved his resourcefulness and bravery on many occasions. Not only recently here in Korea but also in WW2, where he had the Navy Cross awarded to him for his near-suicide attack on Japanese landing craft trying to land behind Marine positions on Saipan. With him flying a PBY no less.

"Will I be flying with Leyden's team?"

"Yes, sir. They are close by and have the Top Secret equipment. Setting up your plane shouldn't be too difficult."

"So basically, Nick, you need a crazy-ass driver that is willing to fly in bad weather, over mountains he can't see, on a continuous set route over enemy territory for many hours without any fighter support."

"Yes, sir. I think you nailed it."

"I'm honored. And yes, I'm good to go and so is my plane. She just got finished being patched up. I'm here in Taejon, and so is my plane. A copilot and navigator arrived yesterday to ferry the plane back to Japan for additional refitting, but she's okay, and I'll have additional support. So, tell me where and when."

"Thanks, commander! Go wake up your crew, Leyden's team will be showing up within the hour."

Ronnie burst into his room. "Nick! Somethings happened to Colonel Nelson!"

Both ran into the hallway and saw the medics wheeling the stretcher away. A fully capable hospital was close and had been alerted.

Ronnie was crying. Nick put his arm around her. "Don't worry, Ronnie. Only a bullet or old age can kill him. Trust me!" Nick hoped to God he was right. He didn't let his deep concern show.

Chapter Sixty Seven

Saturday, July 11, 1950 - Day Seventeen of the Invasion Korea – Taejon – On a Small US Military Base on a Lake a few miles away – 0145 – (1:45 am)

Initially constructed by Japanese occupation officers in the 1930s as a retreat, the base fell into disrepair after the war. Once discovered by America's occupation forces a few years later, its pier, extending well out into the lake, as well as its main building was refurbished. A great place to rehab from the dreary duty they said, and oh yeah, it was on a beautiful lake. They renamed it Lakehouse.

The main building was a rustic lodge resort, housing 20 rooms, a full dining room, a fireplace meeting area, and a pool table. A massive generator powered the building. A lone telephone line connected it to the US Military switchboard in Taejon ever since the US took control of the facility in 1948.

It was on this Lake that Naval Commander John Muzich landed his shot up PBY to return Leyden's team from their successful mission of blowing up the Han River Rail Road Bridge in Seoul, a mere seven days ago.

Besides recuperating from his wounded arm, Muzich stayed at the resort with his plane and supervised its repair. His only guests at the vast resort were the repair crew and

Army MP's, lots of them, all heavily armed. The repair guys had left yesterday morning. Early last night, two navy airmen arrived to assist him in flying his PBY back to Japan for significant refitting. It was a cursory greeting, just handshakes to his copilot and navigator, a little small talk and agreement to meet early the next morning to begin the flight to Japan.

From the moment he hung up the phone with Nick, Commander Muzich moved like a rocket.

Waking his copilot, then his navigator, he ordered them to meet in the dining room, in twenty minutes, ready to fly. Change of plans, he told them.

When the two men came into the brightly lit room, coffee was on a side table. Muzich had alerted the MPs, and they had abruptly awakened the staff to get breakfast going.

Muzich sat with his coffee at a big table with maps laid out.

"Sorry to mess up your night! But shit happens. Get coffee and come over."

After they each grabbed a cup, they came to his table and sat. Neither said a word.

"I'm sorry, but I forgot who's who, you're Leo, right?"

"Yes, sir, your copilot."

"And I'm Gene, your navigator."

"I'm sorry to say gentlemen, but you got yourselves into a top secret operation over enemy territory. I hope you're up to it?"

Muzich got up and refilled his coffee cup and returned.

"Men will join us shortly with specialized equipment that we'll use to spy on the North Koreans. Our flying area will focus within 50 miles or so of Taejon, but we'll hang long, trying to intercept their communications, maybe six or eight hours."

"What's our job, if anything?" Asked the copilot.

"I got the takeoff, Leo," pausing to take another sip of coffee. "Been studying this lake for the last few days. Compass headings and timing. I'm good in total darkness, so I'll drive until we get in position. You'll take over to start running our grid pattern. Then we'll alternate every two hours."

For the first time since they arrived late yesterday, Muzich looked closely over at Gene, his new navigator. His first quick impression of the baby faced young man was as a recruit, but that was way off the mark. His youthful looks hid his age well, but when he looked into his eyes, he realized this young man was older and old before his time and looked like he'd witnessed things that a young man should never have seen. He needed to probe his history.

"You're got a difficult task here, Gene. I need to trust you. Can you tell me a little about your experience?"

"No need to worry about me, Commander. Two years on three decks of sunk carriers in the Jap War, flying Torpedo planes and Dive Bombers."

"Damn! It sounds like you had it pretty rough."

Gene looked up at Muzich. "You have no fucking idea how a Carrier pilot feels when he loses his home, his friends, three times for me."

"I got an idea, Gene. Sorry. Glad you're aboard."

"Sorry to be so rude, sir. You hit a nerve. I'm exceptional at my job."

"You must be, you're still alive. We probably flew close to each other over Saipan."

"Yeah! Probably, I was there. That was a rough campaign!"

Muzich leaned over the table, pulled a map closer, and pointed. "See these mountains to the east. These have receiving towers. We need to establish a flying grid to continually send directed signals to the towers from an orbit near this Hill 102. Can you do this?"

Gene sat back, thoughtful. "You said 'directed signals,' to towers, that I don't see here on the map. I'm confused. I'm not aware of any 'directed signals.' You got something else to tell me?"

Muzich was surprised by the question and sat back to think about what he was going to say next.

"Leo, can you work out a grid pattern to fly this route and then get started on the pre-check, make sure everything's buttoned up. Please do this onboard the plane now."

After he left, Muzich faced Gene. "Our mission is complicated and very secret, but you're a key to it, so you've got to know."

Gene perked up. "I like a good mystery, is there a dame involved?" His smile was broad.

Muzich laughed, "I wish! But no. I'm hoping this is the most boring mission you or I have ever been on if all goes according to plan."

"I'm already disappointed."

"Don't be. **IF** is a big word, and I've learned not to rely on it. Anyway, I don't know a lot about this technology our guests are bringing aboard, but I do know it's unique and ultra-secret. I've seen them use a cone-shaped device to send and receive these directed signals to a tower. I think that's what they want us to do. Use us as a moving sending platform to a stationary tower. I hope they know how to do this, because I sure don't."

Gene squinted his eyes and nodded at Muzich, then lowered his head in deep thought. Having only a high school education didn't help, but his high IQ and navigator training kicked in. Remembering a class about high-frequency radio waves that the new technology of radar emitted, he followed the thread to maybe condensing those frequencies into something narrow. Wow! He thought somebody discovered how to do that.

Within only a brief amount of time, Gene raised his head and smiled.

"Holy shit, Commander. If what you say is true, we got ourselves one hell of a weapon. I think I know how to get it to work in the sky."

He told Muzich his idea.

Ten minutes later, Muzich was talking to Nick.

Chapter Sixty Eight

Saturday, July 11, 1950 - Day Seventeen of the Invasion Korea – Taejon – On the Banks of a Lake a few miles away – 0300 – (3:00 AM)

As the truck abruptly stopped, in the black of night, in a rainstorm, Tech Sergeant Tom Leyden was as pissed off as one could be, and jumped out.

He was rousted out of a deep sleep by a no-nonsense squad of Army regulars in the dead of night. A lieutenant got on a phone attached to his corporal's backpack, asked for a priority patch into NSOPU headquarters, Japan. Waiting a few seconds for somebody expecting his call, "Wait one for Sergeant Leyden, sir," as he handed the phone to Leyden.

"Sorry to fuck up your night, old friend, but duty calls."

"Nick! Jesus Christ! Armed guards? What the hell?"

"My assistant may have gone a bit overboard in stressing the urgency and need to protect your team, sorry. But it is so. Need you to get your team up, with all the Secret equipment and immediately leave with this escort unit. And I mean right now. No extra clothes, food, or anything but the equipment and self- defense weapons. I'll explain later, now move." The line went dead.

The pent up frustration of feeling useless for the last day, knowing that your friends were fighting and you weren't helping them, still festered in Leyden.

In the truck, Leyden sat in the corner next to JP, who wouldn't stop bitching about the entire ordeal, asking questions about his worst fear of being on the water again. JP almost got sick just thinking about it. Phil sat across from them. He was the electronics expert and ran the secret intercept CIA equipment. It wasn't a difficult job until a circuit or something went haywire. Greg sat in the back, a peacemaker at heart but a fierce defender of his team, calm but efficient, respected by his teammates.

A jeep and two trucks escorted Leyden's unit to a resort cove on a lake just north of Taejon.

Trying to get his bearings, Leyden stood away from the truck as the rest of his men started unloading their equipment.

"Is that you, Leyden?" Yelled Commander Muzich.

Tom was momentarily stunned. "Muzich! Never thought I'd ever hear your voice again. It's a welcome sound, my friend, so good to see you." They embraced. "How's the arm?"

"It's fine. Just don't grab it." Pausing to look at him in the rain. "Glad you're alive, Tom." Another brief pause. "We need to move. The PBY is down the path here at the end of the dock. I think you might remember it. It's all repaired. Get your equipment on it and hurry."

"Is she still gunned up with all those machine guns like before?"

"Ah, no. The repair guys stripped her of all unnecessary weight for the trip back to Japan for extensive repairs. But we won't need any weapons on this trip. It's a milk run."

"I don't trust anybody anymore, Muzich, so, where the fuck are we going? I'm not jumping into another a pile of shit like last time without somebody telling me something!"

"Nick didn't tell you? It's just flying around, gathering Intel with your secret stuff?"

"Damn! That doesn't sound so bad." Leyden paused. "Wait a minute! You're telling me we're going to be flying over enemy positions, aren't you?"

"Well, yes. But they can't see us in this weather."

"Just the same, I don't like it. I'm bringing a 50 caliber machine gun with us, just in case."

"Tom, after we take off, have your tech guy get with my navigator, names Gene, It's about sending the signals to the towers."

As the plane powered off the dock, Leyden yelled out above the engine noise to his team. "Listen up! We're doing something that's never been tried before. Phil, after we level off, Muzich says to see the navigator, Gene's his name, has an idea about how you can send the signals to the towers."

Phil stiffened immediately, didn't know what to say for a few beats. "This is all on me? Who the fuck is this guy, Gene? Who issued this crazy order? Never mind finding a fucking relay tower, I can't even see out of the goddamn plane. This mission is so FUBAR!"

As the plane slowly made its way across the lake, Leyden came over to Phil and spoke loud enough for all in the open space to hear.

"Phil, you better get your head on straight and get your ass in gear! We've in a fucking war, and we aim to win. Whether you like it or not, you're a key man in that outcome, so get to it. FUBAR or not, we got to try! Now go set up the receiving unit in the front gunner position while we're still level. Then talk to Gene about the sending unit. Move! Greg, help him! JP, wire the receiving unit back to the sending unit and get it set up back here! Phil will come back to positon it."

Tech Sergeant Tom Leyden didn't know shit about what he was doing but knew he needed to lead, and it felt right. He hoped like hell that Muzich knew more about this operation then he, and could get this plane in the air, off of this lake, in the rain, in total darkness and find the enemy position.

Jesus Nick, he thought, what have you gotten me into this time?

A few minutes later, the plane powered through the lake in the pitch dark.

Chapter Sixty Nine

Saturday, July 11, 1950 - Day Seventeen of the Invasion Japan – Eighth Army HQ, G-2 Section - Colonel Nelson's Conference Room – 0330 (3:30 am)

General Walker, Eighth Army Commander, and now Commander of all forces in Korea, came in the room. A total surprise, Walker yelled as he entered. "Stay as you are! Please relax!"

Colonel Nelson's entire staff, who had been working around the large conference table, suddenly froze at the General's words, they feared the worst.

General Walker quickly moved to the coffee pot and poured a cup. As he did that, he turned to the anxious faces at the table.

"I have good news!" The general grabbed a seat and took a gulp. "Wish it were scotch," he said with a crocked head. "Been a tough few hours, but Colonel Nelson is fine."

You could hear the air escape from the lungs around the table.

"I came here to tell you personally because I know how much he means to you, but also how much he means to me. He's a friend. Jim's been with me for a while, shown exceptional brilliance in many ways, and has helped the Eighth Army and me. You here at this table, have demonstrated the guts of America's strength and ingenuity in the face of defeat. You all have impressed me. You should all be proud of yourselves."

Taking another gulp of coffee, General Walker leaned back in his chair.

"If you know anything about me, you would know that I don't blow smoke, nor do I give praise often. So, keep going and do what you're doing!" He stood.

"Oh, Major Jarvis! As number two, I hold you personally responsible for ensuring Colonel Nelson gets adequate rest and that he stays off coffee for at least a week. Stressed out without sleep, he overdosed on caffeine. No permanent damage, thank God. He'll be released at noon."

General Walker walked out. As the door closed, the room erupted. Everybody was so happy. Then it hit Major Hank Jarvis. He sat down in a daze.

Nick noticed immediately and came over. "You okay, Hank?"

"No! Colonel Nelson without coffee! Are you kidding me? I'm screwed."

The group laughed.

"It'll be a joint effort, Hank. An intervention by the entire staff." Nick looked around, "Right!" The group at the table stopped laughing, just nodded their heads. "See Hank, don't worry, everybody's got your back."

Thankful for the excellent news about Colonel Nelson, Nick was on a high as he entered his NSOPU secret area. His three assistants at the front desks were all on the phone. The noise of machines clanking out messages in the background added to the busyness of voices.

Nick entered his office and closed the door then slumped into his chair. Tried to clear his head. Moments in his life flew by, he strained to focus. Yeah, he thought, few men filled the role model of the man he wanted to be. Colonel Nelson was someone who captured that by his commitment and his trust. It's been a good day so far, he thought, hope it continues. Then he wondered if Muzich and Leyden got airborne.

His door suddenly opened. Ronnie stood there. "You better tell me something about Colonel Nelson!"

Chapter Seventy

**Saturday, July 11, 1950 - Day Seventeen of the Invasion
Korea – In the PBY, Flying a Grid Pattern at 7,000 Feet
around Hill 102 – 0400 – (4:00 am)**

Muzich did his thing on the lake, amazing his copilot as he watched Muzich check his stopwatch at multiple times and various turns, finally throwing the throttles to the stops. The plane quickly powered up and began its increasing lumbering speed across a black surface with rain pelting on the windshield, gradually increasing momentum, and, like the broad-winged eagle, lifted into nothingness.

It took 15 minutes to climb above the high clouds and level off. The sky filled with millions of stars but no moon. Muzich liked seeing the stars, flying at night reminded him of being a kid, dreaming of flying off to distant planets.

Turning to his copilot, "Leo! You got the controls, start your plot, I've got to check on our guests."

Passing his navigator, Gene, on his way back to see Leyden, he asked, "Anybody see you yet?"

"No, sir."

"Follow me."

As Muzich passed behind Gene's navigation section, he went through an un-replaced destroyed door opening into the rear section. It reminded him of his last mission with Leyden, where a shell exploded and killed the previous navigator.

"Everybody," yelled Muzich, "This is Gene, my navigator, the most important man on this plane."

The noisy, spacious area didn't hide Muzich's booming voice as he made his way to Staff Sergeant Tom Leyden's side, Gene following, sitting on the floor.

"Where's your tech guy?"

"Phil! Come over."

"Ah!" Said Muzich, as Phil sat on the floor next to Gene. "You crawled through the cockpit while I was maneuvering before takeoff?"

"Right! Damn glad you kept turning and taking your time. Got the receiving antennae hooked up inserted into the gun port just as you gunned it. That was quite a ride, sir. Can't say I want to do it again, though."

Muzich tapped Leyden on the shoulder to lean in as he addressed the three of them.

"I've been talking to Nick, the CIA, and back and forth for two fucking hours before you arrived, we're out of time, so I'll cut this short. Gene knows what's going on, and you don't need to know shit about the details, but to just follow his directions. Now, that's an order from Nick and the CIA. You guys copy?"

Leyden looked closely at the young looking boy named Gene, and he, too, realized that he wasn't young. Phil felt relieved because he had no screaming idea of how to find a tower to send the intercepted messages.

"I guess it's my turn," said Gene. "Per the CIA, and on a potential life in a no-name prison, I think I have the answer to the tower problem because I asked a simple question. Here's the short of it."

Gene talked to Phil, then the group, because they were going to have to continually shift the sending cone as the plane flew the grid. Phil had a compass. Gene had a better one. They set up a system hoping the plan would come together.

The PBY glided slowly through the black night, Leo at the controls, flying a big grid, at 7,000 feet among the stars.

At 0428 precisely, Gene turned on his RDR (Radio Direction Finder) to a specific very high-frequency radio channel that's never used. Then he aimed it at the mountains to his east and waited. Two minutes later, even though expecting it, Gene jumped at the sound of the faint signal. He stayed calm, adjusted the RDF until the signal was the strongest then wrote down its bearing and time into the grid pattern. His heart beat like a drum.

Leo ran his grid for the next hour. At 10 minute intervals, Gene recorded the same high-frequency signal and plotted it.

With that, Gene had multiple plots and could maintain continuous contact with the receiving tower throughout their entire grid run.

"I got it, Phil," Gene said to his anxious sidekick by his side. "Leo will make the turn on his grid in 3 minutes. Go set up your sending cone on the port Plexiglas with this baring," handing him a paper, "It will change one degree every 2 minutes, you must keep track. Got your stopwatch?"

Chapter Seventy One

**Saturday, July 11, 1950 - Day Seventeen of the Invasion
Korea – On the Main Highway to Taejon – Before Dawn**

Now about three miles away from Hill 102 heading toward
Taejon, the long column of men moved in the darkness and a
slight drizzle. The jeep artillery platoon stationed on the ridge
nearby led the advance, followed by a lone duce and a half
packed with equipment and ammunition.

All the seriously wounded had left earlier on the last
remaining trucks but the one. Despite the loaded vehicle, each
man carried a heavy load as they didn't know what to expect
when they reached Taejon.

During the preparation to evacuate, Rusty spent a lot of
time on the radio with Colonel Haskins, who had refused to
reposition out to Taejon and join the Jeep Airborne Artillery
unit preparing to leave his location. He referred to his duty and
original orders to stay with his assigned 21st Regiment. Colonel
Haskins figured the enemy could come at Hill 102 through the
side pass and slaughter Colonel Doller's men if they left. So,
unless the 21st pulled back, he would stay. Rusty gave up and
wished him well.

Rusty was suddenly alerted by a commotion at the rear of
the column. He stepped out of the middle of the column with
Red and started walking back. Still dark, they couldn't see but

wondered what Mario and Snake, placed at the very rear, had encountered that was causing a fuss. Soon the grape vine of marching men caught up to them when they overheard the word coming forward.

"Missing G I's showed up!"

Rusty looked at Red. "Holy Shit! Could it be?"

They took off at a run and finally got to the end of the column. Back at the end of the column, standing in the road, were Mario and Snake still slapping and embracing the missing Dean and Frenchy. Stepping apart after seeing Rusty and Red approach, all were still smiling.

"Damn good to see you both!" Rusty said as he slapped their shoulders. "And if you ever disappear like that again, you better come back with a North Korean General's head in a sack, or don't come back!"

He turned and walked back to catch up to the column.

Red stood with them and watched Rusty walk away and turned to sniper Dean and Mario.

"I don't give a shit about what you were thinking, nor do I care what, if anything, you accomplished. You're in a family now, a special family. Fuck your past Ranger shit and all that bravado bull crap. Rusty wasn't the only one that was worried sick about you two. Don't ever go off on your own again! Got it!"

Nodding, "Yeah, we got it." They both said.

Looking at them, Red cracked a small smile, "You both look like shit. Glad you made it."

Later on in the march, Rusty's team slowly filtered back to the rear to welcome back the MIA's. Tully was the first, ecstatic that his Rangers were back. And that's when it hit him. They were no longer *his* Rangers. It was strange that he even thought of them in that way because he hadn't in a while. He'd become fully assimilated into Rusty's Team and liked the feeling.

He again pondered the time when he volunteered his Ranger squad to help Colonel Nelson's small intelligence force in Korea before the invasion. It seemed like a long time ago. But it wasn't but less than a month ago. And what a month it's been. Non-stop action on a scale he never envisioned. He smiled.

Joe slid in next to Dean and punched him lightly in his arm. "Asshole! Snipers don't get lost. You're long-range assets, like artillery. Do you need to go back to basic fucking sniper school?"

"Good to see you too, Joe. Maybe I picked up a fungus from you. Maybe it was a Gene Autry movie."

"But can you sing?"

Mario was marching next to Frenchy. After the last of the well-wishes fell in around them, Frenchy turned to Mario, "Some of my friends are missing. Tell me, is Tracker okay? And where are Foxy and Moose?"

Mario knew this question would come. A skilled mountain climber, he wished for a cliff to climb rather than answer the question. But facts were facts, and he knew Frenchy could take the hard truth.

"Tracker got shot and is in critical condition in Taejon. Foxy got badly wounded in a mortar attack and is also in Taejon. Moose didn't make it."

Frenchy didn't miss a step, but his heart pounded, he thought of his friends, then tears slipped out.

Mario waited a minute, put his arm around his friend's shoulder as they marched on together in silence.

It was an emotional march for most of the men, a good deal of whom had lost friends, but all wondered about where they were going and what the rather grim looking future held.

Chapter Seventy Two

Saturday, July 11, 1950 - Day Seventeen of the Invasion Japan – Eighth Army HQ, G-2 Section - Colonel Nelson's Conference Room – Just after Dawn

Major Hank Jarvis, as Deputy Director, was now in charge of all G-2 operations of Eighth Army until Colonel Nelson returned and sat at the head of the conference table. He looked and felt exhausted, as did the other two men in the big room.

Master Sergeant Nick Beloit and his deputy at NSOPU, Captain Sam Haran, sat to his right.

"You're something, Nick." Said Major Jarvis, "CIA said you solved a major puzzle." Pausing, "Unlike anything I've ever heard from them, they don't wax it ever, sounded like maybe you invented the A-Bomb or something."

Nick smiled at him. "So, I'm guessing it all worked out?"

Major Jarvis just looked at him, straight-faced, and smiled. "Yeah, Nick. Whatever the hell you pulled off was something special. We're getting direct intercepts of North Korean units from the CIA translators as of an hour ago."

Nick digested that. Not one to prolong a discussion, "Do I have to beg, Major!" Using his military rank to address him rather than his name showed his edge and maybe his exhaustion at an admired and respected leader.

After just having given Nick a significant complement, he wondered what just happened. Major Jarvis sat back in his chair and thought about this young man he faced, 20 years his junior and given so much responsibility, with only one foot and only a master sergeant. He laughed in his head. Jesus! I'm jealous.

"You're a damn bulldog, you know, and I'm sure as shit glad you're on our side."

Nick sat back, "I'm an asshole sometimes, Hank. Sorry."

"No need. Probably should have started with the results first. The reports coming in are startling. The North Korean command structure is very confused. They think we've somehow deployed significant forces to defend Taejon. Rusty's counter-attack caused a major disruption in their thinking. The ambush by Colonel Haskins completely freaked them out. They're reassessing their next move."

"Good news, I'd say." Said Captain Sam Haran, "Buys us a little more time."

"On that note," said Major Jarvis, "in light of these new developments, General Walker wants to know if defending Taejon is worth a more serious effort or do we keep staging a fighting withdrawal without sacrificing needless causalities. He wants more options. Get your heads clear. We'll meet back here at 0900 (9:00 am) and discuss this."

Chapter Seventy Three

Saturday, July 11, 1950 - Day Seventeen of the Invasion Korea – In the PBY, Flying a Grid Pattern at 7,000 Feet around Hill 102 – 0830 – (8:30 am)

With over five hours flying a standard grid pattern, every man on the PBY was fatigued by the monotony and exhausted by the constant need to focus. Phil and JP were not bored; they were overworked and terribly strained because of the need to adjust the cone-sending sphere to new tower bearings regularly. So they worked half-hour shifts

There was no autopilot on the PBY. The constant demands of maintaining a steady course, timing the turns, and maintaining level flight were taxing. Commander Muzich and his copilot, Leo, decided a forty-five minute shift would work better than anything longer.

Navigator Gene took only occasional breaks, earnest in his efforts to keep the plane on track in its pattern.

Tech Sergeant Tom Leyden was like a cat with an allergy, couldn't sit still, always moving, going to the front gunner position where the receiving antennae now protruded, then to every Plexiglas canopy to check the surroundings. Along the way, he made sure everybody was awake and engaged. He was fighting his numbness to the monotony, figured everybody felt the same.

Muzich entered the rear area and sat next to Leyden. "Good news, Tom. We're heading back early to the lake. We're Just making the turn, heading southeast on the grid, we'll keep going."

"About damn time!" Leyden smiled. "How's the weather at the lake?"

Now it was Muzich who smiled. "Beautiful! Sun's out, flat calm." Then he winked.

JP got up, his turn to spell Phil on the cone. He stretched out. Then the noise of metal ripping through their compartment was sudden and ear-splitting. JP's body exploded, the large Plexiglas window across from Leyden and Muzich disintegrated, heavy plastic pieces flying everywhere. The shot out window let in 150 mile winds to the rear section, creating a maelstrom where anything loose flew around.

Muzich instinctively grabbed Leyden at the outset and pulled him to the floor. But the four-second burst was over; they were just lucky. The plane immediately dipped to the left on a slow descent.

Ivan Suchkov, a Russian Captain, had been training North Korean pilots for the past 18 months. At 28, he was considered a war hero in his homeland and one of the best fighter pilots of the Big War. He was flying one of the best fighter planes of that war, the YAK-3, considered by most to be superior to the Allies P-51 fighter.

He loved his Yak-3 almost as much as he loved his wife and kids, but with only two weeks left in his tour, the anticipation of seeing them far outweighed his joy of flying. Besides, his distaste for the North Korean culture, its men he trained, their food, and the dismal country, added to his hunger to return home. He couldn't wait.

The urgent call came into his base that an enemy plane was heard circling high above a battlefield where several North Korean divisions were attacking, Ivan was ordered to check it out. He was picked because the weather was terrible, and the Russian colonel in charge had no confidence in any of the North Korean pilots. Besides all of that, the Russian general in charge of Korea ordered this recon mission. He was upset by the recent punch in the nose that the North Korean advance just took and felt maybe something was up, and he wanted the best of the best to check it out.

Ivan was pissed at first, having to fly out in this weather in what he thought was a bullshit mission, but when he spotted the American plane, his adrenaline kicked in like old times. Then he was filled with the excitement of action, after just having jumped the American from behind. It had been over five years since he'd been in combat, he'd forgotten the thrill. Maybe he got too excited, he thought, as he came in too close before opening fire and didn't get the kill shot as he zoomed past the slow plane. Still, had his cannon not jammed, he figured, it would have died. But the twin machine guns had done their job as the aircraft dipped after his pass and knew he killed people inside when the plane started down.

Climbing after the first attack, he did a long barrel roll to come at it again from the rear, but this time he'd take a side angle, giving him a chance to strafe the plane across most of its side.

His first victory after so many years went through his mind, Ivan wanted to savor every second as he rolled out of the high end of the barrel maneuver to position his plane for the final attack.

The chaos inside the PBY was something that not many men ever experienced, and Tom Leyden was on the top of that list. Disoriented by the sound of the rushing wind, lying on the floor, he saw JP's blood pumping out on the floor; his torso almost severed in half. He wanted to retch.

Next to him, Muzich yelled in his ear, "Move Leyden! He's coming back to kill us!" Muzich then clawed up, got a hold on something, and slowly crawled through JP's blood to get to the cockpit, as the PBY increased its angle of descent. The noise was roaring.

"Holy shit!" Said Leyden, as he got his bearings. "Phil!" He yelled above the roar.

"Jesus! What just happened?" Phil yelled back from the other side, at the right side Plexiglas where he'd managed the cone sender. Then he saw his longtime friend. "Oh, no!" He sat frozen.

Leyden went over and grabbed him, yelling in his face above the whirlwind, "He's dead, Phil. We may be dead soon too. Where's the 50 caliber we brought?"

Muzich was soaked in JP's blood as he passed through the rear cabin into the cockpit area, he saw Gene leaning over the copilot's chair.

The cockpit was no different than the rear as the wind blew through the blown out copilot's window caused by the same bullets that took off the top of Leo's head, his blood and brain matter everywhere.

After the explosion in the cockpit window, the PBY lurched downward, Gene instinctively jumped up to grab the control wheel of the copilot, just in front and next to him. Initially sickened at the sight of the partially headless Leo, he knew survival meant controlling the plane before it went into a death spiral. He leaned over Leo's bloody body pulling on the control wheel yoke, trying to right the plane and get some lift, hoping that Leo's dead feet weren't stuck on any of the rudder petals.

Muzich crawled around Gene, the downward angle of the plane made it difficult to get to his seat, but he found a way and grabbed the yoke. Yelling at the top of his lungs, "Get him out of the chair!"

Gene now quickly unbuckled Leo and placed him on the floor.

At Leyden's 'in his face' reality shout, Phil got straight real fast as the angle of the plane was telling him survival took precedent over sorrow.

The machine gun was on the floor in a corner, and it was close. Phil didn't take long to get it and the ammo.

Leyden grabbed it and went to the blown-out Plexiglas side window and tried to balance the big gun on the window frame as Phil loaded the first belt and set about the other belts if they were needed.

As Leyden was finishing setting up, the PBY nosed up. It was still going down but not as steep, and it seemed to be trying to level off.

That's when Leyden saw a spec appear, far off to his left. Leyden was Army infantry and had never been in a fight against an aircraft, especially from another plane. He was so angry at seeing JP's dismembered body that he went into another state of mind, thought of nothing but retribution.

He got into an almost trance-like state, quiet and focused on his machine gun training, the guns range, its destructive power, his experience about leading a moving target, and he waited.

Ivan leveled off well behind the slow American plane and angled his attack, still thinking this plane was unarmed. He started to move in close, directly on the side where the Plexiglas was blown out, for his final kill shot.

Leyden felt the dread of a fighter plane coming directly at him, at me! He didn't care now, then drew a bead on the approaching fighter but had no idea of distance and speed. Holding off for as long as he possibly could, Leyden opened fire.

Ivan pressed his gun trigger at the same time.

Leyden kept his finger on the trigger as the 50 caliber machine gun decimated the fighter cockpit and the plane's engine.

Ivan did the same in his death. His bullets tore through the skin of the PBY just to Leyden's left, where Phil was feeding his 50 caliber machine gun belt.

Leyden was blown back by the explosion of metal fragments, as chunks of the fuselage of the plane at his side disintegrated. He landed in a pool of blood, tried to raise his head, and then passed out.

Muzich had just regained control when the shudder of additional shells piercing the plane caused him dread. To his left, he saw a flaming fighter plane zoom past in a death spiral.

"Damn!" He shouted. He wondered if there were more fighters.

He believed the damage he felt had all happened where Leyden's team was, in the rear section.

Gene got into Leo's bloodied copilot seat.

"I've got the coordinates, Commander, bring your heading to 175 degrees."

"Are you sure?"

"Pretty sure." Pausing a moment, "Sir! I can't sit here, the wind in my face is blinding me!"

Then the right engine burst into flames, the final tribute to Ivan Suchkov's last attack.

"Oh God!" Yelled Muzich as he shut the engine down. He wondered what happened in the back. Thought maybe another enemy fighter might come in for the final kill. They usually flew in pairs. Putting that out of his mind, he focused on known facts and how to save his plane. Realizing he'd die if he couldn't.

Turning to Gene, he yelled, "Check out the rear!"

As Gene left, Muzich struggled with his controls to remain level and did. The PBY was one of the most forgiving of any aircraft ever built. With its long wingspan and light construction, it didn't need two engines. Grounds crew often joked that a motorcycle engine would be a good spare in case the main two engines got screwed somehow.

Now in control of the plane, he brought his heading back to 175 degrees. Thinking back to his miraculous crash landing off of the Island of Saipan in the Big War, when he knew he would die, but didn't, he wondered if history might repeat. But then again, he did lose his entire crew. Not again! He swore to himself.

He brought the PBY down into the clouds to hide if there was another fighter. Then Muzich wondered if they made it that far, where and how he was going to land.

The whirlwind in the cockpit was terrifying because of its noise and debilitating effect on one's vision, and now flying blind through clouds made his heart beat so hard he thought it might explode.

He was startled when Gene yelled in his ear. "I think I got Leyden stabilized, but it's bad. Everybody else is dead. Both side skins of the plane are chewed up, don't know how we weren't cut in two." He then moved into the copilot's seat, strapped in, and took out his stopwatch, and yelled over to Muzich.

"Two minutes, sir! Bring her down to 500 feet."

"You know where we are?" He yelled back.

"Only if you stayed on that heading."

"We moved a bit, Gene."

"You got enough lift if we're off somewhat?"

"Don't think so. Too much drag from all the openings, I can barely control the plane now."

Gene nodded and made the sign of the cross.

Rapidly descending, they broke through the cloud cover into a light rain, which wasn't light coming through the copilot's blown-out window. Protected by goggles, Muzich saw the lake to his left and knew he had only one chance. As he turned and increased his descent for a landing, the plane started to shake violently.

"Gene! Bring Leyden into the cockpit. Hurry!"

Gene jumped out of the seat and quickly dragged Leyden into the cockpit area.

"Strap in!"

It felt like being on the inside of a washing machine. Muzich thought they'd break apart any minute, but doing his best, he had only enough control to keep the plane's nose up as they hit the lake really hard. Glass from Muzich's window shattered into his face. A loud screeching bang echoed into the cockpit as the plane bounced twice on the water then abruptly stopped. Its rear section completely separated and sank.

"Out!" Yelled Muzich, blood pouring down his face, as he pulled on a lever that actuated an emergency inflatable that blew out from the side of the cockpit door. He grabbed a rag to wipe his eyes.

A tether line held the raft to the plane, which Gene pulled close as he pulled Leyden into the raft, then he got in.

At the door, with the plane angled up and starting its journey to the lake bottom, Muzich yelled out, "Need to check the nose!" He then disappeared.

As the plane started to sink rapidly, Gene cut the line to the aircraft as the emergency door exit was almost submerged.

Coughing, Muzich appeared, his face covered in blood, dragging a body. Gene paddled in close as the PBY went under, lifted the body into the life raft and then helped his commander aboard.

Chapter Seventy Four

Saturday, July 11, 1950 - Day Seventeen of the Invasion Japan – Eighth Army HQ, G-2 Section - Colonel Nelson's Conference Room – 0900 – (9:00 am)

The entire G-2 and Nick's section were about to start their meeting when the conference door burst open, startling everyone at the table, as Colonel Nelson rushed in.

He looked around, "Rest is overrated!" He exclaimed, as he moved to his chair, where his number two, Major Jarvis had been sitting, who promptly got up. "Thanks, Hank. I'll never drink tea! So would you please get me a coffee?"

Major Jarvis shook his head, looked out to the table of faces staring at him. "I told you all! You're complicit in this."

"What complicit?" Said Nelson as he sat.

"It's a long boring story, Colonel, not important now."

Starring at him and around the table, he decided not to pursue it and settled into his chair.

"So you all realized by now that I don't take orders well, never have when I thought they were wrong. Like from my doctors. It gives me perspective. I've learned that most high-level orders are flawed because they're usually made by men to far away from the field, in essence, from reality."

"These orders are not made by the Captain of his company, nor the Colonel of his Regiment. Most significant orders are made by a General who commands a Group or an Army. These men are so far up the chain of command that they have no idea of what's happening on the ground."

The men at the table had no idea where this was going but knew it was going somewhere that would affect them.

After a long pause, while Colonel Nelson took a big gulp of coffee, he continued.

"We're losing this war!" He angrily said. "This bullshit analysis request about Taejon from General Walker was not from him. It came from his boss, General MacArthur.

"This man has screwed up this war so much that we might actually get kicked out of the country.

"Sitting on his throne in Japan for five years ignoring Korea. Never bothering to check what the North Koreans were up to or seeing to the proper readiness of the South Korean forces.

"Underestimating the North Korean strength when they invaded. Then putting an inexperienced General Church in charge, then General Dean, who I admire greatly, and who is knowledgeable about Korea. But he's a division commander! In charge of all of Korea! Jesus!"

Shaking his head, he paused a moment.

"Finally, he makes the right call! It's now our mess, Eighth Army, and General Walker in particular. If you think that this may have political overtones in the military sphere in the blame game, well, maybe you're a thinking person."

Colonel Nelson then looked around the table and sat back in his chair.

"Guess I needed to get that out of my system. It just shows what too much rest can do. Sorry for my rant. So what did I miss?"

The room was deathly quiet for a few moments as each member looked to each other, wondering what to say or who should start.

Nick decided he should. "Damn glad you're back, boss! And with strong feelings that we need. Just don't put any of what you just said in writing."

That broke the tension as everybody clapped. Then the group got down to business and updated Nelson on events.

After 45 minutes of updates, the conference door opened, and Ronnie, Nick's NSOPU secretary, burst in, distraught and out of breath, holding a paper in her hand.

"Sorry!" She cried out. "It's important!" As she handed the telex to Nick. Then she saw Colonel Nelson and gave him a big smile.

Nick read the short message. "It's from the CIA, Japan." Pausing to read it. "Oh, shit! Their man stationed at the Lakehouse Lodge in Taejon reported that our PBY crash landed on the Lake and sunk. Survivors have been brought to the Lodge and are awaiting medical help from the city. Security and a dive team are also on their way to retrieve the sensitive equipment."

Nick looked up, "I'm going to Taejon."

Colonel Nelson turned to Nick. "I'm going with you."

After a momentary pause, Colonel Nelson stood and turned to the group.

"Let there be no doubt about our resolve to defend Korea." He said forcefully. "Taejon will be defended. We need time until Eighth Army can come to strength in Korea. That's our report to General Walker."

Chapter Seventy Five

Saturday, July 11, 1950 - Day Seventeen of the Invasion
Korea – Taejon Airfield - Mid-Morning

All flights were grounded in Japan because of bad weather. But Colonel Nelson, being who he is, commandeered a C-47 ammunition supply plane scheduled for Taejon and overrode orders after questioning the pilots and asking them if they would volunteer to fly in these conditions. Affirming their qualifications and willingness, they took off in foul weather and landed in horrible weather. It was a real white knuckle flight from start to finish.

Colonel Nelson preceded Nick to the exit but stopped to congratulate the 23 year old pilot and his 22 year old copilot who stood, white faced at the door.

"You'll never forget this heroic flight, son. And I bless your instincts on getting us here safely."

Stepping off the plane, he heard a familiar voice.

"My favorite Colonel!"

They embraced, "Let's get out of the rain," said "Wild Bill," Captain William Stands, a longtime friend and operative of G-2 Eighth Army under the Colonel.

Looking around, Nelson saw four jeeps with pedestal-mounted 30 caliber machine guns and at least a platoon of armed soldiers.

`

"How did you know, Wild Bill?"

"You have a leak, my Colonel."

"Care to share?"

"Only if you are who I believe you are?"

"What the hell does that mean?" Asked an annoyed Nelson.

"She sounded more than concerned, so I wondered if you were staying true to your professed loved family."

Nelson stopped, the rain beating down on them. "I love you, Bill, but you can be a huge asshole sometimes."

"Let's keep walking. My mind does stray into dark circles from time to time, so I apologize for any inference of indiscretion. I believe it may be that my brain has succumbed to The Korean Influence."

"So, who's the mole?"

"Works for Nick, names Ronnie."

"Aah!"

In the airfield hanger, was a Colonel Nathan Harper, Deputy Commander of General Dean's 24th Infantry Division, now in charge of the defense of Taejon. Next to him was a captain with no identifying unit patch.

"Where is General Dean?" Asked Colonel Nelson rather abruptly.

"North, setting up the defense perimeter. I was unable to contact him concerning this meeting."

Pausing a moment but still staring at Colonel Harper, his face now growing seriously red, Colonel Nelson exploded.

"General Walker ordered him to be here! What the fuck is he doing on the perimeter, and why haven't you been able to get hold of him in the last few hours?"

"General Dean takes a hands-on approach to serious matters, likes to get out front. Besides, our communication equipment is vintage WW2. It's old, breaks down often, and or simply dies."

Wild Bill laughed. "I'm not sure whether you should shoot this misguided bastard or give him a medal for absolute loyalty."

Nelson nodded. "I'll hold off on that decision for a little while. But what he says about the equipment is true, and I know General Dean is a meticulous guy that deeply cares about his men. Who's this guy?" Pointing to the captain.

"He's with me, boss." Said Nick. "And I need to speak with him privately."

"Go."

"Colonel Harper, after you make a call to your headquarters ordering every man, woman, and child under your command to find and bring General Dean back to HQ, then you will take me to your medical facility. Go make that call."

Nick came back into the room with the unknown captain. "Boss! I need to speak with you alone."

In the corner of the hanger, Nick started, "The captain is CIA Station Chief of Korea, I asked for his presence and some analysis."

"Analysis of what?"

"A few things boss, but hear me out, because what I'm about to tell you will upset you, as it did me."

"Go on."

"It's mostly about General Dean's erratic behavior since his Osan's unit demise and subsequent regiment's defeats."

"That's enough for now, Nick. We'll get into this later, right now we're going to the medical unit to see our men."

They reconnected with Colonel Harper and entered a jeep outside the hanger. Two jeeps were in front and two in the rear. The no-name captain rode in the first jeep. All the vehicles had heavily armed Army sergeants.

The building they arrived at was a Korean High School at the south end of Taejon. Colonel Harper explained on the way over that the only small hospital in Taejon was overloaded when the 24th Division set up headquarters in town, so they commandeered this empty two story brick building as their medical facility.

MP's and ROK armed guards were everywhere.

"Why such security?" Asked Colonel Nelson.

"We've had infiltrators, and we're close to the front. But this heavy protection is new."

After passing through security, the no-name captain said, "Follow me." He led them past classrooms now filled with patients in beds with IV drip lines and nurses in the halls pushing gurneys and finally arriving at double doors at a back section of the first floor. Four robust-looking men bearing Thompson automatic weapons at the ready stood at its front.

They nodded at the no-name captain as two stepped aside, and the other two opened the doors to the school gym.

"Jesus!" Said Colonel Nelson, at the sight of the gymnasium filled with men in hospital beds, with doctors and nurses moving about.

Nick grabbed the no-name captain, "Where?"

He led him into a semi-isolated area, "Your men are here. But two just came out of surgery."

Colonel Nelson saw Nick go off but then saw a familiar face off to his right.

"Arron! Damn! How're you feeling?"

Smiling, "Like a woodpecker that just got skunked by a rattler, sir."

"Sounds like you're healing fine, son."

"Yes, sir. We southern boys don't like laying around. Tell the docs I'm good. I'm really pissed I let that Northern communist bastard get the drop on me, I need some payback."

Looking over to the next bed, Nelson realized that Foxy was lying on his stomach.

"Arron! Do you know how Foxy is?"

"No. He cries a lot, then I cry."

A doctor appeared, Nelson asked him about Foxy. "Colonel, he's got a severe concussion, maybe a more severe brain injury, but we have limited capabilities here. His back wounds are healing fine."

Nelson reacted. "Doctor! Prepare these two patients for immediate transport. I'm taking them to Japan."

Nick came back to Nelson, "Come with me, sir." He led him to a screened area with a guard at the opening, standing next to the no-name captain. Entering, he saw four beds. Two had men wrapped in bandages from head to toe with IV drip lines and other tubes attached, and a doctor beside one. The next two beds had one man sitting up, his head bandaged, the second man was smoking, with no outward show of wounds. A guard sat in the corner with a Tommy gun on his lap.

"Boss, the doctor has just brought Staff Sergeant Leyden and his unit member Sergeant Greg Foles out of surgery here not long ago. Sergeant Foles is the last surviving member of your secret Post # 4 at the invasion border."

"I hired Greg; he's a damn hero. Shit! They both are." Said a sad Nelson. Turning to the doctor, "Will they make it?"

"We've done what we could, Colonel. They both got chopped up pretty good. We've got them stabilized for now, and I believe we got all the shrapnel out, stopped the internal bleeding, but damn, they got chewed up. Not sure about some limbs. They need to get to a major trauma hospital, real fast."

"I already have two patients set for transport to Japan, doctor, please include these two. We'll leave in about an hour."

"Sir." Nick, directing him to the next bed, "This is Commander John Muzich."

Extending his hand, "You're an impressive man, Commander. Glad I finally get to meet you."

"Heard a few good things about you as well, Colonel." Muzich moved to his right. "Now you should meet the man that made our mission possible and why I and these brave men, Tom and Greg, are still alive, please meet Gene, Chief Petty Officer, Eugene Tadaldi, my navigator."

They nodded.

"Can you walk, Commander?"

"Just got glass and crap in my head, nothing in my legs, got no trouble walking, Colonel."

"Good. You and Tadaldi are supervising the transfer of Leyden and Foles to our plane and coming to Japan."

Five minutes later, the Nelson entourage was back at 24th Division HQ.

"No luck, Colonel, we can't find General Dean." Said a major to Colonel Harper, as they entered a conference area filled with wall maps.

Colonel Nelson and Nick exchanged glances. "So, I guess you're in charge, Colonel. Tell me about plans for the defense of Taejon."

Colonel Harper had a quizzical look on his face.

"Not sure what you mean by that, Colonel, but we plan no defense of Taejon, only a holding action and fast withdrawal."

"What!"

"We have no other orders but that. We plan to delay and fall back and delay again, preserving our force and keep delaying until we achieve more reserves in our rear."

Colonel Nelson was stunned, speechless.

Nick came to his rescue. "Colonel Harper, I believe you have a combined force of about 10,000 or so men under your command in and around Taejon. Is that not so?"

"What's your point, Master Sergeant?" He said disparagingly.

Colonel Nelson responded. "The point, Colonel, is that you have a substantial force here, and if directed properly, could put up a stout defense of Taejon. Perhaps delaying the enemy for many days."

"And get the 24th Division decimated."

"Possibly. But maybe you'd be saving Eighth Army from defeat at Pusan."

Colonel Harper nodded to the higher calling. "I need an order from General Walker."

"Do you have coms to Japan?"

"You're kidding, right? I'm sorry to be a cynic, but we occasionally do have communications. But it's often interrupted and sometimes incoherent."

"Nick, any idea where Larry is?"

"Be back in a minute."

Nick exited the room and met with his CIA captain.

Ten minutes later, they were all at a three-story building in the center of town, a cone-shaped device on the roof, guards at the door.

Larry was on the third floor sitting at a table filled with equipment. A young Korean soldier sat on a wood box next to him with a foot-powered electric generator at his feet.

He jumped up on seeing Colonel Nelson enter the room. "Holy shit!" Joyous, yet befuddled. "Is Rusty okay?"

"Hi, Larry. Don't know about Rusty. Glad you're okay. Are you operational to Japan?"

"Yes, sir. The CIA guys have been using me since I got here. I've tried to get info from your office, but nobody has acknowledged."

"Yeah, they probably thought you were captured. Try again, this time say it's me calling."

He keyed in the protocol message but signed Colonel Nelson. A message came back, asking who was with him. "Tell them, Nick." A confirming "go" message quickly followed.

Nelson then dictated a long message for General Walker explaining the situation and asking for clarification of orders for the 24th Divisions' mission around Taejon based on the latest needs to reinforce Pusan. When finished, Larry turned to Colonel Nelson, "Sir, that's the longest damn message I ever coded. I hope I didn't miss anything."

Nelson smiled. "Jesus, Larry, if you got half of that, I'll give you a medal. We'll be over at the 24ᵗʰ HQ. Bring the response in written form, ASAP."

"Sir! This Korean here is waiting for his boss, a sergeant in the ROK named C J. He was with Rusty at Hill 102. Do you know anything about him or Rusty?"

"No, sorry, I don't. Listen, Larry, you are coming with us. After you receive the answer and deliver it to me, break down this equipment and proceed to a waiting truck in front. This Korean must go with you; he knows too much." Nelson left.

A few minutes later, they were back at divisional headquarters and were surprised at General Dean's presence. He was in full battle gear and looked wet and filthy. The greetings were brief.

"Jim, I've been eating shit sandwiches for a while now, and it sure looks like I'm about to eat another one. So what's on your mind?"

"You're right, General. But it's not a sandwich. It's a full course dinner with blood sauce, yours. You are that proverbial lamb ordered out to sacrifice yourself to save this country and Eighth Army. God, I hate telling you this, I'm sorry, but we are soldiers."

Dean looked at his assistant commander and then back at Nelson.

"What the hell are you talking about, Colonel?"

"You're not withdrawing from Taejon, sir. Eighth Army needs more time. You've got to stay and fight.

A dumbfounded General Dean glared at him and finally said, "Jesus Christ! My division will be destroyed. I need orders from General Walker." Distraught, he flopped into a chair and covered his face with his hands.

Colonel Nelson felt for his colleague, a fellow warrior, but he knew what leaders had to do. And it was time for leaders.

A knock at the door and then a quick opening announced a message from General Walker, as Larry walked in with a paper in his hand. He stood at attention and addressed Colonel Nelson.

"Sir, I have your reply from General Walker."

"Give it to me, Larry." He started reading it.

"To General Dean, Commanding General, 24th Infantry Division: I understand confusing orders as situations change. But they have changed as the enemy's rapid advance has overwhelmed our timeline to build up sufficient forces so we can stop them before they defeat us at Pusan. We must slow them down by any means possible. The fate of Korea and Eighth Army depends on it.

"I thus order you to hold Taejon for as long as humanly possible, so that the US 1st Cavalry_Division and the US 25th Infantry Division can establish defensive lines along the Naktong River, forming the Pusan Perimeter. When no further resistance proves effective, you are to withdraw and link up with available forces near the Naktong River.

"God bless you and your men."

"Signed, General Walker, Commanding General, Eighth Army and All Forces in Korea.

Dean straightened himself, sat silently for a few seconds, then stood and turned to his number two.

"Colonel Harper, we need to realign our force dispositions immediately. Bring up those battalions assigned to protect our withdrawal. Get runners out if the phones are down. I'll start the planners on the details."

Colonel Nelson checked his watch. "Shit! We've got to go. Good luck, General."

Dean looked at him and smiled a friendly smile and saluted. "Please don't revisit me for a while, Colonel."

Exciting the headquarters, Colonel Nelson did a double-take. He abruptly stopped, as he saw a familiar face across the street, leaning against a pillar, under a shelter protected from the rain. He smiled, and Rusty smiled back. A moment in time where both men just stood, looking across a busy street, at each other.

They finally broke into a run and joined in the middle of the street, like a dad meeting his kid after being long estranged.

"Damn it all, Rusty! So glad to see you! Glad I found you. We don't have a lot of time, where are your men?"

"Jesus! Why are you here? The guys are around the corner. Why?"

"Because all of you are coming with me. I'm taking you home. Go get the men."

"Home? We can't leave now. We've got too much to do!"

"You've done enough, Rusty. Besides, I've got something special cooked up for you and your men, much more suited to your talents than playing infantry soldier."

"Well, since you put it like that, okay. But I've got wounded here?"

"They're on the plane already; you need to hurry."

"I'm running!" Rusty took off, found the men, said goodbye to Colonel Daniels, and a few officers, and then brought the team to a waiting truck.

The C-47 had lots of wounded on stretchers. Besides the four Colonel Nelson ordered out of the hospital, an additional 14 severely wounded were added by the hospital surgeon. All were mounted three high against each side, still leaving enough room for all the rest of the men in the spacious plane.

After Rusty's men said their hello's to the Colonel and greeted their wounded guys lying in stretchers, they sat. Joe sat next to Dean. He suddenly went from being excited to being numb. All the killing flashed before him, like a movie. Maybe it didn't happen at all. It was just some bad dream.

The starting of the plane's engines snapped Joe awake. He then saw the men hanging in the stretchers and knew it wasn't a dream.

"Hey, Dean!" Joe wanted his attention.

Dean saw the strange look on Joe's face. "Do you feel as weird as I do?"

"Maybe more!" Said Dean. "But I wanted to ask you. Will you go back?"

"Damn it, Dean. I'm not sure I figured out what happened there yet. So I don't know. Maybe it depends on who I go back with."

The fighting men were exhausted, wet, dirty, and hungry. Nick sat to the left of Colonel Nelson with Rusty on Nelson's right. Tully was next to Rusty with Red next to him.

Colonel Nelson had to yell above the roar of the engines. "Hell of a job you and your boys did. Sorry about your losses, I know what that means."

"You need us back there, boss, I don't understand why you're pulling us out?"

"I'd expect nothing less from you. Fact is, I finally realized just how valuable you and your team are. Much like I discovered Nick here, Master Sergeant Nick Beloit, whom you never met, but I hope, will soon become quite a dynamic duo. Please say hello."

Each reached across and shook hands with Rusty saying, "finally meeting the smart son of a bitch that saved my ass a few times, oh, no offense, boss."

"Nick has saved a lot of asses in this war so far, besides yours. He's like you, Red and Tully all rolled up in one clear mind that knows how to fight and wishes he could, but can't."

Nick blushed. "Jesus, boss, this might be just the right time to ask for a small bed to replace the cot in my office."

Rusty felt like he just met a kindred soul, wondered why Nick couldn't fight anymore because he sure looked dangerous.

A long silence ensued, as each man gathered his thoughts, knowing they'll have time to get or give answers in Japan.

Chapter Seventy Six

Sunday, July 12, 1950 - Day Eighteen of the Invasion
Early Morning
Japan – Eighth Army Headquarters – Japan

The ambulances took the wounded to a nearby military trauma hospital. The rest of the men mounted two covered duce and a half's and with two jeeps loaded with heavily armed MP's, headed over to Eighth Army headquarters inside one of the largest US military bases in Japan, just outside of Tokyo.

Colonel Nelson decided that a hearty dinner, hot showers, and a night's rest were a requirement for all, so he had called ahead from the plane.

Entering the guarded mess hall, the aroma of hot food cooking just about sent Rusty's men crazy. They forgot how tired and filthy they were; they were almost starving. As they piled into the empty hall, cooks were to the right overseeing the food preparation, tables off to the left were all set up with utensils, and there, set in front, was a table with beer bottles in an ice bucket. Next to that were selections of hard liquor, glasses, and various mixers.

Just behind the bar setup, on a slightly raised platform, was a podium.

Colonel Nelson had led the men in, and when all had entered, turned to the small group, "This is my treat, but first, someone wants to say hello."

Just then, a major dressed in his Class A uniform came out from the right side of the podium, stopped ten feet away, and announced, "Attention! General entering!"

The large mess hall reverberated from the small group of men coming to attention. Something they did on reflex but had not done for a very long time, it somehow felt right.

The stout, short, General Walker, cigar in his mouth, came walking to the podium.

"You'll stand at ease. And I mean, relax. Welcome home! Now I don't want to steal any thunder from Colonel Nelson, but I just want to say how grateful I am for the incredible job you men have done. I thank you!" Pausing to a silent room, he went on. "So you should know, you're all on extended, much-earned furloughs, so enjoy the food and the bar." He left the room.

The men responded with loud yells and whistles.

After steaks disappeared as well as generous portions of side dishes and all, with cold beer chasers, the men settled at the bar. Later, everybody, even Rusty, had to be carried into badly needed hot showers and then brought to their quarters and finally tucked in.

At 0800 – (8:00 am), Army MPs entered Rusty, Red's, and Tully's quarters and assisted them into cold showers and gave them coffee from thermoses. They further supervised them as they shaved and helped them dress in new military class A's they brought along, appropriately adorned with their clusters of service ribbons and medals.

Outside their rooms, their MPs escorted them away.

A still bleary eyed Red turned to Rusty. "I asked these guys what the hell's going on, but nobody said anything except hurry up. Did we do something last night? I don't remember a whole lot after a while."

"Don't think it's anything like that," said Rusty, "but it can't be good."

They were brought to the mess hall where the rest of the men were chowing down, also dressed in class A's.

Finishing breakfast and feeling better, the three of them were led to Colonel Nelson's G-2 Intelligence section and finally his conference room. The outside guard knocked, opened the door, and announced their arrival.

The MP stood aside as the guard fully opened the door; the three men entered.

"Attention to the men entering!" Commanded Colonel Nelson.

A sharp snap from the men around the long conference table ensued as they stood from their chairs.

All the men around the table wore their military A's, their ribbons and clusters on display. They saluted the three men.

Momentarily stunned, the three non-coms snapped to attention and returned the salute.

Colonel Nelson smiled, "At ease and welcome home!"

The group around the table started clapping. The three men felt uncomfortable.

Colonel Nelson then made introductions and asked everybody to sit.

"We have a lot of ground to cover before the ceremony begins at noon, so let's start.

The day was bright; beautiful clouds rolled under a light blue sky, and the temperature was mild. The men followed Colonel Nelson and his entire staff to the parade grounds where they preceded to the front of stands with a raised podium at its center front. The platform was partially filled with officers of different ranks and from all the Services.

Colonel Nelson stopped, directed his staff into the stands, and directed Rusty and his men to form a single line facing the podium. He then joined Rusty at the end of the line.

Positioned around the parade ground were about fifty groups of men in formation, each carrying a unit flag that came from all the Services, Army, Marines, Navy, Air Force, Seabees, Airborne, Submarine, Coast Guard, and other specialized units stationed in Japan.

The band struck up a salutation theme.

General Walker came out from behind the stands and walked to the podium.

Everybody on the grounds and in the stands came to attention.

"At ease!" He spoke, turning to the offices in the stands, "please sit."

Rusty's head was still banging with a hangover, so he pretty much tuned the General out for a while, then came back to listen.

"As I said, if I had to give these men a medal for each incredible act of bravery, there'd be no room on their chests. Let me recount just a few, not all mind you. It starts with the defense of the listening Post at the very beginning of the invasion, then the capture of the secret North Korean Death squad headquarters and killing of its general, then the destruction of the two major bridges over the Han River at the capital of Seoul, delaying the enemy's advance for many days. There is more, but I think you get the idea."

The general went on for a while.

Each man then received the Silver Star Medal, including Colonel Nelson, for his leadership.

After the ceremony and extensive glad-handing with the men on the grounds and friends from various units stationed at the Eighth Army facility, Rusty asked and got permission from Colonel Nelson to take his team over to the base Non Commissioned Officers Club.

Walking over, the group was somber; events at the ceremony were overpowering. Nearing the club, Tully asked Rusty, "Think we'll have any trouble getting Commander Muzich in?"

Rusty looked at him like he had two heads. "Are you cracked?"

At the double doors to the club entrance, Rusty heard the rowdiness of the large crowd inside and wondered if this was a good idea to come here but went in anyway. When half the team cleared the doors, they became noticed, and the club noise fell off quickly and suddenly became silent. The team looked at one another, perplexed.

Joe pushing Arron's wheelchair was the last team member to enter the now ghostly quiet club. Despite his wound, Arron was feeling chipper to be out and about. Having missed dinner and the party last night because they took him to the hospital, he was looking forward to getting drunk for the first time in a very long time.

Arron was bewildered at seeing all the men in the club staring and being so quiet. So he yelled out, "Hey y'all, don't mean to bust up your party, just came in to have some brews!"

The cheers started, then clapping and yelling as men came up, hands grabbing them with friendly pats; they were surrounded by men who knew what surviving horror was all about, and they were honoring their valor.

"Make way! Make way!" Yelled a brawny old-time master sergeant as he came through the crowd and finally stood in front of Rusty as the patrons went quiet.

Addressing Rusty, he said, "You did good, First Sergeant! Come in. Drinks are on the house for all of you."

A big cheer went up, and then they were escorted to the bar.

After a few rounds and many toasts, Rusty requested a private room so his team could talk. The master sergeant led them to a back area, where a side room jutted off the back. It had two big doors for privacy and three big tables with chairs put together in a U form.

"I'll bring some setups, ice, and glasses. Be back in a few."

They were silent. The setups came, they helped themselves.

Rusty stood, raised his glass for a toast, "To those who didn't come back."

They all toasted and chugged it down. He sat.

Mario spoke. "I was happy General Walker honored our dead, naming each and giving them medals."

Tully raised his glass, "To the Airborne! Without them, who knows?"

"That's for damned sure!" Said Arron, as all toasted.

The toasts went on for a bit then got quiet.

More silence.

"Have we heard anything about Foxy?" Asked Tracker.

"Only that his brain got scrambled. They got a specialist working on him." Said Rusty.

They drank and thought.

Dean leaned in, "Say, Rusty, what do you think about Colonel Nelson's proposal?"

Rusty just looked at his drink.

Red, sitting next to him, said to Dean, "That's a good question. I think it's pretty crazy, but we should all give it serious thought."

Looking across the table at Tully, Red asked, "What about you?"

Tully raised his glass, "We Rangers love adventure!"

Rusty finally stirred, then stood with a drink in his hand.

"Never served with a crazier bunch before. So here's to you all, that maybe, with some R & R, we may come to our senses and realize that Colonel Nelson's idea may not be so nutty after all. Because right now, I'm starting to think it sounds pretty cool."

The End.